**He felt her small hand grip his wonderfully
coiffed hair—coiffed by her with
such love and attention.**

She pulled his head back, then wrenched it downwards as she
brought up her hard little knee to meet it. He felt his nose pop.
Blood blinded him.

Then he felt her arms around him.

"No!" she cried. "They've killed Chamberlain Hatho!"

But I'm still alive, he thought. But oh he was tired. So tired.
But he was warm in her arms. As good a place as any to sleep,
he thought, drifting away.

Praise for Angus Watson

AGE OF IRON

"Watson's tale is gore soaked and profanity laden—full of visceral combat and earthy humor, and laced with subtle magic." —*Publishers Weekly*

"Unflinchingly bloodthirsty and outrageously entertaining." —Chris Brookmyre

"It simply grabbed me by the throat and wouldn't let go." —*BiblioSanctum* (5 stars)

"Would I read the next one? Yes, absolutely. Bring me my hammer, bring my beer, bring it on!" —*SFcrowsnest*

"A fun and addictive read." —*Fantasy Faction*

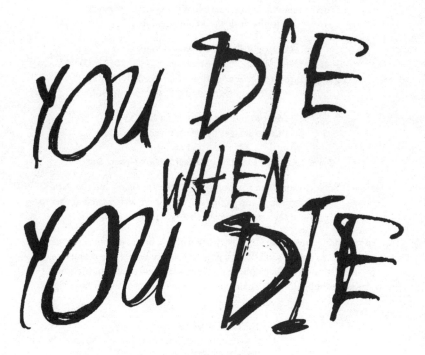

YOU DIE WHEN YOU DIE

West of West: Book One

ANGUS WATSON

www.orbitbooks.net

Copyright © 2017 by Angus Watson
Excerpt from *The Fifth Ward: First Watch* copyright © 2017 by Dale Lucas
Excerpt from *The Court of Broken Knives* copyright ©
2017 by Anna Smith-Spark

Cover design by Ceara Elliot LBBG
Cover images by Larry Rostant
Map by Tim Paul
Cover copyright © 2017 by Hachette Book Group, Inc.

Orbit
Hachette Book Group
1290 Avenue of the Americas
New York, NY 10104
orbitbooks.net

Simultaneously published in Great Britain and in the U.S. by Orbit in 2017
First U.S. Edition: June 2017

Orbit is an imprint of Hachette Book Group.
The Orbit name and logo are trademarks of
Little, Brown Book Group Limited.

The publisher is not responsible for websites (or their content) that are not owned by the publisher.

The Hachette Speakers Bureau provides a wide range of authors for speaking events. To find out more, go to www.hachettespeakersbureau.com or call (866) 376-6591.

Library of Congress Control Number: 2017939636

ISBNs: 978-0-316-31738-2 (trade paperback), 978-0-316-31737-5 (ebook)

Printed in the United States of America

LSC-C

10 9 8 7 6 5 4 3 2 1

For Nicola, Charlie and Otty

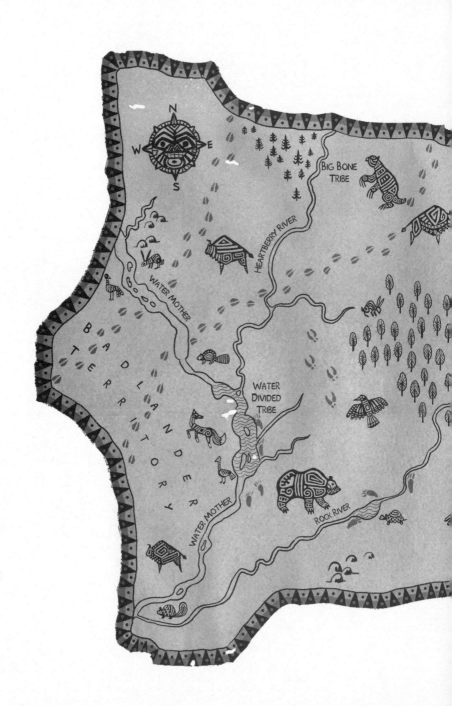

LAKCHANS

ROCK RIVER

HARDWORK

GOACHICA

OLAF'S
FRESH
SEA

CALNIA

©2017 by Tim Paul

YOU DIE WHEN YOU DIE

Part One

Hardwork, a
Town by a Lake,
and Calnia, a
City by a River

Chapter 1

Finnbogi Is in Love

Two weeks before everyone died and the world changed for ever, Finnbogi the Boggy was fantasising about Thyri Treelegs.

He was picking his way between water-stripped logs with a tree stump on one shoulder, heading home along the shore of Olaf's Fresh Sea. No doubt, he reasoned, Thyri would fall in love with him the moment he presented her with the wonderful artwork he was going to carve from the tree stump. But what would he make? Maybe a racoon. But how would you go about...

His planning was interrupted by a wasp the size of a chipmunk launching from the shingle and making a beeline for his face.

The young Hardworker yelped, ducked, dropped the stump and spun to face his foe. Man and insect circled each other crabwise. The hefty wasp bobbed impossibly in the air. Finnbogi fumbled his sax from its sheath. He flailed with the short sword, but the wasp danced clear of every inept swipe, floating closer and louder. Finnbogi threw his blade aside and squatted, flapping his hands above his head. Through his terror he realised that this manoeuvre was exactly the same as his rabbit-in-a-tornado impression that could make his young adoptive siblings giggle so much they fell over. Then he noticed he could no longer hear the wasp.

He stood. The great lake of Olaf's Fresh Sea glimmered

calmly and expansively to the east. To the west a stand of trees whispered like gossips who'd witnessed his cowardice in the face of an insect. Behind them, great clouds floated indifferently above lands he'd never seen. The beast itself—surely "wasp" was insufficient a word for such a creature—was flying southwards like a hurled wooden toy that had forgotten to land, along the beach towards Hardwork.

He watched until he could see it no longer, then followed.

Finnbogi had overheard Thyri Treelegs say she'd be training in the woods to the north of Hardwork that morning, so he'd donned his best blue tunic and stripy trousers and headed there in order to accidentally bump into her. All he'd found was the tree stump that he would carve into something wonderful for her, and, of course, the sort of wasp that Tor would have battled in a saga. He'd never seen its like before, and guessed it had been blown north by the warm winds from the south which were the latest and most pleasant phenomenon in the recent extraordinary weather.

If any of the others—Wulf the Fat, Garth Anvilchin or, worst of all, Thyri herself—had seen him throw away his sax and cower like Loakie before Oaden's wrath, they'd have mocked him mercilessly.

Maybe, he thought, he could tell Thyri that he'd killed the wasp? But she'd never believe how big it had been. What he needed to do was kill an animal known for its size and violence...That was it! That's how he'd win her love! He would break the Scraylings' confinement, venture west and track down one of the ferocious dagger-tooth cats that the Scraylings banged on about. It would be like Tor and Loakie's quest into the land of the giants, except that Finnbogi would be brawny Tor and brainy Loakie all rolled into one unstoppable hero.

The Scraylings were basically their captors, not that any Hardworker apart from Finnbogi would ever admit that.

Olaf the Worldfinder and the Hardworkers' other ancestors had arrived from the old world five generations before at the beginning of winter. Within a week the lake had frozen and the unrelenting snow was drifted higher than a longboat's mast. The Hardworkers had been unable to find food, walk anywhere or sail on the frozen lake, so they'd dug into the snow drifts and waited to die.

The local tribe of Scraylings, the Goachica, had come to their rescue, but only on two big conditions. One, that the Hardworkers learn to speak the universal Scrayling tongue and forsake their own language, and, two, that no Hardworker, nor their descendants, would ever stray further than ten miles in any direction from their landing spot.

It had been meant as a temporary fix, but some Scrayling god had decreed that Goachica continue to venerate and feed the Hardworkers, and the Hardworkers were happy to avoid foraging and farming and devote their days to sport, fighting practice, fishing, dancing, art or whatever else took their fancy.

Five generations later, still the Goachica gave them everything they needed, and still no Hardworker strayed more than ten miles from Olaf's landing spot. Why would they? Ten miles up and down the coast and inland from Olaf's Fresh Sea gave them more than enough space to do whatever they wanted to do. Few ever went more than a mile from the town.

But Finnbogi was a hero and an adventurer, and he was going to travel. If he were to break the confinement and track down a dagger-tooth cat . . . He'd be the first Hardworker to see one, let alone kill one, so if he dragged the monster home and made Thyri a necklace from its oversized fangs surely she'd see that he was the man for her? Actually, she'd prefer a knife to a necklace. And it would be easier to make.

A few minutes later Finnbogi started to feel as though he was being followed. He slowed and turned. There was nothing on the beach, but there was a dark cloud far to the north. For an alarming moment he thought there was another great storm on the way—there'd been a few groundshakers recently that had washed away the fishing nets and had people talking about Ragnarok ending the world—but then realised the cloud was a flock of crowd pigeons. One of the insanely huge flocks had flown over Hardwork before, millions upon millions of birds that had taken days to pass and left everything coated with pigeon shit. Finnbogi quickened his pace—he did not want to return to Hardwork covered in bird crap—and resumed his musings on Thyri.

He climbed over a bark-stripped log obstructing a narrow, sandy headland and heard voices and laughter ahead. Finnbogi knew who it was before he trudged up the rise in the beach and saw them. It was the gang of friends a few years older than he was.

Wulf the Fat ran into the sea, naked, waving his arms and yelling, and dived with a mighty splash. Sassa Lipchewer smiled at her husband's antics and Bodil Gooseface screeched. Bjarni Chickenhead laughed. Garth Anvilchin splashed Bodil and she screeched all the more.

Keef the Berserker stood further out in Olaf's Fresh Sea, his wet, waist-length blond hair and beard covering his torso like a sleeveless shirt. He swung his long axe, Arse Splitter, from side to side above the waves, blocking imaginary blows and felling imaginary foes.

Finnbogi twisted his face into a friendly smile in case they caught him looking. Up ahead their clothes and weapons were laid out on the shingle. Bodil and Sassa's neatly embroidered dresses were hanging on poles. Both garments would have been Sassa Lipchewer creations; she spent painstaking hours sewing, knitting and weaving the most stylish clothes in Hardwork. She'd made the blue tunic and stripy trousers that Finnbogi was wearing, for example, and very nice they were too.

The four men's clothes, tossed with manly abandon on the shingle, were leathers, plus Garth Anvilchin's oiled chain-mail. Garth's metal shirt weighed as much as a fat child, yet Garth wore it all day, every day. He said that it would rust if the rings didn't move against each other regularly so he had to wear it, and also he wanted to be totally comfortable when he was in battle.

In battle! Ha! The Hird's only battles were play fights with each other. The likelihood of them seeing real action was about the same as Finnbogi travelling west and taking on a dagger-tooth cat. He knew the real reason Garth wore the mail shirt all the time. It was because he was a prick.

Despite the pointlessness of it, many of the hundred or so Hardworkers spent much time learning to fight with the weapons brought over from the old world. All four of the bathing men were in the Hird, the elite fighting group comprising Hardwork's ten best fighters.

Finnbogi *had* expected to be asked to join the Hird last summer when someone had become too old and left, but Jarl Brodir had chosen Thyri Treelegs. That had smarted somewhat, given that she was a girl and only sixteen at the time—two years younger than him. It was true that she had been making weapons, practising moves and generally training to be a warrior every waking hour since she was about two, so she probably wouldn't be a terrible Hird member. And he supposed it was good to see a woman included.

All Hardwork's children learnt the reasons that Olaf the Worldfinder and Hardwork's other founders had left the east, sailed a salty sea more vast than anyone of Finnbogi's generation could supposedly imagine, then travelled up rivers and across great lakes to establish the settlement of Hardwork. Unfair treatment of women was one of those reasons. So it was good that they were finally putting a woman in the Hird, but it was a shame that it had robbed Finnbogi of what he felt was his rightful place. Not that he wanted to be in the stupid Hird anyway, leaping about and waving weapons around all day. He had better things to do.

Out to sea, Wulf the Fat dived under—he could stay down for an age—and Garth Anvilchin caught sight of Finnbogi on the beach. "Hey, Boggy!" he shouted, "Don't even think about touching our weapons or I'll get one of the girls to beat you up!"

Finnbogi felt himself flush and he looked down at the weapons—Garth's over-elaborately inlaid hand axes the Biter Twins, Bjarni's beautiful sword Lion Slayer, Wulf's thuggish hammer Thunderbolt and Sassa's bow which wasn't an old world weapon so it didn't have a name.

"And nice outfit!" yelled Garth. "How lovely that you dress up when you go wanking in the woods. You have to treat your hand well when it's your only sexual partner, don't you, you curly-haired cocksucker?"

Finnbogi tried to think of a clever comeback based on the idea that if he sucked cocks then he clearly had more sexual partners than just his hand, but he didn't want to accept and develop the him-sucking-cocks theme.

"Fuck off then, Boggy, you're spoiling the view," Garth added before any pithy reply came to Finnbogi, curse him to Hel. Garth might be stupid but he had all the smart lines.

"Leave him alone," said Sassa Lipchewer. Finnbogi reddened further. Sassa was lovely.

"Yes, Garth," Bodil piped up. "Come for a wash, Finnbogi!"

"Yes, Boggy boy! Clean yourself off after all that wanking!" Garth laughed.

Wulf surfaced and smiled warmly at Finnbogi, the sun glinting off his huge round shoulders. "Come on in, Finn!" he called. Finally, somebody was calling him by the name he liked.

"Come in, Finn!" Bodil called. "Come in, Finn! Come in, Finn!" she chanted.

Sassa beckoned and smiled, which made Finnbogi gibber a little.

Behind them, Keef, who hadn't acknowledged Finnbogi's presence, continued to split the arses of imaginary enemies with his axe Arse Splitter.

"I can't swim now, I've got to...um..." Finnbogi nodded at the stump on his shoulder.

"Sure thing, man, do what you've got to do, see you later!" Wulf leapt like a salmon and disappeared underwater.

"Bye, Finn!" shouted Bodil. Sassa and Bjarni waved. Garth, towering out of the water, muscular chest shining, smiled and looked Finnbogi up and down as if he knew all about the wasp, why he was wearing his best clothes and what he had planned for the stump.

"I don't know why you give that guy any time..." he heard Garth say as he walked away.

He didn't know why the others gave any time to Garth Anvilchin. He was *such* a dick. They were okay, the rest of them. Wulf the Fat had never said a mean word to anyone. Bjarni Chickenhead was friendly and happy, Sassa Lipchewer was lovely. And Bodil Gooseface...Bodil was Bodil, called Gooseface not because she looked like a goose, but because Finnbogi had once announced that she had the same facial expressions as a clever goose, which she did, and the name had stuck. Finnbogi felt a bit bad about that, but it wasn't his fault that he was so incisively observant.

He walked on, composing cutting replies to Garth's cock-sucking comments. The best two were "Why don't you swim out to sea and keep on swimming?" and "Spoiling the view am I? You're the only person here with a good view because you're not in it!"

He wished he'd thought of them at the time.

Chapter 2

A Scrayling City

Three hundred and fifty miles to the south of Hardwork, Chamberlain Hatho marched through the main western gateway of Calnia, capital of the Calnian empire and greatest city in the world. After almost a year away, the teeming industry of his home town was such a joyful shock that he stopped and shook his head. Had he been one of Calnia's uncouth Low, he would have gawped and possibly cursed.

He inhaled slowly through his nose to calm himself, swelling his chest with sweet Calnian air. By Innowak the Sun God and the Swan Empress herself, Calnia was an impressive sight.

As the Swan Empress Ayanna's ambassador to the other empires, Chamberlain Hatho had travelled thousands of miles. Some of the cities he'd seen did in fact rival Calnia in size and splendour, but for the last few weeks he'd been travelling by dog-drawn travois and boat through less sophisticated lands. The greatest settlements he'd seen for a good while had been casual collections of crooked cabins, tents and other meagre dwellings. Staying in those village's finest lodgings had made Chamberlain Hatho itch all over. How did the Low live like such animals?

"Chippaminka, does Calnia not rise above every other town and city like an elk towering over a herd of deermice?"

His young alchemical bundle carrier and bed mate Chippaminka gripped his arm and pressed her oiled torso against his flank.

"It is truly amazing," she replied, her bright eyes satis-
fyingly widened.

He held the girl at arm's length. She was wearing a breechcloth embroidered with an exquisite porcupine-quill swan,
the gold swan necklace that he'd given her to reflect light
and her new allegiance to Innowak the Sun God, and nothing
else. She held his gaze with a coquettish smile then licked
her top lip.

He had to look away.

He was pleased with his new alchemical bundle carrier.
Very pleased. The woman who'd fulfilled the role previously
had disappeared early on his embassy, in the great port
town at the mouth of the Water Mother. Walking along,
he'd turned to ask her something and she hadn't been there.
He'd never seen her again.

That evening a serving girl had seen he was morose and
claimed her dancing would cheer him up. He'd told her to
clear off and protested as she'd started to dance anyway,
but his angry words had turned to dry squeaks as her
sinuous slinkiness, smouldering smile and sparkling eyes
had stunned him like a snake spellbinding a squirrel.

At the end of her dance he'd asked Chippaminka to be
his new alchemical bundle carrier. She'd been at his side
ever since. She was the perfect companion. She knew when
he needed to eat, when he wanted time on his own, when
to let him sleep, when to talk, when to stay silent and, most
joyfully of all, when to make love and how to leave him
smiling for hours.

Chamberlain Hatho was forty-five years old. He'd always
thought that love was at best a delusion, at worst an affec-
tation. But now he knew what love was. Chippaminka had
shown him. At least once every waking hour and often in
his dreams, he thanked Innowak that he'd met her.

She gripped his hand. "It is a wonderful city. But what
are all these people *doing*?"

He pointed out the various stations of industry that lined the road running into the city from the western gate. "Those are knappers knapping flint, then there are metalworkers heating and hammering copper, lead and iron nuggets dug from soil to the north. Next are tanners curing skins with brains, marrow and liver, then there are artisans working with shells, clay, marble, feathers, chert, porcupine quills, turquoise and all manner of other materials to create tools, pipes, baskets, carvings, beads, pottery and more. That next group are tailors who sew, knit, twine, plait and weave cotton, bark fibres and wool from every furry animal in the Swan Empress's domain."

"They seem so *diligent*. They must be very intelligent."

"On the contrary," smiled Chamberlain Hatho. "These are the Low, the simple people who perform mundane but skilled roles so that people like me—and you, dear Chippaminka—might soar higher than our fellow men and women."

The girl nodded. "What are those Low doing?" She pointed at a team of women spraying white clay paint from their mouths in ritualistic unison onto leather shields.

"They are using paint and saliva as alchemy to create magic shields."

"Magic! Whatever next?"

Chamberlain Hatho surveyed the wondrous, teeming array of sophisticated industry and nodded proudly. "Yes, you must find it simply amazing; like something from one of your tribe's legends, I should imagine. And this is just the artisan quarter. As you'll see when we explore, there are thousands of others beavering away throughout Calnia, all dedicated to the tasks essential for keeping a city of twenty-five thousand people clothed, fed and ruling over the empire."

"So many?"

"The empire stretches north and south from Calnia for hundreds of miles along the eastern side of the Water Mother, so, yes, that many are needed."

"And what are those mountains, Chamberlain Hatho?"

Chippaminka nodded at the dozens of flat-topped pyramids rising from the Low's pole and thatch dwellings like lush islands in a muddy sea. The flanks of the largest were coated with a solid-hued black clay and topped with gold-roofed buildings blazing bright in the sun.

"They are pyramids, constructions of great magic that house Calnia's finest. The highest is the Mountain of the Sun, where we are headed now to see the Swan Empress Ayanna herself. You see that pyramid behind it?"

"The little one on the right? The much less impressive one?"

"Yes...That is my pyramid. It is not as high as the Mountain of the Sun, but broad enough that its summit holds my own house, slave dormitory and sweat lodge. It is where we will live."

"*We?*"

"If you will consent to live with me?" He felt the surge of fear, that terrible fear that had grown with his love, as if Innowak could not allow love without fear. The terror that Chippaminka might leave him dizzied him and loosened his bowels.

"I would *love* to live with you," she said and he resisted the urge to jump and clap. That would not look good in front of the Low. He'd never known such a swing of emotions was possible. He'd been terrified. Now, because of a few words from a girl, he had never been happier. Had humans always been so complicated, he wondered, or had the Calnians reached a pinnacle of cultural sophistication which was necessarily accompanied by such conflicting and high emotion?

"Come, let us report to the empress, then you will see your new home."

He headed off along the road with Chippaminka half walking, half dancing to keep up. Her dancing walk was one of the thousand things he loved about her.

He wrinkled his nose at the acrid whiff from the tanners and turned to Chippaminka. She'd already delved into the alchemical bundle and was holding out a wad of tobacco to render the stench bearable. He opened his mouth and she popped it in, fingers lingering on his lips for an exquisite moment. He squashed the tobacco ball between his molars, then pressed it into his cheek with his tongue. Its sharp taste banished the foul smell immediately.

Industry banged, chimed and scraped around them like a serenading orchestra and the joy in his heart soared to harmonise with its euphoric tune.

Ahead on the broad road children who'd been playing with bean shooters, pipestone animals, wooden boats and other toys cleared the way and watched open-mouthed as he passed. As well they might. It was not every day that the Chamberlain, the second equal most important person in Calnia, walked among them. Moreover, his demeanour, outfit and coiffure were enough to strike awe into any that saw him.

Chippaminka had plucked the hair from his face and the back of his head with fish-bone tweezers that morning. Tweezers gave a much fresher look than the barbaric shell-scraping method of the Low. Long hair fanned out like a downward pointing turkey tail from the nape of his neck, stiffened with bear fat and red dye. The hair on the top of his head was set into a spiked crown with elk fat and black dye, enhanced by the clever positioning of the black feathers plucked from living magnificent split tail birds. He could have used ravens' feathers, but those were for the Low. Magnificent split tail birds were long-winged creatures that soared on the tropical airs in the sea to the south. Young men and women would prove their skill and bravery by collecting feathers from the adult birds without harming them. It was nigh on impossible, so the feathers were fearfully valuable;

the six in Chamberlain Hatho's hair were worth more than the collected baubles of every Low in Calnia.

His breechcloth was the supplest fawn leather, his shoes the toughest buffalo. The crowning garment was as wonderful as any of Empress Ayanna's robes, commissioned in a fit of joy the day after he'd met Chippaminka. Six artisans had worked on it for months while he'd travelled south. It was a cape in the shape of swans' wings, inlaid with twenty-five thousand tiny conch beads. The whole was to honour the Swan Empress, with each bead representing one citizen in her capital city. He hoped it would impress her.

Despite his splendid cape, his most subtle adornment was his favourite. It was his strangulation cord. He hoped that he would die before Empress Ayanna. However, if she were to die before him, he would be strangled with the cord of buffalo leather that he'd tanned himself, cut and worn around his neck ever since. He might love Chippaminka with all his heart, but that did not dim his devotion to Ayanna, Swan Empress and worldly embodiment of the Sun God Innowak who flew across the sky every day, bathing the world in warmth and light.

"Will we be safe from the weather now that we are here, Chamberlain Hatho?" Chippaminka asked. Their journey had been plagued by mighty storms. They'd seen two tornados larger than any he'd heard of and passed through a coastal town which had been destroyed by a great wave two days before. The root of the astonishing weather was the chief finding of Chamberlain Hatho's mission. He hoped that Empress Ayanna already knew about it and, more importantly, had laid plans to deal with it.

"Yes," he said. "You will always be safe with me."

They passed from the industrial zone into the musicians' quarter, where the air vibrated and shook with the music of reed trumpets, deer-hoof and tortoise-shell rattles, clappers, flutes and a variety of drums. A choir started up. The singers held a high note then stepped progressively lower, in a sophisticated, well-practised harmony so beautiful that every hair that Chippaminka hadn't plucked from Chamberlain Hatho's body stood on end.

Two other voices rang out, sounding almost exactly like screams of terror. Hatho looked about for the source, intending to admonish them and to have them executed if they did not apologise to a satisfactorily fawning degree.

Instead, his mouth dropped open.

Several of the choir had stone axes in their hands and were attacking other singers. It was no musicians' squabble over a muddled melody; these were full-strength, killer blows to the head. Blood was spraying. Time slowed as a chunk of brain the size and colour of a heartberry arced through the air and splatted onto Chamberlain Hath's eye-wateringly valuable cape.

Further along the road, more men and women were producing weapons and setting about unarmed musicians and other Low. By their look, the attackers were Goachica.

Chamberlain Hatho guessed what was happening. This was the Goachica strike that he'd warned about for years. The northern province of Goachica had been part of the Calnian empire for two hundred years. Many Goachica lived and worked in Calnia. One of Hatho's direct underlings— which made her one of the highest ranking people in Calnia— was Goachica.

Five years before, a few Goachica had stopped paying tribute. This happened every now and then in the empire and it was simple to deal with. You either flattered the rebels into restarting their payments with a visit from a high official such as himself, or you found the ringleader or ring-leaders and tortured him, her or them to death in front of the rest.

However, the previous emperor, Zaltan, had overreacted with the Goachica. He'd sent an army with the orders to kill all who'd withheld taxes. Dozens of Goachica had failed to give tribute only because Goachica's leaders had told their tax collectors not to collect it. To any objective eye these people were as near to innocent as makes no difference; many even had the bags of wild rice that was Goachica's main contribution stacked and ready to go to Calnia.

The Calnian army had killed the lot of them.

Many relatives and friends of the slain Goachica lived in Calnia and many more had moved there since. Chamberlain Hatho had warned that these people would make trouble and advocated either apologising and giving reparations, or slaughtering them. Other issues, however, had taken precedence, not least Ayanna slaying Zaltan and becoming empress herself.

Because the massacre was entirely Zaltan's doing, and because actions like that one had been the chief reason for his assassination, people had thought the Goachica would have forgiven Calnia. Chamberlain Hatho's had warned that this was unlikely. He was less happy than usual to be proven correct.

To his right, several of the choir were fighting back with their instruments as weapons and the attackers were held.

Up ahead, he saw to his relief, three of the Owsla—Malilla Leaper, Sitsi Kestrel and the Owsla's captain, Sofi Tornado—had appeared. They were making short work of the attackers.

Malilla Leaper leapt over a man, braining him with her heavy kill staff as she flew. Sitsi Kestrel was standing on a roof, legs planted wide, her huge eyes picking targets, her bow alive in her hands as she loosed arrow after arrow. Sofi Tornado was dancing like a leaf in a gale, dodging attacks and felling Goachica with forehand and backhand blows from her hand axe. They said that Sofi could see a second into the future, which made her impossible to kill. Certainly none of the attacking Goachica came close to landing a blow on her.

Chamberlain Hatho felt a thrill to see the Owsla again. He had been ashamed when Emperor Zaltan created an elite squad based on his perverted desire for seeing attractive young women hurting and killing people in varied, often grim ways. However, the Owsla had proven to be a fearsomely effective squad of killers. More than that, the unbeatable ten had come to symbolise the success, power and beauty of Calnia.

Just as their chief god Innowak had tricked Wangobok and stolen the sun, so Calnia's rise to power had begun with alchemy-charged warriors rising up and freeing the ancient Calnians from imperial tyrants. Now Calnia ruled its own, much larger empire and the Owsla were its cultural and martial pinnacle; the beautiful, skilful, magical deterrent that kept peace across the empire. No chief dared antagonise Ayanna, knowing that a visit from the Calnian Owsla could follow.

There was a roar as a crowd of Goachica warriors rushed from a side street and charged the three Owsla.

Chamberlain Hatho gulped. Surely even Sofi Tornado, Malilla Leaper and Sitsi Kestrel would be overwhelmed by such a number? This was a much larger attack than he'd imagined the Goachica capable of.

He turned to Chippaminka, determined to save her. Their escape lay back the way they had come, surely, into the industrial sector where the Low craftspeople would be better armed and more inclined to fight than the musicians.

Chippaminka smiled at him sweetly, the same look she gave him before they made love. Had she not seen what was happening?

Her arm flashed upwards and he felt something strike his neck. A gout of blood splashed onto Chippaminka's bare chest.

What was this?

A second pump of hot blood soaked his smiling love. He

saw that she was holding a bloodied blade. No, not a blade. It was her gold Innowak swan necklace.

She'd slit his throat! His love had slit his throat! With the necklace he'd given her!

She winked then nodded, as if to say *yes, that's right.*

The world swirled. He collapsed to his knees. He reached up to Chippaminka. This was wrong, it must be a dream, she wouldn't have, she couldn't have...

He felt her small hand grip his wonderfully coiffed hair— coiffed by her with such love and attention. She pulled his head back, then wrenched it downwards as she brought up her hard little knee to meet it. He felt his nose pop. Blood blinded him.

Then he felt her arms around him.

"No!" she cried. "They've killed Chamberlain Hatho!"

But I'm still alive, he thought. But oh he was tired. So tired. But he was warm in her arms. As good a place as any to sleep, he thought, drifting away.

Chapter 3
A Prophecy

Finnbogi the Boggy tramped across the next low headland, still composing put-downs that would have sunk Garth Anvilchin into Olaf's Fresh Sea. The long town beach stretched out ahead of him, a good deal wider after the great storm that Frossa the Deep Minded had claimed was Tor's punishment for some nonsense that Finnbogi couldn't remember.

To the west were low, grassed dunes. Golden sandy paths cut through the green hummocks and led to the semi-walled group of huts, longhouses, hardly used smithies and other buildings that comprised Hardwork's main settlement.

On the far headland Finnbogi's aunt Gunnhild Kristlover was pouring holy water into the graves of her ancestors. Aunt Gunnhild was the only person in Hardwork who still worshipped Krist. Her husband Uncle Poppo Whitetooth was meant to be a Kristlover, too, but he didn't count because he didn't give a crap about anything. Krist, as far as Finnbogi could see, was the least of all the gods; a dreary, weak entity. Clever but misunderstood Loakie was Finnbogi's favourite, much better than patronising old Oaden and that brainless thug Tor. Loakie had outwitted giants, fathered a monstrous wolf and a snake that circled the world, and battled the pomposity of the old order. Krist's greatest achievement was helping to supply a badly planned party.

Gunnhild jammed the pole back into the holy water hole that led to one rotting corpse and moved onto the next.

Finnbogi had lived with Aunt Gunnhild and Uncle Poppo since his mother had died giving birth to him, shortly after his father had been killed by a bear. They weren't his real uncle and aunt, but he'd always called them that. He'd had little to do with his Aunt Gunnhild and she'd watched his development with an air of mostly silent disapproval. Poppo had been more like a fun, friendly but not that bothered older brother than a father.

Finnbogi walked a little further and the town beach came into view. Down by the edge of Olaf's Fresh Sea, the children were hanging fish on frames to smoke. Nearer, next to Olaf's Tree at the edge of the beach, was Thyri Treelegs.

She was battling an imaginary foe with her shield and sax, darting and prancing confidently, swishing the blade through the air, thrusting the iron shield boss into the faces of pretend enemies.

Strictly speaking, she shouldn't have been attacking Olaf's Tree. While all other trees of any size within a couple of miles of Hardwork had been felled for fuel and building material, this large ash had been preserved because Olaf Worldfinder had decreed that it was a descendant of the World Tree Iggdrasil and therefore sacred. Like most Hardworkers, however, Thyri was much more into Tor than Oaden, and Iggdrasil was more of an Oaden thing. So nobody minded if she gave Iggdrasil a bit of a kicking and a chopping, least of all her.

None of the children further along the beach had spotted him yet—they were busy arguing about something—and neither had Thyri, so he stood and watched her for a while.

She was barefoot, as always, wearing the Scrayling fighting garb that she'd made herself: a short leather jerkin and a breechcloth made from two squares of leather hanging from a belt, one at the back, one at the front. On her head was the padded felt and horn hat which she'd made herself too, copying the design of Garth's iron helmet which the ancestors had brought from the old world.

As far as Finnbogi was concerned, Thyri had the sort of figure that men sung songs about, but she could not be called a slender girl. Everyone said it was because of the maple syrup and sugar which the Scrayling boys had been bringing her for years. She didn't pay much attention to the donors, but she gobbled their gifts readily enough.

Still prancing about in mock battle, she threw her sax aside as if it had been whacked out of her hand. She ripped her two small axes from their holders on the back of her shield, tossed the shield away, leapt at Olaf's Tree, dug her axes into the trunk, gripped the bark with her feet and scaled the trunk in the blink of an eye, like some demon insect.

Maybe, conceded Finnbogi, if he was being entirely objective, she did deserve to be in the Hird more than he did.

She paused near the top of the tree and caught sight of him.

"Hey there, Boggy!" she shouted, hanging out from the trunk on one axe and waving the other.

Finnbogi winced and muttered, "It's Finn" through gritted teeth and waved with his free hand. To show that he wasn't standing there staring at her, he walked on towards the arguing children, the tree stump on his shoulder suddenly heavier than before.

The children had stopped hanging fish to concentrate on bickering. The argument was between Freydis the Annoying, Finnbogi's sort of sister, and all the rest of the little buggers. This was no surprise. It was about Ottar the Moaner, Freydis's older brother and Finnbogi's sort of younger brother. That wasn't a surprise either.

Freydis stood, feet planted in the shingle, fists on her hips, shouting up at the larger girls Raskova the Spiteful and Marina the Farter, twin daughters of Jarl Brodir the Gorgeous.

"No, Ottar can't speak," Freydis declared in her high-pitched, sing-song voice, "but he doesn't need to to be a lot cleverer than both of you put together. You *can* both speak but neither of you has ever said anything interesting or useful, ever. And you smell. Especially you, Marina the Farter."

Finnbogi smiled. She might be only six, but you did not want to upset Freydis the Annoying.

"We are Jarl's daughters and your mummy and daddy are dead and you will not speak to us like that!" spat Raskova, poking Freydis in the chest. "Ottar's said stupid things and scared people and we're going to punish him by throwing him in the lake."

"Where we will hold him under until he's sorry!" squeaked Marina.

Behind Freydis, Ottar picked up a stone, threw it in the air, watched it rise and fall, then repeated the procedure.

Freydis laughed. "What did Ottar say, Raskova the Spiteful? He can't speak, you just said it yourself, you racoon-headed dimbo!"

"We mean what you said he said!" Raskova tried to poke her again but Freydis dodged.

"Which bit of what I said he said? I say he says a lot of things."

"You said he said that we're all going to be killed! By Scraylings! Which is stupid because the Scraylings look after us. Their gods tell them to. They'd never kill us. My daddy said that what Ottar said—I mean what you said Ottar said—is dangerous, and he needs to be punished."

"He doesn't need to be punished. We all need to run away. If he says the Scraylings are going to kill us, then they are going to kill us. He's right. He's always right."

"He's always a silly boy who can't talk and you just make

up what he says and you're stupid." Raskova took a step forward and towered over little Freydis. Freydis glared up at her.

Ottar put a hand on his little sister's shoulder and gestured at her to come away.

"What's he saying now? That you should scurry off like baby chickens and cry about your dead mummy?"

"No," Freydis grinned. "He said that you look like a fish's bottom, and that your daddy goes into the woods and begs the bears to put their pee-pees up his bottom but they won't because he doesn't know how to wipe his bottom and it's covered in crusty old poo!"

"That's it!" Raskova's eyes looked as if they were going to explode out of her head. "Marina, hold Freydis. I'll drag the moron into the lake."

"All right, all right," said Finnbogi, "that's enough now."

"Shut up, Boggy," squeaked Marina.

"Yes, *Boggy*," chimed in Raskova. "You can't talk to us like that. We're Jarl Brodir's children and you and your silly sister and your sillier brother are orphans and—"

"He said that's enough. Go home, the lot of you." It was Thyri Treelegs. She strode past Finnbogi, felt helmet in one hand, shield in the other, her scabbarded sax slapping her leg every other stride. Her black hair was sweat-glued to her forehead and swinging in a long plaited tail behind her. Finnbogi caught a whiff of her musky, maple-sugary scent.

She loomed over Marina and Raskova.

"Off you go, now, both of you."

"But we're meant to be smoking the fish!"

"Then get on with that. If I hear that you've been troubling Ottar or Freydis again, I'll smoke you on the racks."

"But Ottar has been saying the Scraylings are going to kill us all."

Thyri raised an eyebrow. "What's this, Freydis?"

Freydis sighed exaggeratedly. "Ottar says that a lot of Scraylings are going to come and kill us."

"The Goachica?"

"No. Different Scraylings."

"You see!" shouted Raskova.

"Fish." Thyri pointed at the smoking racks. The sisters stomped off. "Go on, Freydis."

"He says we have to leave now, head west, west of west, and go to The Meadows. We'll find a home there."

"The Meadows?" Thyri wrinkled her nose. Finnbogi looked at her, then out over the vast lake. He shivered. There were not many Hardworkers, about a hundred in all, and the unknown land all around them seemed endless. There could have been an army ten thousand-strong coming to attack from any of a hundred directions and they wouldn't know until it was on them.

What was more, Freydis often reported Ottar's prophesies—that there was a bear coming, that there'd be a storm the day after tomorrow, harmless things like that—and, as far as Finnbogi knew, he'd never been wrong. He'd predicted that they'd all get covered in shit, or poo, as Freydis had put it on his behalf, the day before the flock of crowd pigeons had started to fly over.

"Yes, we have to go west of west to The Meadows. That's what he said."

"Where is The Meadows?" asked Finnbogi.

"West of west, that's all he says. I don't know what it means but I know we have to go. Stay here and we die."

Chapter Four

Sofi

Sofi Tornado ducked and smashed one attacker's knee with the blunt face of her stone axe. She continued the swing to bring the weapon's sharp side into the temple of the man who'd come at her from behind and was wondering how she'd known to duck.

She heard another warrior running at her and leapt to meet him. An arrow zipped into his neck and he staggered. She glared up at Sitsi Kestrel, standing on a roof with her bow.

"Sorry!" shouted Sitsi, the youngest and shortest of the Owsla, her abnormally large eyes even wider than usual with what might have been sincerity.

Sofi Tornado, the Owsla captain, had trained to fight every day since early childhood. Like all the Owsla, she had her own alchemy-given skill which gave her an edge in battle. While Sitsi Kestrel could see as well as the bird that provided her nickname and shoot the legs off a wasp from a hundred paces, Sofi had preternatural hearing and could anticipate the moves of twenty attackers by the sound of feet shifting on the ground, by the swish of sleeves, by catches of breath and in a thousand other ways. Everyone said that she could see a second into the future. That wasn't true. But it suited her to let the rumour roll.

The arrow-struck attacker fell. There were no others nearby who weren't either dead or as good as, apart from the two that Malilla Leaper was fending off with her battle staff. They were large men, brothers by the look of them, armed with hefty wooden clubs the shape of a bird's wings. Malilla could have finished them in moments, but she was enjoying herself. Despite her height—she was taller than most men—she was leaping about like a cat on hot stone, blocking every attack and jabbing painful strikes through every gap.

Sofi wanted those men dead, and now. She whipped her obsidian knife from its sheath. Bumping Malilla aside with an exquisitely weighted nudge, she slit one man's throat and drove her knife up through the jaw of the other.

As the men fell, she heard Malilla prepare for a leaping strike—against her. She sidestepped and Malilla flew above, her heavy battle staff flashing through the air where Sofi's head had been a moment before. The Leaper landed and snarled at the Owsla leader, battle staff twitching and ready. Dark eyes bulged and high cheekbones looked even sharper than normal. Malilla had a hard face at the most benign of times. In her rage she looked like she was carved from the same obsidian as the Owsla captain's knife.

Sofi Tornado smiled. "Come on then."

Malilla Leaper smiled back and lowered her staff. "I'm joking."

She hadn't been joking. Malilla had meant to hit her with that blow, that wasn't the question. The question was whether it had been an instinctive retaliation because she'd had her prey snatched from her—which Sofi could relate to—or whether Malilla wanted her dead.

Whatever it was, the answer would have to wait because she could hear thirty or so more Goachica coming in hard from the south. She leapt round to meet them, half an ear on Malilla Leaper.

Chapter 5

Erik the Angry

In Lakchan territory, three hundred and fifty miles to the north of Sofi Tornado and Calnia, twenty miles to the west of Finnbogi the Boggy and Hardwork, Erik the Angry strode up a woodland path.

The bright air trilled with birdsong, the morning was warm and Erik was naked, apart from a small leather backpack containing a few tools. He'd hide if he heard any of the local Lakchan tribe approaching. The Lakchans deemed nudity highly offensive, which Erik still found a little surprising, given how foul-mouthed they were. It was something to do with their chief god Rabbit Girl. Or was it her enemy Spider Mother? One of those two gods hated nudity anyway, so the Lakchans did, too. More fool them. Their lives must have been much the less without ever experiencing the liberating shiver of a morning breeze on the bollocks—or across the vagina. He guessed it was the same for women, or at least similar. Perhaps better? Maybe a breeze across the tits was a delight? Whatever, Erik still thought it odd that the Lakchans found nudity offensive, given that the foul-mouthed fuckers swore every other word. Twenty years with the Lakchans, and he was a long way from working them out.

Cottontail rabbits ran as he approached, zigzagging away along the path, then stopping, looking back, starting fearfully as if seeing him for the first time and zigzagging off again, still along the path. *If you want to escape, run off the path, into the undergrowth* he tried to tell them, but cotton-tails never listened, or at least they never heard. Like all herbivores, rabbits were dumb.

Erik arrived at his hillside clearing, sat on his bee-watching bench and enjoyed the glow of the sun on his skin. It was the first time he'd gone naked that year, and it was definitely the day for it. The winter had been a shocker, with two snowstorms worse than even the oldest Lakchan could remember. The Hardworkers had said the sun was some lady with a cart. The Scraylings reckoned it was Innowak the swan, permanently fleeing Wangobok the lion, who was the moon, or something along those lines. Whoever was right, Erik was glad that the swan or the lady was actually gener-ating some heat for once.

Bees buzzed about the wicker hives. Some headed out, flower-bound, others returned from floral missions, all working hard to make mead for Erik.

Although little more than a rise, the hill was the highest ground for miles. Beyond the bees the view stretched out over grassland, lakes, reed-beds, woods, spinneys and lone trees, all edges softened by shrouds of morning mist. Dozens of white-tailed deer picked their way through long grass. The elder ones stopped regularly, ears pricked and heads high on taut necks, scanning for danger. None spotted the lion slinking towards them from the west, despite the obvious stirrings in the grass. Deer probably weren't as stupid as rabbits, but there wasn't much in it.

Erik began to sing, a song he'd learnt as a child about a man who was too fat to sit on a horse. He knew that a horse was a beast from the old world that people sat on to go about the place, or at least the slimmer ones did—it was the same beast that drew the sun's cart—but he had no idea what the animal looked like. He could hardly remember what a Hardworker looked like. It had been twenty years since he'd seen someone from his old tribe. He saw Scraylings often enough, and knew that Hardworkers were pretty much the same shape—same number of legs, arms and so on—but he knew from his reflection in the lakes that a Hardworker was a larger, paler, lighter and shaggier-haired creation than your average Scrayling.

As he sang, the buzzing of the bees throbbed along in harmony. When he reached the chorus—*And that's why they called him Igor the Walker*—the bees rose in a buzzy cloud and flew away, down the hill to the stand of broadleaved trees where Erik had built another set of wicker hives.

He nodded to himself, standing and singing the last of the bees out of the hive. It was a neat trick. Was it neat enough to get him back into Hardwork? Would Tarben Lousebeard, or whoever was Jarl now, see his ability to muster bees and allow him back in? No, Hardwork law was clear. If any Hardworker saw an exiled man, it was their duty to kill him. It wasn't like Erik wanted to go back anyway. He liked it here and the idea of complicating his life by rejoining the Hardworkers made him shudder.

He took his knife from his backpack, lifted the top off the hive and sliced out two lumps of honey-dripping comb. As he returned to his bench, a gigantic she-bear padded into the clearing. On all fours, she was as tall as Erik, with a head the size of a buffalo's. She lifted her short snout, sniffed the air and moaned.

The huge animal walked over to the hives, limping a little on her front left paw. She spotted Erik and roared, displaying fangs that could have bitten through his torso with as much trouble as he had biting through honeycomb. Erik stood still.

The bear paced towards him, dropped heavily on its bottom, placed its forepaws on its knees and sat, regarding him evenly.

"Good morning, Astrid," said Erik. "Something in your paw then?"

"Aaarrrrhgggghhh," agreed Astrid the bear, lifting said paw.

As Erik examined the gigantic foot, he heard it again. A voice from nowhere and everywhere filled his mind.

"Come and find The Meadows," it crooned. "Come west and find The Meadows."

"I'm fine here, thanks." He shook the voice out of his head and plucked a thorn from the thick pad of grey skin on the bear's paw.

Chapter 6

The End of the World

In her private court at the centre of her palace on the Mountain of the Sun in Calnia, Swan Empress Ayanna welcomed her chief warlock Yoki Choppa and bade him sit on a duck-down cushion. Heavily pregnant, she was already seated and feeling, she imagined, not dissimilar to an overweight buffalo that had been stampeded for miles, driven over a cliff and was lying with its legs broken and waiting to die. Some women talked about a pregnancy glow. Ayanna felt the opposite of a glow, if "disabled, dying buffalo" was the opposite of "glow."

While most other Calnian warlocks dressed as whitecap eagles in white and black feathers, their leader Yoki Choppa's outfit of choice was an old leather breechcloth—two squares of leather hanging off a belt, one at the front and one at the back—and nothing else; no jewellery save a gold sun necklace, no tattoos, no animal parts sewn into his skin or dangling from pierced holes. Generally Calnians who wore very little did so because they had a physique they wanted to display. Surely the dough-bodied old warlock couldn't think that people were keen to ogle his greying flesh? She didn't mind—he was such a fine warlock that he could have worn nothing but a furious rattlesnake as a hat for all she cared—but she would remember which cushions he sat on and have them burnt.

They were alone, apart from a huge gold-plated swan

representing Innowak the Sun God, a gigantic crystal on a wooden scaffold which could concentrate the rays of the sun to light her fire, the two largest humped bears killed in Calnian territory stuffed and standing in menacing poses, plus her usual retinue of six superbly formed young men fanning her with swan's wings. Her fanners were men with good reason to wear very little.

Yoki Choppa sat across two cushions, placed his alchemy bundle beside him and his alchemical bowl on his lap, and waited. Ayanna tried not to think about the warlock's balls dangling between the gap in the cushions.

"I have a dream," she said, "which is why I have summoned you. I have the dream every night. It has been a month and a half, perhaps two. Always the same dream."

"What happens?" If Yoki Choppa was surprised that she didn't want to talk about that morning's Goachica attack, it didn't show.

She placed her hands on her enlarged stomach. "It is not pleasant. I am Innowak the golden swan. Although I am flying high above the world, I can see small details. Strange people emerge from the Wild Salt Sea. They are not Calnians, nor from any tribe I have seen. Their skin is pale, their features narrow and sharp, their clothes are unadorned and colourless, yet many have yellow hair that shines like gold in the sun.

"These men, women and children come inland, devouring plants, trees and animals as they walk, stopping only to urinate and defecate in great sprays. Everything that their effluent touches—plants, animals and people—dies. Some tribes befriend them, others attack them, but the result is always the same. The tribes die. The pale-skinned people walk on, gorging and growing all the while until they are fat giants towering over the land. Their urine dissolves forests. Clods of excrement pulverise mountains.

"Steam from their discharge rolls across the land in a

ravening fog, killing all. The putrefying cloud spreads up the
Water Mother like infection consuming a limb. It spills over
the river's banks, along Calnia's streets and over its pyramids.
When the foul mist clears, almost everyone is dead.

"The few survivors capitulate and mimic the ways of the
invaders, drenching the world with their waste. The last
plant and the last beast die and the land is gone.

"Finally the people are consumed by their own filth.
Everyone and everything is dead. The world is one stinking
slurry sea. That is my dream."

Yoki Choppa nodded. He poked about with pudgy fingers
in his alchemy bundle, hooked out a variety of oddments
and crumbled, flicked and dropped them into his alchemical
bowl. He added a smouldering nugget of charcoal from the
Innowak-lit fire. Stirring the mix with a bone, he peered
into it with narrowed eyes, lower lip protruding even further
than normal. At one point he grunted with something
approaching surprise, but other than that he mused and
prodded silently.

After perhaps ten minutes he put his bowl aside and said,
"Can we have a pipe?"

No "please." His manners were appalling, something else
Ayanna had to tolerate. She raised a hand. A pipe attendant
arrived moments later holding a lit clay pipe. She inhaled
the pleasant smoke twice, then handed the pipe to the pipe
attendant, who walked around to Yoki Choppa.

He took a long draw and held it for a good while. Finally
he breathed out slowly, then said: "The obvious inter-
pretation is the correct one. You have seen the end of the
world. It will be destroyed by these pale-skinned people.
They will kill everything, including us and themselves."

"When?"

"That is not clear."

"There is a tribe of pale-skinned people living in Goachica
territory, is there not?"

"The Mushroom Men."

"Is my dream linked to the Goachica attack?"

"I don't think so. That was a result of Zaltan's mistreatment of the Goachica, and I have seen no pale skins among the dead or captive."

"What do you know about these Mushroom Men?"

"They arrived by boat on the south-west shore of the Lake of the Retrieving Sturgeon in Goachica territory around a hundred years ago. The Goachica decided that they were spirits from another world, loved by the gods. They treated them like children, or perhaps pets, providing protection, food and fuel."

"But that would have ruined the Mushroom Men." The empress clicked her fingers twice to summon iced water. "Give someone everything and you take away all that they are. Why did they allow it to happen?"

Yoki Choppa shrugged.

"What else do you know about them?"

"They number around a hundred. They are very tall, with pale skins. Many have yellow hair. The men grow beards. They have a ten-man Owsla called the Hird, of which they are misguidedly proud. The Goachica cossetting has indeed rendered them lazy, fat and stupid, other than their Owsla, who train a great deal and are not fat."

"How do you know all this?"

"Your predecessor Zaltan took a brief interest and asked me to find out about them, but events overtook his plan to see them for himself."

"Events?"

"His assassination at your hands."

"Oh yes, that. So, we must slaughter these Mushroom Men to prevent them destroying the world."

The warlock moved his head non-committedly, neither a nod nor a shake. It was an annoying gesture.

"It's obvious," Ayanna continued. "And could not be easier.

I am already about to send an army to destroy the Goachica for this morning's attack. They can deal with these Mushroom Men, too."

Yoki Choppa lifted a blowpipe, pressed it to his lips and pointed it at her.

She felt a rush of panic. Was this assassination? The dart in the pipe would be dipped in the poison of a frog from a southern empire. It killed instantly.

Her body froze, but a herd of thoughts charged through her brain.

Was this revenge for her slaying of Zaltan? Was Yoki Choppa a Goachica, and this part of their attack, or was this about something else? Would her physicians be able to cut her baby from her dead body and save its life or would it be poisoned, too?

And why, by Innowak's shining arse, had Yoki Choppa waited until now to kill her? He'd had a thousand opportunities before.

She remembered playing with blowpipes when she was a girl. Even then she'd wanted to be empress and she'd fantasised about slaying the emperor with a poisonous dart. And then she'd fulfilled her ambition. Not many people got to do that. She'd lived a good, lucky life.

She remembered Zaltan gripping his chest with a clawed hand, the other reaching towards her while he stared at her in disbelief and rage. He'd said "glurk!" and fallen dead.

Could she somehow engineer a more elegant death and a finer last word? Perhaps she could swoon gracefully and say something like "I die as I lived—beautifully?" Or was there no choice? Was "glurk" all one could manage as the poison stopped one's heart? So should she stay silent instead of trying to speak? It was something of a shame that she was only going to get one go at it.

Yoki Choppa blew with a *per-choo!*

The dart flew over her shoulder.

"Glurk!" said someone.

She twisted around to see one of her fanners topple. His swan wing fans fell to the ground with surprising "thunks." The man twitched and was still.

"Goachica," said the chief warlock. "Hand axes hidden in his fans. Saw it in the alchemical bowl when I was looking at your dream."

"I see. Are there more?"

"Not here."

"I see." Ayanna relaxed back into her cushions again. "Thank you, Yoki Choppa."

The warlock shrugged.

Chapter 7

The Swing of the Thing

Back at the old church of Krist, where he lived with Uncle Poppo and Aunt Gunnhild's family, Finnbogi the Boggy prepared for the Thing, the quarterly Hardwork meeting when business would be discussed and everyone over the age of twelve would get drunk.

He tried on his second smart outfit, another Sassa Lipchewer creation, but decided on his blue tunic and striped trousers again. To change it up a bit, even though nobody would notice probably, he swapped his rawhide-soled shoes for his all-leather ones and added his red and blue headband, which helped to disguise the broadness of his forehead and covered up a couple of spots that he could feel glowing like fires on a beach at night. The headband also pushed up his brown hair into something of a mushroom, but one had to make sacrifices.

His Uncle Poppo Whitetooth, Aunt Gunnhild Kristlover (who weren't really his uncle and aunt), his sort of sisters Alvilda the Aloof and Brenna the Shy and his sort of little siblings Ottar the Moaner and Freydis the Annoying were waiting for him outside the church next to the life-sized wooden cross of Krist. Gunnhild said it was "life-sized" anyway. Finnbogi had asked a few times if the fellow stuck to it wasn't meant to be dead, so wasn't it really death-sized? Gunnhild had always ignored him.

"Are you beautiful enough for the Thing yet, Finn?" asked a beaming Uncle Poppo and they all laughed, apart from

Ottar, who was at the edge of the woods, flapping his arms and shouting at a butterfly.

"Uh, yes," said Finnbogi. He didn't mind Uncle Poppo's teasing much since it was always good-natured, and Poppo was always happy to be mocked himself. He didn't know why Alvilda was laughing, though. She always spent about a week beautifying herself before a Thing.

They headed for Hardwork along the path that burrowed through an untidy woodland of tangled trees strangled by rampant, aggressively green undergrowth that wanted to be overgrowth.

Poppo and Gunnhild were kind and he was grateful that they'd taken him in after his parents' death, but they'd never treated him like their own. Uncle Poppo had never cared what anybody else got up to, and Aunt Gunnhild had been too busy worshipping her god Krist and looking after her own twin daughters Alvilda and Brenna—particularly weird, shy Brenna—to waste any time on Finnbogi. Even when they'd found out that he'd taken some of Bjarni Chickenhead's hallucinogenic mushrooms, Uncle Poppo had laughed and Aunt Gunnhild had just looked at him in her tight-lipped way.

Alvilda and Brenna, three years older, had been pretty kind, too, or at least not unpleasant. He couldn't complain.

The only problem had come when he'd fallen sandals over breechcloth in love with Alvilda. Her trim waist, pertly round bum, over-pronounced cheekbones, hair tied into a high, bouncy tail and her withering haughtiness combined to make him dizzy with lust and there'd been a period when he'd had to run into the woods to be on his own for a while pretty much every time she'd spoken to him.

He'd tried to hide it from Poppo and Gunnhild, but he was sure that they'd known and been disgusted. She wasn't his sister or even cousin, so his cravings were totally acceptable... was what he'd tried to tell himself, but for about a year he fluctuated between being thrilled at living in the same building as Alvilda and being mortified by his own contemptible and semi-incestuous lasciviousness.

Then he'd fallen even more deeply in love with the sparklingly beautiful Sassa Lipchewer. But she was Wulf's, so that came with its own variety of self-loathing. Even though he knew it wasn't right as he was doing it, he'd fantasise about Sassa being menaced by a dagger-tooth cat. He and Wulf would fight it off. Wulf would be killed, Finnbogi would slay the beast and Sassa would confess to having always loved him secretly and immediately drop to her knees to show her gratitude.

So it was a great relief when one day he'd suddenly decided that Thyri Treelegs was hot enough to stop a herd of stampeding buffalo and he could focus his lust on someone who wasn't his sister in any way, or a friend's wife. Alvilda and Sassa still popped up in his fantasising, but he usually managed to shoo them away, or, at the very most, they'd play a secondary role to Thyri.

His other sort of siblings, Ottar the Moaner and Freydis the Annoying, had joined the family as a baby and a toddler when Finnbogi was twelve. There'd been some sort of scandal, which Finnbogi hadn't paid much attention to, and the children's parents had been executed. Finnbogi had been forbidden from ever talking about it to the kids, which he didn't mind because he wasn't at all interested in a weird toddler and a baby. The only major thing he'd contributed to their lives was their nicknames, which suited them well.

All Hardworker children were given unpleasant nicknames to keep demons at bay. Most people got new ones when they grew older, but some people, like Wulf the Fat, didn't. Finnbogi had been called "the Shittyarse" as a kid, so it had been a mixed blessing when people started calling him "the Boggy." He wished it could have been something less hateful and more suitable, like "the Strong Minded" or "the Man who Notices Things."

A gigantic black and yellow bumble bee buzzed heavily across the path. It was a hot and soggy evening. A sultry breeze shoved its way through broad leaves and knotted vegetation and a few fat raindrops splatted down. Finnbogi thought for a thrilling moment that the Thing might be ruined by a rainstorm, but the gathering clouds seemed to decide that it was too hot to bother and buggered off. The sky brightened.

Aunt Gunnhild fell back to talk to him.

"How many animals have you seen on the way down here, Finn?"

Finn pointed up at the dozens of swift, dippy-type birds gathering in anticipation of the clouds of mosquitoes that would bloom nearer sunset, then at a fat, orange-brown squirrel whirling its tail slowly and snarling at them from a nearby tree. "Quite a few." He held his hand to his ear. The woods were alive with birdsong. "And I can hear even more."

"Not birds and squirrels, proper animals like deer or wolves."

Finnbogi knew where this was going, and knew it was going to be boring, but he humoured her. "I have seen no proper animals like deer or wolves."

"My great-grandfather—the one who was in Olaf Worldfinder's Hird—told me that when they arrived there were thousands of animals everywhere. Under Olaf they were conserved and their killing managed, but the next generation had no respect for the land and slaughtered everything that they could see, not for food but for fun."

"Did they? That's terrible."

"Yes. Your generation must take better care of the animals. The animals are our friends."

Finnbogi thought of the wasp that had attacked him earlier, but said, "We will take care of them."

"And I'd like you to look after Brenna at the Thing. Ottar's silly tales about Scraylings killing us all have got her all het up." She glared at the little boy's back, up ahead on the trail. "So please make sure she's all right. She's your sister."

She's not my sister, but she is your daughter, he thought. Brenna became anxious in the company of anyone other than her family, and even with her family sometimes, so the Thing gatherings were a living nightmare for her. It was her problem, and entirely caused by Gunnhild's coddling, so Finnbogi didn't see why he should have his fun ruined by having to nanny Brenna.

"I'll keep an eye out for her," he said.

"And remember, *let a man drink moderately, speak sensibly or stay silent. No one will admonish you for going to bed early.*"

Finnbogi rolled his eyes. He always behaved himself, at least compared with the Hird men. At the last Thing, Gurd Girlchaser and Garth Anvilchin had bound Bjarni Chickenhead's hands behind his back and tied his balls to a white-tailed deer. Bjarni had been quite badly hurt and the deer had been killed. It was that sort of "fun" that made Finnbogi glad he wasn't in the Hird.

"Got it." He nodded at her.

"And you know that *buffalo know when to stop eating. A foolish man never does?*"

"I will be a buffalo."

"Hmmm. *Never laugh at an older speaker; often wise words issue from a shrivelled hide,*" she said, waggling what Finnbogi supposed was meant to be a wise finger before speeding up to rejoin her husband.

They walked on. Finnbogi half hoped that they'd stumble across a gang of ravening lions to prove Gunnhild wrong about the lack of big animals, but they didn't. By the time they passed Olaf Worldfinder's burial mound, which had been looted by Jarl Brodir the Gorgeous a few years before, they could hear trumpets, flutes and harps playing at the same time but not together.

Then they smelled the roasting buffalo. Sharing the land's bounty with Tor was the best thing about the Thing. They called it a sacrifice, but since the buffalo came ready-killed from the Scraylings, it was more like an exercise in group gluttony, which Finnbogi reckoned Tor preferred anyway.

They emerged from the darkening woods. The clouds over Olaf's Fresh Sea were huge and tinged pink. Oversized torches burnt triumphantly on those parts of the town wall that hadn't been permanently borrowed to repair other buildings. They wandered through the ever-open gates, between regularly spaced wooden houses and halls lining the broad main road, and into Olaf's Square—the wide, bank-ringed clearing at the centre of town. The town and the clearing had been designed by Olaf Worldfinder himself, to create somewhere central and safe for everyone to gather. Even though the cleared area was circular, it was called Olaf's Square. Considering he'd died almost a hundred years before, Finnbogi thought that everyone went on about Olaf Worldfinder a bit too much.

Almost all the other Hardworkers were already there, dressed in a mix of old- and new-world clothes: wool capes and shawls held together with silver brooches, furry boots, baggy trousers and so on from the old world, then garments like fringed leather shirts and quill-decorated dresses from the new. Several people were wearing Sassa's colourful creations, which were generally a mixture of the two.

All were chatting and drinking wine and mead from birch-bark and horn cups. Finnbogi's mouth filled with saliva at the delicious aroma from the buffalo roasting over the sacrificial fire pit, and he looked about for Thyri Treelegs.

"See you in a minute!" he said to the others. Gunnhild opened her mouth to say something—about looking after Brenna no doubt—but he skedaddled.

He hadn't got far when he was stopped by Chnob the White, Thyri's brother. Chnob was a couple of years older than Finnbogi, smaller and weedier but with the biggest beard in town and probably for thousands of miles, since the Scraylings didn't much go for facial hair. Chnob thrust his beard at Finnbogi as if it were a weaponised shrubbery.

"Your brother Ottar is an idiot," he declared. "And his prophecy is full of crap! The Scraylings would never hurt us!" he spat—probably, it was impossible to tell behind all that beard.

Finnbogi nodded.

"You're not defending him?"

"You're saying he's an idiot and you don't believe he can see the future?"

"That's exactly what I'm saying." Chnob nodded aggressively, his beard bobbing.

"Well, that's your opinion and I don't give a crap. See you later." Finnbogi strode away. He'd adapted his witty riposte from something he'd heard Keef the Berserker say, so it wasn't exactly his line, but he was still thrilled by how marvellously he'd snubbed Chnob the Knob.

Thyri Treelegs was on the far side of Olaf's Square with the Hird men. Several were dressed in their iron-reinforced battle leathers. Garth, as always, was wearing his mail shirt and iron helmet. Ogmund the Miller looked like he was already drunk, which was no surprise; he was already drunk most of the time. All were holding weapons which had never been used in real combat, at least not in their current owners' lifetimes.

Despite their redundancy, Finnbogi had to admit that the Hird made an impressive sight, the iron and steel of their well-preserved weapons reflecting firelight and their muscles glowing in the evening sun. Of course, Finnbogi would have had muscles like that if he spent all day leaping about, and anyone can dress up and hold a weapon. But how many of them would keep their cool in a real fight? Not all of them, by any means. Finnbogi knew that he would. And he reckoned he'd beat all of them in a running race, too.

Thyri was talking to her fellow Hird member, the fork-bearded Gurd Girlchaser. She laughed and placed a hand

on one of his beefy biceps. Gurd said something else and
loomed over her like a troll over a fawn. Thyri laughed all
the more, her hand lingering on his arm. It was disgusting.
Gurd must have been fifty years old. Despite his age, he
still thought it important to brush his beard into two separate pointy beards every morning and plait his greying
dark hair into a tail at the back.

Finnbogi dragged his eyes from them and saw Sassa
Lipchewer. Her lips were pursed obliquely as she chewed
the inside of her mouth. It wouldn't have been a good look
on anyone else, but the way her permanently twisted lips
interrupted Sassa's otherwise flawless beauty paradoxically
enhanced that beauty. That's what Finnbogi thought, anyway.
She was wearing a simple, bright dress embroidered with
flowers, which Finnbogi guessed she'd made specially for
the Thing. The way it gathered at her narrow waist made
him feel a little faint.

Sassa spotted Finnbogi and smiled brightly. He raised a
hand in reply. Bodil Gooseface, standing with her, grinned,
waved with both hands and gestured for him to come over.
Finnbogi held up a finger to indicate that he'd join them in
a minute, then went back to staring at Thyri. Tor's tits, Gurd
was a disgusting man, letching all over Thyri like that. And
she was lapping it up. Her hand was on his chest now!

Finnbogi spat onto the packed earth ground, looked up
and saw Garth Anvilchin, standing behind Thyri and Gurd
in his stupid helmet and smirking right at him. He knew.

"You are dead!" Finnbogi jumped as something poked his
back, hard. He spun around. Keef the Berserker was standing
there, his long-handled axe Arse Splitter held across his
broad chest as if he was ready for inspection.

"Hi, Keef."

"Kneel, mortal, and kiss my axe! Ya!" With this last word,
Keef swept Arse Splitter forward so its leading point was
inches from Finnbogi's midriff.

"Kneel!"

"Uh...?" Finnbogi managed. Keef's jaw was set, his small eyes narrow but shining with promised violence. He looked like a hero from a saga, albeit one with a strangely small head and very long hair. If he hadn't known Keef, he would have been terrified. As it was, it was still unsettling.

"I said kneel, dog. This is your final chance."

A few people gathered to watch, all smiling. Finnbogi was not going to kneel.

"Why should I kneel?"

"Your little bro says we're going to be attacked. You look like the sort of person who'd attack us."

"He said we'd be attacked by Scraylings. I'm not a Scrayling."

"That's not what he said, your little sis just added that bit because it seems the most likely. But she doesn't have the brain of a warrior god. I, Keef the Berserker, do. I've analysed every possible scenario and you are the most likely attacker. So kneel!"

"But I..."

"KNEEL!" Keef pressed the tip of his axe into Finnbogi's blue tunic.

By Loakie's sleeves, he was serious. He'd finally gone mad. Slowly, Finnbogi bent his knees.

"Ha!" said Keef, leaping back, face split by a manic grin. "I was joking, fool! Ha!" He relaxed into a Thing-going demeanour. "Why don't you have a drink in your hand? Come, follow, let us drink!" Keef slapped a big hand onto his back and propelled him drinkwards.

Finnbogi breathed out. "Shit, you mustn't do that."

"Do what?"

"Freak people out like that."

"I had to check it was you and not a demon."

"Ha ha."

"No, really. We are about to be attacked."

"You believe Ottar?"

"Yup! Kid's never been wrong. Last year he said a diamond-sided monster was coming. Next day, biggest fish I ever saw, biggest fish anyone ever saw, lying dead on the beach. And the pattern all down its flanks? Diamonds."

"It was a sturgeon. Not that unusual. Poppo caught one a couple of years ago. That's where Ottar had seen one before."

"Not that unusual that there's a sturgeon in the lake maybe, but there's never been one dead on the beach, before or since. And the tornado? Same deal. He said there was a circle wind coming, and the next day there was a big bastard whirlwind out on the lake. The boy's a prophet, no doubt about it."

"But who's going to attack us? The Scraylings—"

"Let me stop you there." Keef darted off between two groups of Hardworkers and disappeared. Finnbogi realised after a long moment that Keef wasn't coming back and had done something he considered hilarious, so he gave up on the strange man and walked on alone towards the drinks table.

"Look around!" said Keef, appearing back at his shoulder. "Notice anything off? Anything a tad untoward?"

Finnbogi scanned Olaf's Square, unsurprised at Keef's reappearance. The man did enjoy arseing around. Finnbogi was flattered that he should want to arse around with him.

All around them were laughing, chatting Hardworkers enjoying the Thing. The trio of trumpet, harp and flute was playing (they sounded a little more together up close, or perhaps they'd drunk more and found some harmony) and the buffalo were roasting away. He couldn't spot anything particularly unusual.

"Nope, nothing wrong here."

"You look but you do not see."

"I do see." Finnbogi was proud of his observation skills.

"Do you see any Scraylings?"

There were no Scraylings nearby. Finnbogi turned, then leapt to get a view over everyone's heads. No Scraylings at all. Usually a load of the Goachica came to Hardwork for the Things; most of them, it seemed, to try it on with Thyri. But that day there were none.

"Wow," he said.

"Wow indeed," said Keef.

"They must be gathering to attack us."

"Yup."

"So what do we do?"

"We leave, man. We go west, like the boy told us to."

"Leave? West? But the Scraylings say—"

"They lost their right to tell us what to do when they decided to kill us."

"But we don't know—"

"I trust the boy. You should, too. He's your brother."

"He's not."

Keef shook his head. "More to brothers than blood, my friend."

"But where will we go?"

"To The Meadows."

"Where?"

"To where Ottar said we should go. The Meadows. West of west. Do you listen to your family?"

He didn't much. But that wasn't the point. This was madness. "But you've heard what's west of here—dagger-tooth cats, man-eating beasts that make bears look like chipmunks, cannibal tribes, one-legged giants who'll kick you to death, three-headed trolls, rivers too wide to swim, mountains too high to climb, plants that'll catch you and suck the flesh from your bones, swarms of wasps which can kill you with one sting, fire-beasts with—"

"Arse Splitter will split all of their arses."

"Arse Splitter will split a wasp's arse? And a mountain's? And a plant's?"

"No problem."

"So you'll head west and die trying to split a wasp's arse while all its friends sting you to death because of something a six-year-old girl told you her mute brother said?"

"It's not just the prophecy. This place is finished. Where do those buffalo come from?"

Finnbogi looked across. Two busybodies dressed in the purple tunics of the people who volunteered to help out at the Things had swung one of the buffalo away from the fire and were carving its cooked edges. One was capering around to show what a jolly fellow he was and the other wore a self-satisfied "oh look at me, I'm *helping*" expression. Finnbogi didn't like the purple-clad volunteers.

"The buffalo come from the plains to the west."

"Do they? That's what the Scraylings tell us, but we've never been there, so we don't know. But I have to know! I *need* to explore! All of Midgard and beyond! The Scraylings bring us all our food and hem us in. We're no better than farm animals here and I wasn't born to be an animal. I am a hero and I mean to act like one. I am going. You should come with me. We'll be like Tor and Loakie going to the land of the giants. But don't tell anyone. And now I must leave you, I have important people to impress."

Finnbogi stared after him. As much as he wanted to leave, the idea of actually doing it was terrifying.

Frossa the Deep Minded climbed effortfully onto the platform. The Fray-cursed steps got higher every Thing, or perhaps her new smock and hat were heavier than last time. Her huge, brightly coloured garments were very much part of the Frossa that everybody loved, so she couldn't disappoint. Every Thing, she considered it her duty to wear a bigger and brighter outfit than last time. Sassa Lipchewer had outdone herself with this latest, spectacular creation. Just a shame the girl with the unfortunately twisted face hadn't had the intelligence and consideration to use lighter material.

Lawsayer Rangvald the Wise, or Rangvald Tuberhead as everyone amusingly and accurately called him behind his back, followed her onto the platform. He was dressed very boringly in black trousers and a white shirt, which fitted his boring role.

Rangvald took his seat and Frossa walked to hers, on the other side of Jarl Brodir's throne. All three chairs were built with wood from Olaf the Worldfinder's own ship. She nodded to the trumpeter. He brought their dirge to a halt with a blaring flourish and all faces in Olaf's Square turned to the platform to await the arrival of Jarl Brodir the Gorgeous.

The Jarl bounded onto the platform with the energy of a much younger man, but the cheers were more muted than usual. Frossa knew why. There was trouble brewing. By the time the Jarl sat on his throne, the crowd was sullenly silent, other than for the cheery purple-clad volunteers trying—and failing—to gee everyone up.

Frossa scanned the sea of surly faces and sought the cause. There he was, standing and staring at the cooking buffalo and flapping his hands in some mad excitement or possibly despair. You never could tell what the poor little halfwit was thinking. Ottar the Moaner, the dangerous little boy who should have been killed at birth. Who, in fact, had nearly been killed *before* birth.

Frossa loved all children, but living like Ottar must be dreadful, and the sooner the boy was helped from this life, the better. It was something of a shame his parents hadn't managed to kill him in the womb when they'd tried. People had bleated horror at their actions, but anyone intelligent enough to separate practicality from emotion could see that it would be easier for everyone if the moron had never been born.

Freydis the Annoying skipped up to her brother and directed Ottar's attention to the platform. There was something about that little girl. It was downright weird that she could understand what her brother was saying when nobody else could. Everybody simply accepted it, but Frossa was not called the Deep Minded for nothing. Who was to say that the girl wasn't a mischief-maker who was inventing all Ottar's pronouncements? And besides, the boy's predictions were laughable when compared to Frossa's own divinations. The tornado and the great fish had been lucky guesses. Frossa had divined much more impressive prophesies from her offerings to Fray. Who had foretold the cold of the previous winter? Who had foreseen the death of Skapti the Old?

Frossa suspected that her skills came from being part Vanir, the family of gods that included Fray and Fraya. She never told people her suspicions, modesty was the Vanir way, but her divine heritage did afford her a private and justified sense of superiority.

"Welcome all, to the Thing!" shouted Jarl Brodir. There were a few half-hearted whoops. "Will you all please join me in praising Tor by sharing these two buffalo with our god and protector!"

Frossa sought Gunnhild's face in the crowd. It was always satisfying to see the Krist lover's reaction to people praising Tor. She found her, and, sure enough, Gunnhild looked like she'd just taken a deep sniff from a sackful of a fox shit. Frossa stifled a grin.

"It was Tor's arm that guided Olaf Worldfinder across the Salt Sea, up the Mighty River, past the Waterfall of Certain—"

"What about Ottar's prophecy?" Some young, ill-mannered fool cut him off. Brodir graciously ignored her. "Past the Waterfall of Certain Destruction and—"

"And where are the Scraylings?" yelled someone else.

"Yes! Are they coming to kill us right now?" asked another. Soon everyone was shouting questions at the Jarl.

Frossa smiled benevolently at the simple people, stifling her urge to scream at them. It wasn't their fault that they were so gullible. She loved them all like a mother but, like a mother, sometimes she became exasperated by them. Sometimes, for their own good, they needed to be spanked.

Jarl Brodir raised his hand. He would know what to say

to quell the ignorant. "All right people, all right. I see we'll get nothing done until I address your concerns. You chose me as leader and I lead you for your benefit, not my own. I have other matters to talk about, important matters, but if you all want to talk about Ottar's prophecy, then I will be guided by your wishes, as always."

The crowd quietened. Frossa looked over them. That idiot boy Ottar and his smug sister were smiling and taking nothing seriously as usual. Behind them Wulf the Fat, Keef the Berserker and Jarl Brodir's unfortunate son Bjarni Chickenhead were talking to each other, rather than helping the Jarl control the masses. Why couldn't all of the Hird be like Garth Anvilchin? He'd make a much more fitting Jarl's son than the mushroom-eating, bouffant-haired dimwit Bjarni Chickenhead.

"First," said Brodir, "you've asked where the Scraylings are. There is a very simple answer. As you all know, our local Scraylings, the Goachica tribe, are part of the Calnian empire. Every few years there is a gathering at Calnia, three hundred and fifty miles to the south. That is where they are."

"They've never missed a Thing before!" came a shout.

"A Thing has never coincided with their pilgrimage to the south before."

There were nods and shrugs in the crowd. That had appeased the fools.

"And Ottar's Prophecy?" yelled Poppo Whitetooth, Ottar's adoptive father and a trouble-maker. Frossa loved the people of Hardwork *so* deeply, she was their spiritual mother, but she'd have loved them even more if she could have removed a few individuals like Poppo Whitetooth.

Brodir gave him a hard stare and said: "Let us have no mystery. Where is Freydis the Annoying?"

"Here I am!" shouted Freydis, cocky as ever.

"Young Freydis, I know that you're a clever girl, and you understand just how much trouble you could get into for making up stories, especially stories that upset so many of the more credulous adults. So please tell us, what is it *exactly* that you're claiming your brother has said?"

The crowd in Olaf's Square spread away from Freydis and stared back at her. That should have isolated and intimidated the girl, but she stood defiantly unflapped. *Such arrogance!*

"He says that we must leave and travel west of west to The Meadows," said the girl. "If we stay here, we will all be killed."

"By Scraylings?" said Brodir.

"That's right."

"I see. We will be killed by the Scraylings, allies for a hundred years and more. And this place, The Meadows, did your brother say where it is?"

"West of west."

"What does that mean?"

"You go west and when you've got there you go west some more."

A few people laughed.

"Can you try giving an adult answer?"

"She's six!" Poppo shouted.

"And she has spread a rumour that is disrupting the Thing," said Brodir reasonably, "so she must answer my questions. Now, Freydis. How far away, in miles, is The Meadows?"

"I don't know."

"I see. Can you ask Ottar?"

"That's not how it works."

Jarl Brodir chuckled. "That's not how it works...I see. So you understand his prophesies when it suits you to?"

"It doesn't matter how far it is." The girl was still aggravatingly calm. "We are all going to be killed if we don't go, so we have to go."

"Freydis, do you know what lying is?"

"Yes."

"Are you lying now?"

"Right now?" The girl cocked her head in a pose of mock confusion. She was so precocious! Frossa would have spanked that right out of her.

"Er, no. Were you lying when you said Ottar said we're all going to be killed by Scraylings."

"I was not."

"You were."

"Was not."

"Well, I know you were. Ottar's prophecy is simply the creation of this small girl's mind," said Brodir. "I'm sure that Poppo will punish the silly child appropriately."

No he won't, thought Frossa, and that was the root of the whole problem—that brat had never been spanked in her life.

Gunnhild, standing next to Poppo, muttered something.

"What's that, Gunnhild?" asked Brodir. "Do share it with all of us, please!"

The lover of Krist coloured. As well she might, butting in like that, thought Frossa.

"I said, *For the weak man, rudeness is substitute for strength.*"

"Oh. Thank you for more meaningless nonsense from the old world. Now, let us ask a genuine prophetess, Frossa the Deep Minded, whether Ottar's prophecy has any merit."

"Frossa the Fat, you mean!" some cruel idiot shouted and several people laughed but the Jarl ignored them and turned to her.

"Frossa, is there any truth in Freydis's lies?"

Frossa smiled, enjoying the sensation of being at one with the Jarl in front of everyone. She'd known the question was coming—they'd discussed it earlier. "None, Jarl, none whatsoever."

"How do you know?"

"When I heard that the dear young boy and his marvellously caring sister were spreading such troubling—such dangerous—rumours, I took it seriously. I care deeply for all the children of Hardwork and willingly give my time when any of them have troubles, but this case particularly concerned me because of its potential consequences. If anyone was encouraged to leave because of the stories of a six-year-old girl—if anyone was to die in the wilds, savaged perhaps by a pack of lions or eaten by frost giants—that would be awful. So I made three sacrifices, to Oaden, Tor and to my own god Fray, to whom I am closer than any might guess. I looked into the entrails of a raven, a fox and a red-winged blackbird. Each one told me of no impending disaster, only of peace with the Scraylings for decades to come."

"So what? You're usually wrong," said Poppo.

A lesser woman would have dived off the platform and gouged his eyes out, and that was Frossa's first instinct. But she would avenge Poppo's insults in time. She exhaled slowly. "The sacrifices are proof enough that Freydis is making up tall stories. No doubt, in your marvellous but alternative parenting of the poor orphan, you have encouraged her to tell stories. This is one of those."

"It's Ottar's prophecy, not Freydis's!" said Poppo.

Frossa smiled. "It is charming and endearing that you believe that she can understand her poor little brother's grunts. But even if the stories do come from him, my sacrifices are proof enough that he is mistaken. However, if more proof is required, then I have it. Because he could see danger in this silly little story to the settlement he founded, danger to his own children, Olaf the Worldfinder left Tor's right side and visited my home last night."

"How could he bear the smell?" someone yelled. Frossa looked about but she couldn't tell who had spoken. It was so unfair. Her hut might well have a distinctive aroma, but if she didn't hang all her sacrifices up inside it until they had rotted fully, the gods would be angry and she'd have trouble with all sorts of demons. Why couldn't the horrible peasants understand that? She put up with the smell of decay because she loved them. It wasn't such a bad smell anyway, sweet and homely once you got used to it.

"Olaf Worldfinder told me that there was no danger," she continued. "He also told me that anyone who left Hardwork and headed west would be killed, horribly."

"There we have it," said Jarl Brodir. "There is no—" Lawsayer Rangvald touched his arm and pointed to the crowd, where Poppo Whitetooth's arm was raised.

"If any man over fifty years of age raises an arm during a Thing, he must be allowed to speak," intoned Rangvald.

"Indeed, indeed," said Brodir. "What is it, Whitetooth?"

"Thanks!" said Poppo, smiling brightly. "My point is this. We should all leave Hardwork whether Ottar's prophecy is true or not. With the Scraylings away, now would be a good time to go."

"And why would we do that?" Jarl Brodir's reply was dangerously snappy and loud. Frossa placed a gentle hand on his arm. They'd discussed this. No matter how right you are, when you show anger you lose an argument.

Poppo continued: "The exchange of compliance for food was a temporary arrangement made by Olaf while we found our feet in a new land. He was an explorer, an adventurer, a pioneer. We should be the same. Olaf never intended us to live like farm animals."

"Would you insult everyone?" Brodir's eyebrows arched as he made the excellent point.

"I would," said Poppo, "myself included—I'd insult myself more, in fact. We have become shamefully idle. It is more the fault of generations that have gone before our current crop of young men and women. When I was a child we had wheeled carts, which moved with ease along good roads. Now we drag our goods along rough tracks on travois like the Scraylings because none of my genera-tion, nor my father's generation, could be bothered to learn how to make a wheel. None of us could be arsed to help maintain the roads, let alone learn how to. And look at our weapons and tools—fine they are, but all are over a hundred years old. Why? Because the knowledge of how to make them is lost. Brodir, the sword that you looted from Olaf's grave—"

"Olaf's ghost gave him that sword!" Frossa could take it no longer. Poppo smiled at her infuriatingly and looked to Rangvald.

"Please be quiet," Rangvald said to her—*to her*! "Poppo has invoked the right to speak." Rangvald gestured for the man to continue. Frossa fumed.

"As I was saying, the sword that Brodir stole from Olaf's grave has a core of iron, and is coated with something called steel, which I think might be a type of iron, I'm not sure, my great-grandfather did explain it to me but I never understood. Both materials, and the weapon itself, were made by burning rocks." A few people laughed at his preposterous claim.

"Yes, it is amusing how ignorant we've become," said Poppo.

"*Please* get to your point," implored Brodir.

"He must be allowed to speak unimpeded," said Rangvald.

"I will get to the point. We have become lazy, useless people. My son Finnbogi is a good example." He pointed to the boy, who reddened. "He has no goals, no hardships to overcome, not even the challenge of finding his own food or making his own shelter. The Hird might look good from all their training, and I'm sure that they would fight well, but they will never have the chance. As things stand, they are display pieces, nothing more. So we should leave, not because of Ottar's prophecy, but to make us better people."

A murmur of assent emboldened the usually timid Poppo. "To make us heroes!" he continued. "The Scraylings may decide one day that we are no longer loved by their gods and to be protected, and they may decide to kill us, but I think we should be long gone before then, forging our own lives in a place of our choosing."

Frossa had dreaded that the people might cheer this ridiculous speech, but thank Fray they didn't. There was more muttering, however, and a few half-hearted shouts of support.

"Can I speak now?" asked Brodir.

Poppo nodded.

"Good. I also spoke to the elder generation when I was a boy, who in turn had spoken to the original settlers, people who had lived in the old world. In that old world, you would not have had the right to speak, Poppo. You would have been a thrall. Thralls were slaves, who worked their whole lives for masters who were allowed to beat them or kill them as they chose. If your master wanted your daughter, he took your daughter. Would you like it if I took Alvilda or Brenna, Poppo?"

"I would not."

"No, but that's what happened in the old world, and I'm sure still does. If you complained, it was your master's right to kill you. If there wasn't enough food one year, which happened often because productivity and food storage were dependent on the whims of potentially incompetent overlords, then the children of the thralls would be thrown into the sea to drown. When a thrall reached the end of his or her useful working years, their master was allowed to kill them. Yes, they had laws like we do, they had many more, but the purpose of every single one of these laws was to ensure that the few stayed comfortable and well fed and the many stayed downtrodden. That is why our ancestors left the old world. Are you all glad that they did?"

A few shouted agreement and the purple volunteers whooped.

"I thought as much. We do not have thralls in Hardwork. All men and women are equal here. We do not murder children so that adults may eat. There has never been a murder or a rape in the history of Hardwork. Nobody has starved. We do not make our women wear their hair in ways that show whether they're married or not, as they did in the old world. In the old world a woman could not be a witness, nor a chief—okay, so we've had no women chiefs yet, but a woman *could* be chief and I'm sure will be one day."

Frossa saw many in the crowd turn to Thyri Treelegs, who pretended not to notice and nodded seriously as if agreeing with the Jarl's point. Treelegs was the first ever woman in the Hird, took great interest in the running of Hardwork and got on well with the Scraylings, all of which might make her a good Jarl, and Frossa could tell that the girl yearned for authority. But Thyri was a quarter Scrayling, and a mongrel like that could never be Jarl, not while Frossa had breath in her body.

"Yes," Brodir continued, "we have had crimes and punishments—including two executions and one banishing—but we are a society of humans so these things will happen. Our lives here are immeasurably better than they were for our ancestors in the old world, but only if we *stay here*."

Frossa thought back to the banishing, some twenty years before, when the previous Jarl, Tarben Lousebeard, had banished that oaf Erik the Angry for wanting to leave. Brodir was too kind. He should have already banished Poppo for the same crime.

"Yes," continued Brodir, "it's true that the Scraylings feed us. They say it's because their gods demand it, and I believe they think that, but between me and you all, the real reason they feed us is because it's so easy for them to do so. In the old world people grew their food. They planted seeds, tended to crops and kept pests at bay. That was the life of most thralls. Here the Scraylings do have crops, but they also have wild rice. It grows itself, needs no tending and it's easy for the Goachica to harvest more than enough. They have no need to farm animals because game is so bountiful.

This is not going to change. We will always be fed.

"On top of all of that are the recent storms, which are getting worse. Would you rather be out in the wild in one of these storms, or huddled by the hearth of your sturdy, watertight house? Leave here and you'll be dead before the week is out.

"So you see, Poppo, I understand the complexities of the situation. You do not. That's why I am Jarl, and you live in a church in the woods where nobody but you has praised any gods for years. That's why the people will listen to me and not the ravings of your unfortunately afflicted child."

People cheered. Poppo tried to say something else but the purple-clad volunteers gathered round him and drowned out his voice with their triumphant hollering. Frossa smiled.

Finnbogi didn't know who to believe. Uncle Poppo Whitetooth had sounded convincing, but so had Brodir the Gorgeous. On balance, he swung towards Brodir, because Brodir hadn't accused him of being lazy and useless in front of the whole town.

But then again Ottar the Moaner had never been wrong before . . .

He set off to find Thyri Treelegs. He'd ask her what she thought. He spotted her—talking to that helmeted idiot Garth Anvilchin now! He quickened his pace but someone grabbed his elbow and stopped him. It was Wulf the Fat.

Wulf looked about to check others weren't in earshot and leant in conspiratorially.

Finnbogi was thrilled. Wulf was the coolest guy in Hardwork by about a thousandfold. What could he want with Finnbogi?

"Keef tells me you're keen to leave Hardwork?" Wulf's pudgy face, white-toothed smile and curly golden locks said friendly, but his great muscles, padded leather jerkin, shield, and most of all his hefty hammer Thunderbolt said something more sinister. Did he want Finnbogi to join a leaving gang, or was he about to shop him to Brodir? Wulf might be a very cool man and a decent fellow, but he was also captain of the Hird.

"You mean leave the Thing and go back to the church?" squeaked Finnbogi.

"No. Leave Hardwork. For good. A group of us are preparing to go. If you want to come, meet us by Olaf's grave at dawn tomorrow."

"You're going *tomorrow*?"

"No no no. There's no rush, mate. Your little bro is a fine little man, but he's wrong this time. No one's going to attack us. It's just time to explore a bit. We're getting stuff together, making plans, you know...So, if you want to leave Hardwork, drag yourself out of bed before dawn and come along. If you don't want to, no worries. But don't tell anyone else about it." Wulf grinned like his lupine namesake and managed to look sincerely friendly and sincerely threatening at the same time.

It could be a trap.

"I..."

"Treelegs will be there." Wulf winked then strode away.

Chapter 8
Clever Chippaminka

Swan Empress Ayanna stood atop her viewing tower at the base of the Mountain of the Sun, on the edge of the Plaza of Innowak, the vast, sandy rectangle that they used for sports and displays. She surveyed the bloody spectacle.

Below her and pressed against the Plaza fence, the lower Calnian orders were watching the same event, cheering and oohing like a herd of drunk buffalo. Most of them were watching the Owsla and their victims, but many were gawping up at her, alone on the platform but for six fan men. Above her and her fanners, held up on gold-coated legs, was the great crystal, the largest in the world, which focused Innowak's rays to light the cooking pits.

The spectators were lower orders, but not the lowest, obviously, since the Low were allowed within Calnia's inner walls only to carry out Low duties like food delivery and waste removal. These were the high-born and elevated Low, so they carried themselves with a rudimentary attempt at graceful deportment that set them above the knuckle draggers who populated outer Calnia.

The men wore a variety of belted shirts and leggings that they probably thought were well cut. The women were in bright dresses, blouses and skirts, some sash-tied and almost all decorated with porcupine quills, beads, shells and other bright and shiny baubles. Both sexes had their hair styled in various complicated ways—a spiralled pile here, a multicoloured triple fin coupled with a pointed beard there—and all wore a dazzling range of jewellery fashioned from glass, turquoise, bone, horn and more. Many wore representations of the sun god Innowak—gold swans, swans of corn sewn into the back of dresses and other decorations. One woman had grown and waxed her long hair into huge mouse ears.

Her predecessor Zaltan had maintained that the Calnian upper middle orders' idea of sparklingly individual sophistication was simply their version of conformity. Maybe he was right. Ayanna thought that the commoners' efforts to mimic the elite were simply hilarious.

Ayanna herself was dressed simply, tastefully and originally, in white fawn leather sandals and a long white dress of white buffalo calf wool that both smoothed and displayed her pregnancy. A golden swan rendered in porcupine quills on the back of her dress had taken the finest quiller and her team a month to dye and embroider. The empress's hair was short, brushed to one side, coloured silver but otherwise unadorned. Her only jewellery was a black slate gorget around her slender neck, both reflecting and absorbing light like a bottomless forest pool.

The people gawped at her. So they might. She knew how to dress. At the next sacrifice many of them would mimic her new style with varying degrees of ineptitude.

She returned her attention to the Plaza. The captured Goachica raiders had provided a plentiful sacrifice, the largest since the day early in her reign when Chamberlain Hatho had had to build a new mound to house the partially eaten bodies of three hundred raiders from the south. Ayanna held far fewer sacrifices than her predecessor Zaltan. He had enjoyed filling the burial mounds with large groups of young women, allies and enemies alike, killing them in a variety of horrifying and perverted ways that were humiliating and debasing for all concerned, including the gods. Ayanna had put an end to his wanton cruelty. She sacrificed only people who deserved it, like these Goachica rebels.

Some two dozen Calnians had been killed before the Owsla had suppressed the raid. They'd all been Low, other than her deputy Chamberlain Hatho. His loss was badly timed and she cursed him for letting himself get killed. He had been on a long embassy to the southern empires and she'd been keen to hear his report. Right now, his alchemical bundle carrier was waiting in her palace for debriefing, but a servant was unlikely to know much. Ayanna sighed and resolved to watch the show for a while, before heading back up the Mountain of the Sun.

The ten women of the Owsla were spread out at the nearest end of the Plaza of Innowak. In between the alchemically charged warriors and the crowd, downwind from the empress's viewing tower, were five Innowak-lit roasting pits. Two of the fires already had people cooking above them. At the third pit, a trio of burly Low gutted a slain Goachica man with practised efficiency, ran the roasting pole through him from anus to mouth and trussed his legs.

The finest cuts of meat would be sent to the Mountain of the Sun for Ayanna's consumption. If your flesh was cooked in Innowak's fire and consumed by another person after you died, your soul was destroyed: no afterlife, no reincarnation. If you ate someone else's Innowak-cooked flesh, you were strengthened in the spirit life and the next life. Empress Ayanna had eaten human meat equivalent of several large families in her time, and she would eat more. There was no limit to how strong she intended her next incarnation to be.

Beyond the cooking pits, nine of the Owsla were facing a corral that contained around thirty remaining Goachica. All the women were barefoot, dressed in the standard Owsla uniform of leather leggings laced tight with rawhide thong to above the knee, leather breechcloth and a short leather chest piece belted under the arms. Their uniformity ended at their uniforms. Each was armed differently and each had her own skills.

The tenth member of the Owsla, the giant Chogolisa Earthquake, closed and re-lashed the gate of the corral with one hand. Her other hand was around the neck of a young captive. He writhed and pummelled her massive arm. He was tall, well-built and no doubt a capable warrior in normal circumstances. But Chogolisa was more than a head taller, with biceps as wide as the Goachica man's thighs and thighs as wide as his torso. She marched him towards the line of waiting Owsla, oblivious to his blows, as if she were carrying a chicken to a chopping block. Chogolisa Earthquake really was an extraordinary looking woman, thought Ayanna. Despite being a good measure taller and broader than any man, she had the clear-skinned face, bright eyes and shining hair of a teenage girl. The size of the woman! Like Sofi. Her Owsla nickname Earthquake came from the devastation she left in her wake, but it was easy to believe that if the massive girl jumped up and down a few times the earth really would shake and split.

Sofi Tornado, captain of the Owsla, walked to meet the giant and the man she was carrying, each step prime with magical verve, her hand axe and knife dangling from loops of leather at her waist and bouncing off firm thighs. She said something to Chogolisa, who repeated her words in a booming voice audible to all of Calnia:

"This man will be spared if he can reach the south side of the Plaza of Innowak. He will have a head start of thirty counts."

She didn't need to tell the crowd that he would be pursued. They were already holding their collective breath in anticipation.

She dropped the raider. He lunged to punch Sofi, but she slinked past his fist, grabbed his arm and shoved him in the buttocks with the sole of her foot, propelling him on the first few steps of his journey to the far end of the Plaza.

Without Sofi Tornado's support, and the support of her squad that came with it, Ayanna could never have become empress. Sofi must have known this, but had demanded nothing—no favours, no baubles, no pyramid of her own—nothing. The woman seemed to require only a simple life of exercise and killing.

"Go!" shouted Chogolisa. "Stay here and you'll die. Flee, and you have a chance. Thirty. Twenty-nine. Twenty-eight."

The man fled, sprinting like a deer from a lion. The crowd buzzed. All eyes turned to Paloma Pronghorn.

Paloma was considered the most beautiful of the Owsla, which was saying something next to the likes of Morningstar, Talisa White-tail and Sofi Tornado herself, but that was not her skill. Her nickname was accurate. Pronghorns were the fastest animals in the Calnian world; had there been a faster one, Paloma would have been named after that.

"Three, two, one!" shouted Chogolisa Earthquake. The fleeing Goachica was fast. He was a good three hundred paces away, sprinting for his life.

Paloma Pronghorn did not rush at first. She linked her hands above her head and stretched at the waist from side to side. Dropping her arms, she pulled a slim wooden club from a loop on the belt of her breechcloth.

Then she rushed.

By the Sun himself, did she rush. She tore across the arena with the speed and sound of wildfire through dry scrub in a gale.

The crowd reversed Chogolisa's count. "One! Two!"

The *eight!* died on their lips as Paloma caught up with the Goachica and cracked her club into the back of his head. His legs tangled and he crashed down, rolled in a cloud of sand and was still. The fastest woman—the fastest person—who had ever lived slowed and turned in a wide circle. Ignoring her dead victim, she jogged back to the other

Owsla at twice the pace that her unfortunate victim had sprinted.

Ayanna had seen this format before. Each of the Owsla would display their particular skill on individual captives. She was tempted to stay and watch Chogolisa Earthquake crushing the skull of a living man with one hand, and to see Morningstar punching through a man's torso so that her fist protruded from his back... but her desire to find out what Chamberlain Hatho's alchemical bundle carrier could tell her about his embassy to the south overrode all.

She made a signal to Sofi Tornado, who called an order to her women. Owsla and crowd turned to their empress and bowed.

Ayanna ascended the log steps of the pyramid, buffeted by waves of cheering from the Calnians below as the next victim was freed to be slain. Her fan bearers went ahead of her, sweeping the already spotless ground and laying newly woven reed mats for her to walk on. After this one use the reed mats would be sent to worthy citizens in the provinces who'd treasure them for the rest of their lives and be all the more loyal.

Yoki Choppa was waiting in her private court. He introduced Chippaminka. The girl was dressed in a swan-embroidered breechcloth. She had a lithe torso, pert breasts and an elfin face, but the spark of mischief and wisdom in her deep, dark eyes made Ayanna wonder if she wasn't a good deal older than she looked. Her eyes had more of a slant and her cheeks were broader than those of the typical Calnian. If the empress had had to guess, she would have said she was from the east, perhaps a Badlander.

"Sit, Yoki Choppa," said the empress, sinking down onto a cushion herself. It was a great relief after climbing the pyramid but she resisted the urge to let out a satisfied sigh. She might be pregnant, but it was only her first child and there was no need to behave like an aged matron quite yet.

"Chippaminka, I prefer you standing. How old are you?"

"I do not know, Empress."

"Where are you from?"

"I do not know, Empress. I was captured as a child."

"Captured where?"

"I do not know."

"Who brought you up?"

"Two Water Mother merchants."

"How did you come to be in Chamberlain Hatho's service?"

"He saw me and asked for me."

"Do you miss your adoptive parents?"

"No."

Ayanna liked the girl already. She appreciated honesty and despised flummery.

"Are you sad that Chamberlain Hatho was killed?"

"He was good to me and I will miss him."

"Did you see his death?"

"I was next to him."

"What happened?"

"His throat was slit."

"How did you survive?"

"I ran and hid."

"Good. Can you tell me anything about your embassy to the southern lands?"

"I can repeat Chamberlain Hatho's report word for word. He practised and honed it by performing it to me."

"Excellent." This was far better than Ayanna had dared hope. "Tell me what he would have said."

"Would you prefer a precis with the facts retained and arranged more efficiently, and superfluous embellishment removed?"

"...yes."

"Chamberlain Hatho detected no desire in any of the southern empires to encroach on Goachica land, and saw no opportunities for Calnia to expand southwards. Taking each empire, starting from the south..."

The girl continued. The general theme was that the empires of the south were increasingly worried by the growing strength of the Badlands empire to the west of the Water Mother. This was no surprise. The Badlanders worried Ayanna, too. Calnians did not venture west of the Water Mother and the Badlanders did not come east of it. That had been the convention for decades. But, with rumours of government-sponsored raiding and dark alchemical experiments in the Badlands, how long would it last?

While the girl talked, the empress munched on crisp, salty morsels of Goachica, carried by servant boys from the sacrifices below. Yoki Choppa poked about with a bone in his alchemical bowl. It looked like he wasn't listening, but Ayanna knew the sour-faced little warlock would remember every word.

Potentially troubling were rumours of mass upheaval beyond the Shining Mountains in the Desert That You Don't Walk Out Of.

"Information is scant," said Chippaminka, "due to inaccessibility of the Desert That You Don't Walk Out Of, but it seems that the tribes have coalesced around two warring empires. The stories are from unreliable sources, but they speak of war over a great power, which is growing greater. Some claim that the recent freak weather events, which I understand have also been happening here, are caused by this power. Some say it is centred in a place called The Meadows."

At this, Yoki Choppa looked up and raised one eyebrow, which was the undemonstrative warlock's version of leaping up, screaming and waving his arms around his head.

Ayanna held up a finger for the girl to pause. "What are The Meadows, Yoki Choppa?"

"Don't know."

"Will you investigate?"

"Yup."

The rest of Chippaminka's report was mostly about advances in farming and building technology. The empress listened to these with half an ear.

"Repeat all the technical details to the Head of Administration. Ask any lackeys where to find him, and ask someone to send Kimaman to me now. When you have been to the administrators, come back. I will find a role for you on my staff." And perhaps in her bed. Ayanna usually slept with men, but the girl had an appeal.

"Thank you." Chippaminka bowed and left, her small but plump bottom dancing below a graceful, slender back. By the way she moved, thought Ayanna, she *had* to be older than she looked.

Kimaman, her chief lover and the father of her unborn child, entered a few minutes later. He was so startlingly attractive and well proportioned that many thought he was a god. He wasn't. In fact he'd become a little irksome. Ayanna liked him, perhaps even loved him, but she'd seen far too much of him recently, and, more importantly, he seemed to think that impregnating her had made him her equal, or perhaps even her superior. He needed to be reminded that it had not, and that the child would be hers, not theirs.

"You will lead . . . how many, Yoki Choppa, four hundred?"

"Yup."

"You will lead four hundred warriors to Goachica lands on the banks of the Lake of the Retrieving Sturgeon. You will kill all the Goachica and their pet tribe of pale-skinned Mushroom Men to their north. The latter is particularly important—none of them must be left alive and you must raze their village and any outlying structures, leaving no trace."

"Are you sure I'm the right man to lead the . . ."

"Yes. Stay away from the thick of the fighting, let the captains lead the men into battle. Take geographers to help you plan the attack. You may go."

"Will I take the elite troops? And the Owsla?"

"You will not. Goachica's finest warriors died attacking us, and the Mushroom Men will be easy to kill. Four hundred of the standard army will be more than enough for your task."

"It will take, what, two weeks to get to Goachica territory?"

Ayanna looked to Yoki Choppa, who nodded.

"So I could miss the birth."

"Are you a midwife?"

Kimaman shook his head.

"Then why will you be needed?"

"I . . . don't suppose I will."

"Indeed. Now go."

"I . . . I am already on my way. Consider the Goachica destroyed."

"And the Mushroom Men," she added.

"Especially the Mushroom Men." He winked at her, then swept from the room.

"There is a lone Mushroom Man," said Yoki Choppa, "exiled by the Hardworkers. He lives with the Lakchan to the west of Goachica territory."

"Why didn't you mention that before I sent Kimaman away?"

"Lakchan are allies. It would be counterproductive to send an army into their lands."

"All the Mushroom Men must die! All of them!" Ayanna was losing her cool, which she hated, but she felt very strongly about this.

Yoki Choppa regarded her levelly.

Calm, she told herself, calm. "What should I do?"

"Have the Lakchan kill him."

"Of course. Send a runner to tell the Lakchan to kill their Mushroom Man," she ordered the warlock. "In fact, send runners to all the northern tribes, in case any Mushroom Men escape Kimaman. Any tribe harbouring a Mushroom Man will . . . what would be the best threat?"

"All be killed and eaten?"

"Yes, that should do it."

Chapter 9

Bear Paw

Frossa the Deep Minded walked with Jarl Brodir the Gorgeous back to his longhouse. It had been the most dispiriting Thing in her lifetime, all because of one stupid little girl and her family.

They ducked under the low door. Frossa helped Brodir light the torches that jabbed out from sconces along the wall. The dancing light brought life to the thousands of carvings that coated every inch of the interior. The carvings were mostly animals, real and fantastic, many of which had each other's tails in their mouths in representation of the circle of death and life. They were everywhere, even places like the underside of chairs where nobody would ever see them. Carving was a popular activity in Hardwork.

Jarl and warlock sat on two huge buffalo-wool cushions, next to the empty hearth.

"This is a crisis," said Brodir, stress etched into his fine features. "Unless we take action it could be the end of Hardwork. So take action we will."

"Don't concern your fine mind with this triviality," said Frossa, "I already have the answer. We remove the children."

Brodir nodded. "I agree. We could discredit their claims further, but while they keep making them there will always be those who take them seriously. But we can't kill them, can we?"

"*We* can't." Frossa held up a finger, struggled to her feet, walked over to a chest, opened it and took out a huge, white-furred bear's paw with thick, sharp black claws, stuffed and mounted on a short pole. It was one of Olaf's grave treasures, liberated by Brodir.

"But Tor can send a bear to kill them as punishment for false prophecy."

"I like it," said Brodir. "But who would do it?"

There was a heavy rap on the door.

"I've arranged that," said Frossa. "Come in!"

The door swung open. Garth Anvilchin ducked under the lintel and stood, massive and powerful, the beautifully inlaid heads of his axes the Biter Twins at his hips glimmering in the torchlight. He was beardless, not because he couldn't grow a beard, but because he'd adopted the Scrayling custom of shaving with a sharp shell. His great anvil of a chin made him look like a saga hero or perhaps even a god. Frossa could never have sex—she would lose her magic if she did—but if she ever decided to take a man, it would be this one. He would no doubt be honoured to make love to her.

Frossa handed the bear paw to Garth. "It's for the children."

He nodded. "Both of them?"

"Yes."

"No," said the Jarl. "There's no need to kill the girl. With the boy removed she will have no credence."

Frossa shook her head. "I'm certain she'll continue to make dangerous claims and people might believe her. And we must remember that the little mite loves her brother so dearly. Orphaned so young, they only have each other. It would be cruel to leave one alive."

"So be it," Brodir sighed. "But use the claw and nothing else, Garth, then lose it where it will never be found."

"It will be a pleasure. It'll probably take a few days to find an opportunity. If you want it done more quickly, the bear could break down the church's door and kill all of Poppo's lot tonight—him, the brats, Gunnhild, Alvilda, Brenna and Boggy."

"No." Frossa shook her head. "I do like that idea, but we need to show that Tor is punishing the children specifically."

"Agreed," said the Jarl. "Don't rush and take care not to be found out. If you have to wait a few days, so be it. You may go now. Find Chnob the White and send him to us."

Chnob arrived a few minutes later. Despite the ridiculous beard, or maybe because of it, Chnob was so much less of a man than Garth. While Garth had dominated the longhouse with his presence, the longhouse dominated Chnob.

Chnob seemed to realise this and jutted out his beard in an attempt to compensate. It did not work.

"When and where are the plotters meeting?" Brodir asked.

"Tomorrow at dawn, next to Olaf's grave."

"Have they set a time to leave?"

"No. They've gathered a few supplies, but it's still theoretical. They don't have the balls to go."

"Is it the same group?"

"I saw Keef the Berserker and Wulf the Fat talking to Finnbogi the Boggy so it's possible they've asked him, but I doubt it. I think it's still the original fools—Wulf the Fat, Keef the Berserker, Sassa Lipchewer, Bodil Gooseface, Ogmund the Miller, my sister Thyri Treelegs and, sorry, Bjarni Chickenhead is still with them."

"That idiot boy." Brodir shook his head. It pained Frossa to see the distress that Bjarni caused his father. When there was a suitable gap after the deaths of the children, she would have to slip some poisonous fungus into Bjarni's stash of magic mushrooms.

"How will you punish them?" asked Frossa. "Wulf, Keef, Ogmund, Bjarni and Thyri are half the Hird."

"I don't know, yet." Brodir sucked his teeth. "I hope I

won't have to. We've all gone through the stage when we wanted to leave"—Frossa had not—"but none of us acted on it—apart from Erik the Angry, of course. Besides, you never know, something frightening like a wild animal attack might happen to dissuade them."

He looked at Frossa meaningfully and she looked back uncomprehendingly. It was dangerous to speak like that in front of Chnob.

"What will you do if they go?" she asked.

"If we don't manage to stop them, we'll tell the Scraylings and let them do the work for us. Would you like immunity for Thyri, Chnob, in return for your help?"

"Why would I want that?"

"Because she's your sister?"

"She's a traitor and I can see no reason to treat her differently from the other plotters. Will you banish them?"

What an idiot question, thought Frossa. When Erik the Angry had been banished twenty years before, it had been a totally different situation. Besides, if you banish a group of people who want to leave, it does rather play into their hands.

"I haven't decided," said the Jarl. "But it shouldn't concern you. You may leave. Return to report on their meeting."

Chapter 10

Twin Columns

The first dawn meeting by Olaf Worldfinder's grave mound had been Finnbogi's favourite hour of his life so far. Most mornings Gunnhild said: "*He should rise early; seldom a sluggish wolf finds prey or a sleeping man victory.*" For the first ever time Finnbogi had seen the sense in that particular trite spouting.

People who'd been there were Wulf the Fat, Sassa Lipchewer, Bodil Gooseface, Bjarni Chickenhead, Keef the Berserker, Chnob the White, Thyri Treelegs and . . . him! The only person in that group he didn't like was that prick Chnob the White, and actually Bodil was a bit of an idiot, but the rest of them were the best people in Hardwork. And they'd accepted and chosen him! Garth Anvilchin, Gurd Girlchaser, Fisk the Fish and others hadn't been chosen. But he had!

They'd listened to his ideas. He knew that the land was marshy to the west, so had theorised that it would become marshier as they got further from the Fresh Sea since there was nowhere for the water to go. Everyone had nodded and hmmed at this, so he'd suggested taking Keef's little birch-bark boat with them to ferry their provisions across rivers and lakes. They'd all thought it was a great plan. Wulf had even slapped him on the back and Keef had run off to get his boat straightaway to add it to their hidden stack of provisions. Best of all, Thyri had smiled at him like a proud wife when her husband does a good job.

He'd walked home that day with a spring in his step and a grin on his face.

Two weeks later, Finnbogi went to the second meeting of what he liked to call The Leaving Gang. It was also totally brilliant, but not quite so good as the first, because they didn't seem any closer to actually going. Provisions were very nearly prepared, they were more or less ready to go, but nobody would commit to a day.

Ottar's prophecy that they'd be destroyed by the Scraylings was more than two weeks old now and everybody had accepted that it was only a strange little boy's fantasy, so there was no urgent reason to depart. When Finnbogi suggested that they leave in a week's time, Wulf had told him not to be so hasty. He didn't mind too much; it was good enough knowing that they'd be going at some point, but he wished they'd hurry up and get on with it.

They left the meeting at different times, so as not to arouse suspicion. Wulf asked Finnbogi to wait until last, which kind of marked him out as the least important, but he didn't mind. *The least important man at the Jarl's table is still at the Jarl's table*, as Gunnhild might have said. He strolled back to Hardwork, through woods and clearings glowing golden in the dawn light, smiling like a loon.

As he clambered through the branches of a tree that had fallen across the path, an enormous yellow and black bee buzzed him aggressively. He swiped at it, then decided No! No more will you frighten me, big black and yellow bees. Where they were going, he would have to deal with bees and probably worse every day. He would toughen up, learn how to fight...he'd get Thyri to teach him, as they journeyed together across the land!

He was one of them, accepted, and they were all going to run away together. He was going to spend hours and hours, weeks and weeks—the rest of his life—with Thyri Treelegs. Three other single men were going, but surely she'd pick him over those oddballs? Bjarni and Keef were good blokes, sure, but there was no denying how weird they both were, and Chnob the Knob was Thyri's brother, and he was a bellend. The odds were good.

Bjarni and Keef had raided a neglected store and found leather sleeping sacks brought over from the old world. Each one could hold two people. Keef had wanted to take one each, but Sassa had said that they should keep the weight of their equipment to a minimum and share sleeping sacks. Everyone had agreed. Finnbogi tried not to think about it so he didn't jinx it, but he hoped more than he'd ever hoped anything before that he'd be sharing a sack with Thyri.

He paused to calm his breathing and heard shouts up ahead, in Hardwork. That was unusual, especially so early in the morning. He quickened his pace. A mournful bleat pealed through the woods. It was the alarm trumpet, the one that called the Hird to town in times of trouble and attack. He waited for the second trumpet call, which told you it was just a practice. That call didn't come.

Finnbogi the Boggy broke into a run.

He burst from the trees outside the town. Nothing looked amiss. Hardwork wasn't burning, there were no armies of Scraylings smashing down what was left of the walls and massacring the lot of them. Perhaps the trumpet call had been a practice after all.

Doors banged open as he jogged along the main street. Everyone was running to Olaf's Square. Someone pointed to the north. Finnbogi stopped and turned.

Two tendrils of smoke were rising from the forest into the pale sky.

Much later, Finnbogi would remember that image of

ominous smoke against the pristine, peaceful blue as the moment that his life changed for ever. It was the moment, he'd come to think, which separated his childhood from his adult life.

But he didn't know that then.

He couldn't be sure, but it looked like one of the smoke strands was rising from the farm where Sassa Lipchewer's family lived. The other, he was pretty certain, was coming from his home, the old church. He'd left Uncle Poppo, Aunt Gunnhild, the older girls Alvilda and Brenna and the kids Ottar and Freydis there when he'd headed off to the dawn meeting. All had been asleep. They never cooked their breakfast, and rarely did any work around the place that would require a fire, certainly not at this time of year. So why the smoke? Just one fire could be explained away, but two of them...

He began to run to the farm, then checked himself. He wouldn't be much use on his own. He'd go to Olaf's Square and find out what was happening. Maybe his family would already be there, or maybe there'd be an explanation for the smoke.

"I don't think you should commit us all," Wulf the Fat was saying when Finnbogi joined the throng gathered around Jarl Brodir and the Hird. "It could be a diversion, to lure our fighters out of town before the main attack. I'll take the trumpet and run alone to Sassa's place. I'll blow it if I need help."

"Do you presume to order?" shouted Jarl Brodir. The spittle that Brodir sprayed up into Wulf's face glinted in the early sun and Wulf took a step back. Brodir followed, poking him in the chest. "I was captain of the Hird before you were a baby and now I am the people's choice of ruler! I am the people and they are me and my word is not to be questioned! The Hird will do as I have ordered. Lion squad will go to the farm, Wolf squad to the church. Find out what is happening, deal with it and come back!"

"I think that..." said Wulf.

"Now!" shouted Brodir, purple with rage. Behind him, Frossa the Deep Minded, or Frossa the Smelly Ogre as Finnbogi preferred to call her, smiled.

The Hird arranged themselves into two companies.

Finnbogi grabbed Bjarni Chickenhead's arm. "Who's going to the church?"

"The other lot, the Wolves" said Bjarni. "And don't worry, man, I'm sure it's all fine."

"Okay, thanks." That was annoying. Thyri was in the Lions, as were Wulf, Keef and Bjarni. The Wolves, who Finnbogi would have to follow up to the church, were led by Garth Anvilchin and included four others that Finnbogi didn't like much: the slimy fork-bearded wanker Gurd Girlchaser, nasty little Fisk the Fish, creepy Hrolf the Painter and boring Frood the Silent.

The Lions left first, followed by Sassa Lipchewer, who was chewing her lips with even more dedication than usual, and Bodil Gooseface, who followed Sassa everywhere. The paths to the farm and the church were the same until they split a couple of hundred paces into the woods, so Finnbogi and the Wolves followed behind.

Finnbogi led initially, but Garth grabbed his shoulder, yanked him to a halt and said: "Bugger off, Boggy. This is man's work."

"They're my family and I'm coming. You can't stop me."

Garth looked down at him, nostrils flaring, but then smiled. "All right, you little prick, come. But don't get in the way. And know that I'm letting you come. I could stop you and I'd enjoy doing it." With that friendly booster, Garth jogged off into the woods.

Finnbogi felt hot and faint, but proud that he'd stood up to Garth. He may not have thought of anything clever or funny in reply, but soon all Garth's friends were leaving Hardwork for good and Finnbogi was going with them and Garth wasn't, so whatever happened Finnbogi would win.

He ran on.

"Wait for me!" Freydis's voice called as he reached the trees. She appeared over a dune with Ottar, both of them carrying smoked fish. They'd been robbing the smoking racks on the beach before everyone woke up.

Finnbogi had to swallow a sob of relief on seeing that they were fine, which surprised him. Clearly he liked the tykes more than he thought he did.

He waited. Freydis dropped her fish and ran as fast as a six-year-old girl could and Ottar came behind, shouting as he bounded down the dune.

Finnbogi expected Freydis to ask what was happening.

"So," she said instead. "It's started."

Chapter 11

Red Fox One and Red Fox Four

Erik the Angry was dreaming about the weird world of twisted, multicoloured hills and hot red sand again, and the child's voice imploring him to go west to The Meadows. He walked around a phallic tower of red rock and saw a stone arch, crazily long and spindly, and the child cried out. No, it was a different child, higher and more pained...

The cry rang in his ears again and he was awake and it wasn't a child, it was Red Fox Four yipping somewhere down the hill, near the path leading from the Lakchan village. What was Red Fox Four up to, making all that noise so early in the morning when Erik and his new brew of mead had been up so late the night before? The exiled Hardworker lay on his bed in the wall of his shorthouse, pressing his eyes shut in an attempt to squeeze the headache out of his head, trying to work out what Red Fox Four was trying to tell him.

When the animals had first communicated with him—or he with them, he wasn't sure who'd started it—he'd given them all Hardworker names like Thorvald and Snorri—and Astrid. Then he'd found himself bereft every time one of them died, so he'd stopped naming them. In many ways it made it worse. Hearing Red Fox Four scream, for example, reminded him of the previous Red Fox Four, a good-natured but feisty little animal who'd been killed by the Lakchans for eating a sacred turkey. He could have given each one a new number, but that would have made Red Fox Four something like Red Fox Thirty-Two, and every new day that Erik spent alone, the less clearly he remembered higher numbers. Very few things in his life came in batches of more than six or so, so he no longer had any call for seven and beyond.

Red Fox Four yelped again and Red Fox One called out from even closer. Buffalo's piss, thought Erik, that meant there was danger. But what could it be? There was never danger. Animals didn't trouble him and he was more or less one of the local Lakchan tribe now, good friends with Chief Kobosh. He grabbed his war club Turkey Friend from its hook, rolled off his bed and then under it, slid a bolt, pushed a plank and rolled out of the back of the shorthouse into his backyard. He sat up with a groan of effort. Rolling around like a child playing Hird and Scraylings wasn't as easy as it had been a few years before.

Astrid the bear was sitting on the yard's packed earth looking as if she'd been expecting him. He told the huge animal that he'd shout if he needed her, and crept around the side of the building.

There was nothing immediately terrifying in his front yard and he was about to return to bed when Red Fox Four yipped yet again, more urgently this time.

He headed down the animal track that ran more or less parallel to the trail from his home to the Lakchan village. He was a large man—tall, big-shouldered, barrel-chested and paunchy—but he ran lightly and almost silently, in the way of wolves and foxes. It wasn't hard, once you knew how.

It wasn't long before he spotted the cause of the foxes' angst.

Five young Lakchan warriors, three women and two men, were heading for his shorthouse, armed with bows and stone axes. He recognised all of them from the nearby village, but couldn't remember their names, which wasn't great because he'd slept with one of them the previous summer.

They looked nervous. As well they might, coming at him armed like that.

He'd thought that the danger might be people from another Scrayling tribe, or maybe even Hardworkers come to finish him off after all these years, but there was no mistaking Lakchans. They had two main gods, Rabbit Girl and her arch enemy Spider Mother. Generally, Rabbit Girl was good and Spider Mother was evil, but it wasn't that simple. Rabbit Girl was the kind of irritating goody-goody who'd stop you having that third mug of mead, and you could understand why Spider Mother hated her. Spider Mother was bad, but often in amusing ways that you could relate to. She'd be pushing that third mug of mead, and a fourth. Many Lakchans, most of the older ones in fact, found greater affinity with Spider Mother than Rabbit Girl.

To represent these gods and reflect the good and evil in all, every Lakchan wore a pair of rabbit fur rabbit ears on their heads and six leather spider 'legs' attached to their breech-cloth belts.

So, the Lakchans had turned on him, just as the Hardworkers had. He sighed. It was disappointing. And confusing. Three days earlier he'd shared the last of his previous batch of mead with his, or so he thought, old friend Chief Kobosh, and had a good old laugh.

"Kobosh must be fucking mad to send only five of us after the cunt," said one of his would-be attackers.

"That fucking bear of his—"

"It's not so much the cunting bear as the fucking lions."

"The lions aren't friends with the cunt like the fucking bear is," said the oldest person in the group, the woman who he'd slept with. What *was* her name? "Hopefully the bear won't be there, but keep your arrows ready. Stick your fucking flint deep enough in a male bear and the cunt'll run."

"And female bears won't? Are female bears fucking *better*?" sneered a high-pitched young man, who Erik had known since he was a toddler and who'd been an irritating little shit at every stage of his life so far.

"A female won't run if she's got cubs nearby, no. The males don't have anything to do with the cubs, or any other bear, so will run if it suits them. Have your fucking parents taught you fuck-all?"

"I wish they'd taught me how to avoid suicide missions like this fucker."

"The cunt was up drinking last night. He'll be asleep. A couple of arrows in him and we're done. Now quiet, no more fucking talking, we're nearly there."

A great Lakchan hero of yore had sworn a lot, so now they all did to honour his memory. Erik had found it offensive for a while, but now he shruggingly accepted that all of them, from toddlers using words for the first time to wise old grandparents telling tales of old, swore almost every other word.

He slipped from the bushes onto the track and silently followed his sweary, would-be killers up to his home.

He caught up with the backmarker, clonked him on the head with Turkey Friend, caught the toppling man and lowered him into the undergrowth.

As he'd hoped, the others ran on to his front door without realising anything was amiss. As one of them pulled at the barred door, he charged them from behind, arms wide, and knocked all four off their feet. After a brief wrestle, a few punches and a couple of club-whacks, the young Lakchans were unconscious.

Erik went round the back of his house and found Astrid, yawning widely to display a mouthful of teeth that could eviscerate a buffalo with one bite.

"Go to your winter cave. I'll come and find you when I know what's up," he said.

The bear dropped forward onto all fours and lumbered away.

Erik crawled back into his shorthouse through the escape hatch, grabbed some twine, slung the sheath that held his double-bladed obsidian knife over his shoulder and unbarred the door. It was a bit of a struggle to push the door open because he'd left two of the Lakchans sitting against it. He'd been feeling a bit cocky after knocking them all out, but the error of blocking his own door reminded him that no matter how impressive they might seem for brief moments, all humans will regularly do something dumb. That was your Rabbit Girl and Spider Mother for you.

Half an hour later he was neck deep in the cold water of a lake, watching the Lakchan tribe eat their breakfasts.

The village was mostly domed reed huts covered in buffalo skins, dotted about with carvings of rabbits and spiders. There was one large building, Chief Kobosh's timber and daub longhouse. Erik had designed and mostly built that longhouse, using old world methods that had both impressed the Lakchans and made them complain about how much timber he'd used.

Why on Oaden's green earth had they tried to kill him?

He waited until most people had headed into the fields and woods to farm and forage, then crept between empty huts to the back of the longhouse, shivering after his morning dip. When he'd built the longhouse, he'd felt a bit guilty sticking in a secret panel like the one in his shorthouse, but he was glad he'd done it now.

It took a moment for his eyes to adjust when he stood up inside, so he had a blissful second of feeling successfully stealthy, before realising he was surrounded by a dozen or so warriors, arrows strung and pointed at him. Chief Kobosh sat on the Spider Throne, his rabbit ears towering imperiously, long-stemmed pipe in one hand.

"Ah," said Erik.

Chief Kobosh sucked deeply on his pipe and blew out a cloud of smoke. "Good morning, Erik, you old cunt," he said in his rough, bubbling voice, "why are you wet?"

"Came via the lake."

"You, my friend, have always been fucking strange. It's a fucking shame we have to kill you."

Chapter 12
Caterpillars

Sassa Lipchewer ran behind Wulf the Fat, Keef the Berserker, Bjarni Chickenhead, Ogmund the Miller and Thyri Treelegs. She felt sick.

Next to her, Bodil Gooseface was babbling away: "I'm sure they're just burning cleared *leaves* or something and it's a *coincidence* that Poppo and Gunnhild are doing the same thing. What was it that Finnbogi said the other day about *coincidences*? He said it would be *more* unusual if coincidences didn't happen...hang on, that's not it. And maybe it wasn't Finnbogi. But *somebody* said that coincidences—"

Bodil prattled on. Sassa pictured herself arriving at the farm and finding her mother sewing in the yard, her brother Vifil the Individual doing his own thing and her father tending to the fire that was causing all this worry. He had burnt things before. But not, she had to admit, at this time of the year. And, apart from their own hearth, which they never lit in the morning, Poppo and Gunnhild up at the church had never laid a fire. Two unusual fires at the same time was no coincidence and Sassa could not think of a reason for it. Fuck a duck, it was frustrating to have no idea what was happening. She ran on.

Two red-winged blackbirds alighted on a nearby branch. Had they seen what was happening? She wished she could ask them. What if it was raiders? There had never been

raiders before, but they were all aware of the concept...
She wished she'd taken her bow to the dawn plotters'
meeting. She wished she hadn't gone to the dawn meeting.

She'd really thought that she wanted to leave. She wanted
a baby more than anything, but no matter how many times
she and Wulf made love—or shagged, as Wulf insisted on
putting it—they had no luck. She thought that if she left—
made a change, breathed different air, ate different food—
then Fraya might see her need, respond to her offerings
and answer her prayers.

Now she knew that she could never leave her parents
and her brother. It had taken this scare to realise it. She
prayed to Fraya that it was only a scare.

She emerged from the trees into the farm's lower field, a
good way behind the Hird. There was no need for a farm
when the Scraylings gave them all the food they could eat,
but the buildings and fields had been in her family since
Olaf Worldfinder's day, and they'd always kept a few animals
and grown some crops. Her brother Vifil the Individual was
too much of an individual to carry on the family work, so
her father hoped that Sassa and Wulf would settle down
into the agrarian life. The thought of it appalled her. It was
another reason that she'd been planning to leave. Another
selfish reason.

They crested a rise and she saw the source of the smoke.
The barn next to their longhouse was on fire.

"Hold!" Wulf shouted up ahead.

The first thing she took in when she ran through the
gate into the farm's yard was the five Hird facing outwards,
weapons ready. Next she noticed that the small barn was
almost burnt to the ground.

The final major thing she was aware of, perhaps, she
thought later, because her mind refused to accept it, was
that her mother, father and brother were lying dead in front
of the longhouse.

Her brother and father's throats were slit so deeply that they were all but decapitated. Her mother looked unharmed, but her eyes were open and staring milkily, like the eyes of a fish on a smoking rack.

She ran and knelt by her mother. She couldn't see an injury, but neither could she find a pulse. There was a trickle of blood from under her head. She felt for a wound and found one. The back of her mother's head was a soggy mess. Sassa thought of that morning, when her mother had caught her nipping out, kissed her and told her to be careful. Her mother knew that Sassa didn't want to farm, and she would never have stopped her from following her desires, including leaving for good. She felt the tears come. As long as she could remember her mother had listened while her father had commanded, and she'd never—

"Yah!" Keef the Berserker shouted, startling Sassa. A Scrayling was charging him. Keef used the hook of the axe to pull his attacker off his feet and slammed the blade round into his chest—a manoeuvre that Sassa had seen him practise a thousand times. Despite her shock and horror, she found herself thinking that it was nice to see that Keef's constant drilling seemed to have borne fruit.

"My finest regards to your ancestors! Tell them Keef the Berserker sent you!" Keef wrenched the axe from the dying Scrayling's chest and looked around for the next adversary.

He had plenty of choice. A large gang of Scrayling warriors had burst from who knew where. They wore breechcloths and were armed with stone-headed spears, stone axes and flint knives.

Bodil ran over to cower next to Sassa.

Around them, the Hird fought.

Thyri Treelegs leapt and spun, punching with her shield and slashing with her sax. She opened one raider's throat and kicked another so hard in the groin that Sassa heard the crunch over the battle clamour. A Scrayling thrust his spear and Sassa was sure that Thyri was done for, but the girl melted aside, spun like a squirrel, whacked the spear aside with her shield, twisted around and struck low to chop off her attacker's foot. Thyri had spent countless hours sharpening that sax.

Keef the Berserker roared and chased after two Scraylings, his axe Arse Splitter held aloft.

Two men attacked Bjarni with hand axes and he defended desperately with his lovely sword Lion Slayer.

Ogmund the Miller, already drunk or perhaps still drunk from the night before, swayed and lurched, but somehow managed to not only keep two Scraylings at bay with his long, flanged spear, Alarmed Calf, but also to wound them. One of his attackers had a gushing gash in his thigh and surely wouldn't last long, and the other was clutching his arm.

Wulf felled a third with his hammer Thunderbolt then ran over to help Bjarni. Two Scraylings armed with flint knives took after Wulf. He hadn't spotted them.

"Behind you, Wulf!" Sassa shouted. He leapt round and dispatched one with a backhanded hammer blow. The second was cannier, leaping from foot to foot, eyes sly. He circled Wulf, blood-stained knife alive in his hands. Wulf swung, the Scrayling dodged and lunged.

Seeing the threat to her man finally jolted Sassa into action. She jumped up and ran into the longhouse to fetch her bow.

Frossa the Deep Minded followed the Hird and their tagalongs a little way down the road from Hardwork towards the two pillars of smoke. She reached the top of a dune in time to see Ottar and Freydis join Finnbogi and head after the Hird into the trees.

Good, she thought. Somehow the children had avoided Garth thus far, but with everyone panicked and spread through the woods it would be easy for two little children to become separated and torn apart by a bear. Possibly Garth wasn't bright enough to work out that this was the perfect opportunity—Frossa had been let down many times by overestimating others' intellects—but he'd been carrying the bear paw under his mail shirt as a reminder, so surely he'd seize the day?

Frossa practised the face she'd make when she was told about the children's deaths. If she remembered all the injustices she'd suffered, she might be able to squeeze out a genuine tear or two. The people looked to her as a mother figure as well as a spiritual leader, so it would help them heal if she could lead the grieving.

She turned to return to town and tell Jarl Brodir that the deed was all but done.

Her mouth fell open.

Out on Olaf's Fresh Sea was a fleet of canoes, bigger canoes than she'd seen before, with bizarrely high prows and sterns. They were slicing silently through the dawn-lit, puddle-calm water towards Hardwork. There were well over a dozen boats, each carrying more than a dozen warriors.

She felt her breakfast sink to the pit of her stomach. Suddenly she knew that it didn't matter whether it was Ottar or Freydis who had prophesied Hardwork's destruction. What mattered was that he or she had been right. Hardwork, with its broken walls and the few defenders it did have off in the woods—lured by decoys as Wulf had suspected and Brodir had pooh-poohed—wouldn't stand for a moment against so many attackers. They were doomed.

She tried to persuade herself that maybe, just maybe, there was a peaceful explanation. Perhaps these were merchants? However, as if to make the raiders' intentions clear, a warrior stood up in the nearest boat, pulled back on a bow and loosed an arrow at her. It missed by about ten feet, but he'd definitely been trying to hit her.

"Scraylings!" she screamed, waddling down the slope to town as fast as she could. "Scraylings!"

Freydis and Ottar were aggravatingly slow, so Finnbogi ran ahead. He soon caught up with the Wolf section of the Hird, who weren't going nearly as quickly as you'd expect given the urgency of the situation, and sprinted past them.

"Wait, Boggy!" shouted Garth.

Bugger off, thought Finnbogi, you have no authority over me.

He ran on through the trees. He'd nearly reached the church when a horrible, throaty yell brought him to a shocked standstill. It had sounded like his Aunt Gunnhild. What by Loakie was happening up there? He looked round for the Hird, but he'd turned a corner a hundred paces back and they hadn't even got that far yet. They were in no hurry, the buggers.

He stepped one way and then the other, then thought *screw it*, put his head down and ran as fast as he could towards the church.

Thumps and whacks and a Scrayling-sounding scream sounded out ahead. He stopped, pulled his sax from its scabbard with a shaking hand, and ran on. Lying in bed, he had often fantasised about dispatching hordes of enemies with the little sword. Now that he might really have to use it, he felt weak and sick.

He almost collapsed when he reached the churchyard. It looked like a tornado had ripped through it. Uncle Poppo, Alvilda and Brenna were on the ground, looking dead, alongside perhaps eight Scrayling warriors. The life- or death-sized cross of Krist had been knocked over and there was a dead Scrayling pinned beneath it.

He heard a shout from the side of the church and ran there.

Two Scraylings with stone axes were advancing on

Gunnhild. She was dressed in her cotton nightgown, swinging her heavy clothes beater at them. Family legend said that the jewel-encrusted clothes beater had once been a warlock's sceptre in the old world. Judging by the Scrayling with his head caved in at Finnbogi's feet, it was now a Scrayling beater.

A Scrayling lunged. Gunnhild whacked his axe away. None of them had spotted Finnbogi. He raised his sax high and tiptoed up behind the rightmost attacker. The other swung his weapon at Gunnhild. She stepped back, tripped over the tree stump that Finnbogi had put there a couple of weeks before and never got round to carving, and fell. She yelled as she went down, her head cracked onto a stone, and she was silent.

Finnbogi closed his eyes and slashed his sax.

The blade struck, and stuck. He opened his eyes. His sax was deep in the Scrayling's shoulder. Finnbogi wrenched it free and took a step back. The man turned, eyes mad, a hand flailing at his horrible, blood-pulsing wound.

"Sorry," Finnbogi heard himself begin to say, but the word caught in his throat as the other warrior jumped round and raised his axe. Finnbogi lifted his sax. His opponent was short, but all sinew and muscle. He had blood smeared over his face and chest. Behind him, Gunnhild lay still.

Finnbogi lunged with his blade. The Scrayling caught his wrist and squeezed. The Hardworker yelped, dropped the blade and stepped back. His attacker smiled and bent to pick up the sax. Straightening, he licked blood off his lips, jutted his head forwards and made a very alarming noise— something like a large, angry, cornered lizard might make. Finnbogi guessed it was a war cry, meant to terrify him.

It worked.

He turned and ran into the woods. Something tangled between his calves and he went down. He heaved his face off the ground and spat out a mouthful of soil. He was face to petal with yellow, purple and white flowers, their prettiness jarring with his situation.

"Thank you for the blade, Mushroom Man," came a voice from behind him, speaking the universal Scrayling tongue in a strange accent. "You have earned a slow, coward's death, and it begins now. It will last a while."

Finnbogi tried to get up but the Scrayling kicked his feet away and he collapsed onto his face. He turned over. On a bush's slim branch to his left was a large silk caterpillar nest, full of black eggs and crawling with black, white and brown caterpillars. He grabbed the branch and thrust the seething mass at the Scrayling. The man chopped the top off the branch and the nest fell onto Finnbogi's face. He spluttered and clawed at it, pulling silk, eggs and hairy caterpillars out of his mouth.

He stopped when he felt a blade—his own blade—press into his neck.

Chapter 13

All Old Friends

"Good morning," said Erik, looking round at the archers, and nodding hello. They were all old friends. He'd slept with one of them—Sittiwa—several times, and had thought that they might even marry, but her parents had got involved. For some reason they hadn't wanted their daughter to hook up with a large shaggy alien who lived on his own in the forest. He'd seen their point and actually been a little relieved. He'd liked Sittiwa but, honestly, he liked solitude more.

Neither Sittiwa nor the other archers responded to his cheery greeting. They kept their arrows trained on him, looking deadly serious, or at least as serious as a group of Scraylings dressed in rabbit-ear headbands and spider-leg skirts could look. Twenty years he'd been with the Lakchans, and still he found their rabbit/spider outfit somewhere between gently amusing and thigh-slappingly hilarious, depending on his mood. This was one of those more gently amusing times.

"I came to ask why you sent people to kill me," he said.

"I thought you would," said Chief Kobosh, breathing out a cloud of smoke. His words bubbled hoarsely in his throat; a result, Erik reckoned, of his constant pipe use. Couple that with the swearing, and he did not have the most delightful speaking voice. "You didn't kill any of the fuckers I sent, did you?" he rasped.

"You'll find them tied up by my place. They'll have head-aches, but no permanent damage." (He hoped; he had hit one of them pretty hard in the heat of things, and if a lion, wolf or any number of other animals found them, they might be in trouble...)

"Good. I didn't think you'd hurt them."

"I see. But you did send them to kill me?"

"Yeah. And now I'm going to kill you. Someone pass me a bow." Sittiwa gave him hers, which upset Erik a little, given all that he and Sittiwa had been through.

Kobosh pulled back the string and aimed the arrow at Erik's heart. Then he lowered the bow.

"Doesn't feel fucking right, killing you in front of these cunts like this, you being an old friend and all." He waved at his archers dismissively. "Fuck off the rest of you, I want to do this in private. Go and collect those useless cunts from up at Erik's place.

"Right," said Kobosh when they'd gone, putting the bow on the ground next to the Spider Throne. "You're in fucking trouble."

"I'd guessed." This was proving to be one of his more confusing mornings. "Why?"

"Runner came from the Calnians. They want you dead."

"What did I do to them?"

"It's what you will do. You and those Hardworker fuckers you came from are going to destroy the world."

"Are we?"

"Yes. Dunno how. To be frank, I can't see you managing it. But the cunt empress of Calnia had some vision. So that's it. We've got to kill you or they'll send a fucking army to do you, and us while they're at it. They're not bad as over-lords go, the Calnians, they leave us alone most of the time. But they are no fucking fans of direct disobedience."

"I see. So you'd better kill me."

"Don't be a cunt. You've been a good friend. An odd fucking friend, but a good one. So, here's the deal. You have to fuck off."

Banished, again! What was it with him and groups of people? Everything seemed fine, then after twenty years they told him to leave. "Where to?"

"A long fucking way. You've got to go west, across the Water Mother." First the voice in his head, now Kobosh—everyone wanted him to go west. "The Water Mother is a big fuck-off river that the Calnians don't cross. Head towards the setting sun and you'll come to a river that you'll think is the Water Mother. That'll be the Rock River. There should be boats around, but if there aren't, find one. Do not try to swim the cunt. It's full of fucking fish that'll fucking eat you. Then you'll get to another river and say: 'fuck me, that's a big fucking river, that Rock River was a fucking streak of piss in comparison.' That'll be the Water Mother."

Erik had in fact journeyed across the Rock River and to the bank of the Water Mother the previous summer, but he understood that all men love giving directions, so let Kobosh continue.

"Cross that. You'll be safe from the Calnians there and, once you're across the Water Mother, they won't know I spared you."

"How come?"

"I said. Calnians don't cross the Water Mother."

"Why not?"

"Everyone knows the Calnians don't cross the Water Mother. I don't know why, they just fucking don't. It's probably because of the fucking Badlanders. You're safe from the Calnians on the other side of the Water Mother, but you're a long fucking way from safe. Do not fucking dally. Go as fast as you can, west, west and west some more until you're through Badlander territory. To the west of the Badlanders, the Black Mountains are safe. I suggest you settle there. Do not, whatever you fucking do, go beyond the Black Mountains and into the Shining Mountains.

"It'll be dangerous. Fucking dangerous. And it's a fuck

of a long way across Badlander territory, not far shy of a thousand miles, and you've got to keep clear of the Badlanders the whole way. Don't even try to talk to them. If they see you, hide. If you can't hide, run. You think the Calnians are cunts? The Badlanders make them look like pussies. Do not go near them."

"Okay. Can I have a few days to pack up?"

"You've got until noon."

"Noon tomorrow?"

"Today, you silly cunt!" Kobosh chuckled wetly. "Go back the way you came and don't let anyone see you. And don't think about going back east to warn your tribe. They're already dead. You're the last of them left alive."

"What?"

"Runner said. The Goachica launched some big fucking attack on Calnia, the cunts, so the fucking Swan Empress sent a massive army to do for the Goachica, and the Hardworkers while they were at it. Killed them all, he said."

"Shit."

"Yeah, man, you're the last fucking Hardworker. If you want to die too, head east. Otherwise it's west. You'll enjoy it. You're like a caged bear here, it'll do you good to run free. Look after yourself. I'm going to miss you. Goodbye, Erik the Angry."

"I'll miss you too, Kobosh, and thanks for everything. Goodbye." Erik shook his head, still trying to come to terms with the idea that all of his old tribe were dead.

"Wait a minute," rasped Kobosh, "I can't remember. Were you ever Angry?"

"Aye, when I first got here. I was fucking Angry."

Chapter 14
Sassa's First Kill

"Ottar, shush!" Freydis whispered. She was clinging to his shirt. He was trying to stand up.

Ottar giggled. It was a funny game, the big man Garth chasing them with the animal hand. It had been fun running, and it had been fun hiding in the long grass. But now the grass was itchy, he was hot and he didn't like Freydis holding him. He wanted to stand and see where the big man was. He hit Freydis's arm.

She pressed her face very close to his, eyes wide, and shook her head.

"It's not a game," she whispered so he could only just hear. "He wants to hurt us. You must stay quiet."

Ottar hated being hurt.

"Come out, come out!" shouted the big man, nearby. "I've got maple sugar!"

Maple sugar! Ottar tried to stand but Freydis held him. He raised his arm to hit her again, but her eyes were big and he stopped. "He's lying," she said, so quietly that he had to watch her lips to hear. "He doesn't have any maple sugar. If you're quiet and he doesn't find us, I will give you some maple sugar. But only if he doesn't find us. *Please* stay quiet."

She was scared, which scared Ottar. He felt his lips curl and wobble and he was going to cry, but Freydis shook her head. He mustn't cry. He could see Garth through the grass now, wearing his metal shirt and helmet, coming closer and closer. Ottar didn't want to be hurt. But Garth was right on them. He'd find them any moment.

Sassa Lipchewer ran out of the longhouse with an arrow strung, but the fighting in the yard was over. Scraylings lay dead: skulls smashed, guts spilled.

"Got any booze in there, Sassa?" asked Ogmund the Miller. He was holding his arm, blood seeping through his fingers and eyes narrowed in pain, but he was grinning as always, cheeks ruddy. The other Hird and Bodil Gooseface were unharmed.

"Sassa!" Wulf pointed at a Scrayling fleeing across the big field, then at her bow. He wanted her to shoot him, in the back. She shook her head. No way.

"Sorry, my love, but he mustn't escape. Give me your bow and I'll do it."

Wulf was a terrible shot. Screw a shrew, she thought. She raised her bow and drew the string. She aimed high because of the distance. There was negligible wind, so no need to allow for that. She had shot smaller deer at greater range in harsher conditions. But she'd never hurt a person, let alone killed one. Yet here she was, aiming her bow at a man who had parents, siblings, probably a wife. Probably children.

As she loosed, she knew she'd hit him.

The man fell. She heard the thwunk of her arrow into his back a moment later. He flailed an arm at the sky, then lay still. Thyri was already sprinting towards him, bloodied sax blade aloft, presumably to finish him off. It was turning out to be a very strange day.

"Awesome shot!" said Keef, "You totally—"

"That'll do, Keef," said Wulf, putting a hand on his shoulder.

Sassa stood stunned, staring at the crumpled little shape

in the field. Thyri reached him and chopped down with her sax. Sassa remembered her dead parents. Killing a man had made her forget for a moment. She walked over to her mother's body. Somebody had closed her eyes.

Wulf took her arm gently. "We have to go, right now. There's nothing more we can do here and—"

The Hird trumpet rang out from Hardwork.

"Well, that," said Wulf. "We have to go."

"I don't think I—" Ogmund the Miller stood, wobblingly. "I feel..." His knees crumpled and he went down.

"Bodil, tend to him," said Wulf. In all their years together, Sassa had never seen him like this. His permanent air of boyish frivolity had dispersed to reveal a calm, commanding and charismatic man. "Find a shirt in the house and use it to bandage the wound, then prop his arm up on something."

"Which arm?"

"The injured one."

"Sure thing." Bodil nodded. "What should I prop it on?"

Wulf picked up a log and placed it next to Ogmund. "That."

"Okay!"

"Good. Bring him to Hardwork if he can walk any time soon, otherwise we'll come back for you."

"I'm to stay here?"

"Yes, with Ogmund. Don't leave him."

"Got it."

"Unless he wakes up and is well enough to make the journey to Hardwork."

"Sure thing."

"Right. Come on the rest of you."

Finnbogi heard a crunch and lumpy spray blatted into his face to join the tangle of silk, caterpillars and moth eggs. The pressure of the blade released from his neck. He opened one eye. The Scrayling was toppling, his head destroyed.

"Buck up, boy!" said Gunnhild, clothes beater in hand. *"Man is not born brave, he acquires bravery by acting bravely.* Are there more?"

Finnbogi clambered to his feet, scraped the worst of the gunk off his face and stared at his aunt. She was smeared with blood, there were chunks of Loakie knew what stuck to her nightgown and face, but she was apparently unharmed.

"...more?"

"Scraylings."

"I don't know. I don't think so."

His aunt shook her head in her standard "isn't Finnbogi useless" manner and headed back to the churchyard. He mopped the remaining gore and caterpillars from his face— the caterpillar silk acted like a cloth, which was handy—and followed her. She walked around the dead Scraylings, whacking each of them on the head with her jewelled club.

Finnbogi saw movement out of the corner of his eye and jerked around. It was his uncle Poppo Whitetooth, raising an arm. Finnbogi ran over and knelt next to him.

"Ah, Finnbogi."

He lay grey-skinned in a pool of blood.

"Uncle Poppo. Where are you hurt? What can I do?" He felt tears spring into his eyes.

"First of all you can stop grieving. You die when you die, and today is my day. Hardworkers do not mourn the dead, not for a moment. Secondly you can listen. We have not made a brilliant job of bringing you up in place of your own parents, and for that I'm sorry, Finnbogi."

"That's okay..." Finnbogi could not help the tears.

"As a result, you've become what one might call a bit of a twat. You're a good lad deep down, Finnbogi, but you are judgemental and superior."

"I'm not, I..." Finnbogi shook his head. His uncle calling him a twat with his dying breaths would make it easier not to grieve for the man.

"Shush. Listen. You are more than you think you are. You are better than you think you—"

"I think I'm all right. I could have stayed in the town but I came running back here to the church and I sped away from Garth when I could have—"

"Finnbogi," Poppo cut in, shaking his head weakly, "you're the sort of fellow who interrupts a dying man's last words."

He had a point. Finnbogi squashed his lips and widened his eyes into an "I'm sorry, please go on" expression.

"You can change, but that's not what I wanted to tell you. I have something important to say about your parents. Your father . . . your father . . . is . . ."

Poppo's eyes rolled back into his head and he died.

Crap, thought Finnbogi.

Gunnhild knelt for a moment next to her two daughters and husband, whispering words that Finnbogi couldn't hear, then stood.

"Right, Finn," she said, "you and I will go to Hardwork, fetch the Hird and—"

She stopped as Gurd Girlchaser appeared from the town-ward path, followed by Hrolf the Painter, Fisk Fisheye and Frood the Silent, all brandishing swords and spears.

"You took your time." Gunnhild pointed her club at them. "Two of you head in that direction, two in the other," she pointed to either side of the church. "Go slowly, watch for hidden Scraylings. If you come across more than two of the buggers, shout. If you hear a shout, run to help but go carefully. They're not above a trick or two. That's how they got Poppo. All right. Gurd and Hrolf, you—"

Where was Garth? Finnbogi wondered. And where were Ottar and Freydis for that matter? He opened his mouth to interrupt Gunnhild's orders and tell her that the children were missing when there was a wap! sound.

Frood the Silent, a rat-faced man who Finnbogi had hardly

ever spoken to, put a hand to his neck and found an arrow in it. He fell, gurgling nastily. Finnbogi stared at him, feeling weak. The rest of them shouted and ran at the Scrayling who'd shot him.

Hrolf got there first. The Scrayling dodged the spear thrust and swung his axe into the Hardworker's face with a sound like a hammer hitting a sack stuffed with wet fish and dry twigs. Hrolf turned slowly. His jaw was hanging by a strip of skin from his cheek. His spear tumbled to the ground, he gripped his jaw with both hands and looked down goggle-eyed at the ruined mess of teeth and bone. A keening whine sung out from the blood-gushing hole which moments before had been a mouth.

Finnbogi stared at him, his own mouth open.

Hrolf staggered away. Lithe little Fisk and lumbering Gurd circled the Scrayling. The raider lurched at Gurd. Fisk speared him in the side. The Scrayling dropped his axe, grabbed the spear shaft with both hands and pulled the blade from his torso, all the while staring into Fisk's eyes. The spearhead suck-squelched out of the man and black blood flowed from the wound. The Scrayling ripped the spear from Fisk's grasp and for an instant Finnbogi thought the Scrayling was some kind of immortal demon who was going to use the spear on its owner, but Gurd whacked his iron axe into the Scrayling's chest, through skin and ribs and into lungs, and he fell.

"Bunch of idiots," said Gunnhild. "Hrolf, come over here and I'll see—"

Finnbogi shook his head. He'd always pictured battle as a lot more glamorous and a lot less disgusting and terrifying. He looked around. Where, by Tor's tits, were Garth, Ottar and Freydis? Had they been caught by another group of Scraylings?

"Fisk, will you bring your spear and come with me?" he asked.

"Why?" Fisk narrowed his eyes.

"I think Garth and the children might be in danger."

Fisk looked at the corpses of Finnbogi's adoptive family and nodded.

Finnbogi ran back into the woods. Fisk pounded along behind him.

"Scraylings! The Scraylings are coming!" yelled Frossa as she jog-wobbled along Hardwork's main street, huge colourful hat slipping askew on her sweat-slicked head.

"What are you talking about?" shouted Brodir, running from Olaf's Square, then, when he reached her: "Quieten down, you're scaring everyone."

"They need to be scared! They're coming," she panted, "in boats. They'll be here—"

She was interrupted by a yelp from Olaf's Square. "Arrows!" somebody shouted. Others screamed.

"Follow me!" Jarl Brodir ran towards the square.

Frossa took a step after him, then stopped. If anybody survived this attack, they would need care and spiritual guidance. As the Hird trumpet parped for a second time that day and Hardworkers yelled, Frossa squeezed through the large gap between two houses. She knew a hiding place over on the edge of the town.

The next street was empty, apart from a solitary Scrayling, advancing towards her, stone axe raised.

Jarl Brodir the Gorgeous saw that the Hardworkers in Olaf's Square were panicking like cooped turkeys who've smelled a lion. They needed direction. They needed leadership. They needed a hero. And that hero had arrived. Cometh the hour, cometh Brodir the Gorgeous.

"Everyone take weapons! To me!" he shouted as he drew Foe Slicer, the beautiful, pattern welded sword that Olaf the Worldfinder's ghost had given him. Scrayling Slicer— that's what he'd rename his sword after this famous day!

He ran past two Hardworkers lying still and another slithering for cover with an arrow sticking from his back. "Frossa, tend to the wounded! The rest of you, to me!" He didn't look back, he knew they'd be leaping to obey his orders, caught up in his majesty, in his gorgeousness.

He fizzed with confidence and battle lust. He'd dreamt often that the Scraylings might attack and his Hird might finally be put to the test. This was even better. The Hird were away and he would be the Hird. He had been in the Hird for half of his life, he still had the skills and now he had wisdom, too. He was invincible. He would lead the defence against the inferior natives. What were they thinking? No matter what numbers the Scraylings attacked with, how could they hope to triumph against the old world blood of the Hardworkers?

The first Scrayling attacker ran into Olaf's Square, dressed in a breechcloth and brandishing a stone axe. Brodir ran to welcome him with steel. Steel always beat stone. He swung Foe Slicer.

The Scrayling ducked. Something flashed at the Jarl's face and struck his chin. Light flared, narrowed into a point and disappeared.

He opened his eyes. He was lying on his back. Above him was the bare sole of a raised foot. The foot slammed down. Brodir the Gorgeous's head cracked to the side.

He could see the other Hardworkers, the ones who'd stood back when he charged. They were gawping at their felled leader.

So his fight had started with something of a setback, but he'd soon show his people what happened when a Scrayling messed with a Jarl.

His hands didn't respond. He couldn't get up. He couldn't move! That wasn't good. Something thudded into his ear, hard. That foot! What foot? Everything was cloudy. Why was everyone watching him? Oh yes, the Scrayling's foot.

He was about to defeat the Scrayling to show his people how easy it was. But what kind of underhand fighter stamps on your ear? He'd show him, just as soon as he could get up.

The foot thudded down again. Yes, I'll show him, thought Jarl Brodir the Gorgeous.

The foot stamped again and Jarl Brodir the Gorgeous felt the side of his skull collapse.

"Welcome," said Frossa to the lone Scrayling, "I am a great warlock—therefore above the fighting. If you head that way," she pointed towards the square, "you'll find the normal people, the ones you're looking for. If you're planning to kill them all, then some of you are sure to be wounded. I can tend to those wounds."

"Sorry," said the Scrayling. He was dressed in a breech-cloth and was distractingly good-looking—beautiful, even. A slim, muscled waist rose from his breechcloth into bulgingly defined pectoral muscles. He had great rounded shoulders, and his chin and cheeks could have been carved from the most wonderful brown-blue marble by Heimdall himself. His nose was large but well-shaped and powerful, like a whitecap eagle's beak. His eyes were narrow, twinkling with a knee-weakening mix of manly strength and boyish good humour. "Quite good-looking, for a Scrayling" was a phrase she might have used before, but this man was another level, better looking than any man or woman she'd seen before, Scrayling or Hardworker. Could he be a god?

She gathered herself. He might be a god, but with the Vanir blood in her veins, so was she. "You're sorry? Why are you doing this?" She closed her fingers around her ivory-hilted sacrifice knife. No, his beauty didn't faze one as wise as her.

"It's your fault. The Swan Empress Ayanna herself has seen the Mushroom Men destroy the world and warlock

Yoki Choppa has endorsed the prophecy, so you all have to die before you kill the rest of us. I am leader of the army commanded to carry out the sad but necessary deed. It's all of you, I'm afraid. We can't make exceptions. I can't especially, since I'm in charge. Leading by example, and all that."

Men, thought Frossa. This chap, lovely though he was, could not help telling her that he was in charge, three times. He spoke the shared Scrayling tongue with a lilting accent that she'd never heard before.

"What's your name?" she asked, as he advanced.

"Kimaman."

"Well, Kimaman, I am Frossa the Deep Minded. I have met the Duck Empress several times and we are close personal friends. Take me back to Calnia with you, and she can decide whether I should die with the rest of them. If you agree, I'll show you the hiding places where some of them might have fled and you can be sure that you've killed them all—apart from me. Then you can kill me later if the Duck Empress commands it."

He laughed. Why was he laughing? This was far from funny. "No, sorry." He was right on her. "Hang on, what's that smell? Oh, by Innowak's rays, that's vile! Is that you?"

"No."

It was her. It was the smell of the rotting sacrifices that she kept in her house. Some days it carried with her more resiliently than others. She looked over his shoulder. "It's the town bear. Here he comes." She pointed behind him.

He turned.

Frossa drove her dagger between his ribs, into his heart. He collapsed and sighed as he died.

Built like Tor and just as dumb, thought Frossa. If Kimaman had been a god, he'd definitely been brutish Aesir, not enlightened Vanir like her.

She picked up his stone axe and headed between the next

row of thatched houses. There were more screams from Olaf's Square. A few people were running towards the centre of town, weapons in hand. They didn't notice her as she hurried towards the unused blacksmith. There was a cellar there, with a hatch that was all but invisible.

She was being sensible, fleeing the battle. There was no shame in running away from certain death. If any of the idiots running towards the fight had seen how many Scraylings had come across Olaf's Fresh Sea, they'd have fled, too.

She arrived at the blacksmith's at the same time as Rangvald the Lawsayer and his son Chnob the White—father and brother of Thyri Treelegs. Thank Fray Thyri wasn't with them. These two weaklings she could deal with.

Frossa didn't have a great deal of pity to spare—few people had had it as hard as her, after all—but she did feel a glint of sympathy for Thyri. Her mother had died when she was young and ever since her father Rangvald had put her down at every turn, all the while glorifying the useless Chnob, who joined in demeaning his sister whenever he could. This happened often in public and Frossa guessed it was worse in private. Frossa did not like the girl, but she could not deny that Thyri had reacted well to her father's constant belittlement, by becoming a bold, ambitious young woman and first female member of the Hird. Her father and brother's regular reproaches may have resulted in a positive outcome, but Frossa doubted very much that had been their plan. No. They were weak, nasty, small men, jealous of a more capable woman, even if, or perhaps because of the fact that she was one's daughter and the other's little sister.

"What are you doing?" she asked them. "Why aren't you fighting with the others?"

"Oh, drop your pretence for a second," said Rangvald. "I can see through you. You're here to hide in the cellar just like we are. But there's only room for two. Well, three normal sized people, but there's no way your stinking bulk is going to fit with us and we got here first. So fuck off."

Frossa strode up to Rangvald and whacked Kimaman's stone axe into his forehead as if it was a hammer, Rangvald a wooden post and she was trying to bury a nail with one hard, well-placed hit. The attack was so unexpected that Rangvald didn't even raise his arms. *So he could see through her, could he?* thought Frossa as Rangvald the Lawsayer's eyes crossed and he fell.

Chnob the White was already on the other side of the heavy work table, gripping its sides and ready to flee.

"We two can fit down there," he gasped. "I won't tell anybody what you did to Dad. If anyone else survives I'll tell them I saw a Scrayling kill him, then I made you hide in the cellar with me so that you could tend to the wounded after the battle. If nobody else survives you'll have a better chance of staying alive with me to help. I'll be able to hunt and forage and fish and fetch water... Please don't kill me. Let's hide together."

The idea of cramming into the cellar with Chnob and his big beard did not appeal, but the points he made were good, and she knew he was far too cowardly and self-interested to avenge his murdered father.

"All right. Help me with the hatch."

Finnbogi dug his heels into the earth and windmilled his arms to halt his pell-mell sprint along the rutted woodland road. Fisk ran into his back and nearly knocked him over.

"What are you doing? I could have speared you!"

"Sorry."

They'd just passed the overgrown track that ran between the roads from Hardwork to the church and the farm. Poppo had taught Finnbogi rudimentary tracking and he could tell from the fresh broken foliage around the edge of the track that someone had passed that way recently.

He headed down the narrow path, beckoning for Fisk to follow, hardly slowing despite the clinging leaves and twigs. He was so worried about Freydis and Ottar that he didn't even mind if he ripped his best striped trousers. He hacked at dangly, head-height branches with his sax as he ran.

"Come out, come out! You can't hide for ever!" That was Garth's voice, up ahead. Finnbogi held up a hand, slowed, jogging now as quietly as he could along the vegetation-choked trail, Fisk tripping along behind him.

They burst out of the trees and into a meadow of long grass, dotted with a few spindly young trees here and there. It was an old field that had been part of Sassa Lipchewer's farm but was now abandoned to nature.

Garth was off to the left, holding something large, furry and white in one hand.

"Garth!" shouted Finnbogi. "What are you doing?"

The big man strode over. For a moment Finnbogi thought he was about to whack him with what he could now see was a big white bear's paw, but then he seemed to spot Fisk and decide not to. He flung the paw into the long grass.

"What was that?" Finnbogi asked. "What are you doing? Have you seen Ottar and Freydis?"

Garth looked at Finnbogi's bloodied blade. "Never mind that, what have you been doing?"

"Nothing much. Killed a Scrayling. Wasn't a big deal."

"You? Killed a Scrayling? Was it a child?"

"No. A warrior. They raided the church. I don't know why. Poppo, Alvilda and Brenna are dead."

"Shit."

"Yeah. I got there in time to save Gunnhild. But why didn't you come? What are you doing here?"

"Hello, Finnbogi the Boggy," said Freydis, as she and Ottar stood up from the long grass five paces away.

Garth glared at them. Freydis looked at the big man as if he were a cauldron of water and she was trying to make him boil by staring at him. Ottar smiled and knocked his elbows together.

Finnbogi looked from the children to Garth and back again. What had been happening here? Why by Loakie's tits had Garth broken off from the Hird mission to the farm to chase the children with a bear's paw?

"What's going on?" he asked.

"We were playing," said Garth, sounding about as playful as plague.

Ottar pointed angrily at Garth and shook his head.

"What happened, Freydis?" asked Finnbogi.

"Garth Anvilchin was pretending to be a bear and chasing us. It was fun."

"Naaaah!" said Ottar, shaking his head.

"Ottar doesn't agree."

"He does. He says things differently. Now come on, we have to go and bury Poppo Whitetooth, Alvilda the Aloof and Brenna the Shy."

"How do you know they're dead?" asked Fisk.

"Finnbogi the Boggy said, when you got here."

"Ah."

The far-off note of the Hardwork trumpet sounded through the woods.

"There's trouble in town," said Garth.

"Of course there's trouble in town," Freydis shook her head. "Did you not listen to Ottar's prophecy?"

Garth turned and ran.

"Hurry!" Freydis shouted at Garth's back.

Finnbogi looked down at Freydis. She met his gaze with disturbing equanimity.

"What should we do now?" Finnbogi heard himself asking the six-year-old girl.

Sassa gasped as she ran through the gates behind Wulf the Fat, Keef the Berserker, Bjarni Chickenhead and Thyri

Treelegs. Doors were smashed, walls split, thatch on fire and Hardworker and Scrayling dead everywhere.

She bent down to close the eyes of Thorval, then man who'd taught her to sew. His mouth was open and one hand gripping the arrow lodged in his heart.

"No time for that yet," said Wulf, touching her shoulder. "Listen."

There were shouts from up ahead.

The five of them crept along, weapons ready, towards Olaf's Square.

As they approached, a voice rang out in a strange accent: "Kimaman is dead, as are many more. We will mourn later, but now let us carry out Ayanna's orders. We will burn the Mushroom Men's buildings and scatter their ashes in the Lake of the Retrieving Sturgeon."

"Not while I'm alive, you won't!" shouted Thyri Treelegs, sprinting into the square with her sax aloft, shield bouncing on her back.

Wulf, Keef and Bjarni ran after her, roaring.

Sassa swallowed then followed.

There were maybe twenty Scraylings in Olaf's Square. The nearest one was staggering, clutching his severed throat as Thyri ran on, blood dripping from her blade.

The other Scraylings gathered to meet her. Sassa closed her eyes. Surely the girl couldn't take on so many?

"Back, Thyri!" shouted Wulf. "Four-man diamond formation!" He looked about. The only visible Scraylings were up ahead. "Sassa, stay here, shout if you're in trouble."

Treelegs dashed back, Scraylings at her heels.

The three men advanced, Keef leading, Wulf behind him to the left, Bjarni behind Wulf to his right. Thyri took her place next to Wulf, making the right-most point of the diamond.

The Scraylings came at them with axes, spears and knives. The four Hird advanced. The raiders charged from every direction with yells and courage but no tactics. This might have worked against the untrained townspeople, but against the tightly synchronised Hird it was suicide. Bjarni's sword, Keef's axe, Thyri's sax and Wulf's hammer swung and sliced and crushed and killed Scrayling after Scrayling.

Two bowmen appeared on the far side of the square and took aim at the Hird, but couldn't get a clear shot. Sassa raised her own bow, drew, aimed, hesitated, thought of her murdered family, and loosed. One bowman fell. The other spotted Sassa. Instead of shooting, he dropped his bow, pulled a flint knife from its scabbard and ran at her. She strung another arrow and shot. Her arrow went well wide and he kept coming, screaming an ululating war cry.

There was no time to string another arrow. She tried to shout for Wulf but no sound came. He was right on her. She dropped her bow and held her hands in front of her face.

Something swished over her head.

She opened her eyes.

The Scrayling was headless, blood spurting from his neck. He toppled as Garth ran past her to join the others, axes in both hands, blood dripping from one of them.

'Mini swine five-man formation!" shouted Wulf. They switched about so that there were two at the front and three at the back. The Scraylings were warier now, holding back. The Hird advanced.

Sassa shot one more Scrayling during the battle. The five Hird slaughtered the rest.

Chapter 15

Foe Slicer

Finnbogi the Boggy, Fisk the Fish and the children reached the main path as Gurd Girlchaser ran down from the church.

"Get back up there, Boggy, help your mother with Hrolf. Fisk, you come with me," ordered Gurd, breathing hard, eyes looking all the bluer in his bright red face.

Finnbogi nodded at Ottar and Freydis to follow him up the path to help Gunnhild because he wanted to, not because Gurd had told him to. And she wasn't his mother.

Fisk and Gurd ran off through the woods towards Hardwork.

Gunnhild had fixed Hrolf the Painter's jaw back in place and tied a scarf under it. The injured man's eyes were slits and he was cooing like a bereaved pigeon.

Aunt Gunnhild prepared food for all of them while Finnbogi used an iron spade from the old world to dig graves for Uncle Poppo, his daughters and Frood the Silent. It was hard work, but the mundane exercise certainly beat thinking.

Gunnhild told Ottar to help with the graves but the boy sat, rocking and looking in turn at Hrolf and the corpses of Frood, Poppo, Brenna and Alvilda. Somebody should probably have looked after him but everyone was busy. Freydis sat with Hrolf, telling him every saga that she'd ever heard. Finnbogi almost told her to stop—Hrolf was in no mood to be listening to stories—but actually her babbling little voice lent an air of calm normality to the otherwise horrible task of burying his kind (until the end at least) adoptive father and sort-of sisters.

Finnbogi avoided looking at them as he dragged them into the graves and set up the holy water tubes. He was just doing a job.

It was only when he started to cover them in soil that he looked at Poppo, Brenna and Alvilda's faces and found himself weeping. Ottar came and hugged him on one side, Freydis joined on the other. He put his arms round them both and the three of them stood and cried. Maybe death was fated, maybe everyone died when they died, but it still felt like someone had rammed a spear into his guts and was twisting it.

"Enough of that," said Gunnhild, emerging from the church with an armful of supplies. "There's work to be done."

"I thought Krist lovers mourned the dead? Don't you care about them?" Finnbogi said.

Gunnhild gave him a look that would have curdled a sea of milk and Finnbogi wished he could have swallowed his words. "They are not dead. They are alive with Krist, in a better place. To mourn them would be selfish and weak." Gunnhild's eyes brimmed with tears. "*Cattle die, kin die, we die; fair fame of he who has earned it never dies,*" she blurted, then dashed back into the church.

After the door banged shut, Finnbogi heard running footsteps coming up the path towards them.

"Hide," he hissed to the children as he pulled his sax from its scabbard. He held it with both hands and stood, shaking a little. He'd protect the children, Gunnhild and injured Hrolf, with his life if necessary. He gulped. He'd heard so many different ideas about where you went when you died—Olaf's Hall, Gefjon's Hall, Tor's Hall and plenty more, as well as Krist's Haven. He wasn't keen to find out where he was going to end up just yet.

Whoever it was, he was coming quickly. Finnbogi gripped the hilt of his sax and took a step back.

Thyri Treelegs leapt from the trees, sax in one hand, shield on her back, eyes aflame. She was in her breechcloth and short leather jerkin, soaked in blood. Her raven-black hair was matted with gore. She looked amazing.

"It's you!" said Finnbogi, happy as he'd been all day.

He dropped his blade and hugged her. It wasn't the greatest hug, due to Thyri's shield and her hands held up between them.

Thyri asked what the situation was and Finnbogi told her. She examined Hrolf, nodding at the bandages.

When Gunnhild emerged from the church, Thyri asked them all to sit down. She had something to tell them.

"The Calnians have killed almost everyone in Hardwork, and at the farm."

"What?" Finnbogi couldn't believe it. "Jarl Brodir?"

"Everyone, apart from Frossa the Deep Minded, Chnob the White, Sassa Lipchewer, Bodil Gooseface and all the Hird, apart from Frood the Silent.

Finnbogi nodded.

"How did you and the other Hird survive?" asked Gunnhild.

"Jarl Brodir sent us to investigate the fires here and at the farm. It's clear now that they were meant as diversions. While we were away the main Calnian force attacked Hardwork. The people fought well. By the time we got back from the farm every Hardworker was dead, but so were most of the Scraylings."

As she spoke, Finnbogi marvelled at her. She was calm, wise, confident and ball-achingly sexy. Could she really be two years younger than him?

"Your father?"

"Dead." Her expression didn't waver.

"How did Frossa survive?"

"My brother Chnob and my father protected her. They wanted to keep her alive to tend to the wounded survivors. My father was killed undertaking that duty. Chnob survived." It looked for a moment like her lip might wobble, but it remained firm. Finnbogi wondered if she was upset more by her brother's survival than by her father's death.

Gunnhild did not look convinced. "Do we know why the Calnians attacked?"

"Frossa spoke to their leader at the start of the attack. The empress of the Calnians ordered it."

"Why?"

"Pale-skinned people like us will destroy the world, apparently." Thyri shrugged. She was not much paler-skinned than a Scrayling, but she didn't seem to know that.

It took them an age to walk down to the town, since walking at any pace was agony for Hrolf. Finnbogi didn't mind too much, as he'd been given an absolute ton of supplies to carry in a big leather backpack that weighed quite enough on its own before Gunnhild had stuffed it with dried meat, smoked fish, tools, a couple of blankets and Oaden knew what else. He couldn't complain unfortunately, since Gunnhild was carrying an even larger pack as well as her clothes beater in case they met any Scraylings, and even Freydis and Ottar were weighed down with supplies.

Mostly he couldn't complain though because Thyri was there. She wasn't carrying anything but was supporting Hrolf, arguably the most difficult job of all, given the weight of the man and the disgusting fluids seeping from his bandages. He wasn't quite sure that Hrolf's hands needed to wander quite so much over Thyri's exposed midriff and lower back; surely the man was too badly injured to be making full use of an opportunity to grope her? Finnbogi wondered for a moment if he himself would exchange having half his face smashed off for the chance to paw at Thyri's torso for a while and thought, on balance, probably not.

* * *

Finnbogi knew the smell of roasting human flesh from crema-
tions, but the reek that assaulted his nostrils as they
approached Hardwork was on another level.

It became even more rank as they walked into the destroyed
town and was almost overpowering by the time they reached
Olaf's Square, one end of which was a funeral pyre.

Wulf the Fat and the rest were gathering supplies.

When the workers spotted Gunnhild and the children,
they ran over and there was much slapping of backs. Sassa
Lipchewer gave Finnbogi a big hug, then helped Thyri to
sit the injured Hrolf in the shade.

Finnbogi asked Chnob how he'd survived.

"What are you suggesting?" spat Chnob, poking a finger
into Finnbogi's chest.

"I'm not suggesting anything, just asking how come you're
alive?"

"How come *you're* alive?"

"I went to the farm, where I rescued Gunnhild by killing
a Scrayling. So that's my story. What's yours?

Chnob reddened. "I defended Frossa. The fighting drove
us to the other side of town. By the time we got back to
Olaf's Square all the Scraylings were dead."

Now this was buffalo shit. One, weedy Chnob wouldn't
have been anybody's choice of defender. Frossa would probably have had more of a chance without him. Two, both of
them should have been in Olaf's Square, helping the others
against the Scraylings. Finnbogi knew Chnob was lying and
he knew that Chnob knew that he knew it. Despite the size
of his beard, Chnob had run from the fight. Finnbogi smiled.

Chnob pushed him two-handed in the chest. He staggered.
The little man came at him, fists raised. Finnbogi was not
going to take this, not from Chnob. He gathered himself to
dive at him, but was grasped from behind by somebody
strong.

"What the *Hel* do you think you're doing?" It was Garth,

towering over both of them by a head, a neck and then some more. His helmet gave him even more height and his mail shirt made him seem, Finnbogi hated to admit, like a warrior hero.

"He came at me, I was just defen—"

"We've all lost people, Boggy. And now we're all mucking in to help. And you're trying to fight one of our own? One of the few of our own that are left? You're pathetic."

"I didn't start it. It was him. He—"

But Garth was walking away and it was Chnob's turn to smile.

Bodil Gooseface and Ogmund the Miller arrived at Hardwork safely. Sassa Lipchewer was beginning to worry about Keef the Berserker when he came running back to the square. He'd been to the nearby Goachica village.

"It wasn't a Scrayling and Hardworker thing," he panted. "The Goachica Scraylings are all dead, bar a few children and elderly who hid in the woods. The Calnians—are we still thinking they're Calnians?"

Wulf nodded.

"They must have hit the Goachica first. Lucky for us the Goachica took quite a lot of the Calnians out. Do we know why they attacked?"

"We have an idea, thanks to Frossa. The more important question is what we do now. And I know the answer," said Wulf. Everybody gathered round him. Sassa was proud.

"There's no question," said Keef. He pointed at Ottar. "If you want proof that we should have already done what the little dude told us to do, it's burning over there." He hoicked a thumb over his shoulder at the mass funeral pyre. "Let's go west of west, to The Meadows." To emphasise this, he swished Arse Splitter in a circle, bisected a make-believe adversary, and stood with the weapon pointed to the west.

"To The Meadows!" Ogmund the Miller raised his spear

boldly, winced at the wound in his arm and lowered it again. He took a big swig from an earthenware jug. Sassa didn't know what was in the jug, but, knowing Ogmund, it wasn't water.

"No!" said Frossa. "My children, we must stay here." She smiled benevolently. Sassa was glad Frossa had survived. She was a calming presence, like a mother to the whole tribe, but, spunk on a skunk, why would she want to stay?

"Why?" asked Keef.

Frossa turned to him, her eyes kind. "Dearest Keef. First, thank you and the rest of the Hird for fighting so hard and well. Without your service, we would not be alive to have this discussion. You are heroes."

"True enough." Keef nodded.

"I understand the excitement of change, but there are many reasons to stay and none to go. Our ancestors built Hardwork. We betray them if we leave. Hrolf is too badly injured to travel any distance, and Ogmund has lost too much blood to be heading into the wilds. Are we so selfish that we'd leave them behind?"

"No," said Bodil.

"The real reason that we must remain is what awaits us in the west. I have spoken to Scraylings from as far away as the Mother of the Waters. Once we leave our boundaries, we become prey to bears, lions, wolves, dagger-fang cats, poisonous spiders, snakes, wasps that will kill a strong man with one sting and nature itself—storms, tornadoes, swamps that will suck you down in an instant, rivers too wide and turbulent to cross even in a boat, mountains too high to climb, and plants that kill with one touch.

"If somehow we survived more than a few days, we'd meet other Scrayling tribes a great deal less paternal than our Goachica friends. They would revel in killing us in ways that simple folk like you cannot imagine. If we get past those, the further we go the more dangerous it becomes.

We will face giants, three-headed trolls and other monsters more terrifying than anything from your worst nightmares."

There were murmurs and everybody looked worried.

"Oh, let's stay here!" cried Bodil. "It was a nice idea to go when it was fun, but it's not fun any more. Oh, *please* let's stay here."

"We can't," said Wulf. "All that Frossa said may be true, but we can deal with it. We can fight wild bears and cats, we can tiptoe around Scrayling villages, we can shelter from weather and we can tread carefully to avoid annoying snakes and all the other dick animals. I suspect the only monsters we'll meet are the ones in our minds, but if we do meet real monsters they will be made of flesh and bone. We have weapons that can pierce flesh and smash bone.

"But more pressing than the reasons not to go is the reason not to stay. There are many more Calnians where that lot came from. They sent an army to kill us all. How do you think they'll react when that army doesn't come home? 'Never mind, let's forget about it and put all our focus into next week's sun festival?' No. They'll send another force to finish us off. They might even send their Owsla. If we want to live, we have to go."

Sassa shuddered. They had all heard of the Calnian Owsla, a squad of ten magic-powered demons, any one of which could slaughter a whole tribe on her own.

"That's exactly it, I could not have put it much better myself," said Keef. "Leave and live, stay here and be killed by the Owsla. So who wants to come, right now?" He raised his hand, as did Wulf and a few others. Sassa put her own up, then watched Finnbogi watching Thyri. Thyri raised her hand hesitantly and Finnbogi's shot up immediately. That made Sassa smile despite it all. She strongly approved of Finnbogi's infatuation with Thyri, not least because it had drastically reduced the amount he perved at her.

"We do not need to risk the west," said Frossa. "We can

simply move a couple of dozen miles north, up the coast of Olaf's sea. They will never find us—"

There was a loud pop from the nearby cremation fire and a charred arm fell off. As Keef walked over to prong it back onto the fire with Arse Splitter, everyone else started talking at the same time.

"I'd like to say something," said Sassa. She put her hand up. The others continued talking over each other. Chnob was chanting: "Stay! Stay! Stay!"

"SHUT UP!" she shouted. They all turned to look at her, amazed. Keef stopped in his tracks back from the fire and raised his eyebrows. Wulf took her arm as if she were ill. She felt herself reddening. They'd never heard her shout before.

"Sorry, but there's something important I need to say. Olaf Worldfinder and our ancestors left the old world because they didn't agree with the way the overlords lorded it over them. They braved a sea far larger than ours, crossed an unknown land and faced unimaginable dangers. Why? Because Olaf had foreseen that they'd find sanctuary here, in Hardwork.

"We have *exactly* that situation again. A larger tribe—an overlord—has killed most of us. We have only two alternatives. Go to Calnia and seek vengeance for the slain, or head west. We have the answer. Ottar predicted the massacre. He was *right*. And now he says we must go west and find The Meadows. We have to trust him, as our ancestors trusted Olaf. We cannot possibly go to Calnia to fight them. We owe it to our ancestors, we owe it to ourselves, but most of all we owe it to our unborn children, their children and on. We must survive. We must go west."

Sassa Lipchewer's speech swung it, and what a great speech it had been. Finnbogi had respected her before, but now he thought she was amazing. She was the wise woman that Frossa claimed to be.

After Sassa's excellent points, everybody apart from Frossa

wanted to leave, even Hrolf. Seeing that everyone was against her, Frossa deigned to accompany them. That was a bit of an arse ache. Finnbogi would have left Hrolf and Frossa behind because they'd slow the rest of them down. Still, if he'd been in their boots he would have gone anywhere rather than be left alone with either of them. Garth and Chnob aside, Frossa and Hrolf were Finnbogi's two least favourite people in all of Hardwork. It was terrible luck that all four of his least favourite people had survived.

"Good," said Gunnhild, "Now, let's get to planning and provisioning. Remember everyone, *there is no better burden on a journey than good sense. In a strange place it is more useful than riches.*"

Everybody nodded while Finnbogi groaned.

They spent the day collecting provisions. Finnbogi had thought it wouldn't take more than an hour, but Wulf the Fat said it would take all day and actually it took a bit longer. It was exciting to really be going, with all of his favourite people as well as his least favourite. Out into the wild! They'd have to take everything on their backs, and Finnbogi's pack was heavy, but he didn't think carrying it would be any big deal since they'd have to go so slowly to allow for Frossa and Hrolf.

There were two big highlights of the day.

The first was when Wulf had handed him Brodir's sword Foe Slicer, along with its silver-studded baldric and scabbard. It was the sword that had been strapped to Olaf the Worldfinder's hip all the way from the old world and which the late Jarl had looted from his grave. Finnbogi drew it. The polished blade's iron core was like a fish's skin, with swirling, dark markings flowing along its length. The edges were hard, shining steel and could chop through any armour. The pommel was jewelled and the grip was carved from the tooth of a great sea beast called a walrus that could swallow a man whole. The more you sweated, the grippier that grip became. It was the best weapon in Hardwork, probably the best weapon for thousands of miles.

"You should have it," Wulf said.

"Why?" Finnbogi wanted it, but he didn't have even the beginnings of a claim to the dazzling scabbard, let alone the fearsome weapon.

"Bjarni has his own sword, I have my hammer, Thyri's got her sax and her axes and her dagger. We Hird all have weapons we know and have trained with for thousands of hours, so we don't want to change. Plus I reckon that after the Hird, and Sassa with her bow, you're going to be the most useful in a fight."

"Not Chnob?"

"Not Chnob."

Finnbogi beamed. Wulf arched an eyebrow. "Don't get cocky."

Finnbogi looped the baldric over his shoulder and Wulf buckled it so the hilt was positioned for a quick grab.

"Will you teach me how to fight with it?" he asked, as Wulf showed him how to draw the blade without chopping his own arm off.

"No, not me. I'm a hammer man." He lifted his weighty hammer Thunderbolt. It was an iron lump the size and shape of a large clog, moulded around a shaft of fire-hardened oak a pace long and held in place by a tight criss-cross of leather strips. Both ends of the handle were sharpened into points. It looked like something a child might knock together in an afternoon, but the sagas said that it was hundreds of years old, magically preserved, and that it had seen much heroic battling. Wulf swung it, missing Finnbogi's nose by a finger's length. "All I know is hit them quick and hit them hard enough that they don't hit you back. Swords are a bit more sophisticated than that. Ask Bjarni to teach you."

"Sure," said Finnbogi, although he didn't want to ask Bjarni, because, secretly, although he liked him a lot, he thought that Bjarni had only got into the Hird because he was Jarl

Brodir's son and he didn't rate him as a fighter. No, thinking objectively, the best person for him to ask was Thyri Treelegs. She was amazing with that sax, and a sax was simply a small sword so surely the training would be the same?

The second highlight of the day was even better. It came when they were deciding who'd share sleeping sacks. Frossa worked it all out, so he didn't think he had a chance. He was pretty sure Frossa didn't know he was in love with Thyri, but he knew she was mean enough to put him with the person he'd least like to be with—Garth (Garth pipped it over Chnob as the person Finnbogi would least like to share a sleeping bag with because he was so much larger).

But Frossa decided the sleeping bag allocation on size—after taking out Wulf and Sassa who were obviously going together—and it had fallen by luck (or by the plan of the gods!) that he and Thyri were together.

Thyri shrugged at the news as if she couldn't care less, and Finnbogi tried to suppress his reaction. With so many so recently dead, it was hardly the time for prancing about and grinning like a loon with a bulge in your trousers.

Despite Finnbogi's suggestion that they try out the sleeping bags, everyone slept on beds in the longhouse, built into the wall way back, when Olaf's Hird would sleep in his hall with him. When it was all quiet, Gunnhild's voice rang out:

"Remember: *a foolish man lies awake worrying; he will wake tired with his laments unchanged!*"

Finnbogi lay awake. His fantasies about Thyri morphed into memories of those who had died, particularly Poppo, Alvilda and Brenna. You die when you die. Hardworkers did not mourn death.

But Finnbogi could not help but sob silently until, mercifully, he fell asleep.

Chapter 16

The Crocodile Tribe

Almost all of the sacrifices who were cajoled at spearpoint onto the Plaza of Innowak knew about Calnian Owsla and were suitably terrified. Every now and then, however, the Owsla got to fight people from backwaters where their fame hadn't spread.

Sofi Tornado liked it when that happened.

Today's lot were twenty raiders, all men, from a troop of humans who lived an isolated life in the swamps to the south-east and called themselves the Crocodile tribe. The fools had come north in search of gold and glory, camped without posting a guard and been captured by Calnian farmers. Not so glorious.

The twenty Crocodile tribesmen looked nervous initially, perhaps cowed by the heckling crowd, the great sun crystal and the gold-topped pyramids that surrounded the Plaza of the Sun. However, the moment they saw their opponents were all women, and that they outnumbered those women two to one, they whooped, jeered and slapped each other's backs.

Sofi smiled.

The Crocodiles lined up opposite her women, some grinning, some striking warrior poses, some pointing their axes and knives threateningly. This was standard battle array. Free-for-alls did happen, especially during raids, but the accepted form of battle throughout the known world was one-on-one combat while the rest watched and waited their turn. It reduced casualties and everybody got to show off their fighting skills.

One of the men pointed at Chogolisa Earthquake: "Look, they're not all women. They've got a buffalo, too! Ugly buffalo at that! She's not even armed! What's she planning to do, sit on us? Ha ha!"

The Crocodiles laughed along. The one who'd insulted Chogolisa stepped forward, still chuckling.

"What is your name?" asked Sofi.

"My name is not important, but you may call me Fist of the Jaguar." He spoke the universal tongue in a tough-man growl, his accent tortured and sharp. "I'm the captain of the Crocodile army and undefeated in battle." He was beefily muscled, shaven-headed, with the cocksure smile that Sofi Tornado recognised as the smile of someone who'd never lost a fight. "It seems an awful shame to kill women as lovely as you. There are other ways we could tussle that you'd enjoy a lot more."

"Jaguars do not have fists."

"Ha!" Paloma Pronghorn barked out a laugh behind her.

"...What?" Fist of the Jaguar's muscular brow knitted above his small eyes.

"A jaguar cannot bend its paw into a fist. So Fist of the Jaguar is a bad name because jaguars don't have fists. It's like being called Tentacles of the Rabbit, or Talons of the Worm."

"What's your name?"

"Sofi Tornado."

"That is quite good," he said after a pause.

"I can't claim credit for it, but, yes, I think it is."

"Perhaps I'll take it when I've killed you."

"Kill me and it's yours. First, though, pick any one of my Owsla to fight."

"Including you?"

"Anyone." As she spoke she heard the change in his breathing, grains of sand shifting under his feet, skin moving against skin. She stepped back, slipping her obsidian dagger from its sheath. Fist of the Jaguar's stone axe flashed through the air where her head had been a moment before.

Leaning to avoid his next blow, she slid her cruelly sharp obsidian blade into his chest, then reached round and stabbed him in the back.

Fist of the Jaguar stepped away.

"I..." He sucked in a long, windy breath, then looked down at his chest, confused.

"I've pierced your lungs. You've lost a fight for the first time."

He blinked at her.

"On the bright side, you won't be losing any more."

He raised his axe, but the effort to breathe overtook him and he stood sucking in air, shoulders heaving, looking a great deal less cocksure than he had a few moments before.

Sofi smiled at him sadly, then looked along the line of his men. Boastful distain had been replaced by slack-jawed disbelief.

"Chogolisa?" she said.

The giant woman nipped nimbly forward. "Yup?"

"Finish him."

Fist of the Jaguar raised his stone axe, but Chogolisa Earthquake caught his wrist, plucked the axe from his grip with two fingers and tossed it away. She spun him round so he was facing his men, then crouched and thrust one arm between his legs and another under his arm. She linked her hands and stood, picking him up. He beat ineffectively at her massive arms. She pivoted at the hip, making sure that the Crocodiles all had a good look at their helpless leader. Then she squeezed.

Fist of the Jaguar screamed as his back, pelvis and leg bones cracked, then crunched into his guts. A flush of blood from his mouth silenced him. Still she squeezed. The captain of the Crocodile army's torso crackled and squelched. One final sad sound gasped from his already dead throat.

Chogolisa opened her arms and dropped him. Fist of the Jaguar slapped wetly onto the arena floor. Moments before he'd been a proud, well-built man with a jutting chin. Now he was a bag of pulp with limbs and a head.

The Calnians watching from the edge of the Plaza whooped and cheered. The remaining Crocodiles stared at their destroyed leader, mouths open.

Chogolisa returned to her place in the line, flicking blood and viscera from her arm.

"Right!" declared Sofi Tornado, looking up and down the Crocodile line. "Who's next?"

After the Crocodiles were dispatched—they would not be eaten, as they'd been caught before committing any offences against Calnia so would be allowed an afterlife—a boy ran up, leapt over a couple of corpses and told Sofi Tornado that the Swan Empress wanted to see her.

"Hey, Sofi!" shouted Malilla Leaper, leaning cockily on her blood-caked kill staff, her voice loud so that all the other Owsla might hear. "Chamberlain Hatho's pyramid hasn't been reassigned yet. Tell Ayanna we'll take it."

"Good plan," agreed Caliska Coyote, the woman who never smiled. "Our quarters are cramped. We deserve Chamberlain Hatho's."

"I will consider it."

"Please do," said Morningstar, "our barracks is *disgusting*." She wrinkled her nose as if she'd smelled something terrible. "I'm not sure I can sleep another night there. I grew up sleeping on a *bed*. Surely we deserve *beds*?"

Sofi Tornado walked off wondering what in the name of Innowak that had been about. As those three women well knew, you didn't *tell* an emperor of Calnia anything, not if you liked life. Besides, the quarters they had were perfect for training. Chamberlain Hatho's pyramid was in a higher-status location, facing the Mountain of the Sun over the Plaza of Innowak, but it simply wouldn't have worked as a home for the Owsla. And why would they want a status-enhancing home? Their status was already as high as it could possibly be. Morningstar was daughter of the former emperor Zaltan. Although she despised her father—she'd dropped the name he'd given her to be known only by her nick-name—you could understand that she might miss her early life of opulence. But the others?

No, Malilla Leaper had challenged Sofi Tornado with an impossible task. It was an attempt to weaken her in the others' eyes, an attempt which had the support of Morningstar and Caliska Coyote. It might not seem like much, but she'd keep an eye on those three.

Sofi Tornado put the potentially mutinous women from her mind as she bounded up the log steps of the Mountain of the Sun. A childhood memory of ascending a larger pyramid, made of stone rather than earth, flashed into her mind. She wasn't sure if the pyramids of her childhood had really been larger. She'd been five or six when she'd been shipped north to Calnia as a gift to Emperor Zaltan, so had few memories of her first life. Mostly she remembered men with big hats, people jumping off towers, a beautiful woman whom she assumed was her mother, and jaguars. She remembered the jaguars best of all. Gorgeous, fierce and powerful cats, lining the steps up to the emperor's pyramid, roaring and straining at their bonds, stamping their big paws.

At the top of the steps, she walked towards the shining gold roofs, past guards, the empress's sweat lodge and other pristine buildings. Two sickly looking girls sat next to the empress's bathing pool, chosen for the sensitivity of their skin to monitor its temperature. If Ayanna decreed that the pool was too hot or too cold, the girls might be whipped or even killed, depending on the empress's mood. Everyone in Calnia had his or her place. The two girls looked down as Sofi walked by. Owsla training might be hard, but she preferred her place to theirs.

Swan Empress Ayanna was waiting with Yoki Choppa, looking pregnant and unhappy. Yoki Choppa, one of the people who had helped to give the Owsla their preternatural fighting abilities, didn't look up from poking about in his smoking alchemical bowl.

"Kimaman was killed this morning," said Ayanna, as near to tears as Sofi guessed it was possible for the Swan Empress to be.

You're certain?" She looked to Yoki Choppa. The warlock nodded, eyes still on his bowl. He would have taken a lock of Kimaman's hair before he'd headed north. By mixing a hair with Innowak knew what in his alchemical bowl, Yoki Choppa could see where a person was, and whether they were dead or alive.

"Was it the Goachica?"

"It happened in the territory of the Mushroom Men."

"The little tribe of weird aliens?"

"The same." Empress Ayanna told her about her dreams in which the pale-skinned invaders destroyed the world. Sofi had heard of the Mushroom Men and understood that they were useless oddballs. So this was all a little surprising.

"You are to lead the Owsla and kill them all." Ayanna's lips were thin and bloodless. "Do not return until they are all dead. Kill anyone who helped them."

"Certainly. Although... Kimaman may have died but it doesn't mean his army has failed."

"Does," mumbled Yoki Choppa. "I took hair from twenty other warriors. All are dead. Odds are the whole army is gone. Most were killed in Goachica territory in the night, the rest in Mushroom Men territory this morning. I under-estimated both tribes." Yoki Choppa reported the error that had cost the lives of four hundred Calnian warriors with all the emotion of a man who hadn't prepared enough food for a feast.

"So you are to take the Owsla to the territory of the Mushroom Men and leave no human alive," said the empress.

"The survivors may have fled."

"You will track them and kill them. All of them."

"We will do our best. However, tracking can only do so much. If it rains heavily—"

"Yoki Choppa will go with you."

Sofi raised an eyebrow. This was surely a punishment for Yoki Choppa, for underestimating the Goachica and Mushroom Men's capability. "He will slow us down."

"Won't," muttered the warlock.

"Go." The Swan Empress pointed northwards. "Do not return until you are certain that they are all dead. And raze their town. When you are done there will be no trace that the Mushroom Men ever existed."

Part Two

Westward Ho

Chapter 1

A Bear Cub and an Idiot

Seventeen survivors set out from Hardwork. Wulf the Fat and Garth Anvilchin led, followed by little Freydis the Annoying and Ottar the Moaner. The rest of them were strung along behind, feeling varying degrees of odd to be leaving the life they'd always known and heading into the reputedly terrifying west on the say-so of a six-year-old girl's translations of her eight-year-old brother's unintelligible-to-everyone-else pronouncements. It seemed like the right thing to do to most of them—the boy had predicted the massacre and nobody had a better plan—but that didn't mean it seemed like a good thing to do.

Sassa Lipchewer walked towards the tail of the string of refugees, alongside Bodil Gooseface. Sassa had stopped listening to Bodil's gabbling before they'd left Hardwork's walls, knowing that Bodil wouldn't mind or even notice.

Sassa was trying to focus on the future and not dwell on the horrors of the day before, but it was proving difficult. She didn't have the slightest idea what the next hour would hold, let alone the coming days, weeks and years, nor had she any experience other than life in Hardwork from which to extrapolate. Images of her dead family kept flashing into her mind and she could feel unshed tears gathering.

When she reached a rise in a clearing, she turned to say farewell to her home.

"What's up?" asked Bodil, interrupting her own verbalised stream of consciousness.

"I'm going to stand for a second, you go on."

Bodil opened her mouth to disagree, but then seemed to change her mind. "Finn, wait for me!" she called, and jogged to catch up with Finnbogi the Boggy.

The town of Hardwork and the lake of Olaf's Fresh Sea were obscured by the tangle of trees and undergrowth, so Sassa had to be content with saying farewell to the wheeling gulls and the sky that she'd lived under for the first twenty-two years of her life. Clouds rose in five great columns, like fingers stretching upwards across the vast blue. Was the sky trying to clutch onto her or was it waving her away?

Would she ever be back? They'd gone perhaps a quarter of a mile. How long was the path ahead? What, for the love of Fraya, was this place *The Meadows* that they were looking for? Would they ever reach it? Or, as Frossa had predicted, would they be cut down by wildlife or wild Scraylings as soon as they left Hardwork territory?

She said a silent farewell to her mother, father and brother. She wondered which god's hall they'd ended up in. She hoped they were together and hoped that she'd join them when her time came—which would be pretty soon, if Frossa was right. She hoped it was Tor's Hall. She should really want to be in Fraya's, since she prayed to Fraya the whole time to give her a child, but Tor's Hall sounded a lot more fun, plus very few people were as well suited to Tor's Hall as her husband Wulf, and she wanted to be with him.

Tears sprang, not for her dead family as she'd expected, but for her unborn, unconceived children, who'd surely never live now. Five years they'd been trying and failing to have a baby, and now it seemed that she'd be mauled by a monster or stabbed by a Scrayling before she had the chance to bring life into the world.

Frossa the Deep Minded limp-wobbled out of the trees,

accompanied by Hrolf the Painter. Sassa wiped the tears from her face. The injured Hird man was using his spear as a walking stick to keep his ruined jaw from joggling. Behind them were the rearguard of Keef the Berserker and Ogmund the Miller. Ogmund seemed to have recovered from the Scrayling slash to his arm. He was zigzagging a little along the path, but that was more a result of his mead-based breakfast than his injury.

Frossa was good to help with Hrolf, although Sassa reckoned they'd already gone further than the heavy woman had walked in one day for her whole adult life, so hanging back with Hrolf was possibly more to do with necessity than charity.

Hrolf looked seriously unwell. The lower half of his head and his neck were bandaged. The visible part of his face was bloodless as the corpses they'd burnt the day before. However, when they caught up to her, his infirmity didn't prevent him from staring at her chest, as he always, always did. She shuddered and threw her shoulders forward, trying to suck her boobs into her body to escape his oily glare.

Men looked at her the whole time; they had done for as long as she remembered. Usually it wasn't a big deal, or even a deal. Most men glanced at her figure and looked away apologetically, as if it was something that had to be done, they were very sorry about it, and for everyone's sake they were going to do it as quickly as possible and the less said about it the better. They might have to have another quick peek in a while, but they would do their clumsy best to make sure she didn't notice. She didn't exactly enjoy their meek perving, but if it was the price for being an attractive woman, she could pay it.

Hrolf and a few others, however—Jarl Brodir had been one of them—pushed that price far too high. They stared at her unashamedly and proprietorially, as if her body was a spectacle like a carving or a tree in bloom, and they'd ogle just as much as they liked, thank you very much, with whatever drooling expression they chose. Root a coot, it was loathsome, and, although she felt guilty for thinking it, if she had to choose someone to have half his face hacked off by a Scrayling axe it would have been Hrolf the Painter. Judging by Brodir's flattened skull the day before, the Jarl's death had been pretty nasty. Sassa found it hard to feel sorry for him either.

Frossa the Deep Minded was an interesting contrast to the pale lecher Hrolf; she was so red with exertion that she was almost purple. Sassa reckoned the dead-animal smell from her sacrifices had already lessened somewhat, but the sharp stink of her sweat was already rising to take its place.

Despite Frossa's smell, Hrolf's leering and the frustratingly ponderous pace, Sassa stayed back with them. Partly she wanted to help Hrolf—it seemed the right thing to do even if he was disgusting—but mostly she wanted some peace. Frossa was too puffed to talk, Hrolf's mouth was bandaged and Keef and Ogmund were too fixated on scanning the trees for enemies to chat. So they walked in silence.

It was a mercy to be away from Bodil's constant prating. If she was annoying after a quarter of a mile...how far could The Meadows be? Fifty miles? Sixty? She loved Bodil like a sister, but she wished she'd shut up for a few minutes every now and then.

They plodded on through the morning, treading the path that led to the western edge of Hardwork territory. They walked through woodland and wide clearings, skirted lakes and crossed log bridges.

They stopped often, whenever Frossa said that Hrolf needed to rest, which was always at the top of one of the gentle rises. Every time they paused, Keef yelped an accurate impersonation of a fox scream to alert Wulf at the head of the walkers, and Wulf fox-screamed back.

After an hour they were still in Hardwork territory, but they were further from the town than Sassa had been in years, and already it seemed much wilder. They passed through stands of trees twenty or thirty times her height. Herons with insectoid legs lifted off waterways as they approached, the birdsong in the trees was almost unpleasantly loud and geese honked above, flying off to Fraya knew where. In one clearing three young wolves bounded into the open, saw the humans and turned tail for the trees. In almost every other clearing white-tailed deer stared at them from the long grass, ears alarmed but standing their ground, watching them pass.

"Should I shoot a deer for tonight's supper?" she asked Keef.

"Sure, if you want to drag it behind you all day. Or you could wait until we camp when there'll still be shitloads of deer around and shoot one then."

After one of their breaks, Chnob the White joined the gang of backmarkers. As well as a pack, he was carrying Keef's birch-bark boat on his back.

"They're saying up ahead that the Calnians might use alchemy to track us. Is that possible, Frossa?" he asked.

"They won't need alchemy." Keef pointed at the footprints on the earth path.

"As long as it rains like a bastard at some point, we'll be all right," said Ogmund, smiling broadly. He let out a boozy burp to emphasise his point.

"The Scrayling warlocks believe that...they can see which path a person has taken," panted Frossa, "if they mix the right...herbs and other ingredients with part of a person...Hair is the obvious part to use since...it can be collected more easily than...other body parts."

"Do you think they can do that?"

Frossa shook her head. "No, I don't...I can't do it... and I'm more powerfully connected to magic...then anyone I've known or heard of..."

"More so than Ottar?" asked Keef.

"Yes."

"Even though he predicted the massacre?"

"That was coincidence, not magic...The boy lacks the

wit to speak...how can you think he has the wisdom needed...to use magic?"

"Right." Keef raised his eyebrows, spun around, swung Arse Splitter and chopped a make-believe attacker in half.

Towards the middle of the day Sassa and the others bringing up the rear were skirting the north shore of a lake. On their right was grassland pocked with low bushes and surrounded by woodland. For once, there were no white-tailed deer around, but there were strange swells and swirls on the surface of the lake. Sassa was trying to work out whether they were from a current or an unusually large fish, when Ogmund the Miller shouted:

"Lookie there! A bear cub!" His voice was swollen with drunken wonder.

But he was right. There was a small black bear's head poking above the long grass fifty paces away, watching them. With ears erect above a black face and a light brown muzzle, it was an appealing little animal. However, where there was a cub there was probably a mother. Smaller and shyer than a humped bear, a black bear still weighed more than a big man and was quite capable of killing one, especially if that man messed with her cubs.

"It must be orphaned, like us!" Ogmund cried. "It wants to be our friend!"

"Leave it." Keef put a hand on Ogmund's shoulder. "Every bear attack story begins with a bear cub and an idiot."

"Humped bears maybe. But black bears are pussies. I'm going to ask it if it wants to come with us. Alarmed Calf will protect me if mummy's nearby." He waggled his spear with its metal ears.

"Stop, you foo—" began Keef. But Ogmund was already jogging towards the bear.

"Ogmund!" shouted Sassa, but he wasn't stopping for anyone. She had a bad feeling about this. She strung her bow and pulled an arrow from her hip quiver. Frossa leant over, hands sinking into her big thighs, and puffed, no doubt glad of the break. Hrolf stared at Sassa as she drew her bowstring—a manoeuvre with the unavoidable side effect of puffing out her chest. Hrolf's eyes bulged. She considered shooting him. She could always say it was a Scrayling...

"You're a dick, Ogmund!" yelled Keef, walking on ahead.

"Hello, bear," said Ogmund, reaching out to touch it. The cub wasn't afraid of him. It lifted its twitching nose to investigate the new scent. "Are you all alone? Do you want to—"

Mummy was nearer than any of them had guessed. Ogmund didn't have time even to raise Alarmed Calf. The mother black bear launched out the grass like a creature from the deep, and, with one swipe of her paw, ripped his throat to shreds. Ogmund fell.

The bear leapt onto him. Sassa couldn't see because of the long grass, but from the positioning and the way the bear's shoulders were shaking, she guessed the beast had Ogmund's face in her mouth and was trying to rip it off. She'd heard they did that.

She fumbled the arrow onto the string. "Frossa, Hrolf, get behind me."

The bear looked up. Dangling on a stalk from her bloodied muzzle was one of Ogmund's eyes.

Frossa screamed.

The bear glanced at her cub, then started to gallop towards Frossa, Sassa and Hrolf.

Sassa shot, but the arrow went high, over the bear's shoulder.

The bear hurtled towards them and Frossa screamed again.

Finnbogi the Boggy was walking with Ottar the Moaner and Freydis the Annoying. He'd rather have been walking with Thyri—or Keef, or Bjarni or Wulf for that matter, but the Hird were on guard duty. Thyri had been paired off with

Garth, annoyingly, and the two of them were "scouting the south flank," whatever that meant.

So the Hird got to prance about pretending to be warrior heroes, leaving Finnbogi and the other minions to carry all the crap and look after the children. Finnbogi's backpack was massive, weighed down with three sleeping sacks, a load of cooking equipment and about ten tons of dried fish. Why the fish, for the love of Tor! They were going to hunt and forage! They didn't need to *carry* food. The only person who might need extra food was him, to give him the energy to carry all the extra food. It was very unfair. It was all Gunnhild's doing—she just liked to see him carrying things. The only slightly cheering thing was that Chnob the White was weighed down by Keef's boat, which was even more of a burden than Finnbogi's backpack.

Finnbogi had the best sword, so he should have been on guard duty with the Hird. Now he was realising just how heavy Foe Slicer was. What was the point of carrying it if he wasn't going to use it? It was pointless weight, adding to all the other pointless weight on his back.

To make matters worse, for about the last million hours, Freydis had been telling Finnbogi things about animals that he either knew already or didn't want to know. It was as boring as anything had ever been. He did often fantasise about having children with Thyri, but when he thought about it, he didn't really want children at all. The idea of looking after them the whole time filled him with horror. They were so self-obsessed and selfish. They demanded everything, contributed nothing and had no notion of what other people might find interesting. Why couldn't Freydis consider for a moment what he wanted to talk about? She seemed to think she was the centre of the world.

And why weren't she and Ottar carrying anything?

"Stop!" the girl shouted, making him jump. She bent down. "Look here, Finnbogi the Boggy, these are deer mouse tracks. It's a lovely little mouse, the deer mouse. It lives on its own in trees. Ottar likes them, too. There was one time when I was walking with Ottar and—"

"Shush, Freydis," said Finnbogi. He'd heard something. A scream?

"You shush. I'm telling you about—"

There it was again. A scream, coming from the path behind them.

Finnbogi slid the straps from his shoulder and lowered his backpack into the greenery on the side of the path. "I'm going back."

Freydis rolled her eyes, but said: "We'll come, too. Come on, Ottar. But you shouldn't leave your backpack there. Aunty Gunnhild Kristlover said—"

"Let me stop you there," said Finnbogi and ran back the way they had come, smiling at how clever he'd been. Foe Slicer slapped against his thigh as he ran. He half hoped they *were* being attacked and he could use the heavy sword to win the day, rescuing Thyri in the process, of course, and giving weight to the argument that he should be guarding the march, not carrying stuff.

He hadn't got far when he heard two fox yips, the signal for trouble.

There was a booming SPLOSH! behind her, which Sassa guessed was Frossa jumping into the lake. The bear was thirty paces away. She fumbled for an arrow, dropped it and picked it up. The bear was ten paces closer.

"Run, Sassa!" shouted Keef, sprinting back towards her along the lakeside, his axe aloft. There was no way he'd make it in time. He barked two rapid fox yelps, the signal to bring the other Hird to help. But they were even farther away.

Sassa couldn't run because Hrolf couldn't run and she had to protect him, and Frossa, too; Frossa was in the lake and black bears were better swimmers than people.

She loosed an arrow, hands trembling, and it flew wide. There was no time to string another.

"Yah!" shouted Sassa, spreading her arms. "Yah!"

The bear was ten paces away. Five. And it was on her.

The bear bumped her aside with its head, lumbered past, reared up, came down, knocking Hrolf flat, then bit down into his long-suffering face and shook.

Sassa screamed at the animal, beating its furry back with her bow. It kept right on with its savaging, paying her not one jot of attention. Hrolf's arms and legs flailed as if he was a rice-stuffed doll shaken by a baby.

"Get AWAY!" shouted Keef, finally arriving.

The bear looked up, slices of skin hanging from its blood-dripping muzzle.

"Grrrr-ahhhh!" yelled Keef, lifting his axe above his head and looming over the animal.

"Yah!" shouted Sassa. In the corner of her eye she saw people emerge from the trees into the clearing and hoped it might be Wulf. She glanced up. It was just Finnbogi and the children. They would not be much help.

The bear snarled and crouched as if it was going to attack.

"Grrrr-ahhhh!" shouted Keef again.

The bear changed its mind. Its expression morphed from bestial rage into that of a woman who's walked into her hut then forgotten what she'd come inside for. Shaking its head, it turned and lolloped away, back to its cub. The two of them cantered off towards the treeline.

Keef bent down over Hrolf the Painter. "Shitbags, this is not good."

"Let me have a look. You help Frossa out of the lake." Sassa squatted by Hrolf. The attack had torn his bandages away. His jaw was hanging down by his neck, a mess of white bone, red blood and beard hair. Air bubbled through the gore as he exhaled.

Pole a mole, thought Sassa. What to do?

"Give me a shout if the bear changes her mind and comes back!" said Keef, tossing Arse Splitter aside.

Finnbogi the Boggy emerged from the woods with Ottar and Freydis. He saw a bear menacing Sassa and Keef and was about to run and help, but the bear retreated. Frossa, it amused him to see, didn't know that the bear had gone and was still swimming off across the lake, brightly coloured hat abandoned and bobbing behind her, fat arms splashing more than propelling.

"Pouf!" said Ottar.

"No, Ottar," cajoled Freydis, "that's a bad thing. You shouldn't—"

Finnbogi ignored their prattling because out in the lake an enormous fish, at least the length of a man, leapt fully out of the water, hung in the air for a moment, fell and landed on Frossa's head. Fish and woman disappeared with a deep CLONG! which echoed around the lake.

A moment later, but for the ripples spreading from the centre of the smooth water, all was calm. At the edge of the lake, geese carried on honking and flapping their wings at each other as if they didn't care at all about the plight of humans.

"Wow," said Keef. "Now that's something you don't see every day."

He peeled his sleeveless hooded smock and padded leather shirt over his head and set to yanking off his baggy trousers.

"What is it?" asked Sassa, looking up from blood-bubbling Hrolf.

"A fish jumped on Frossa."

"A fish? Is she all right?"

"I wouldn't think so, it was a big fish. Very big."

"What? How big?"

"I'm going to swim out. We'll talk fish size later. Check Ogmund then see what you can do for Hrolf."

Ogmund the Miller was very dead. His face was gone along

with half his head, and his neck was a mess of cartilage and blood. She ran back to Hrolf, knelt by him and jumped when his eyes opened. At first she thought he was gazing blankly, but his pupils swung downwards and he was staring into the gap between her dress and breasts that gravity had opened as she'd leant over him. Somehow, the mess that was left of his face managed to coalesce into a lascivious grin.

The bears were gone. Keef was wading into the lake. Finnbogi and the children were two hundred paces away at the edge of the clearing. There was no way anybody would see if she did what she was seriously considering doing.

Could she?

The night before, Wulf had attached a scabbard containing a sharp iron knife to her quiver, saying it was bound to come in handy. She reached for that knife now, really thinking that she might be about to prove her husband right.

Could she?

How much of a utopia would The Meadows be if it had Hrolf in it, drooling over her and the other women?

Could she?

He was slowing them, and would slow them more with these new injuries. Every extra moment they dallied, the more likely the Calnians would catch them up and kill them. The slower they passed hostile tribes, the more likely that they'd be discovered. She wanted a child. She wanted children. This unpleasant letch was endangering her future, Wulf's future and the future of her unconceived sons and daughters. And if she had daughters, did she want Hrolf anywhere near them?

She slipped the blade from the sheath, amazed and thrilled by what she was about to do.

Chapter 2

Pink Dawn Mist

The eastern sky was lightening when Sofi Tornado ran out of the citadel's northern gate, a smile on her face. The joy in setting out on a mission was a less intense but deeper and warmer sensation than the fevered excitement of catching her prey and slaughtering it.

Paloma Pronghorn and Luby Zephyr tripped along easily beside her. The seven other Owsla followed, with chief warlock Yoki Choppa bringing up the rear.

They had packs strapped tight to their backs and, other than Yoki Choppa, who wore only a breechcloth, they were in standard battle gear of leggings, breechcloth and short-belted jerkin, greased with deer fat to prevent chafing. They carried their weapons in their hands.

The ten women and one man pounded across the wooded bridge over the stream that ran along the city's northern border, and out into the dew-sodden wilds. Sofi nodded to Paloma Pronghorn and the super-fast woman zipped away up the track like an arrow from a bow. There were no dangers between Calnia and Goachica lands that any of her warriors couldn't have taken care of on their own—other than the very unlikely exceptions of large groups of well-trained and disciplined troops and a few, rare animals—but Paloma did love to scout ahead and Sofi wasn't going to stop her.

Waking waterfowl honked mournfully and flapped swirls into pink dawn mist as the Owsla skimmed past lakes. They ran beneath branches draped with dew-spangled spiders' webs, serenaded by sweet singing birds. Rabbits, racoons, foxes and other mammals saw them coming and skittered for cover. A pack of wolves watched warily from the far side of one flower-filled meadow and a skunk ignored them in another. Sofi saw and heard all these things and searched for patterns, or more specifically changes in patterns that might signify problems. She found none, or at least none up ahead.

There was one behind her, though. She knew the footfall of each of her Owsla. They had no official running formation, but they usually fell into the same positions. By the noise their feet made as they hit the ground, Sofi could tell not only who was where, but who was flagging, who was developing an injury, even who was hungry, excited and so on.

Right now, Malilla Leaper was further forward in the formation than usual and her footfall was more heavily on her toes, as if she had urgent business. Caliska Coyote and Morningstar were out of place, too, at Malilla's shoulders. It probably meant nothing, but after their solidarity against her in the Plaza, she was watching for any signs of dissent from those three. The best leaders and warriors—the best living leaders and warriors—never ignored things that probably meant nothing.

Yoki Choppa was following closely behind the women, his pace steady. She'd told him they wouldn't wait for him and that they were going to run seventy miles a day, every day. He'd nodded, unruffled, and, sure enough, here he was, plodding along and keeping up. It shouldn't have been a surprise. Many of the warriors in the Calnian army were all mouth and no breechcloth. The warlock was the opposite.

They stopped after around twenty miles. While the women drank from a stream and ate berries, dried meat and maple sugar, Yoki Choppa started a little fire in his alchemical bowl and hunched over it, stirring the embers with a bone.

They ran for the rest of the day, breaking several more times before halting for the night after around seventy miles. The women were weary but far from exhausted. Yoki Choppa looked tired, but he always looked tired, and he set about preparing their evening meal without a murmur of complaint. Paloma Pronghorn chased down a white-tail deer while others gathered edible plants.

Chapter 3

Age Is Just a Number

Frossa the Deep Minded woke after Fraya knew how long. A dozen red-faced vultures hopped away and flew up lazily into the dark branches of a dead tree. She opened her mouth to shout at them, but her throat was too dry to form the words. She looked about. It was evening, but was it the same day?

A pair of geese with a gaggle of goslings sailed by on the lake. She hoisted herself onto her elbows. There was no sign of the rest of the Hardworkers. They'd left her! The selfish, selfish bastards.

What had happened? She'd been swimming, then she was underwater, being dragged along at a frightening speed, then she'd surfaced in a river and drifted and finally crawled out...This was a different lake from the one she'd jumped into when the bear attacked. No wonder they hadn't found her...No, not no wonder. They should have looked harder. They had abandoned her.

Assuming it was the same day, she thought she'd be able to find their tracks and catch them up. But she wasn't going to do that. They'd left her, and now she was going to leave them. She'd head back to Hardwork and wait for the Calnians. Kimaman had been a fool. Whoever the Calnians sent next was sure to see her value as a warlock. Especially when she used her magic to tell them exactly where all the other Hardworkers were heading.

* * *

"Watching Wulf wash?" asked Finnbogi the Boggy.

Bjarni Chickenhead jumped. "Doing what? No! Ha ha! No. I'm waiting for him. We caught a couple of trout." He gestured at two dead fish lying on the grass. "I wasn't watching him."

Bjarni was sitting on the hard-earthed bank of a creek, a couple of hundred paces from the camp. Kneeling in the shallow stream was a naked Wulf the Fat, using a handful of grass to rub fat and ash soap lather over his muscular torso.

They'd stopped well before sunset, on the edge of the ten-mile zone in which the Hardworkers had been contained for a century. Wulf had said they'd tackle the new world on a new day. Nobody had disagreed. It would be weeks before news of their survival got back to Calnia, so they were in no hurry.

Wulf and a few others had gone scouting while the rest, Finnbogi included, had washed and made camp. Now the light was beginning to soften, glinting lazily on the stream.

Finnbogi sat. "Bit crap, isn't it? We're not even out of our own territory and three of us are dead."

"Yeah. How many left?"

"Fourteen, I think. At this rate we won't last a week."

"You're right, and it's a real shame about Ogmund the Miller. But what an idiot. You don't hassle bear cubs."

"Yeah. And I suppose Hrolf was more or less dead anyway. But Frossa?"

"I think she would have struggled with more than a few miles a day."

"Sure. But killed by a fish?" Finnbogi shook his head.

Bjarni breathed a laugh through his nose. "If you'd told me this morning that Frossa was going to die today and asked me to guess how, I'd have been guessing until Ragnarok before I said she'd have her neck broken by a fish! Poor woman. Still, it was quick, Sassa tells me."

"I saw it too."

"Did you? Tell me about it, man."

Finnbogi told him what he'd seen, then said: "Listen, Bjarni, I don't like to ask, but after the tough time we've all had...Have you got any...you know?"

"Mushrooms? Are you sure? They don't agree with some people. After what happened to you last time, I'm pretty sure you're some people."

The first and only time that Finnbogi had tried Bjarni's mushrooms he'd become trapped in a net made of light on the beach, been chased all the way home through the woods by a giant crayfish made of smoke and only relaxed when his mother's ghost had appeared at his bedside to soothe him.

"I know I asked you to never give me your mushrooms again, even if I begged, but that was old me in the old place. Maybe I'll be okay and, you know, it's been a weird time. Man."

"Fair enough but sorry, I left all that behind. I've got nothing, not even a bit of baccy. New life, new journey and it's a new, clear me, too."

"Oh."

"Yeah. I'm regretting it already. Do you fancy going back to Hardwork with me to fetch my stash?"

"What, tonight?"

"Yeah, man. If we head now, keep up a good pace, we'll be back here by dawn."

"All right." Finnbogi liked the idea of going on an adventure with someone as cool as Bjarni Chickenhead. And maybe after that, he and Thyri could do mushrooms together. Then, when they got into their sleeping sack..."Let's go now," he said.

Bjarni chuckled. "I'm joking, you idiot. I wouldn't mind a shroom or two, but not so much that I'm going to miss my sleep to run a twenty-mile round trip."

"Oh...can we pick them as we go? They must grow somewhere."

"I wouldn't know where to look or which ones to pick. The shrooms that kill you look a lot like the ones that get you high. I got all mine ready-dried and diced from this Goachica guy."

"In exchange for what?"

"Um, err...nothing. He just gave them to me."

"Nice guy."

"He was."

Bjarni helped Wulf dry off by rubbing him with clumps of grass and the three of them returned to camp, where, in a short time, Finnbogi would share a sleeping sack with Thyri. As they walked, Finnbogi asked Wulf the Fat if he was going to address the group.

"A sort of leader's pep talk?" asked Wulf.

"I suppose. That and remind people of the dangers, talk about food supplies, that sort of thing."

"Nope."

"Why not? You're head of the Hird and that makes you in charge of us."

"Yes, and everyone knows that. Just like they know about food supplies and the dangers—Ogmund and Frossa outlined those pretty well earlier. So the only reason to give a little talk would be for me to say 'Look at me, I'm in charge,' and everyone's had too hard a day for that sort of buffalo shit."

They walked on, meeting Sassa Lipchewer heading the other way, bow in hand.

"I think we have enough meat?" said Wulf.

"I'm going to practise. I missed a bear today, twice."

Back at camp, most people were sitting around a large fire. Some of them were cooking game on sticks. Gunnhild was stirring a pot of roots and wild rice. Perched apart from everyone else on a hummock, deep in conversation, were Thyri Treelegs, Garth Anvilchin and Gurd Girlchaser. That was a bit of an upset, but, Finnbogi reminded himself, neither Garth nor Gurd would be sharing a sleeping sack with Thyri in a couple of hours.

"Right, Finn. Shall I get Garth to teach you how to use your sword now?" Wulf asked.

"Um, well, the thing is..."

Wulf smiled, punched him gently on the arm, and turned to where Garth, Gurd and Thyri were sitting. "Hey, Thyri!"

"Yup!"

"Will you teach Finnbogi how to use his new sword?"

"Sure."

"Where's our dried fish, Boggy?" sneered Garth. "You'll never be a fighter. Why don't you go and practise carrying fish instead of wasting Thyri's time?"

Gurd and Garth laughed.

Finnbogi reddened. The backpack he'd left behind in the woods when he'd heard Frossa's screams had been raided. Freydis had analysed the tracks and, as they'd walked on, given him a little lecture about each of the surprisingly wide variety of animals that had stolen the fish. It hadn't helped a great deal.

"Leave him, Garth," said Thyri, "we've got plenty of food and we can get more. Come on, Finn, let's go and find some space."

He followed Thyri Treelegs to a wide, grassy clearing that sloped gently to the stony stream bank. Sassa was at the far end of it, shooting arrow after arrow into a dead tree.

Thyri cut two sticks, handed one to Finnbogi and whacked him on the ear with the other.

"Ah!" he said. He pressed his fingers to his ear then looked at them. No blood, which was a surprise, because it felt like she'd split the fucking thing in half. "Wha?" he asked.

"First lesson, most important lesson. Strike first and strike hard. Lesson—" A flash of arm and she whacked him again, on the other ear.

"Loakie's cock! What the...?" he touched his stinging ear. This time there was a little blood.

"Lesson two. Strike when they least expect it."

"That's underhand."

"Underhand beats dead."

"You die when you die."

"You could fall onto your new sword right now and prove that wrong."

"Or prove it right."

Whack!

"Fucking...Loakie's bellend! What was that for?"

"For sassing your teacher." She smiled and it was like the sun blasting storm clouds away. Suddenly, the pain in Finnbogi's ears felt good.

"I can't sass you, I'm older."

"Age is just a number."

"No, age is how long you've been alive, numbers are what we use to describe it. Saying age is just a number is like saying the sun is just a word."

She whacked him on the arm. "One." It stung like a bastard. She hit him again and again and again: "Two! Three! Four! Are those just numbers? Five!"

"Ow! Ow! Ow! Stop! You're proving my point! The number of times you hit me matters!"

"Six!"

"Stop!"

"I'll stop when you admit I'm right. Seven! Eight!"

"You're right! You're right about everything! You're amazing and I'll do anything for you!"

"Good. Now are you going to sass your younger teacher again?"

"No!"

"Am I your better in every way?"

"You are."

Whack! On his arm again. At least she was leaving his ears alone now.

"What was *that* for?"

"A reminder of what will happen if you sass me again. I did it to help you. Say thank you."

Finnbogi looked over to Sassa Lipchewer. She was pulling arrows from the tree, paying them no attention and out of earshot anyway. There was nobody else around.

"Thank you," he said, adding, in his mind, "and I love you."

She didn't hit him again that evening. Instead she nearly killed him. She made him sprint, jump, squat and all sorts of other horrors including crawling along with his back legs straight like a bear, lying down and standing up again and again—which was surprisingly gruelling—and many other humiliating routines. After five minutes he was exhausted. After ten he felt sick and angry. Every exercise he did, she did, too. While he heaved and sweated like a fat man shagging in a heatwave she remained dry-browed and unruffled.

"How is all this..." he panted at one point "...related to putting the pointy end of my sword into a Scrayling?"

"You've got to be faster and stronger than the Scrayling you're fighting, and they tend to be pretty fit. We do this every day for a few months and you might be nearly as fit as them."

"*Every day*? Isn't walking all day enough?"

"We'll train twice a day if there's time."

"Loakie's tits."

"Unless you don't want to?"

"No, no. No. I do want to."

"Then shut up and get on with it."

*   *   *

After training, they sat well away from Garth and Gurd and ate delicious deer and fish. Even though his ears throbbed and his limbs felt like they'd been beaten with hammers, Finnbogi was so happy it was hard not to giggle. As he munched, Thyri explained rudiments of fighting. With a spark in her eye, she told him about old world techniques that had been drummed into the Hird every day, moves and theories that she'd learnt from the Scraylings, and various ideas she'd worked out herself.

Her lips were red and plump, her skin was golden in the firelight and her broad face shone with the glee of explaining her favourite subject to a willing audience. He could have listened to her for ever.

Then it was time to climb into their sleeping sack. He almost didn't want it to happen so he could savour the anticipation for longer. He couldn't believe it would actually come to pass. Somebody or something would get in the way. Thyri would decide to sleep in the open, or maybe she'd share with someone else, or the children would demand that Finnbogi stay with them and Gunnhild would make him, or they'd be attacked by an army of dagger-tooth cats . . .

But, no, the time came and she said: "Find a good spot for us by the fire, Finn, I'll be back shortly."

She disappeared into the trees, in the direction of the stream.

Finnbogi cleared away twigs and stones, dragged Ottar and Freydis out of the way—the children were already asleep in their sack so wouldn't mind—and smoothed out his and Thyri's bag in the best place relative to the fire. His and Thyri's bag!

He couldn't decide whether to get in it, or go for a piss himself, which he was going to have to do at some point. He elected to sit and stare broodily into the fire so he'd look hunky and wise when Thyri got back.

After about a thousand years, Thyri returned. "What's wrong?" she asked.

"What do you mean?"

"You look really upset about something."

He'd have to rework his hunky and wise expression. "No, really, I'm fine. Fine as a—" ·

"Okay, your turn at the stream." She hadn't changed her mind. She started to undress and Finn headed for the stream. He couldn't pee. He went upstream to the drinking area, rinsed his mouth, then rushed back.

Thyri was already in the bag, facing away from the fire.

"You were quick," she said.

"That's why they call me Quick Shit Boggy!" He winced. Why had he said that?

"Got it."

"I didn't really shit."

"...Okay"

"Are you all right, Finn?" said Wulf, passing by.

"Yes, I'm fine. Sorry." What was he sorry for?

"Great, but see if you can keep it down. We don't want to wake the kids."

"Sure, right," he whispered. It was a mercy to be told to shut up.

He undressed. Should he take all his clothes off? Had she? Probably not. She'd probably put more on.

He shifted his weight from foot to foot. A few people were in their sacks already, others were getting ready to go down. He pulled off his clothes, electing to leave on his cotton undershorts, then got down on all fours and clambered backwards into the sack, doing his best to brush against Thyri only by accident.

He lay, facing away from her. The sleeping sack was made for two men, and neither he nor Thyri was full man-sized, so there was plenty of room. Nevertheless, he decided it was acceptable to press his bottom against hers. By Tor. It was like pressing against a pair of wooden bowls.

"It'll be more comfortable if you turn the other way," Thyri breathed.

"What, so I'm facing your back?"

"No, so your head's in the bottom of the sack."

"What, really?"

"No, dumbo, so you're facing my back."

He turned. He went for it. Right there and then, straightaway before he could think about it and reject his insane recklessness, he put an arm round her.

"Is that okay?" he whispered.

"It's good." She took his arm in her hand and clasped it to her chest and said, "Mmmmm." He didn't feel cotton. He felt smooth skin. She was topless. She smelled of flowers and maple sugar. She was holding his clenched fist to her naked breast. Surely, he suggested to himself, it's unnatural to sleep with one's fist clenched? Of course it is, nobody could disagree with that. Again, before he could convince himself not to do it, he opened his fingers.

She didn't move!

He lay for a while, cupping her breast, hips pivoted away from her buttocks, hardly breathing, then whispered, "Thyri." No response. "Thyri?"

She snorted.

Oh great. She was asleep.

All around, nocturnal animals squawked, squeaked, screamed and scampered, but Finnbogi didn't notice them as he lay awake for what seemed like hours.

Chapter 4

Crossing Etiquette

Erik the Angry and Astrid the bear came to a swift flowing but wadeable looking river. Erik didn't fancy wading, though. Wet leather was not great for walking. Undressing wouldn't have been a problem, but getting dry enough to dress on the other side would be a bore.

When he'd reached this spot the previous summer there'd been a canoe on either side, as a mobile bridge—and, yes, there they were, two canoes. Both on the other side. He shook his head.

The idea at a crossing like this was that you always left one canoe on each side. That meant you crossed three times; once with one canoe, then back towing the other, then across again leaving one behind. It was a simple thing, didn't take any significant amount of time, but some tit had decided that they were too important to bother. Erik quivered with indignation. He pictured catching up with the transgressor and knocking some river-crossing decency into them with his war club. The club was called Turkey Friend because it gave turkeys a quick death. He'd go more slowly on whoever had broken the boat etiquette.

"Arrrrghhh!" said Astrid.

"I know," said Erik.

He was glad Astrid had come with him from Lakchan lands. There was something reassuring about having an unnaturally large bear as a travelling companion. He'd expected Red Foxes One and Four to come as well, but they'd sniffed him then scurried off, leaving him with the understanding that the Lakchan lands were their territory and leaving them for the hardship of a slog across the world did not appeal. Their fear of mild discomfort outweighed their affection for him. That was foxes for you—neither brave nor loyal, but at least they were honest.

"You won't fit in the canoe, so you'd get wet whatever happens," said Erik to Astrid, "so how about you swim across and fetch a canoe for me?"

Astrid looked at him blankly, as if she didn't understand. Erik knew she didn't want to spend any longer than necessary in the cold, fast water.

He sighed, stripped, laid his clothes on a rock and waded in.

By Spider Mother's eight legs, it was cold as a snowman's bollocks.

"Woooo!" he shouted when the water lapped his own balls. A few more skin-zinging steps and it was at his nipples. Arms aloft, it was hard going. The current was more powerful than it had looked from the bank.

He was just thinking how lucky he was that the riverbed was stable when something gave way underfoot and he slipped and went under. He surfaced a way downstream, spluttering. He swam for the bank, carried further downstream all the way.

As he scrambled out, slipping on mud, he felt rather than heard a voice saying: "Go back, go back." It was similar to the voice that had implored him to head west, possibly the same one. He wished it could make up its mind.

"You want me to go east now, do you? What about going west to The Meadows?"

"Turn around. Go back," said the voice.

Erik walked upstream to the two canoes, shivering. He pushed the nearer one out, stepped into it and paddled across the river.

He dragged the canoe onto the bank, gathered his clothes and headed back along the path they had come on. He'd dress when he'd dried.

He could feel the perplexed stare of the bear boring into his back.

"Come on then, back this way."

"Arrrgh?" said Astrid.

"We're going back east. Don't ask me why."

Chapter 5

Stone Crab Claws

Malilla Leaper jogged along behind Sofi Tornado. Her fire-tempered wooden kill staff felt alive in her hand. She was itching to crack it into the back of her captain's head.

Had it been anyone else but Sofi Tornado she would have brained her as she ran and taken her chances with the rest. She'd persuaded Morningstar and Caliska Coyote over to her side, which left Paloma Pronghorn, Sadzi Wolf, Chogolisa Earthquake, Luby Zephyr and Sitsi Kestrel with Sofi Tornado. There was no point trying to persuade the other five that the leader had to go. They were too loyal. However, once Sofi was dead, they would have no choice but to follow Malilla.

As for Yoki Choppa, well, it didn't really matter what the weird little warlock did. They said that he'd been a key part in using alchemy to create their abilities, but she couldn't see it. He looked so much like an awful, fat child that he simply couldn't have any magic. A few idiots like Sitsi Kestrel had gushed about how amazing it was that he was keeping up with them, but it was no great feat. Chogolisa Earthquake was keeping up and she weighed more than the rest of them put together.

It wasn't that Malilla hated Sofi, although she did; it was simply that Sofi was the wrong person to be leading the Owsla and Malilla was the right one.

Unlike the rest of the Owsla who'd never known real hardship, Malilla Leaper had had a difficult childhood. Her father was a hunter and tanner in a trading village that linked the mainland to a number of islands on the edge of the Wild Salt Sea. Her mother left when Malilla was little more than a baby and moved in with a young fish-spearer who lived on a nearby island, leaving the girl with her father.

Her mother still came to town most days with her new love's catch, but Malilla was forbidden by her father from saying a word to her. One of her earliest memories was of being perplexed that all the other children cuddled their mothers while she never even spoke to hers.

As soon as they were old enough to be able to, the rest of the children mocked her about her family situation. She tried to stop their attacks by breaking the rules and talking to her mother and asking her to come back, but her mother ignored her. So she resorted to countering the other children's verbal attacks by retaliating physically. It took about four years before she started winning the fights. She hadn't become bigger or stronger than the others, she'd just become vicious as a coyote in a snare.

After she half blinded a boy three years her senior by jamming a stick into his eye, then broke his older sister's arm with a branch when she'd come to remonstrate, the elders ordered her father to take his violent daughter away from the village.

They moved to a nearby island, which Malilla wasn't allowed to leave. She spent her days running around, working out her frustration by leaping bushes and developing the beginnings of the skill that would win her Owsla nickname several years later.

Around the age of ten, she told her father that she intended to kill her mother.

"Kill the bastard she ran off with, too," was her father's counsel.

So she did. She crept into their hut on stilts one moon-bright night and rammed stone crab claws into their necks while they slept.

The elders were all for executing her but a travelling merchant was passing through that day. He said that there was a demand for girls like her in the city of Calnia, and offered to buy her.

She never knew what she was sold for, but her father seemed pleased. As she left the village with the merchant, she turned to wave goodbye. Her father wasn't looking. He was smiling and chatting to the girl whose arm she'd broken a couple of years before, a hand around her waist.

"My father made me kill my mother and her lover!" she shouted. "He said I'd have to suck his magic growing snake again if I didn't!" The villagers all looked at her aghast, then at her father.

Mallia walked away with the merchant and never looked back.

From that lowly and troubled start, she'd become one of Calnia's magic-enhanced elite warriors. Her life had become harder in Calnia, the training endless and painful, but it had been worth it. Physically, she and her fellow Owsla were the most powerful people in Calnia. They were the finest fighters in the world.

So they should have been ruling Calnia and beyond. They should have been on the Mountain of the Sun, having every need seen to by fit young men, eating mushrooms in the sweat lodge and being fanned with swans' wings.

Instead they were lackeys for the Swan Empress.

It had to change. It would change. But Sofi Tornado, for all her flair and astonishing fighting skills, was a boring line-toer who would sooner smother herself in mouse blood and lie in a pit full of half-starved rattlesnakes than challenge the status quo. Nothing would happen while she was alive.

So she had to die.

But how? How do you kill a woman who can see a second into the future?

When Malilla had realised the answer, she'd actually slapped herself on the forehead. Of course, you kill her in the same way she'd killed the first two of the hundreds she'd slaughtered. You kill her when she's asleep.

She'd been waiting for the opportunity for a long while, and tonight it would come. Tonight she was on second watch with Morningstar. All the other women would be sleeping deeply after the day's run. Nothing would stop them from striking.

Chapter 6
Who's the Dumb One?

The Hardworkers walked west into the unknown.

There was more of a breeze today, a westerly in their faces, not so strong that it hindered them, but it was cooling and stiff enough to keep the lighter and bitier insects at bay. The birdsong was louder and more varied than any Sassa Lipchewer had heard, punctuated by the cheery barks of ducks. A robin sang with such gusto that it made Sassa's chest swell.

She and Wulf had made love before dawn. Surely this new life would bring them a baby? Fraya favoured the brave, and it didn't get much braver than walking into an unknown land rumoured to be full of monsters and murderers on the advice of a child with a damaged mind. Brave or possibly stupid. Did Fraya favour the stupid, too?

On that beautiful morning it was easy to believe that she did, and hard to imagine that there was any danger anywhere nearby or anywhere else in the world. The air was thick with the pungent, sometimes sexual scents of late spring. The tangled forest was busy with gambolling squirrels and a multitude of inquisitive birds. Turkeys ran like armless idiots and hid behind spindly trees a tenth their width. Rabbits hopped to their holes. A spiny-limbed turtle with a pointed face and panicked eyes slid down a mud chute into a path-side pond.

Every now and then they had to negotiate a tree downed

by the recent storms. Every time they did, Gurd Girlchaser would curse the "lazy Scraylings" for not clearing their paths, then go on to list further failings of the Scraylings. Sassa soon tired of his unfounded vitriol and fell back to walk along with Ottar the Moaner and Freydis the Annoying.

"Can Ottar and I hold your hands please, Sassa Lipchewer?"

"Sure," she said. Freydis's grip was cool and light. Ottar held on with two sweaty little paws. They walked along, breathing in the smells and watching animals scurry and flit. Sassa didn't think she'd ever felt happier, until Freydis asked:

"Why don't you and Wulf the Fat have any children, Sassa Lipchewer?"

"Because . . ."

"Because," said Wulf, jogging up to join them, "children are trouble. When you have them, you have to stop looking after yourself to look after them. Do you like playing, Freydis?"

"I do."

"So do we, but you have to stop playing when you have children. So we're going to play for a few years and look after each other, then we'll think about making some little ones."

"I see."

"And do you approve?"

"Yes, I do, Wulf the Fat."

"Good to hear." Wulf ruffled her hair and Freydis giggled.

"But how do you make the little ones?" she asked.

"Sassa Lipchewer will tell you that one." He ran off back to the head of the procession.

A short time later they were crossing a wide field of waist-high grassland. The swaying vegetation was alive with beetles, myriad hopping insects and the constant rustle of unidentified scurrying mammals and ground-dwelling birds.

To the south, increasingly visible as the orange morning mist paled and lifted, were what Sassa Lipchewer thought were large brown erratic rocks. But then one of them moved and another made a deep throaty lowing, like the sound of a giant frog snoring.

"Buffalo!" Sassa cried. She had never seen a living buffalo before, only the butchered carcasses that the Goachica had given them. They were larger than she'd imagined, their giant heads and great furry shoulders emerging colossally from surprisingly dainty rear ends. Even at this distance she could feel strength emanating from their dark bulks.

"What are those smaller, light brown animals with them?" asked Freydis.

"Calves, I suppose."

"Oh, can we go closer and look, please, Sassa Lipchewer?" The girl tugged on her hand.

"No, let's leave them to their business."

Ottar the Moaner pulled at her, too.

"Ottar says we must go and see them."

"No, he doesn't say that we must, he just *wants* to go." Sassa leant back against their pulling. "There's a difference. Now come on, there will be more buffalo. Many more. You'll be bored of buffalo before long."

More low snorts rumbled across the grassland.

"I will never be bored of buffalo," declared Freydis.

"Never say never." Sassa wagged a finger.

"You just did. Twice!" Freydis jumped on the spot and giggled.

A short while later they came upon a new sound: an excited, high-pitched trilling. Three racoon cubs came bowling out of the long grass onto the trampled path and looped about their feet, sniffing shoes and chittering excitedly.

Here were creatures created by a gentle god, thought Sassa. The children and Sassa crouched down. The young racoons sniffed their hands, licked them and nipped at them harmlessly.

They had little white ears, shiny, bulbous noses, stripy tails, messy, spikey fur and eyes as expressive and imploring as any human child's. Sassa thought they were almost tear-inducingly endearing. The children would have stayed with the little animals for ever had Wulf not popped up and asked them to move on.

The children came, reluctantly, but the racoons followed, across the grassland and into woods.

Ottar pulled at Sassa's hand and jabbed a finger at the racoons.

"He wants to keep them," Freydis translated.

"Their mother will be nearby and missing them," said Sassa.

"Chances are the mother's dead, that's why they're on their own," said Wulf.

Sassa gave him a look. "Perhaps they think Ottar's their mother now? Let's keep going and see what happens."

They walked on and the racoons followed. Sassa looked about; there was no sign of a mother, only Garth Anvilchin and Thyri Treelegs—today's rearguard—catching up.

"I suppose if they want to follow us..."

"Hello," said Garth, reaching them. "I see you've found lunch."

Sassa laughed. She thought Garth was joking, and reaching down to stroke one, but no. He whipped it up and twisted its neck. Crack! The little animal was limp in his hands. He dropped it.

There was a moment's silence, then Ottar screamed, ripped free of Sassa's hand and flung himself at Garth. Garth put a hand on his head and held him. The boy's fists flailed and he screamed louder and louder as Garth chuckled.

"Thyri, get the other two will you?" he said.

Thyri took a step towards the racoons, which were crouched and shaking, staring at their dead sibling.

"Leave them, Thyri," said Wulf.

Thyri shrugged. "Sure."

"Do what I told you, Thyri," said Garth, smiling with about as much warmth as a blizzard.

"Wulf is head of the Hird. I'll do what he tells me."

"We're not in Hardwork territory any more. There is no Hird, so there's no 'head of the Hird.' We're on our own, we need to survive and these animals are meat."

"There's plenty of meat around and these don't have much on them. You want to kill them so badly, do it yourself." Thyri stepped away.

"Fine. I will." Garth moved Ottar to one side.

"No. You won't," said Wulf.

"You can't order me."

"I can. These animals are under my protection. I'll let you off for killing the one because you didn't know. But you won't take the other two."

"And if I do?"

"Then we'll have a problem." Wulf, smiling all the while, gripped Thunderbolt's handle.

Garth's hands went to his axes, the Biter Twins. Sassa's heart was beating like a war drum whacked by a hyperactive Scrayling who'd eaten too many mushrooms. She gripped her little iron knife.

Garth took a step forward. "You're pathetic. Why are those animals any different from the deer we kill for food every day? Because they're pretty?"

Garth did, Sassa had to admit, have something of a point.

Wulf's smile broadened and Thunderbolt's iron head twitched in his grip. "Kill one and we can see how pathetic I am."

Garth laughed and held up his hands. "All right, all right, I'll leave your little pets."

Sassa breathed out again.

"Well done, Garth," said Wulf. "And you'll accept that I'm the chief of our little group."

Sassa sucked that breath back in.

"Why?" Garth lifted his big, helmeted head. Had he spent a lifetime being taught how to look arrogant by the most arrogant men who had gone before, he could not have looked more arrogant at that moment.

Wulf smiled. "Because we need a leader. Because I'm head of the Hird, and most of us are Hird, that leader is me. At the moment I just set watches and guards and choose where and when we stop. However, there will come a time when difficult decisions have to be made and the need for a leader will be more obvious. If you really want to be that leader, then say and we'll hold a vote. But until then, you'll do what you're told. Understood?"

Garth's fingers curled round the shafts of his axes, a smile playing on the corners of his lips. Wulf looked relaxed, but his knuckles were whitening on his hammer grip. Could Wulf beat Garth? Sassa felt sick. Both men had spent years practising with their weapons most of the day, every day, both were young and strong, but Garth was taller and he had two axes to Wulf's one hammer, and metal armour and a helmet to Wulf's leather jerkin and bare head.

"What do you think, Thyri?" asked Garth.

"I don't give a coyote's crap about the racoons, but you should do what Wulf tells you. We do need a leader and Wulf is best suited. Call a vote if you want, but everyone will vote for Wulf. So let the racoons be and do what he says, or answer to the rest of us."

Sassa could have hugged the stocky young woman. She was only seventeen, but she was the most secure and mature of the lot of them.

Garth raised his arms again. "Okay, fine, you're right, I'm wrong. I'm sorry, Wulf, I will obey you from now, and I won't harm these lovely little animals. Well, apart from this one." He poked the dead cub with his toe.

Ottar moaned.

"*Sorry*," said Garth, grinning. "But I will protect the other two as if they were my own gay little pets."

Sassa, Wulf, Ottar and Freydis walked onwards through woods and clearings, the two racoons scampering around their feet, zooming off to sniff interesting things every now and then but always returning to Ottar.

It took a good hour for the adrenaline to drain out of Sassa and for her heart to slow down enough for her to start enjoying the scenery again.

"You don't have to be the leader, you know," she said to her husband.

"Yeah I do. Anybody else could do all the setting of the guard, deciding where we stop and so on, but they miss one key trait."

"Which is?"

"The ability to match Garth in a fight. That's the only leadership skill that'll keep him in line."

"So let Garth be leader if he wants it so badly."

"Can't do that."

"Why not?"

"I've two racoons to think of now."

"Ottar says they're called Munin and Hugin," piped up Freydis. "Like Oaden's ravens."

"So Ottar's just like Oaden now, is he?" Sassa asked.

"Yes," Freydis nodded.

Finnbogi the Boggy marched along near the head of the strung-out parade with a smile pasted to his face, thinking about his night with Thyri Treelegs. The air was fresher and the ground springier than the day before and he felt a great, warm love for all the animals. A small fat bird watched him from a branch, and Finnbogi nearly wept at the idea that the little animal might ever know sorrow, cold or pain.

The day before he'd seen a lone green-headed duck floating along with a dozen or so black and white geese and thought that the duck neatly reflected his own alienation among the Hardwork exiles. Today, he saw two chipmunks chasing each other around a tree stump and then disappearing into the same hole, and thought "that is me and Thyri Treelegs."

The cause of his happiness was rearguard with that bellend Garth, so Finnbogi was up front because on the one hand he didn't want to see them together, and on the other he wanted to make it clear to everyone that he wasn't head over heels in love with Thyri Treelegs.

"It's clear to everyone that you're head over heels in love with Thyri Treelegs," said Gunnhild, catching up.

"With who?" asked Finnbogi.

Gunnhild said nothing. Finnbogi could feel her smug little smirk without turning to see it.

"Do you think I'm an idiot to like her?"

"*Never question another's love; the wise may find beauty where the foolish do not.*"

"You don't think she's beautiful?"

"You do, and that's all that matters. But there is one thing you must try to remember."

"What?"

"You won't listen to this, because you're young, so in your mind you are different from everyone who's ever lived before—more intelligent, with much deeper emotions."

There was no way Gunnhild had ever had an emotion a quarter as deep as the turmoil that plagued Finnbogi every waking minute, but he said: "No, no, I don't think that at all. I'm sure you and Poppo..."

"Don't bother. The important point is that you don't love

Thyri as much as you think you do. I know you don't believe me, but I'm telling you because it would make the future a great deal easier for you if you *could* believe me. If you devote all your thoughts to her, as I suspect you are doing, and she rejects you, you will be devastated. I also know that the more besotted you are, the less appealing she is likely to find you. I had my heart broken when I was young because I loved somebody who was never going to love me back, and I'd like you to avoid treading the same path."

"Before Poppo?"

"Yes."

"Who?"

"You . . . don't know him."

"I know everyone."

"Not this man."

That was weird, but Finnbogi didn't care enough to probe any further. As if the Krist-loving crone could ever have felt about anyone the way that he felt about Thyri! But why was Gunnhild saying all this? She'd never spoken to him like this before. Did she know something that he didn't?

"Do you know something I don't?"

Gunnhild didn't answer.

"Well?"

"I'm sorry, Finnbogi, but I think Thyri may be in love with someone else."

"Who? Not Garth?"

Gunnhild's silence confirmed his suspicion. Stupid old woman, poking her nose in. Did she know what had happened the night before in their sleeping sack? She did not. He didn't want to tell her, but neither did he want her thinking that Thyri was after Garth.

"There are things that Thyri and me have done that you don't know about."

"Thyri and *I*."

"What?"

"You say 'that Thyri and I have done,' not 'Thyri and me.' It's easy to work out. Say it in your head before you say it out loud and remove the word 'Thyri.' You get 'things that me have done.' Sounds wrong, but 'things that *I* have done' sounds right. So you say 'things that Thyri and *I* have done.' Easy, is it not? We really should have put more effort into bringing you up."

What by Loakie's shiny helmet had this got to do with anything? Gunnhild was managing to be boring, heavy and insulting all at the same time.

"I'm fine," he said.

"*Are* you?"

"Yes! Look, there are things about Thyri and me—I mean Thyri and I—"

"No, you were right that time. Try the trick. Remove Thyri. Does 'things about I' work?"

Loakie's tits! "Right. There are things about *me and Thyri*, things we've done that you don't know, that nobody knows but us. I'm sure you're trying to protect me, and you think you're doing the right thing" (she wasn't, she was just trying to poke her nose in and stop him being happy and she knew it) "but I am okay and I'm going to be okay. We're going to be okay. You'll see."

"All right," said Gunnhild, in the same tone of voice that Finnbogi might use with Freydis when he couldn't be bothered to argue any more about whether or not she'd seen a purple dragon eating a goblin earlier.

"*Never question another's folly; desire makes fools of the wise,*" she added.

Well exactly, thought Finnbogi, then thought about it some more and became confused.

They walked on in silence until a white-tailed deer leapt on the path a few paces ahead. The deer stood square for a good couple of seconds with a surprised look in its shining eyes, then leapt away again and crashed off through the undergrowth.

"How did a creature that dumb get to be that big?" asked Finnbogi.

"What do you mean, dumb?"

"We could have easily put an arrow in it, or jumped on it if we were wolves or lions and it just stood there."

"Did you put an arrow in it or jump on it?"

"Well, no."

"So who's the dumb one?"

Loakie's *tits*, thought Finnbogi.

They saw more animals and birds that day than Finnbogi usually saw in a month, but, after his depressing lecture from Aunt Gunnhild, he didn't pay them much attention. He didn't see Thyri all day, apart from in his mind every moment of every hour. When he wasn't imagining their new home at The Meadows, he was picturing himself besting Garth in an epic battle while Thyri watched.

By the time they stopped to camp, Finnbogi's Thyri-related fantasies had turned sour. He was imagining waking up and finding that she and Garth had run off together, or that they reached The Meadows and Garth and Thyri were king and queen and he had to be their servant. He cursed Gunnhild for putting such ridiculous ideas into his mind.

But all was well. Thyri came bounding up as soon as she arrived in camp and insisted that she and Finnbogi began their weapons practice immediately.

The training was an absolute bastard, especially after all the walking, and she made their exercises even harder, but he loved every moment. Being with her made his heart sing with joy, plus she didn't hit him this time.

When sleeping sack time came, he pressed against her and curled his arm around her before she asked him to. She said "Mmmm," and, if anything, went to sleep even more quickly than she had the night before.

Chapter 7

Disarmament

Sofi Tornado heard Yoki Choppa padding down to the stream, paused her washing and waited.

"You know about Malilla?" he asked.

"That she's planning to kill me?"

"With the help of Morningstar and Caliska."

"When?"

"Tonight. During Morningstar and Malilla's watch."

"Makes sense."

"Shall I—?"

"No need. But thanks."

Yoki Choppa nodded and turned back up the hill.

Malilla Leaper crept silently into the clearing where the women of the Owsla were sleeping, Morningstar at her side. She had her kill staff at the ready. Morningstar held her double-headed punch-club and had a shield strapped to her back.

Noises always seemed louder at night, but they were even more amplified when your blood was hammering in your veins, the spirits of your ancestors were powering your limbs (Malilla liked to imagine that her distant ancestors had been nobler people than her shitty parents) and you had murder planned. The clamour of woodland insects was as loud as the baying crowd in the Plaza of Innowak, yet she could hear the soft snores of the women as if they were shouting in her ear. Loudest of all came from Chogolisa

Earthquake, her silhouette on the far side of the sleeping group more like a recumbent humped bear's than a woman's. Quietest was Luby Zephyr's, sleeping next to Sofi Tornado. Malilla hoped to avoid killing any other women, but if Luby or any of the others got in the way, they would die, too.

A shape rose on the far side of the camp and waved an axe; Caliska Coyote, as planned. Malilla Leaper herself would slay Sofi, Morningstar would be on hand as backup and to keep others at bay. Caliska was wide cover, watching over the whole camp with her throwing axes at the ready.

Malilla and Morningstar stole towards Sofi.

The captain's chest was rising and falling, so peaceful. Soon she would find a deeper peace.

Malilla raised the kill staff and struck.

Sofi rolled and tucked. Malilla's staff cracked onto rock and jolted her arm, shocking her enough that she didn't see Sofi's kick coming. It struck her in the midriff and blasted her backwards.

She drove a heel into the earth to regain her footing. Morningstar jogged in, punch-club swinging, but the captain twisted away and felled her attacker with a backhanded blow from the blunt edge of her stone axe.

Caliska Coyote dived and threw an axe at Sofi, who caught it and said: "Stay where you are and I may let you live. Move and die."

Caliska did as she was told.

Luby Zephyr ran at Malilla, but Malilla met her with an underarm blow to the head and the woman crumpled. Then she hesitated. There was little point in attacking further, now that Tornado had the initiative. But there was no point stopping, since she'd be executed and eaten for her treachery, especially now that she'd felled Luby Zephyr. It was almost a relief when she felt Chogolisa Earthquake's unmistakably large hands grip her upper arms and the chance for making a decision was gone.

The other women were awake, weapons in hands.

The leader glanced at the prone woman, said, "Sadzi, tend to Luby," and strode over to Malilla. "Hold her arms out."

Chogolisa Earthquake did as she was bid. Malilla Leaper tried to pull free but had no hope. The giant's hands slipped from her biceps to her wrists, holding her arms wide, no give in the granite grip.

Sofi Tornado held her stone axe aloft.

"Don't you want to know why?" Malilla had a tale ready, a plot involving the empress, that just might buy her life or at least enough time to escape.

"I know why." A flash, and the axe was buried in Malilla's shoulder. Sofi wrenched it free and smashed it into the other shoulder. Stone cleaved flesh and crushed bone. Malilla felt surprise, but no pain.

"Pull her arms off," said Sofi.

Chogolisa wrenched. Malilla felt muscles pull and pop, sinews strain and snap, flesh stretch and tear as the giant ripped her arms from their sockets.

Her right arm came free with a sucking smack. Her vivisector flung her arm away, high into the trees. Malilla almost fell from the force still pulling her left arm, but Chogolisa gripped her by the back of the neck and wrenched her left arm free, too, hurling this one into the trees on the other side of the camp.

Still Malilla felt no pain. She saw the whole scene as if she were a bird watching from a branch. Perhaps she was a bird on a branch? Perhaps she was already dead and her soul had occupied the bird's body?

She stood, armless. Everyone was watching. She felt light-headed and lighter all over. She took a step. *The longest journey begins with one step.* She took another. How far was it to Calnia? If she carried on like this and didn't trip, then surely she'd make it home? She was a good deal lighter without her arms. That would help.

Malilla Leaper walked five steps then fell, to leap no more.

Chapter 8

Rimilla and Potsi

"Birch bark is best," explained Keef the Berserker, although Sassa Lipchewer didn't know why. All she'd done was remark on how light Keef's boat must be for Chnob to carry it with such ease, but Keef seemed to have thought she'd said: "Please tell me everything about your boat and the construction of boats in general. Don't skip anything. If I look bored at any point, consider that a sign that I couldn't be more fascinated and would love you to go back over what you've already said in even more excruciating detail."

"If you can't get birch, you can use elm, spruce or animal hides for the hull," Keef continued, "but birch wins because it's awesome."

"How is it awesome?" Sassa heard herself asking. She and Wulf had made love again that morning and she was certain she was pregnant this time, so she was happy enough to humour Keef.

"How is birch *not* awesome? It doesn't stretch or shrink. It's a regular grain without knots. It peels off the tree in good wide strips. See?" He nipped forward to where Chnob was carrying the canoe and tapped it.

"I do see. Is it all made of birch?"

"All birch? Are you mad?"

"I must be."

"Oaden spare me from simple women! You need cedar for the frame, because it splits easily and it's light. You want maple for the paddles and the cross pieces because...here, I'll show you. Chnob, put the boat down a minute."

Chnob the White did as he was told, and Sassa saw that his gigantic beard, the one he seemed so proud of, had lost some of its length.

"What happened to your beard, Chnob?" asked Keef.

"What do you think happened? I got too hot carrying your stupid boat so I cut some off."

Keef raised an eyebrow. "You look a bit more normal now. It doesn't suit you."

"Ha ha ha."

"So, Sassa, compare the colour and grain of the frame to the struts and you'll see—"

Sassa stopped listening and wondered what she and Wulf would call their child. Maybe Vifil, after her brother, if it was a boy and Wulf agreed. Not Chnob or Keef, that was for sure.

Towards the middle of the day they caught up with the advance guard, who had stopped because they'd met some people.

It was a Scrayling woman around Sassa's age and a boy who was perhaps two years old. The woman looked nervous, as well she might with Wulf, Bjarni and Garth hulking over her. She was dressed both normally and weirdly; normally, in that she was wearing the sort of Scrayling dress that a Goachica woman might have worn, simple but prettily decorated with porcupine quill flowers and gathered at the waist by a leather belt; and weirdly, in that she had ears made of rabbit fur poking up from her head and six buffalo leather strips with the fur left on hanging from her belt. The little boy was wearing a leather smock and rabbit ears.

"Rimilla and Potsi, this is my wife Sassa Lipchewer," said Wulf. Sassa nodded hello.

The woman smiled timidly and the boy looked up with huge eyes. "Sappa Lip-La," he said.

"Close enough." She winked. He giggled and hid behind his hands.

"And Sassa Lipchewer, this is Rimilla and her son Potsi."

"Hello, Rimilla and Potsi," said Sassa.

"Rimilla was just saying that she's from the Lakchan tribe," said Wulf. "Their main village is about five miles that way." Wulf pointed south. "And her rabbit ears and spider legs— the furry strips are the legs—represent Rabbit Girl and Spider Mother, two of the Lakchans' gods."

"They're not really gods," said Rimilla. Her accent was similar to a Goachica woman's. "But in a way they are. It's simplest for visitors to think of them as gods. The important point is that they represent people's dual character."

"Good and evil?" asked Sassa, looking from Wulf to Garth.

"Sort of, but it's not that simple. Potsi here has rabbit ears and no spider's legs. It doesn't mean he's all good, he can be mischievous and wilful, but his misdeeds are inno-cent. So he can do things that might be considered evil, but he hasn't yet developed Spider Mother's premeditated wickedness and self-serving spitefulness. When he does we'll put some spider legs on him and give him a new name. It's a day that every Lakchan parent dreads."

"*Vices and virtues mingle in the breasts of mortal men; no one is so good that no failing attends him, nor so bad as to be good for nothing,*" chipped in Gunnhild Kristlover.

"Indeed," said Rimilla.

"Babbit Girl," said Potsi, pointing inaccurately at his deco-rative ears.

The woman still seemed scared, not helped greatly by Gurd Girlchaser and Fisk the Fish arriving and joining Garth to form a "looming over and staring menacingly at the little woman and her toddler" gang.

"Why don't you join us for lunch?" asked Sassa, trying to make it sound like an invitation and not a threat. "You can tell us all about the Lakchans. We're from Hardwork."

"I know who you are," said the woman.

"What do you mean by that?" Garth took a step towards her.

The Lakchan woman stood her ground, pulled Potsi to her hip and looked up at the Hardworker. He was around twice her height. "We trade with the Goachica. They tell us things. It was fairly big news when aliens arrived a hundred years ago and we keep an eye on you. What's interesting is that you don't seem to know about us, even though our territory borders yours. Not a particularly inquisitive bunch, are we?"

"We haven't been," said Sassa, steering the woman away from the Garth gang. "But we're changing. So why don't you tell me all about the Lakchans while Wulf and I get lunch ready?"

They ate well and Sassa learnt about the Lakchans. Rimilla was about the most intelligent, level-headed woman that Sassa had met, and she seemed to have a real sense of fun. There was one odd thing, though. Sassa didn't tell her about the massacre at Hardwork or any reason for them leaving home, and Rimilla didn't ask what they were doing in Lakchan territory. Sassa guessed that she was being polite.

As they were finishing up, Rimilla asked:

"Why are you called Wulf the Fat? You are not fat."

"I have a fat cock," Wulf said, straight-faced.

Rimilla looked at him in shock for a moment, then laughed melodiously.

"It's because he was a fat child," said Sassa.

"With a fat cock," Wulf winked.

"But he's got a lot slimmer since. All over."

Rimilla laughed so much at that Sassa thought she was going to choke.

Sassa left the Lakchan woman talking to Wulf and joined Freydis and Ottar playing with Potsi. The boy liked rudimentary hiding games best, it seemed. Sassa joined in, self-consciously at first because Gurd, Fisk and Garth were looking on disapprovingly, but soon all four of them were running around a tree and laughing, followed by the two yipping racoon cubs.

Wulf came over, dragging a reluctant Finnbogi with him. They had races on all fours, each adult with a child on their back, racoons running alongside. By the way they laughed and screamed happily, the children seemed to think this was the most marvellous thing that had ever happened. The normally sour-faced Finnbogi laughed more that afternoon than Sassa had seen him laugh in all his life, although the laughter became a little more measured and manly when Thyri joined in.

Some of the Hardworkers looked on with smiles. Garth and his cronies kept up the scowling. Screw them, thought Sassa. Only the dimmest and dullest adults can't let themselves behave like children every now and then.

When the time came to part, Potsi wailed as if someone was tearing his arms off. Ottar was snivelling and even brave little Freydis was red-eyed.

Sassa turned to wave one last time, and Rimilla shouted: "Wait, wait!" The little woman hauled Potsi onto her hip and jogged towards them.

Sassa walked back to her, along with Wulf and Garth.

Rimilla flicked a nervous look at Garth, seemed to resolve something and said: "The Calnians have ordered your deaths."

"We know that," said Garth. "They've already killed most of us."

"Yes, but you survivors are in terrible danger. The Calnians have commanded all tribes to kill any Mushroom Men on sight or face death themselves."

Sassa felt her stomach sink.

"Mushroom Men?" said Wulf.

"That's what the Calnians call you."

Garth stepped towards her. "So you'll go back and tell your tribe where you saw us and which direction we're headed in?"

"No! On Potsi's life I won't tell a soul. You must travel carefully. In a perfect world you'd stay off the paths, but the woods are impenetrable to all but those who know them best, so stay on the path but use scouts. If you see someone, make sure they don't see you. But if you head north-west from this clearing, you shouldn't meet anybody."

"Until the next tribe." Garth's hands, Sassa noticed, were on his axes again. She looked to Wulf. He'd noticed, too.

"Well, yes. But now you are warned and can be more wary. Hopefully that will be some protection."

"Why didn't you tell us this before?" asked Wulf.

"Because I was afraid you'd kill me to stop me telling the tribe about you."

"And you were right!" Garth swung an axe at Rimilla. Wulf's hammer shot up, knocking Garth's weapon aside. Rimilla fell back, clutching her son. Sassa stood away, took her bow from her back, bent it on the ground to string it, then slotted an arrow, all in a moment. She'd practised the move the night before and was pleased that she didn't muck it up under pressure.

Garth and Wulf squared up. Garth had an axe in each hand. Wulf's weighty, ancient hammer Thunderbolt was dull in the midday sun, as if it was too serious an item to do something so superficial as reflect light.

Garth spoke first. "This is what we were talking about. A difficult decision for a leader. Difficult morally, anyway. Intellectually, it's easy. She has to die, Wulf, for our safety."

"She has given her word and I trust her."

"You are weak."

"Come at me. Find my weakness."

Garth shook his head, spun around and strode off up the hill, axes still in his hands.

"Go now," Wulf said to Rimilla, his eyes on Garth, "and go quickly."

Rimilla gathered up Potsi and ran for the trees. Sassa and Wulf followed Garth Anvilchin up the hill.

"What are you going to do about Garth?" asked Sassa.

"We'll see," said Wulf.

Up ahead, Garth caught up with Fisk the Fish and Gurd Girlchaser. All three men looked back at Wulf, then at the fleeing woman.

Wulf halted the march and told everyone what they'd learnt from Rimilla.

"Can we trust her?" asked Gurd Girlchaser, eyes bright blue in his doughy face. "She's clearly as thick as day-old gravy, and so is the rest of her tribe."

"Why do you say that?" asked Wulf.

"She said those six leather strips were meant to represent spider's legs."

"Yes?"

"Spiders have eight legs."

"And how many do people have?" asked Wulf.

"...Two."

"And two plus six is?"

"It's ...oh."

"So the point is," Wulf continued, "look out for Scraylings and don't let them see you."

"And if you do see a Scrayling, man, woman or child," said Garth, "kill them."

"No, do not," said Wulf. "Use your judgement. If a Scrayling sees you and immediately flees, then, yes, stop them. But much better for us all to tread carefully and stay hidden. There will be no more talking as we walk. At night we will use small, sheltered cooking fires and no large campfire."

That means Thyri and I will have to huddle closer, thought Finnbogi, feeling an immediate twitch lower down.

"And keep an eye behind," said Garth. "Wulf let the Scrayling woman live, so she will no doubt return to her tribe and tell them all about us."

"She will not, Garth. I trust her."

"Do you trust her child? Did he strike you as someone who's good at keeping secrets? Or do you think he's a child who'll blab to everyone about anything unusual that he's seen?"

Garth's point struck home. Finnbogi could see that Wulf hadn't thought of it, and that he realised Garth was right.

But did that mean they should have killed Potsi? Would *he* have killed the boy in exchange for all their lives? Well, thank Loakie he didn't have to deal with a poser like that. What a bugger it must be to be a leader.

Wulf shook his head. "We move on, a little faster than before."

"The woman is slowed by a child. The Lakchan village is five miles away. I could run now and silence them both."

"No."

Finnbogi looked from man to man. There was serious tension between them. He looked at Gunnhild to see what she thought. By the way she was focusing on making circles in the dirt with her toe and not meeting anyone's eye, she agreed with Garth. Finnbogi, however, was on Wulf's side because Garth was a bellend.

"You and Gurd will be this afternoon's advance guard, Garth," said Wulf. "Stay hidden and use the duck call if you see Scraylings."

Gurd Girlchaser looked to Garth, as if to check it was okay with him, and Finnbogi hated them both a little more.

"All right," said Garth.

"Good, now let's hear both your duck noises so we know what to listen out for."

Garth smiled, nodded and quacked, then Gurd copied him.

"Well done. Garth. Thyri and Finnbogi, you'll be rear-guard."

Finnbogi's heart leapt. Had he heard that right?

"Boggy's not Hird," spat Gurd.

"He's a fast runner, and there are too few of us to worry about who's Hird and who isn't." Wulf turned to him and Thyri. "The two of you will watch our rear like hawks who've had stuff stolen recently and are determined to never let it happen again. When you come to a good vantage point, stop for a few minutes and watch for movement. Then run until you find the next vantage point. If you see anyone, Thyri will keep an eye on them while Finn runs to tell me."

Finnbogi nodded, stifling a grin of glee. *Finn.*

"We'll go now," said Thyri.

As Finnbogi turned to follow her, he saw Garth nod to Fisk the Fish. What was that about?

"On shoulders, now," said Rimilla. Her tired arms couldn't hold the child clasped to her chest any longer.

Potsi screamed and kicked as she lifted him off her hip and up to her shoulders.

"Be a good boy and ooof!" His flailing foot whacked her in the mouth. She tasted blood, thrust the boy upwards, then down onto her shoulders. She gripped him by the ankles and set off at a jog. Potsi wailed with some great grief that only he understood. Rimilla tried to soothe him but every time she said anything he screamed all the more. *Well,* she said to herself, *if the Hardworkers do change their minds and follow us, they're not going to find it too tricky.*

And I might just leave Potsi here for them.

She didn't mean that, but her mouth hurt and she wished the little fucker would stop screaming.

She'd been *such* a fool to tell them about the death command from Calnia. She'd been overwhelmed by their friendliness and how good they'd been with Potsi.

Of course they had to kill her now, and Potsi.

She wouldn't tell her tribe about the Hardworkers, but Potsi was yet to be constrained by so dreary a concept as discretion. He would tell anyone who'd listen about his afternoon with the Mushroom Men.

Luckily their leader, Wulf the Fat who wasn't fat, hadn't seemed to realise that, and neither had the handsome but nasty one, Garth. Thank Spider Mother they didn't have children themselves or they would have known. But surely they'd work it out? The older woman, Gunnhild, would surely tell them. And as soon as that happened, surely they'd run back to silence them? It was, she hated to admit, what she would have done in their leader's place. The safety of his people had to come before her and Potsi's lives.

What was that? She stopped. Someone was sprinting through the woods behind them, gaining fast. *Spider Mother's venomous piss*, she thought.

She sped ahead until she found a suitable spot. Stepping off the path, careful not to leave a trail, she nipped between bushes and behind a tree. She slipped the boy off her shoulders and crouched low.

She looked into his big eyes. "Now, Potsi, you must see how quiet you can be for Mummy. Don't say anything, just nod if you understand?"

He nodded.

A moment later, she heard approaching footsteps. Whoever it was had slowed. She caught a glimpse of her pursuer through leaves. It was one of the Hardworkers, not one she'd spoken to, but the smaller of the two who'd been in cahoots with Garth.

He had a spear.

"Who dat?" asked Potsi, his voice loud and clear.

She heard the Hardworker stop on the path. "Is that you, Potsi?" he asked.

Potsi opened his mouth to answer. She flicked up a hand

to stop him, but too quickly. Instead of gently closing his mouth, she cuffed him firmly on the chin.

His eyes widened and stared at her with hurt and surprise. He'd never been hit by anyone before, let alone his mother. He sucked in a huge breath, preparing, Rimilla knew, for the sort of scream that stampeded buffalo. There was nothing she could do.

He screamed, as loud as he could, for as long as he could.

When he finally stopped and breathed in, she whispered "stay here," stood and walked around the tree.

The Hardworker was standing on the path, grinning. His hair was cut short on his little, round head. He was small compared to the rest of the Hardworker giants, about average height for one of her tribe's men, and a head taller than her. His limbs were wiry and muscular and he was armed with a short, heavy spear with a wicked head made from the same strange material as the other Hardworkers' weapons. She had a flint knife.

"I'll stay in the wilds," she said, "for three days. You and your people will be well clear by the time I go back to the Lakchan village."

"Sorry, won't do."

"Then I will come with you. I will cook and help. I am a good hunter."

"No."

"Then kill me, but take Potsi with you. Raise him as a son. Wherever you are going you will need young men to help build your new lives."

He shook his head. "I am thirty-five years old. For more than twenty of those years I have been learning how to fight with this." He spun his spear in his palm. "Every day we train for hours. Yet, before you Scraylings attacked, I'd never fought anyone. We'd had fake fights with wooden weapons for hours on end, but, before you lot came to massacre all of us—women and children, too—none of us had ever killed anyone else. I still haven't. I cannot tell you how much I am yearning to kill a Scrayling."

"I understand, I do. But we Lakchans weren't the ones who attacked you. We're a peaceful tribe."

"Scraylings are all the same."

"The Lakchans are as different from the Calnians as you are."

"Buffalo shit."

"You don't need to believe me. Even if we were Calnians, you'll find no satisfaction in killing a little boy." Those last words caught in her throat. The idea of harm coming to Potsi was almost too much. "You'll feel crushingly guilty. Our spirits will haunt you day and night for the rest of your life and you will never know happiness again. Take us with you, we will serve you, then let us go when we have gone far enough. Our tribe's spirits and all the spirits of the forests, rivers, clouds and plains will smile on you for your noble, generous deed."

"I have never known happiness," he smiled sadly. "And your spirits are nothing to me. Tor is more powerful than any of them. Tell them that when you see them."

He lowered his spear and came at her.

She pulled her knife from its sheath.

He looked at it and laughed.

She lunged.

He jabbed his spear into her thigh. She felt it pierce muscle, hit the bone and send a horrible expanding and contracting pain from foot to hip. She gasped.

He pulled the spear clear and danced away, grinning.

She looked down at her leg. Blood was pulsing. Wooziness swam up from the wound, up through her stomach and chest and into her head. She swayed.

"Wah?" said Potsi, toddling from the undergrowth.

"Go back into the trees!" she shouted.

She'd never shouted at him before. First the blow to his

face, now this. It was too much for his young mind. He stared at her with shocked surprise, sat down hard, gripped his feet, and sobbed, rocking back and forth as if the sorrow and unfairness of it all was weighing on his narrow shoulders.

"Run, Potsi, run!" she shouted. He wailed all the more then choked on snot. She knew that once he was like this it would take an age of comforting before he would relax.

"On the bright side, you'll be free of that wailing brat," said the Hardworker, lifting his spear.

"What was that?" asked Finnbogi.

"Shhhh." Thyri held a finger to her lips. Finnbogi held his breath. They heard nothing else. "I think it was Potsi screaming. Run and tell Wulf. I'll go and see what's happening."

Finnbogi opened his mouth to tell her to be careful, but she was already gone.

Chapter 9

A Misplaced Sense of Superiority

The rebellious Morningstar and Caliska Coyote sat next to Malilla Leaper's armless corpse. Morningstar's eyes were closed, unable to face the light after the blow to the head that Sofi had felled her with. Caliska Coyote was looking at her own feet and scowling.

The most badly injured in the assassination attempt, Malilla Leaper aside, was Luby Zephyr. She was asleep after Sadzi Wolf had knocked her out with a hefty dose of herbs and stitched her head wound with deer-gut sutures. Sadzi had said that she would probably live, but that she wouldn't walk for a few days and shouldn't run for a few weeks.

The punishment for the leader of the mutiny was simple. Already Yoki Choppa was roasting one of her arms and the aroma of burning flesh was mixing with the woody morning air. They would all eat a little to kill her spirit and ensure that Malilla Leaper would never live again. It was the harshest penalty possible. Sofi Tornado had not wavered for a moment from ordering it.

Punishments for the other two were trickier. Malilla had headed the rebellion, it wouldn't have happened without her, but her followers were far from blameless. Theoretically Sofi should kill them slowly to dissuade further insurrection. However, cruelty was only one way to assure loyalty. Clemency could also be effective, and, perhaps more importantly, she didn't want to lose more Owsla.

Kill these two and she'd be down from ten to five for the mission to the north, since she'd have to leave someone behind to tend to Luby Zephyr.

"Caliska Coyote," she declared. "You followed Malilla Leaper because you think that your fighting skills make you more important than the rest of the Calnians, so you should have more power and wealth. You will learn humility and dilute your arrogance through healing Luby. You will stay here with her. You will build a shelter and tend to her every need, following Sadzi's instructions. When she is well enough to return to Calnia, you will escort her home. When I see her again I will ask her if you have treated her well. If you have, you will rejoin the Owsla and we will never mention the events of last night. If you have not, or if I do not see her again, I will kill you and eat you. Understood?"

"Understood."

"Morningstar, you followed Malilla for the same reason—a misplaced sense of superiority. Yours is more understandable, you being Zaltan's daughter. That does not make it excusable. However, your father founded the Owsla and for his sake I'll give you another chance. But, if I even suspect you of further insurrection, I will torture you, kill you and eat you. Is that clear?"

"Yes. I'm sorry."

"You will be if you try anything like it again."

"I won't."

Sofi Tornado nodded. "Good. Sadzi, instruct Caliska. The rest of you prepare to leave."

They packed up. Sofi watched as Yoki Choppa prepared two different mixes in his alchemical bowl and handed them to Caliska Coyote, instructing her to eat a small amount of one of them every day and to feed the other to Luby Zephyr.

Chapter 10

Sax and Shield vs Spear

Rimilla took a step on her stabbed leg. The pain made her feel faint and terrified her. She had to beat this man or he would kill Potsi. But what hope did she have? She cursed herself for warning the Mushroom Men. Her blind stupidity had killed her lovely son.

The round-headed Mushroom Man spun his short spear on his palm. "I'm going to take some time on you and the brat, enjoy my first kills."

He took a pace towards her.

"Oh yes, almost forgot—do tell your gods that Fisk the Fish sent you."

"Please let my—" she fell to her knees.

"What are you doing?" The Hardworker's face crinkled in confusion. He was not a bright man. Was it possible that her brains might yet beat his strength?

"I feel..." she rolled her eyes up into her head, fell onto her side and lay still.

"Mummy!" She watched through narrowed eyes as Potsi recovered from his wailing fit in an instant, clambered onto his feet and tottered over to her. *Go away go away go away*, she tried to tell him without speaking. His little hand gripped her hair and pulled. "Mummy!"

"Get back, you little shit!" Fisk the Fish ran at her son and kicked him in the chest. Potsi flew and thwumped against a tree trunk.

Rimilla roared and stabbed her knife into the Mushroom Man's leg.

It was Fisk's turn to scream. She tried to keep hold of her knife but it was lodged in the bone and yanked from her grip as he staggered away.

Potsi sat where he'd landed, wailing. By the amount of noise he was managing to make, he couldn't be too badly hurt. But, now that she'd seem him kick the boy as hard as he could, for the first time she really believed that this evil man might be capable of killing a child a long way from his Spider Mother day.

Their attacker placed his spear on the leafy ground and used both hands to pull the knife from his leg.

He tossed the weapon away, wiped tears and mucus from his face, and smiled. "Thank you. Now I'm *really* going to enjoy killing you. And I had been thinking about sparing the boy. Now I'm going to kill him all the more slowly. In fact, I'll do him first so you can watch."

Rimilla scrabbled back on her hands, searching for a branch, a rock, anything. She found leaves and twigs.

The Mushroom Man walked towards her son. She tried to get up but her leg buckled.

He grabbed Potsi by the hair. Rimilla screamed.

"That's enough, Fisk," said a woman's voice.

It was the stout young female, the darker skinned one who looked more Lakchan than Mushroom Man. She was vital and fit, and her felt hat made her look like a warrior. Rimilla felt a rush of hope.

"Piss off, Thyri," said Fisk.

"Wulf told us to leave them."

"Wulf's a fool. If she gets back to the Lakchan village with little blabbermouth here, we're all dead before sunset."

"Walk away, or I will kill you." Thyri pulled a blade from her scabbard. It was beautiful—a long, slim knife made from the same material as Fisk's spear's head—but it was a delicate little weapon compared to the hefty spear.

"A sax is no match for a spear, and you are no match for me."

The young woman pulled her shield from her back. It had a picture of a tree on it.

"Sax and shield beats spear every time."

"It depends who's holding them." Fisk charged. She batted his spear aside with her shield and slashed her blade across his face. Rimilla felt a surge of hope.

He reeled away, clutching his opened cheek. He snarled and came back at her, swinging the spear wildly but powerfully. Thyri ducked and sliced her blade into his torso. Fisk ignored the wound and swung an overhead blow at the girl's head.

She leapt back, landed, slipped on a blood-slicked rock, fell and cracked her head against another rock. She lifted her head, eyes spinning. Her padded hat had been some protection, but not enough. Her irises disappeared into her skull and she sank back.

"Ha!" cried Fisk. He stood over the unconscious woman and raised his spear two-handed over her chest for the killing thrust.

Finnbogi soon left Wulf, Sassa and Bjarni behind, sprinting back the way he'd come. The gratification of proving how much faster he was than the others almost outweighed his concern for Thyri.

He reached the clearing where they'd had lunch and played with Potsi. There was an opening into the woods on the southern edge, which had to be the path that Rimilla had taken back to the Lakchan village.

He ran into the opening and sprinted downhill, deeper into the woods, leaping roots and rocks. He was cursing himself for going to get the others. He should never have let Thyri go on her own. He could have had an adventure with her.

* * *

He skidded to a halt when he came to a leafy glade splashed all around with gore and parts of person. In the middle of the path was a head attached to an arm. Was it Thyri? It looked more like Fisk's little round head and there was no felt helmet. He rolled it over with his foot. It was Fisk, or at least part of him, white with blood loss, mouth open in a scream.

"For the love of—"

He spotted Thyri, propped up against a trunk, out cold.

"Thyri!" He ran over and knelt down.

She opened her eyes.

"Finnbogi..." She pushed him away and leapt to her feet. "Where are Rimilla and Potsi?"

"I don't know, I just found Fisk...all over the place. Maybe whatever ripped him apart got them, too?"

They found Thyri's shield leaning on her sax, which was jammed into a large chunk of torso.

Thyri poked a severed foot with a toe then inspected a hand and the lower portion of an arm that was hanging from a tree.

"This mess is just Fisk. I think the other two must have got—"

Someone was running towards them.

"Sword out, Finn. Be ready." Thyri held her own blade aloft, hefted her shield and stood with her legs wide, bouncing on bent knees. Finnbogi drew his sword, gripped it two-handed and copied her ready stance.

Sassa Lipchewer ran into the clearing, bow in hand, followed by Wulf and Bjarni.

"Wow!" said Wulf. He knelt down to examine the bits that had once been Fisk. "He was killed by a bear. By the depth of the wounds and the gaps between them it was a very, very big one. Impossibly big. What happened, Treelegs?"

"I don't know. We heard a scream so I ran back, and

found Fisk the Fish about to kill Rimilla and Potsi. We fought. I had him, but I fell. The next thing I saw was Finnbogi."

"Finn?" asked Wulf.

"I didn't do it."

"I'm glad we can rule you out, dude."

"I got here a minute before you, I found Thyri out cold and—"

"You can track, can't you, Finn?"

"Sort of."

"Look around, tell us what happened. And be quick, the Lakchan village can't be far."

Finnbogi scanned the ground. At first he was too aware of Thyri, Sassa, Wulf and Bjarni watching him, but then he spotted an odd print. Then he found a trail, then another and soon the whole pattern was clear.

"Fisk had Thyri beaten," he said.

"I had *him* beaten. Then I fell." Thyri was examining her felt helmet.

"Then Fisk was killed by the biggest bear in the world and possibly the largest man."

"What?"

"I'm just telling you what the footprints are saying. There was a big man with the bear. Look, this print is fresh."

He picked up one of Fisk's feet, still in its leather shoe with two white bones poking up from the severed ankle, and held it against one of the prints on the ground. The print was double the area of Fisk's foot. He looked up at Wulf with a "you see?" expression.

"So the bear had a friend, and he was Rimilla's friend, too."

"Pah," said Thyri, "that would be—"

"What the land is telling Finn and the best explanation we've got. And now we've got to go."

Wulf ran and Finnbogi followed. He turned to make sure

Thyri was coming. She wasn't. She was hunched over the largest part of Fisk's torso, using her sax to saw out a section of his ribs.

"What are you doing, Thyri? Come on!"

They found the others waiting.

"Where's Fisk?" was Garth's first question.

"Killed by a bear," said Wulf.

"That's convenient."

"You die when you die. Let's move on."

Finnbogi spent the rest of the day guarding the rear with Thyri. Wulf had asked them not to talk, but even taking that into consideration she was subdued, moving with less than her usual bouncy confidence.

At that evening's camp the mood was like a sodden blanket smothering the group. Garth and Gurd sat on their own, glowering at Wulf. Wulf was his normal genial self, or at least doing a good impression of it, but so sullen were the rest that even Wulf's social beacon was only as bright as a sickly firefly on a stormy night.

Thyri told Finnbogi to train on his own. He didn't. He sat and watched her clean Fisk's ribs then sew them into her felt helmet.

After a while, Wulf and Sassa stood up from a quiet conversation. Sassa picked up her bow and headed into the trees. Wulf walked up to Garth and Gurd and asked them to follow him. They did, leaving the camp. Everyone looked at each other.

"Don't worry," said Gunnhild, nodding wisely, "*A cowardly man thinks he will live long by avoiding war, but old age will give him no peace.*"

Finnbogi groaned at that—what in the name of Hel Loakiesdottir did it mean and how was it relevant here? But the others seemed to lap it up. Chnob the White nodded as if he were in Oaden's hall and the chief god had made a particularly wise and worthy comment. Finnbogi noticed that Chnob's beard was shorter. When had he done that? And why?

A surprisingly short time later, the three men returned, all smiles, chatting away as if nothing had ever gone wrong. Finnbogi wondered what Wulf had said to them.

"Training?" he asked Thyri when she'd finished with her helmet.

"I told you. You're on your own today." She set about sharpening her sax and her axes.

An hour later, when he climbed into the sleeping sack next to her, she was wearing her cotton undershirt. He knew she wasn't in a good mood, so he faced away. He lay awake for an age, certain that she was awake, too. He told himself again and again to turn and put his arm around her, but he couldn't muster the courage.

Chapter 11

The Path to Valhalla

Shortly after sunrise the next morning they came to a wide expanse of grassland. The vegetation was taller than Finnbogi in places but mostly it was thigh-high and sparse and the land dipped, so he could see several deer walking around, doing whatever it was that deer were so busy with first thing.

At the far side of the sea of swishing grass was a wooded bluff. Finnbogi knew it wasn't a mountain like the ones from the sagas, but it was the highest rise of land he'd seen in his life. If any Scraylings happened to be up there, they'd have to be blind not to see thirteen pale-skinned people, some of whom were very large, crossing the couple of miles of open grassland.

"Thank Tor we'll be out of the trees for a while," said Garth, "we'll be able to see who's coming."

"Yeah, genius, and they'll be able to see us from miles away," said Thyri.

"That, my bouncy-arsed beauty, is a good point." Garth smiled like a Niflheim troll and Thyri, to Finnbogi's horror, winked at him.

Finnbogi felt himself redden. As if to prove that he was an evil spirit sent to torment decent men, Garth turned to him and grinned. Finnbogi reddened all the more.

Wulf stood at the edge of the treeline and looked pensive. Finnbogi could see his dilemma. Sticking to the treeline in one direction would take them a good mile south, back towards the Lakchan village. In the other direction they'd either have to backtrack miles or swim across a wide lake, which would expose them even more than crossing the open grassland.

Ottar leapt about, spindly legs spread wide, and jabbed a finger to point across the grass, towards the bluff. He was wearing rabbit ears. Finnbogi guessed that Gunnhild must have made them for him. He didn't have spider legs.

"Ottar says we have to go across the grass," said Freydis.

"Whoopee fucks for him," said Garth.

"Uncle Poppo had a word for people like you," said Freydis, hands on hips.

"Oh yes, and what was that?"

"He would have called you a cock."

Everybody laughed heartily, apart from Finnbogi because he was too painfully in love with Thyri for frivolity.

"Which way to The Meadows, Ottar?" said Wulf, crouching to be eye level with the boy.

"Jish!" Ottar pointed straight across the grassland. He was wide-eyed and red-cheeked, saliva shining from his chin. Hugin and Munin, hidden by the long grass, trilled squeakily as if to back him up.

Wulf nodded and stood. He told everyone to stay quiet as they crossed the slice of prairie, to give a pigeon call if they saw anyone, and to be ready to drop down into the grass the moment anyone else gave a pigeon call.

Off they set, their shadows long in front of them. Birds chirred and whirred, spider webs strung between grass stems glistened in the dew and yellow, pink and blue flowers shone in the green.

Chnob the White lingered under the trees and watched them go. He knew nobody would notice, and nobody did.

How he hated them. They all thought his sister Thyri

was so great, practically worshipped her, and why? She was a woman, weak and stupid like all women. But she was a show-off who'd convinced the gullible morons to believe in her abilities as much as she believed in them.

He was the more intelligent, and he'd beat her in a fight if ever he put his mind to it. His father Rangvald the Wise had known that. He'd treated Chnob with the respect he deserved, and he'd quite rightly treated Thyri with contempt. These other fools were all as stupid as Thyri.

He'd show them.

He slipped his knife from his belt, sliced off a couple of inches of beard and jammed the knot of hair into the fork of two twigs at around eye level, where anyone following them could not possibly miss it.

Then he watched them walk away. It was *so* stupid to cross the open like that. He prayed to Loakie that a passing army of Scraylings would spot them.

Clinging clouds of dawn mist dissolved in the pristine air. The female deer and fawns skipped away. The big bucks held their broad-antlered heads high and sauntered lazily from the path of the advancing Hardworkers, as if they were heading that way anyway and they certainly weren't scared of humans, or anything else for that matter.

Finnbogi caught a glimpse of a brightly coloured bird through the grass and was trying to work out where it had gone when Wulf cooed like a pigeon.

Finnbogi dropped.

He looked up. Bodil was still standing, turning around with a "where did everybody go?" look on her face.

"Get down!" Finnbogi whispered through gritted teeth.

"Why?"

For the love of Loakie... "*Just do it! Now!*"

She rolled her eyes as if *he* were the idiot and crouched down next to him, her head still above the level of the grass.

Finnbogi grabbed her squirrel-skin jerkin and pulled her down. She squeaked, then lay facing him, her face inches from his. She smiled. Her breath was warm and sweet. She was actually not bad looking, just a shame she was so—

She put a hand on his hip, smiled wider, and slipped her hand round onto his arse. Finnbogi's stomach lurched and he found himself pushing his hips towards her as she pulled him in. Her head leant towards his. Her brown eyes were bright and intense. Her lips parted. Finnbogi closed his own eyes and let his mouth fall open.

"Everybody up!" cried Wulf. Finnbogi shook his head and stood. Bodil sprang up next to him. She looked at the bulge in his trousers and winked.

Tor's balls! thought Finnbogi, commanding his off-message erection to subside. *Why is everything so weird?*

"That was a test," Wulf continued. "Everyone well done, although it shouldn't have been that tricky—unless you're Bodil. What happened, Bodil?"

"Finnbogi pulled me down into the grass!" she tittered. A few others, Sassa included, laughed and Finnbogi reddened and wished that someone would pull him down into the grass and hold him there for ever.

"Well done him. But why didn't you drop when you heard the pigeon noise?'

"Was that what it was? It sounded more like an owl."

"I see. From now on, if you hear anyone make any bird noise, or you think they might be trying to make a bird noise, drop so that you're hidden in the grass. Got it?"

"But why would they make a bird noise?"

"A pigeon call is the sign if we see a Scrayling."

"Oh! I see. Coo coo!"

"Yes, like that, although a pigeon is more of a cu-cu-caroo! Cu-cu-caroo!"

"Cu-cu-caroo! Cu-cu-caroo!" Bodil spread her arms and flapped her hands.

"Good, but only do it again if you see a Scrayling."

"Cu-cu-caroo! Cu-cu-caroo!"

"Bodil, only if you—"

Bodil pointed to the south, where a good fifty Scraylings were walking towards them through the long grass, all carrying strung bows, rabbit ears bobbing. They were a hundred paces away. They must have run in, thought Finnbogi, while they were all hiding in the grass. Clever of the Lakchans. Not so clever of the Hardworkers.

He turned to the north. Two dozen more rabbit-eared Lakchans were wading through the long grass towards them.

They were trapped and outnumbered five to one. And that was including Ottar and Freydis as two of their ones.

"Cu-cu-caroo!" said Wulf.

They all dropped.

Sassa Lipchewer slipped her bow from her back and crouched next to her husband.

"Knob in a robin," she whispered.

"Yup," said Wulf the Fat, then stood and said, "Good morning!" to the Lakchans.

Sassa peeked over the grass. Several arrows zipped in their direction. Both of them dropped again.

"Tor's helmet," he said.

"Rear a deer," she agreed.

There was a ruckus and a muffled crash. Keef the Berserker barrelled into the grass next to them as a small flock of arrows swished overhead. "Too many," he panted. "We're screwed," he added.

"Thanks, Keef," said Wulf.

"If we attack, we'll get maybe two or three of them. But that's only if they're really shit with those bows. They're probably not."

"They probably hunt with them every day."

"They probably do."

Sassa tried to think. What to do? They were trapped by people who were going to kill them. Despite Keef's gloomy assessment, their only option was to fight. She strung her bow, pulled an arrow from her quiver, slotted it and stood, intending to thin the enemy's number by one. Before she'd picked a target something punched her arm, hard. Her bow fell from her hand. She thumped down into a sitting position. There was an arrow in her arm.

Wulf pulled her head down as another arrow zipped over.

"Jab it in a rabbit," she gasped. The pain was extraordinary.

"This is what we get for following the advice of a moron," said Garth Anvilchin, crawling over to join them. Even in her agony Sassa was about to leap onto him and kill him, when she realised he meant Ottar, not Wulf. It was still a hateful comment, but what with the situation and the arrow in her arm, she'd let it slide for now.

Wulf took her shoulders and turned her gently to look at the wound. His wide-eyed concern morphed into a face of stone and he stood, grabbing his shield from his back as he did so. Sassa knelt to watch him.

"I'd like!" he shouted, taking a step towards the Lakchans. Two arrows thunked into his shield.

"You to imagine!" He pivoted his shoulders and an arrow fizzed past.

"That this hammer!" he held Thunderbolt aloft, jinking his head to let an arrow fly by.

"Is a white feather." The white feather was the Goachica symbol of peace, so, Sassa hoped, should work for the Lakchans too.

"Hold, you cunts!" shouted one of the Scraylings, "Let's hear what this fucker has to say!" His voice was rough, as if he had a throat disease. Sassa quite liked his swearing, though.

"Stay down, you lot." Wulf walked towards the Scraylings, swinging his hammer.

He came back a short time later. "Stand up, everyone."

Finnbogi watched Sassa rise slowly, one hand holding the flesh around the protruding arrow. Her face was grim but tough. She looked fantastic. He looked about for Thyri. She was over to the right, next to Garth.

"He's actually not a bad fellow, the Lakchan chief," Wulf continued. "His name's Kobosh."

"Is Kobosh going to let us go?" asked Gunnhild.

"Actually no, sorry. They're going to kill us. They don't have a choice. It's like Frossa said. The empress of the Calnians has prophesied that people with pale skins like us are going to destroy the world. I pointed out that there weren't many of us and we had no intention to destroy anything. Kobosh admitted that he wasn't convinced by the prophecy, but, if they let us go, the Calnians will slaughter all of them and eat them. Like the Goachica, they believe that if someone eats them after death, it kills their spirits and that's it—no afterlife, no reincarnation, no anything. So you can see their point. They have to kill us. They're not going to eat us, though."

"Thoughtful of them," said Keef.

"They could just let us go and not tell anybody," suggested Bjarni.

"Yeah, I tried that but Kobosh said the Calnians would probably find out and he couldn't take that risk. Like I said, he's a nice guy, but he's got to put the hundreds of people in his tribe before us and he's not going to change his mind. What he will do is let us die in battle. We have five minutes to say our farewells, then we charge. They will shoot us down, but we'll die fighting and meet in Valhalla in time for lunch. Kobosh has sworn to finish off any injured as painlessly as possible and burn our bodies."

"Will he spare the children?" asked Gunnhild.

"I did suggest that, but he won't. Sorry."

"But it's a stupid prophecy. There are thousands more like us in the lands that Olaf Worldfinder left behind! If anyone is going to destroy the world, it's them, not us. *Never smite a wasp lest its brethren swarm behind you.*" Gunnhild was a lover of Krist, Finnbogi reminded himself, so didn't have quite as certain an afterlife as the rest of them. He wasn't looking forward to being struck by arrows and then maybe head-whacked with an axe himself, but it seemed a small price to pay for an eternity with Thyri in the awesome drinking hall of Valhalla.

"Yes, but the Calnians only know about us and they've decreed that we have to die. Buck up, we'll be together again before we know it. You die when you die."

Indeed, thought Finnbogi, heading for Thyri. The time had come to declare his love.

Chnob the White had seen the Scraylings before the rest of them, dropped before any has seen him and crawled back to the treeline. Now he watched from the shadows, a smile twitching on his face. This delay was a little annoying, but surely the Scraylings were going to kill them all, as the Calnians had commanded? This was Oaden's reward to them for not realising Chnob's greatness, for promoting his idiot sister ahead of him and for being silly, self-obsessed wastes of life.

He resolved to watch them die and then set off west himself. He'd find The Meadows on his own. He was certain he'd discover a better class of Scrayling there. He'd befriend them at first, then rule over them. The men would admire him and the women would know their place.

Bodil Gooseface was excited because she was going to see her mother and father again. Hardworkers didn't mourn the dead, but she had been missing her parents and she regretted following Sassa to her farm when she could have stayed in town and died with her mum and dad.

She headed for Finnbogi. She'd always liked him and now, after their moment in the grass, she knew he liked her. He was walking away, though, towards Thyri and Garth. She followed him.

Keef took her arm: "Bodil..."

"Sorry, Keef, no time!" She shook him off.

Finnbogi stopped when Garth and Thyri started kissing. Garth and Thyri kissing! How long had that been going on?

Finnbogi turned to meet her, tears in his eyes. Oh, she liked him even more for being so sensitive!

"Don't you worry," she said, putting her arms around him and giving him one of her really good hugs. "You die when you die! It's the beginning, not the end."

He hugged her back and heaved with a big sob. What was this? Was he a Krist-lover like Gunnhild and scared of death?

"All right, you cunts, time is up," shouted the gravelly voiced Lakchan chief. "Line up. I'll shout 'go' and we'll get this fucker over."

Finnbogi pulled his face from Bodil's shoulder, dragging out a string of snot between her squirrel-skin jerkin and his nose. She smiled at him, not seeming to mind. He wiped his eyes and glanced over to Thyri and Garth. They were standing shoulder to shoulder, weapons out, ready to charge. Thyri's glare was fixed on the enemy, but Garth spotted him looking and winked.

Loakie's *arse*!

He blinked tears away. This was not how he wanted to go to Valhalla! If he dropped his sword and refused to fight, he would go to a different hall, maybe Gefjon's hall of virgins, but more likely he'd go to Hel Loakiesdottir's realm, which was meant to be shit. But what could be shittier than having to see Garth and Thyri together?

"Cheer up, Finnbogi, this is a happy time." Keef was gripping Arse Splitter, face ablaze with a small-toothed grin. "In Valhalla we'll fight all day and drink all night!"

"Whoopee." He joined the line next to Bodil. She was unarmed.

"You have to have a weapon to get to Valhalla!"

"Do you?"

Finnbogi thought for a second. "Actually I'm not sure."

"Here, take this." Keef handed her a knife.

"What do I do with it?"

"Run at the Scraylings. Die."

"Oh."

Finnbogi looked along the line to his left. There was Wulf and his hammer Thunderbolt and Bjarni with his sword Lion Slayer. Sassa had her bow on her back, a knife in one hand, the other hand on Freydis's shoulder. Gunnhild was brandishing her Scrayling beater and holding Ottar to her hip. Ottar had his racoon cubs clutched to his chest but he was unarmed, as was Freydis. Children didn't go to Valhalla. They went to a friendly, comfortable place. Finnbogi wondered if he'd be allowed to visit them? Or even stay with them so he wouldn't have to see Thyri and Garth? Maybe he'd be able to have a word with Tor and get transferred.

Gunnhild whispered something to Ottar. The boy crouched and stood, no longer holding the racoon cubs.

The image of Thyri kissing Garth sprung into Finnbogi's mind like a lion leaping out of a tree onto a baby. He tried to tell himself it was good to know now, before he embarrassed himself in front of the gods, but he'd much rather it hadn't happened. Why did such terrible things always happen to him? Everyone else just had the pain of dying to deal with. None of them knew what it was like to have your heart ripped from your chest and chopped into a million pieces by two sharp axes called the Biter Twins.

"Ready?" shouted the Lakchan chief from the centre of his fifty archers. A couple were looking at Finnbogi, and he guessed they'd chosen him to shoot. He hoped they were good shots. He wanted to go down with an arrow in the heart. An arrow to the gut then writhing around and waiting to be banged on the head did not appeal.

"Ready," said Wulf the Fat.

The Lakchan chief raised his hand. "When I drop my hand, you fuckers charge."

Chapter 12
A Big Cat

Sitsi Kestrel jogged along next to Morningstar in the middle of the bunched runners of the Calnian Owsla. They crested a rise and a new, wide view of trees and lakes opened before them. As they headed down the slope, the women sped up and became more strung out.

Sitsi had been waiting for an opportunity when everybody else was out of earshot: "I think you're very lucky. Sofi would have been well within her rights to kill you and eat you. What *were* you thinking?"

Morningstar shook her head.

"And why didn't you tell me?" Sitsi continued. "I thought you were my best friend. I would have talked you out of it."

"That's why I didn't tell you."

"What did you hope to gain?"

"I was born on the Mountain of the Sun, Sitsi, and I don't like living like a Low. We're the best fighters in the world but we eat Low food and sleep on Low beds and we live outside the citadel—alongside the nasty, stinking Low. We should have everything that the empress has. More. And we could have it. We could take it with ease."

"Look at us now, running through the land with our friends, headed for adventure. How many Low get to do that? What more do you want?"

"Slaves, a palace, as much honey and maple syrup as I

can eat, my own sweat lodge, not to be ordered about the whole time—"

"You'd be bored."

"Oh, I would not. A team of fan men would be good as well."

"You *would* be bored. I know it doesn't compare with your dad being emperor and everything, but my mother and father are pretty high up—my mother might be the next chamberlain. Compared to ours, their lives are extremely boring. And I'm sure they're not happy. They spend their days talking about crop yields and wall height. Their only excitement is watching us in the Plaza of Innowak. And my big brothers, they've got something wrong with their minds. They sit by the window, smiling at the sun and every now and then they hit themselves and scream at shadows. We're *really* lucky to be who we are and do what we do. Why would you try to spoil that?"

"You're right, I'm sure. I know you are. It's just...Do you know how we got our powers?"

"Training and well...no, I'm not sure what they did to us. I can't remember much. I remember it wasn't very nice."

"I know."

"How do you know?"

"Can you keep a secret?"

"Of course."

"I used to give hand jobs to my father's chief warlock Pakanda in exchange for information."

"You did *what*?"

"I'd pull at his—"

"Yes, I know what a hand job is. I'm just surprised. And disgusted."

"He wanted more, but I would *never* have done anything else. Hand jobs are easy. Bit of a shake, then you wash your hands. He was *really* quick. Afterwards it was like he hated me, but Pakanda would tell me anything to get one. I learnt loads of good stuff."

"Hang on...that's why Pakanda was exiled!"

"Yes, we got caught. He would have been executed if I hadn't sworn that I'd persuaded him, rather than the other way round."

"Is that true?"

"He was difficult to persuade at first but I knew he wanted it, and there were things I needed to know."

"Wow. You are...disgusting. How did we get our powers then?"

"It's more of a how *do* we than a how *did* we. You see—"

She was interrupted by a shout from the forward scout Paloma Pronghorn. "Dagger-tooth cat, coming fast!"

The two Owsla looked at each other. Chatting, they'd dropped back so that only Yoki Choppa was behind them. They sprinted to catch the rest.

They reached the other five on the crest of a hill. Grassland stretched away down a gentle north-facing slope. Usually a landscape like this would be busy with grazing buffalo, white-tail deer, elk or any number of animals. But there was only one beast in view, a dagger-tooth cat, three hundred paces away and galloping towards them.

Sitsi Kestrel's serious-minded parents had taught her everything they knew about Calnia, its empire and the world around, and sent her to a variety of wise people to learn what they couldn't teach themselves. They were determined for her to rise high enough in Calnia for her own good, for their pride, but mostly, she thought, to protect her older brothers. Because of their defective minds, Zaltan had ordered her brothers' deaths. Shortly before they were due to be executed, Ayanna had killed Zaltan. The new empress did not find her brothers offensive—quite the opposite, she believed they should be indulged and protected—but she might not last for ever.

As a by-product of her parents' protective pushiness, Sitsi knew more about Calnia and its empire than the rest of the Owsla's women put together. So, although she had never seen a dagger-tooth cat, she knew all about them. There were two types. Most common, spotted every couple of years around Calnia, was known simply as a dagger-tooth cat. They were bigger than lions, with the two great teeth that earned them their names curving down from their upper jaws, but generally they were timid. They had killed people, but almost all those people had been idiots—young men, in other words—who'd cornered or otherwise threatened them.

The other type, monstrous dagger-tooth cats, were much larger and were thought by most to be a myth. Some said that they were as common as the normal dagger-tooths, but, because they attack and kill humans on sight—or smell—people rarely lived to talk about an encounter. Sitsi believed in them. Plenty of people from Calnia and its empire disappeared in the woods every year. She didn't think it outlandish to believe that an animal was intelligent enough to kill people while steering clear of settlements.

Judging by the size of the animal charging them, monstrous dagger-tooth cats were not a myth.

Sitsi blinked, to make sure she hadn't misjudged the perspective. No, the big cat really was larger than a buffalo, with two great fangs as long as her arm. When he'd remade the world after the great flood, Innowak had created some wonderful creatures, but this, surely, was the most wonderful.

Sitsi Kestrel pulled her bow from her back and an arrow from her quiver. None of the others had bows. The only other projectile weapons were Sadzi Wolf's rabbit sticks, but those wouldn't be much use against such a beast. Neither would arrows, for that matter.

They needed strong spears and lots of them, but they didn't have any. All the other women, bar Chogolisa Earthquake, had short melee weapons which would be next to useless against this creature. Chogolisa carried no weapons. Her strength was enough to defeat any armed man. But any monstrous dagger-tooth cat? Sitsi doubted it.

Fleeing would be the worst option. This animal could smell them a mile off. Perhaps Paloma Pronghorn would get away, but it would track the rest of them down and eat them one by one.

She loosed an arrow. It hit the beast's neck and ricocheted. She looked to Sofi Tornado for command.

The captain was watching the charging beast, looking more like an engineer pondering a broken bridge than a woman about to be attacked by several tons of muscle, claw and tooth.

After what seemed like far too long, she said, "Morningstar, give your shield to Chogolisa and stand here. Paloma, you're there. Sitsi stand here and keep those arrows flying, but use small game blunts and aim for the body, not the head. Your goal is to annoy it, not injure it."

Sitsi did as she was bid, whizzing arrow after arrow into the charging animal's flanks while Sofi Tornado continued instructing the other women.

The monstrous dagger-tooth cat seemed even more colossal as it neared. With her alchemically enhanced eyesight Sitsi could see that its dagger teeth were stained yellow with age but its eyes were clear. Was it *bigger* than a buffalo? Surely not.

The Owsla captain ran to meet the cat, arms in the air. The animal roared and leapt at her.

Sofi dived and rolled, twisting to avoid a swipe from the cat's long claws as it flew overhead.

It landed. Chogolisa Earthquake, with Morningstar standing on her shoulders holding her hair for balance, slammed the shield up into those huge fangs. Morningstar leapt, turned in the air and landed astride the big cat's neck.

The beast roared and shook its head, enraged by the shield stuck to its teeth.

Morningstar raised her punch-club—a stout pole with a ball of polished wood at either end—and slammed it down onto the monstrous dagger-tooth cat's skull. All the women had their skills. Morningstar's was a punch that could fell a buffalo. But could if fell a monstrous dagger-tooth cat?

The animal roared, whacked its teeth into the ground and smashed the shield. It bucked, desperate to throw the head-hitting burden from its back.

Morningstar yelled, pulled back her club then drove it with all the might of her alchemy-given punch into the back of the beast's head.

The cat froze for a moment, then collapsed.

Sadzi Wolf ran in with twine that she'd woven from the long grass. Sitsi dropped her bow and joined Sadzi Wolf, Paloma Pronghorn and Talisa White-tail trussing the cat.

"Don't kill it," said Yoki Choppa, ambling up to join them, casual as a spectator arriving late to a sporting event that he doesn't care about.

"Wasn't planning to," said Sofi.

The unconscious cat's muscular, orange-brown body rose and fell a good foot with each breath. It smelt like murder on a summer's day.

Sofi Tornado cut one of the great fangs from the animal's mouth with her obsidian knife, Sadzi Wolf pressed healing herbs into the wound and sewed it up and Yoki Choppa took clippings from its fur. Sitsi Kestrel ran a hand across its surprisingly soft pelt, then followed the flattened grass back along its attack path to pick up her arrows.

Sitsi admired Sofi Tornado's battle tactics—kill a creature like this and its spirit might chase you for ever, so knocking it out made sense—but she wasn't sure about taking a fang.

"Aren't you worried it might follow us to get its tooth back?"

"No," said Sofi. "He attacked us, so should pay a price. He'll understand."

"Aren't you worried he'll starve?"

"No, he's a canny one. He'll untie himself."

Sofi Tornado jogged on at the head of the column, pleased

with her new dagger-tooth knife, but more so by the way the women had collaborated to defeat the animal. All their training in Calnia, all of it, was based on single combat—one on one, one on two, one on three and more, but always just the one Owsla. It was a failing that had been highlighted by having to fight an enemy like the monstrous dagger-tooth cat. It was possible that one day they'd come across more powerful beasts, or even people more powerful than they were, but their training had never considered than. They'd be much more potent against such a foe if they could fight as a team.

When they'd killed the Mushroom Men and returned to Calnia, the first item on their training agenda would be teamwork.

That evening Sitsi Kestrel followed Morningstar to the camp-site stream.

"So?" she said, once they were out of earshot.

"So what?"

"So how do we get our powers?"

"Sorry, Sitsi, I've been thinking about it. I'm going to keep it to myself for a while."

"Aw. Why?"

"Secrets are useful."

"Oh. We could share the secret?"

"Then it wouldn't be a secret."

"I suppose not. Oh, well, never mind, have a good wash!"

Sitsi jogged back to the camp. She'd never let it show, but she was annoyed with Morningstar because she'd very much wanted to know how they got their powers. Her amazing vision and her skill with a bow was all well and good, but if she could see into the future like Sofi Tornado, and get Paloma Pronghorn's speed *and* Chogolisa Earthquake's strength...

She reached the camp and Yoki Choppa handed her a bowl of steaming stew.

"Thanks!" she said.

Chapter 13
Fatherhood

"Hold!" shouted a Hardworker voice that Sassa Lipchewer had never heard before.

The Hardworkers about to charge to their deaths and the Lakchans about to shoot them paused.

"Well, I'll be Loakie's uncle," said Wulf the Fat.

"That is a large bear," said Freydis the Annoying. "It's not a humped bear, either. I don't know what kind it is."

Walking towards them from the north-west was the biggest bear that Sassa had ever seen. Alongside the bear was a man dressed like a Scrayling and swinging a Scrayling war club, but with the pale skin, blond hair, blue eyes, beard and bulk of a Hardworker. She couldn't decide whether the giant bear or the mysterious man was more surprising.

"I'm going to lower my hand," shouted the Lakchan chief. "But don't shoot the cunts, not yet anyway. We'll hold off killing the fuckers until we've heard what this silly cunt has to say for himself."

Kobosh dropped his hand. Hardworkers and Lakchans alike let their weapons fall to their sides and watched the unlikely pair approach.

At first Sassa had thought the man was unusually short and the bear very big, but, as they approached, she realised that the man was large, at least on a par with Garth, and the bear was foul-an-owl enormous. It was walking next to the Scrayling-dressed Hardworker on all fours, but its eyes were level with his. Hardworker sagas mentioned large white bears in the north, but surely they couldn't have been this big or the sagas would have made more of a fuss about them. And besides, this one was brown.

She blinked, shook her head and looked again, but the bear was still the size of a saga monster. It was an odd-looking creature, too, with a much shorter muzzle than even the shorter muzzled black bear. Could it be a cross between a buffalo and a bear? Or even, with its short face, a human and a bear? Was this the first of the terrifying creatures that they'd find to the west?

As if it heard her, the bear opened its mouth and made a noise like a hundred people yawning. It wasn't an aggressive noise, or particularly loud, but it displayed an effective looking array of knife-like teeth and the reverberations made the hair on her forearms and neck stand up.

She realised who the Hardworker was. There was only one person it could be. She was too young to remember him herself but she knew the story.

Gunnhild said: "Erik the Angry, for the love of Krist."

"Erik the Exiled," said Garth. "We're sworn to kill him if we see him. And I can see him."

"Hold your axes for a moment." Wulf put a hand on Garth's arm. "As a rule, I think it's best to avoid attacking a big, well-armed man accompanied by a monster. Maybe even more so when you have a hundred Scrayling war bows trained on you and his appearance has stopped them from shooting you."

"It's more like seventy bows."

"The point remains."

"I told you to go across the Water Mother and stay there, Erik," growled Kobosh. "What the fuck are you doing back here, cunt?"

"You let me go because you're a good man and the Lakchan are a good tribe." Erik the Angry spoke Scrayling like a

Hardworker, but with a hint of the Lakchan lilt that Rimilla had had in her voice. "You were confident I'd go across the Water Mother and disappear into the west. You can apply the same logic to this lot." He swung a hand to indicate the rest of the Hardworkers. "I really was on my way—I had to come back to get them, that's all. I'll lead them across the Water Mother and far away. You'll never hear from us again, and neither will the Calnians."

"We are planning to go west, as I told you." Wulf walked over to stand next to Erik the Angry, nodding hello to him and the bear. "We'll keep going west and never look back. We've got a prophecy of our own. We have to find—"

"The Meadows?" interrupted Erik.

"The Meadows indeed," said Wulf. "But how would you . . . ?"

"*In dair!*" shouted Ottar.

Erik looked at Ottar and nodded simply and solemnly as if he was agreeing the best herbs to use in a venison strew. "That's right, little fellow," he said, and Ottar beamed. "So, Kobosh, what do you say? You don't want to kill these people. Rabbit Girl doesn't want you to kill them and even Spider Mother would be iffy about slaughtering children and old women." Erik nodded at the kids and Gunnhild.

"I am no older than you, Erik the Angry," said Gunnhild.

Erik's bushy eyebrows jumped like chipmunks spotting a hawk as he recognised Gunnhild, but he recovered quickly.

"Actually I think you're four years older than me, Gunnhild Kristlover, and that probably hasn't changed. But we can discuss that later. Would you mind if I carry on . . . ?" He waved his hand at the Lakchan war party.

"No, please do."

"You're very kind. So, Kobosh, we are going to walk away, to the west."

"And if I don't let you?"

"Well..." Erik looked at the giant bear, who was sitting on its arse like a human, watching the proceedings.

"You can see a big bear, can't you?" Bjarni whispered to Sassa.

"Yes..."

"Phew."

"Oh, Erik." Kobosh shook his head. "You had a chance on the other side of the Mother River when it was just you and the bear. Not much of one, but you did have a chance. Take these fuckers with you and, if you get as far as the other side of the Water Mother, which you probably won't, the Badlanders will definitely hear about you and find you. And then you'll wish the Calnians had caught you."

"Goodbye, Kobosh. I can keep this lot hidden. You needn't worry. Follow me, Hardworkers."

Everyone looked to Wulf, who shrugged. "Let's go."

Erik walked back to his bear and turned.

"And you," he shouted, "hiding back by the trees! You come too."

Sassa followed his gaze. Two hundred paces back the way they had come, almost at the treeline, Chnob the White stood.

What had he been doing back there, she wondered?

Erik the Angry walked up the hill, wondering whether to turn round. He was pretty sure the Hardworkers were following him, and it would look much more heroic if he didn't check. However, he was going to look like an arse if he got halfway up the hill to the treeline and turned and found that they weren't following.

He'd joined a group of his own kind for the first time in twenty years. A few seconds in, and it was already confusing. He'd been glad when he'd first seen them and realised that they must have survived the Calnian massacre. He'd been relieved that Brodir the Slimy hadn't been with them, and both relieved and disappointed that his former lover and betrayer Astrid wasn't there. He guessed that meant she was dead, which was weird.

Astrid and Brodir aside, the future was suddenly just a bit terrifying. Who by Spider Mother were all these people? What was he meant to say to them? What would they say to him? It was the odd little boy, he was pretty sure, who'd called him back. But his was a different voice from the one that called him to The Meadows. Had the magic boy simply wanted to be rescued from the Lakchans, or was there more to it?

He'd been looking forward to a solitary life with only Astrid the bear for company. He glanced back. They were all coming, Gunnhild Kristlover out ahead of the rest of them. He was tempted to run. He'd saved them from the Lakchans, which was good enough. Now he could bugger off.

"Erik, Erik, wait!" she called.

Erik had a flashback of over twenty years, hearing Gunnhild say exactly those words as he'd walked home from a beach party. That time he'd kept going. This time he waited.

"It's good to see you again," Gunnhild beamed at him and he remembered that expression. Suddenly it was like the last twenty years hadn't happened. He could have been standing in Olaf's Square during a Thing and he would have gone about his business without breaking stride.

"Let's keep going before Kobosh changes his mind."

He walked on, Gunnhild half jogging to keep up.

"You must be full of questions?" she asked.

"Hmmm."

"You haven't changed a bit. Still too tough to admit you're itching to know all about what's happened in Hardwork. *Fire burns from brand to brand; man becomes known to man by his speech, but a fool by his bashful silence.*"

"I'm not so tough nor bashful. I just don't know what to ask first."

"Well, I'll tell you. The Calnians attacked four days ago. We're the only survivors."

"Astrid...?"

"By Krist, you don't know?"

"Uh. No?"

"She died, Erik, twenty years ago. Not long after you left."

"No. How?"

"In childbirth."

"Childbirth. So...Oh, Rabbit Girl's bollocks..."

"Yes, your child."

"And the child?"

"Look behind you. See the curly-haired one?"

"The tall one?"

"No, behind him, shorter hair, with a scowl like a constipated owl."

"*He's* my son?"

"Yup."

"Well, I'll be a chipmunk. What's his name?"

"Finnbogi the Boggy."

Erik was stunned. What was that phrase that Kobosh always used? Oh yes, that was it—*What the cunting fuck?*

Chapter 14
Erik's Tale

Finnbogi could not believe that the rest of the world remained the same. The lakes didn't boil, the trees didn't fly up into the sky, the astonishing number and variety of animals still ran around and twitched their noses at him. But all he could see, again and again and again, was Thyri kissing Garth.

He tramped along, following the odd new man Erik the Angry and his enormous bear. Everyone else was excited to have been rescued, abuzz with chat about the newcomer, but Finnbogi couldn't have given the tiniest of craps about Erik. He was seriously considering heading back to those dumb rabbit and spider Scraylings, baring his chest and telling them to do the job the Calnians had told them to do.

Wulf and Erik took the lead. Erik knew the best, firmest routes and they made much better time than ever before but Finnbogi didn't give a shit. When the day's speedy but miserable tramp was finally over after about a thousand years and they stopped to make camp, Keef said:

"We've gone as far today as we did in the first three days put together!" as if it meant something.

Finnbogi couldn't stand being near the rest of them, so he went off to train. He looked at Thyri as he left. She caught his eye and looked away. So she knew. She knew she'd torn his heart out and trampled on it.

He worked hard, doubling the routines she'd taught him,

pushing himself until he felt sick and hated Thyri for teaching him the stupid exercises in the first place.

Afterwards, he washed in the river, exhausted but happier, congratulating himself that his natural resilience was already helping him to get over Thyri. There would be new women when they got to The Meadows, wouldn't there? They'd probably be more lovely than Thyri. And there was always Bodil, who wasn't that bad...Bodil. He'd been about to kiss her. Was that why Thyri had kissed Garth? Was it the goddess Fraya, punishing him for his infidelity? If so that was totally unfair—he couldn't be unfaithful to Thyri if nothing had happened, surely? And he hadn't even kissed Bodil! But he'd wanted to.

Halfway back to the camp he found Bjarni Chickenhead, sitting on a log and whittling a stick with an iron knife. "Hey, Finn, good bit of training?" asked the older man.

"Yup."

"Must be getting pretty skilled with that sword now?"

"Hmmm."

"Ready to take on the Calnian army?"

"I'm ready to fight anybody right now."

"Good, good. Now look, with Erik joining us and everything, we've rearranged the sleeping sacks."

Finnbogi knew what was coming. He told himself not to cry.

"So you're with me now! We're sack mates!" Bjarni beamed.

Finnbogi nodded. He didn't trust himself to speak.

Bjarni put a hand on his shoulder. "Listen, Finn, I know what it's like to love someone and see them with someone else." Did he? How could he? Nobody had ever suffered like Finnbogi was suffering. "Life will go on, you'll become used to it and eventually you'll be happy again. In the meantime, if you want to talk about it, or just get away from everyone else for a while, let me know. How about we spar tomorrow night?"

"I'm meant to be exercising, not sparring, getting fit before learning to fight. Thyri said..." Tears burst from his eyes and a sob exploded from his chest. *Fuck!*

Finnbogi cried and Bjarni said things like "Come on, man, let it all out" and "There you go."

When Finnbogi had recovered, Bjarni pulled a pipe and a leather pouch from his jacket. He stuffed the pipe with brown weed and sparked it up with a flint and his iron knife.

"Where did you get that from? I thought you said you'd left it all..."

"I only brought enough for me. But under the circumstances...deal is you can share it with me every night, but you've got to be on the lookout for more. We meet any friendly Scraylings, try to get hold of some."

"Sure, man, thanks."

"Don't thank me, Finn. You're a good guy. Sometimes shitty things happen to good guys. Times like those are what tobacco's for. Smoke it up!"

Finnbogi returned to camp with Bjarni, feeling a little nauseous from the tobacco smoke but already on his way to being happy again. The sky was beginning to pink in preparation for sunset and this new world of trees, lakes and grassland was undeniably beautiful. Seeing Garth and Thyri sitting together was a jolt, but he could deal with it.

"Ah, Finnbogi and Bjarni, you're back," said Gunnhild. "Take a seat. Erik's gone off scouting with his bear, so I'm going to use the opportunity to tell you his story."

"The story is that he's an exile and we should kill him," said Gurd Girlchaser.

"He saved us," said Sassa Lipchewer.

"So what? The law is the law. Any Hird who sees an exile must try to kill him or be executed himself. We're already in breach. Isn't that right, Wulf?"

Wulf sighed. "You're right, Gurd, about the laws governing

the Hird. But things have changed. There's no more Hardwork, no more Jarl, no more Things—and no more Hird."

"Nothing's changed. We still have to have structure. You're Jarl now. Your role is to enforce the laws, not change them."

"I'm not Jarl. The days of Jarls are over. Let's hear Gunnhild's story, then we can decide what we do with Erik."

"What if he comes back when we're in the middle of it?" asked Chnob.

"He won't. He knows what we're doing and he's going to be away all night. Everyone gather round. Gunnhild, start when you're ready."

Oh great, thought Finnbogi, it's story time. Just what I'm in the mood for. But he sat anyway.

"Twenty years ago," began Gunnhild, "Tarben Lousebeard was Jarl of Hardwork. I'd like to say that people's spirits were stronger and that they worked harder, but the town's name was just as much of a misnomer. We were as lazy as your generation. There was one wheeled cart left, but it was about to collapse and nobody would be able to repair it. The meanings of the runes were still known to a couple of the very elderly, but they were about to die and nobody cared enough to learn from them. By providing all our food and fuel, you see, the Scraylings took away our need to work, and people need to work in order to—"

"Can you get on with it?" asked Garth Anvilchin. "I'd like to hear the end before I'm older than Erik."

Gurd Girlchaser, who certainly looked older than Erik even if he wasn't, laughed.

"All right. As in the Hardwork we left behind, the one thing that thrived, the one thing anybody put any effort into, was the Hird. Just like you lot, they trained all day, every day. Brodir was leader of the Hird. Back then he was called Brodir the Slimy."

"No he wasn't," blurted Gurd. Finnbogi thought "the Slimy" was an excellent name for Brodir, but Gurd was a man who simply loved authority and would always defend people in power.

"He was," said Bjarni.

"He crushed all mention of it pretty effectively when he became Jarl," said Gunnhild, "but it was his name and it was apt. Brodir was Hird captain, but the best fighter, winner of all the bouts and the best-looking man in Hardwork, was young Erik the Angry. His name was apt, too, but he was angry for a reason. He hated Hardwork's apathy. As he told you all, I'm four years older than him. As soon as he could speak, he spoke out against the Jarl and the older people. He wanted to explore. He convinced a few others that they should leave, and, just like you lot did, they began making preparations to go."

"How do you know we were making preparations to go?" asked Chnob.

"Because you're not nearly as clever as you think you are about covering your tracks, because every generation does it—stashes a few supplies and tells themselves that they'll definitely go at some point—and because one of you, Chnob, was telling Jarl Brodir everything."

Chnob reddened. Finnbogi stared at him. Chnob, a traitor! He looked at Treelegs. She was staring at her brother. If looks could pick someone up by the neck and shake them until their head came off...

"It's a cycle. The young plan to leave and the old don't take them seriously, then the young become old and it happens again. It would have all blown over and maybe Erik would even have become Jarl. But everything went wrong when he got mixed up with Jarl Tarben's daughter, Astrid the Fair of Face and Hard of Heart. All the women were attracted to Erik—"

"Even you?" interrupted Gurd.

Gunnhild nodded sadly. "Even me. But Astrid was always going to get him. She was a year younger than him, and,

Angus Watson

so everyone said, the most beautiful Hardworker there had ever been. However, Tarben and his wife brought her up to believe that she was better than everyone else, and, by Krist's cross, did she become a serious fucking bitch."

"Aunt Gunnhild Kristlover!" cried Freydis.

"Sorry, child, I forgot you were listening. Let's say she was nasty instead. However, she won Erik over one night when he was drunk and they made love. The next day, Erik wanted nothing to do with her. To everyone's surprise, Astrid took it very well. It was as if her character had changed. We should have been suspicious. *A woman might change her smock daily, but character changes over decades, not overnight.* So Astrid charmed Erik, and, after a couple of weeks, he came round to her. She persuaded him that they should leave Hardwork together and they did.

"That first night, they camped just outside Hardwork territory. Astrid waited until Erik was asleep, then ran home, claiming he'd taken her against her will. The next day, he followed her back to town and was seized."

"But everyone knew she was lying?" said Sassa.

"Most people did, but Jarl Tarben was blind to his daughter's evil and sided with her, as did Brodir, who wanted Erik out of the way. With those two against him, Erik the Angry probably wouldn't have had a chance even if he had put up a fight, but he went without a fuss. Astrid had her revenge. But that wasn't the end of it."

"What happened to Astrid?" asked Bodil. Finnbogi was surprised and impressed that she'd followed the story.

"Krist is not a forgiving god. He likes to avenge wrong-doers. And so he did. It was soon clear that Astrid was pregnant with Erik's baby. She walked around for the next eight or so months, slowly expanding, looking about as happy as a poisoned squirrel. Then, as she gave birth to her and Erik's son, something went wrong. She bled out."

"Bled out?" asked Freydis.

"She died."

Everyone was silent. Slowly, all the older lot turned to look at Finnbogi, all looking patronisingly supportive. Bjarni put a hand on Finnbogi's shoulder and squashed his lower lip into a sympathetic grimace. What the Hel was this about? Even Gurd was staring at him and nodding in a *we're both men and I feel manly compassion towards you* way.

"What?" he asked.

"Was it Finnbogi the Boggy!" asked Freydis. "It was, wasn't it! Finnbogi the Boggy is Erik the Angry and Astrid the Fair of Face and Hard of Heart's son! You've got a dad, Finnbogi the Boggy! Is that right, Aunt Gunnhild Kristlover? I'm right, aren't I?"

"Yes," said Gunnhild.

That night was the worst night, thought Finnbogi, that anyone had ever had, ever. Crammed into a sleeping sack with Bjarni instead of Thyri, he lay awake trying to deal with the idea of Erik being his dad, all the while horribly aware that Thyri and Garth were sharing a sleeping sack only paces away.

He kept consoling himself with the fact that Thyri always went to sleep straight after getting into the sack, but, when he'd been awake for Tor knew how long, he heard them.

It started with a giggle. Finnbogi tried to tell himself that it was a rabbit vomiting or something, but, no, it was Thyri. Giggling. Why wasn't she asleep? She always went to sleep straight after getting in the sack. After the giggling came the breathing, from both of them. Finnbogi pushed the tips of his fingers into his ears so hard that he was worried they might pop through into his brain. When he took them out, the breathing was louder, harmonised and accompanied by a rhythmic rustling of leaves under sleeping sack.

He pushed his fingers harder into his ears, actually trying this time to break through bone into his brain to silence it all for good.

Chapter 15

Fat Chance

The seven remaining women of the Calnian Owsla and Calnia's chief warlock Yoki Choppa skirted the edge of Goachica territory and arrived in Hardwork in the afternoon. The day was fine, the town was shabby but far from destroyed. A five-day-old aroma of burnt flesh and wood cut the air with a mildly eye-watering tang.

The Calnians walked into the central clearing. An array of corpse-feasting mammals darted for cover. A flock of birds ranging in size from red-throated hummingbirds to red-faced turkey vultures buzzed off or flapped up and away. Swarms of flies lifted, hung in the air, then returned to feasting. One elderly black bear was reluctant to leave but Chogolisa Earthquake roared and it scarpered.

Sofi Tornado stood and listened for a moment, then turned to the largest building on the edge of the square. "Come out of that big hut," she shouted, "or we'll come and get you."

A woman walked out from the dark doorway. She was as broad as Chogolisa Earthquake, but, rather than being made of muscle, this woman was a quivering colossus of fat. Her skin was pale to the degree of sickliness, but her robe and hat were a turmoil of colour, brighter than the outfits of the most vulgar Calnians.

"So *this* is what happens when another tribe brings you all your food," said Paloma Pronghorn.

"You must be the Calnian Owsla!" called the woman. "I am so glad you're here! I am a personal friend of Ayveranna!"

Sofi Tornado waited as the roly-poly woman tottered towards them, then said: "You mean Ayanna."

"Oh, for the love of Oaden, yes, I'm sorry, I haven't had much sleep since the battle and my brain is addled. Ayanna, empress of Calnia, is an old, personal friend of mine. And who do I have the honour of welcoming to Hardwork?"

"I am Sofi Tornado."

"The captain of the Calnian Owsla! We have all heard of you here. Well, I say 'we all' but sadly I am the only one left so I cannot offer you much in the way of hospitality. And I say 'we,' but of course I'm not from here. I was visiting when your army came and meted out what I'm sure was justified punishment for something."

"Who are you?"

"I am Frossanka, a warlock from the north."

"Which tribe?"

"White Bear."

"I see. And what happened here?"

"The Calnian Kimaman came with an army to kill the Hardworkers. When he told me of Ayanna's prophecy about them destroying the world I tried to help him, but, alas, the Hardworkers prevailed."

"How many of them survived?"

"Sixteen. They headed west. One of them, a poor, sickly child, made up a story about a place to the west where they would find a new home, and they all believed it. I guess they needed something to cling to, the poor people."

"What is this place in the west called?" asked Yoki Choppa.

"The Meadows."

The warlock nodded nonchalantly, but Sofi Tornado heard his breathing shorten.

"What do you know about The Meadows?" she asked the woman who claimed to be a White Bear.

"It's a fantasy, nothing more. The child is a moron who makes up stories. Defective mind, don't you know, should have been put out of his misery as soon as the parents realised it."

Sofi heard Sitsi Kestrel bristle and take an angry step towards the fat woman, but she held up a hand. "Do you know any more details about the direction they are taking?"

"They took the west path out of Hardwork territory and they intend to carry on heading west. If you follow their trail, perhaps I could go to Calnia with your blessing and tell Ayanna where you've gone?"

"You're from the White Bear tribe?"

"That's right."

"Tell me the White Bear tribe's last three chiefs."

"I left a good while ago and—"

"The last three chiefs, please."

"...Dogwok, Catapak and...Sofinda."

"Sitsi Kestrel?" Sofi Tornado asked.

"She couldn't be much further wrong," announced the smallest of the Owsla in a crisply smug voice. "The last three chiefs of the White Bear tribe were Smanga Calla, Frozza Polk and a woman whose original name isn't known, but she dressed as a white bear and changed her name to *Oooooom!*. Current White Bear chief is Gayajay. There *was* a Catpak, who was chief of the Corn Triangles from a hundred and five to eighty—or possibly eighty-one—years ago, although the Corn Triangles call them kings and queens, not chiefs, of course. There have never been any leaders, or anybody at all as far as I know, called Dogwok or Sofinda. I suspect that last name—"

"That'll do, Sitsi, thanks."

"I come from a lesser known White Bear tribe. It's a small tribe, many hundreds of miles—"

Sofi Tornado's stone axe slammed into the fat woman's temple. She fell.

"One Mushroom down, sixteen to go," said Paloma Pronghorn.

There was no other sign of human life. Sofi Tornado told Talisa White-tail and Morningstar to check the surrounding countryside and the two small outlying homes that Calnia's geographers had told them about. She sent Paloma Pronghorn to the Goachica town.

Ayanna had told her to raze the settlement, to leave no trace that the Mushroom Men had ever lived on the shore of the Lake of the Retrieving Sturgeon. Sofi had imagined perhaps burning a few straw and plank longhouses and maybe folding up a few skin and pole tents and chucking them in the lake. She looked around and shook her head. These Mushroom Men had a god-offendingly wasteful building style. The lowliest storage hut was made of enough wood to build an entire Calnian neighbourhood.

It would take days of dreary manual labour to erase all traces of this town. It was not a job for the prime fighters of the Calnian Owsla.

Paloma Pronghorn sprinted into the town's clearing.

"There are a handful of survivors in the Goachica town. Old people and kids."

A moment later Talisa White-tail jogged up, beaming a bright smile.

"I didn't find any survivors, but I found the tracks of the sixteen. Interestingly," she nodded at the large corpse, "it was seventeen. Fatty here headed off with them originally, then came back a day or so later. I guess she couldn't keep up."

"Anything else from their tracks?" Sofi asked.

"There are two children, an injured man and fourteen others. Some of them are very large men."

"Good, gather everyone and we'll be off."

"We're following them?"

"We will, but first we're going to pay a visit to the Goachica survivors who weren't bright enough to flee."

Yoki Choppa looked at her. He knew her orders were to level the town and they hadn't so much as kicked over a bucket.

She winked at him. He shrugged.

The surviving Goachica were too miserable a bunch to bother running away from the approaching kill squad. The children were wide-eyed, the elderly sullenly defiant. Sofi Tornado stood with her hands on her hips and surveyed them. The eldest child was perhaps ten, the youngest crone at least sixty.

"Come to finish us off?" said that youngest crone, waddling forward with the aid of a sturdy stick. She had long, hefty breasts like half-filled buffalo bladders, an arse that looked like two children hidden under her dress and the tone of someone who was used to being obeyed.

"What's your name and who are you?"

"I am Cannakoko, leader of the surviving Goachica."

"I am—"

"You are Sofi Tornado, captain of the Calnian Owsla, and that's Yoki Choppa, Calnia's chief warlock. Where are the rest of your Owsla?" Cannakoko waggled her stick at the other women. "You're missing three. I do hope something horrible happened to them." She jutted her chin at Sofi Tornado, as if daring her to punish her disrespect.

"Would you like to live?" asked Sofi.

"No, I'd much rather you tortured us to death. Of course I'd like to live, you strumpet-dressed freak. And I'd rather you didn't kill these poor orphaned children and these defenceless old people, but you're going to, aren't you, you abhorrence?"

"You know I was going to, but you're so charming that I'm going to spare you."

"You'd better get on with it. But you're to slay the children first, and quickly. They've been through terrible times and they will not suffer more than they have to."

"Are you listening? I said I was going to spare you."

"Leave me till last and torture me for all I care. I will return as an avenging spirit and I will make you wish it was you who'd died here today."

"I'm sure you'd enjoy that. But try to listen, I have a proposal for you."

"Just get on with it and kill us."

"I Am Not Going To Kill You."

"Oh?" Finally the woman heard her. "What are you going to do then?"

"All of you are to move to Mushroom Man territory and spend every waking hour destroying their town and the outlying buildings. Burn it all. If anything can't be burnt, throw it into the lake."

"Who are the Mushroom Men?"

Sofi explained.

"Ah, the Hardworkers. I never liked them," said Cannakoko.

"I'm sure that will help you in your task. When I return, there will be no trace that the Mushroom Men ever lived on the shore of the Lake of the Retrieving Sturgeon."

"And if there is?"

"I'll kill you and eat you all."

"You'll *eat* us?" Cannakoko looked more outraged than scared.

"Yes. You're dreadful enough in this life. I don't want your spirit haunting me or you coming back as some irritating animal."

"I see. But we are the very old and the very young. Have you seen their town? We are not suited to such work."

"Are we more suited to dying?" Sofi waggled her axe.

Cannakoko snorted like a frustrated buffalo. "We'll do it for the children."

"Noble of you."

"When will you be back?"

"Soon, so you'd better do it as quickly as you can."

Sofi Tornado could feel the disappointment of her Owsla behind her. They'd expected killing and they'd been denied. She was a little surprised herself that she'd been able to hold back from slaying people who she had every right to slay, but the Hardworker town wasn't going to level itself, she couldn't be arsed to do it and they could always kill this lot when they got back from slaying the Mushroom Men.

Chapter 16

Shelter

Wulf the Fat was a good guy. Finnbogi the Boggy asked him if he could be rearguard again and Wulf agreed, putting him on with Keef the Berserker.

If Keef knew about Finnbogi's woes, it wasn't obvious. He certainly didn't mention them or offer any consoling words. He darted around with Arse Splitter, menacing every squirrel and chipmunk. When he did walk next to Finnbogi, he walked backwards or circled crabwise, scanning the trees for imaginary foes.

Finnbogi tramped along. He didn't mind if the Lakchans caught up and killed him, not when the two worst things that had ever happened to anyone had happened to him the day before.

He was coming to terms with losing Thyri, in the same way you might be coming to terms with losing an arm, the day after you lost that arm. It was painful and raw, he felt unbalanced and sick but, not one for self-pity, he could see that life was going to be possible. It was just going to be very different from the life he'd planned. Although it didn't help, to carry on his arm analogy, that someone else was waving his detached arm around as if to say, 'look, I've got your arm and you haven't,' especially when that someone would be the chief twat of the tribe made up of chief twats from all the twattiest tribes.

And then the discovery that he had a living father, and

that father was some weird outcast whose only friend was a bear, and that father was coming with them to The Meadows? Had anyone ever had worse news?

Having no parents was what Finnbogi was all about. He was the solo hero, the maverick, the romantic loner, his own man formed by his own choices. You could look at others and say, "oh he's just like his father," or even "he's totally unlike his father," but not Finnbogi. He was a man without a reference point.

And now they said that this thick-looking, Scrayling-dressed lunk was his *father*?

He didn't know what to do about it. Avoiding him seemed the best tactic. He couldn't work out why Erik was avoiding *him*, though. Was he biding his time before wandering over and having a manly father-to-son chat? Finnbogi dreaded that almost as much as he dreaded hearing Thyri and Garth shagging again.

Up ahead of Finnbogi, Chnob the White walked along on his own. Chnob's betrayal of their leaving plans to Jarl Brodir and his subsequent pariah status was the only good thing that had happened recently.

"You're a dirty traitor, Chnob!" Finnbogi shouted at the loser's back. Chnob carried on walking, but his shoulders sagged a little. It made Finnbogi feel a lot better, for about three seconds, until he found himself feeling sorry for Chnob and he wished he hadn't shouted at him.

Sassa Lipchewer strode along with Bodil, not listening to her. Bodil had said all she had to say about the arrival of Erik and the other events of the previous day in the first thirty seconds and was now repeating herself in a variety of lengthy ways. Sassa had had a go at turning it into a conversation, but Bodil carried right on saying what she wanted to say without deviation or hesitation or any reference to Sassa's points, so Sassa stopped making them.

The going was a lot less soggy that it had been. From Hardwork well into Lakchan territory there'd been as much lake as there was land, perhaps more. Now it was a great deal dryer, which meant they could follow a straight path. The patches of grassland were similar, but the trees in the woods and copses were larger and less tightly packed. If anything, there were even more animals than before, filling the woods with their calls.

Sassa's arm, where she'd been hit by the Scrayling arrow, was surprisingly painless and mobile. Erik had rubbed a gunky salve onto it and wrapped it in leaves and a cotton cloth. "Lakchan healing is better than Hardworker," he'd said. It seemed he was right.

Up ahead, Wulf walked next to Erik, asking questions, then nodding and saying the odd "By Tor!" during the answers. It was endearing to see how much her husband enjoyed talking to the man. Erik was the adventurer and traveller that Wulf had always wanted to be. Sassa had plenty of questions for him herself—she wanted to know how far west he had gone and what lay ahead—but her husband could have his fun first.

The only cloud on the horizon was literally that. The sky to the north was an ominous blue-black.

Shortly after lunch, the first large raindrop fell. It heralded the sort of rainstorm that had inspired humans of old to create waterproof dwellings. They were soaked within seconds. The path became a stream. It was raining so hard that they could hardly see. Sassa had never known anything like it. It was impossible to go on.

Erik suspended a long branch between two trees and supported it in the middle with a forked stick. Under his instruction, everyone gathered shorter branches, leaves and twigs and built a sloping roof onto the long branch. He sent the children and Bodil to gather dry kindling from sheltered spots while he and Wulf dragged a fallen tree up the hill.

In no time at all they had a shelter with a log fire running the length of its open side. The Hardworkers crammed under their waterproof roof, joking and jostling for space. Sassa ended up between Gurd Girlchaser and Wulf.

Ottar's racoons Hugin and Munin seemed the most put out by the wet weather. Again and again they sprinted out of the shelter, squeaked their rage at the clouds, then tore back and burrowed under a giggling Ottar.

Sassa laughed at the cubs. It was the happiest she'd been since leaving Hardwork. Chnob the White and Finnbogi the Boggy were miserable, of course, but Chnob deserved to be and Finnbogi's anguish would pass soon enough. Besides, it was nice to have miserable people around to remind the rest of them how happy they were.

Chnob had cut more of his beard off, in, Sassa guessed, some weird attempt to show that he was penitent. He was going to have to do more than that before she forgave him. He'd told Brodir they were planning to leave. They could have been executed for that. Why, for the love of Fraya, had he done it?

She put the nasty man from her mind and stared out into the trees. The rain still came down harder than any rain she'd ever encountered but they were warm under their shelter and swiftly drying.

"Horrible weather," she said.

"It's not, it's great weather," said Gurd. "We've been leaving a trail like a herd of buffalo through fresh snow. This rain'll wipe that all out. I've never seen rain like it. It must be Tor's doing."

"Do you think we're still being followed?"

"With what Frossa said about the Calnian empress, and the Lakchans, too... what do you reckon, Wulf?"

"Chances are one or two of the Calnian army fled when they saw they were losing, and are on their way back to

Calnia now. But by the time they get there and report that we're alive, we'll be long gone."

"But won't they follow us all the way to The Meadows?" asked Sassa.

"According to Erik there's a big river ahead called the Water Mother. He says the Calnians won't follow us over that."

"Why not?"

"Everyone knows the Calnians don't cross the Water Mother."

"Do they?"

"So Erik says."

"How far is it?"

"We should be there in a week."

"I hope the Calnians don't work out that the Lakchans let us go," said Sassa.

"Why?" asked Gurd.

"Because they'll kill them all."

"Serve them right."

"Gurd! They let us go."

"They wanted to kill us."

"No, they didn't. It was the lives of a few strangers for the lives of all their friends and families. I'd have killed us if I were them. We were lucky that Erik came along when he did."

"Erik the outlaw, who we should have killed."

"You know that Erik was outlawed for leaving Hardwork, don't you, Gurd?"

"So?"

"What have we done?"

"What do you mean?"

"Shag a stag, Gurd. We've left Hardwork. We've all done exactly the thing that you want to kill Erik for."

"That's different."

"How?"

"It's the law. He broke the law, the Hird are sworn to kill him."

"But he's an outlaw only in name, for doing what we did, too."

"The law is the law."

Fuck a duck, thought Sassa, it was like trying to reason with a particularly dumb rock.

"It's all different now, Gurd," said Wulf. "We are not going to kill him. He saved us and now he's leading us."

"He's leading us? So he's in charge?"

"He's leading us geographically, in the sense that he's showing us which paths to take. He's a good man—decent, adaptable, intelligent, with an open mind. Capable of listening to reason. Capable of adapting his opinions to a new situation."

"We should kill him. The law is the law," Gurd snarled.

Wulf sighed.

Finnbogi the Boggy hugged his knees to his chest. Thyri and Garth were huddling in the middle of the shelter. Finnbogi was at the end, spray from the downpour soaking his left flank. He didn't care.

"Here, move in closer," said Gunnhild, shifting to the right.

"Hmmm," said Finnbogi, but he shuffled in.

"Have you spoken to Erik yet?"

Finnbogi shook his head.

"You should. He'll be pleased. And it'll be good for you to have a dad. Stop you sulking about Thyri."

Finnbogi pondered heading out into the rain and drowning himself in a puddle.

"*Never overconsole nor overcongratulate yourself. Some are worse off, some better, always,*" Gunnhild announced.

Lightning flashed and thunder boomed.

"Not many worse off than me," said Finnbogi when the sky had shut up.

"You didn't pay attention when Freydis and Ottar came to live with us, did you?"

"What do you mean?"

"Do you know their story?"

"Their parents were killed or something?"

"Their parents were executed."

"Wow. What happened?"

Gunnhild looked along the shelter. Freydis was at the other end, talking to Keef and Erik. Ottar was kneeling next to her, arm outstretched and watching raindrops splash off his hand.

"Holger the Dumpy and Aud the Manic were a strange couple. She was always angry or upset about something and she was difficult to talk to because she was always fixated on whatever was upsetting her or annoying her. If you tried to discuss, for example, the lack of animals around Hardwork, she'd simply carry on about whatever it was she was interested in."

Can't say I blame her, thought Finnbogi.

"Holger was a very nice guy, although possibly the dimmest person Hardwork every produced."

"Dimmer than Bodil?"

"Don't be cruel, Finnbogi. The strange thing about their relationship was that if you ever saw Holger on his own, he would do nothing but complain how awful Aud was. He'd seek you out for the sole purpose of badmouthing her. Yet they stayed together."

"And Freydis and Ottar?"

"A story needs background, Finnbogi. So, Holger and Aud were a young couple, unmarried. They didn't want a baby, but Aud fell pregnant."

"So they married?"

"So Holger punched Aud repeatedly in the stomach to kill the unborn baby."

"What?"

"There was plenty of food and firewood, so they couldn't claim that it would have been difficult to look after a child, and if they really didn't want it there were plenty of people—me and Poppo included—who would have taken it in. There was no excuse, but he was stupid and she was evil and stupid. So stupid were they, in fact, that they failed to kill the unborn child. But they did damage his mind."

"Ottar!" Finnbogi felt tears pricking his eyes. "Why didn't I know this?"

"Because up to now you haven't been much interested in anything but yourself."

That simply wasn't true. He just hadn't been interested in anything Gunnhild had to say.

"So they had little Ottar and actually they did try to look after him. All seemed fine, but after a few months he wasn't developing like other babies and it was clear that there was something amiss with his mind. People wondered why and Holger, the idiot, told everyone what they'd done. Brodir sentenced them to death."

"But Freydis..."

"Patience, Finnbogi. They fled. Brodir sent the Hird after them, but the fugitive couple left the ten-mile zone and so escaped.

"Three years later, Aud and Holger came back to Hardwork with two children: Ottar, who was a lovely little boy by then, albeit with a less developed mind, and a new baby."

"Freydis."

"Exactly. She was a year old and already showing signs of being precociously intelligent. Aud and Holger apologised to everyone and said they'd been young and stupid when they'd damaged the unborn Ottar. They'd had Freydis to prove that they could be capable parents."

"But Brodir—"

"Executed them anyway. There were plenty who disagreed with him."

"Including you?"

"No."

"I thought Krist was a forgiving god? I thought that was his main thing? Surely if you follow Krist nobody can ever be punished for anything?"

"Some things cannot be forgiven. So. We already had you and plenty of space at the church, so we took on Ottar and Freydis."

"And Ottar's prophecies?"

"Started as soon as Freydis could speak and tell us what her older brother was saying. They didn't happen very often, but every now and then Freydis would tell us he'd said something like 'dead wolf tomorrow,' and the next day we'd find a dead wolf behind the church. He's never been wrong. That's why I'm certain we have to reach The Meadows. It's why we should have believed that the Scraylings would try to slaughter us all."

"Wow. Poor kids."

"Yes, Finnbogi, exactly. Next time you're moping because your passing fancy has gone off with someone else, put Ottar and Freydis's story in your pipe and smoke it."

My passing fancy . . . she knew nothing about love.

"And here's one more thing to make you feel better. If Thyri's going to go for a wanker like Garth, she's clearly not the sort of girl you want to be with."

"I thought you liked Garth?"

"I don't hate him. I don't hate anybody, Krist tells me not to. *Never pass judgement on your brethren, lest they judge you. Unless that brethren is Garth, for he may be called wanker.*"

"What?"

"I made up the second half of that one." Gunnhild smiled. In an instant, Finnbogi felt a good deal better about Thyri, and respected Gunnhild's opinion much more than he had before.

* * *

Erik the Angry was having two conversations at the same time and thinking about something else. Keef the Berserker was asking about Erik's war club—how did it compare to Hardwork weaponry, how would he use it in a fight against, for example, a long axe like Arse Splitter?

Freydis the Annoying was asking about Astrid. How was it that the bear followed him? Where was she now and was she out of the rain? How come she didn't eat the racoons? He was enjoying both these chats, it was undeniably good to be with his own kind again, especially when he'd spent the last twenty years thinking that his own kind were evil shits and the ones he'd spoken to so far were not.

However, even as he spoke and listened, he was thinking about his son, the odd sulky one who'd helped half-heartedly with the construction of the shelter and was sitting at the other end of it apparently getting wet on purpose. What was Erik meant to do? He'd hardly had a friend for twenty years and now he had a son?

"Whoop!" Ottar suddenly shouted. He grabbed Freydis by the collar of her cotton dress. "In nair! In nair!" he wailed.

"Oh no," said the girl.

"What is it, Freydis?" asked Wulf.

"The Calnians. They're at Hardwork."

"It in nair!"

"They know where we've gone and they're following. Very fast."

Wulf jumped up from his spot under the shelter and knelt in front of the boy.

"Is it another army?"

The boy shook and garbled.

"He says no," said Freydis. "It's their Hird. But they're called something else. Wowsla?"

"Fuck," said Wulf, standing.

"Wulf the Fat!"

"Sorry, Freydis, but I said 'fuck' because it's appropriate in this situation. We have to go, now."

"Carry on in the pissing rain, on his say-so?" said Garth Anvilchin, the biggest of the Hardworkers and, if Erik were to pass early judgement and use a Lakchan term, an overbearing cunt.

"When has Ottar been wrong?" asked Wulf.

"When he told us to cross the meadow and led us right into the Scrayling ambush."

"The result of which was that we made peace with the Lakchans and met a guide who's our best hope for escaping the Calnians."

Garth's mouth opened and closed, fish-style. Erik liked this Wulf fellow.

"Come on, Garth, let's go," said Wulf. "And the rest of you, too, come on. The rain has let off a little, I reckon the storm will pass soon."

"Hey, Bodil, get in the stream," said Bjarni Chickenhead.

"Oh, yes, sorry."

Ottar the Moaner, a boy who'd spent an hour trying to escape his shadow the day before, understood the concept of walking in the stream and not treading on the banks. Bodil, it seemed, did not. Bjarni had been put in charge of making sure that she stayed in the stream, but, despite constant reminders, this was the fifth time she'd left a footprint on the bank and the fifth time he'd had to scoop freezing mud from the stream bed and cover her tracks, heavy drops from the trees above plopping unpleasantly onto the back of his neck as he did so.

"Please don't do it again," he said, straightening.

"What?"

"Step out of the stream."

"Oh, yes, don't worry, I won't."

Bjarni envied Bodil. She had no concept of...well,

anything really, it seemed. The Calnian Owsla chasing them was the worst news they could have had. Why had they come to Hardwork? It was five days since most of Hardwork and all of the Calnian strike force had been killed. They shouldn't have found out about it for a good few days more, let alone had time to get to Hardwork.

Perhaps Ottar was wrong and the Owsla weren't on their trail. Or perhaps the Calnian Owsla had been in the area when they'd heard about the failed massacre. Both of those seemed unlikely. The most likely, but also the most outlandish, was that the Calnian Owsla had found out immediately that their army had been wiped out and somehow travelled sixty or seventy miles a day to Hardwork. If they really could travel that fast, it meant that the Owsla would catch up with their ragged little group by the end of the next day at the latest.

Bjarni knew all about the Owsla from the Goachica, who were in awe of them. Ten women chosen for their cruelty and beauty had been twisted by magic into the perfect fighters. They had no remorse, they loved killing and they had alchemy-given powers which made them very good at it. In a way, he wanted to see them, but it was in the same way that he sometimes wondered what it would be like to be eaten by a bear.

With any luck the rain and then the couple of miles of stream-walking should put them off the scent. But that would only get rid of their footprints. The best trackers would probably still be able to follow them, looking for broken twigs and bent leaves or whatever, and chances were the Calnians had the best trackers. Or maybe they could use alchemy and wouldn't need trackers at all?

"Oh, Bodil!" She'd stepped out of the stream again. If she'd been any brighter, he'd have thought she was actually trying to show the Calnians where they'd gone.

Chapter 17

Dead Warlocks

In her private court atop the Mountain of the Sun, the Swan Empress Ayanna collapsed heavily onto cushions. She looked up at the giant golden swan of Innowak looking down at her. A piercing spasm pulsed excruciatingly across her bulging stomach. She stiffened and sat. The pain eased and she collapsed again, brow and back sweating.

Do you think, the empress thought to Innowak, *that you could make this baby come out very, very soon?*

Her discomfort was made all the worse by the terrible news. The only Calnian warlocks who were anything near as skilled in alchemy as the absent Yoki Choppa had both died. Vong Wapun's heart had stopped in his sleep a day after Kawunger had been murdered in the market in a dispute over heartberries.

It was such bad luck for them to die at the same time, particularly with Yoki Choppa hundreds of miles away. Such bad luck that it simply couldn't be a coincidence, but the head of her guard had insisted that there was nothing to link the two warlocks' deaths, and that there was nothing suspicious about either of them. Vong Wapun had been in his sixties, so it wasn't strange that his heart had stopped, and neither of the women who'd been sleeping with him had seen or heard anything amiss. Kawunger had a famously short temper and had started the argument over heartberries. The warlock had been in the wrong, had been first to draw a knife, then attacked so violently that the other man had had no choice but to defend himself with lethal force. It had been simple bad luck that the other man had been one of Calnia's finest warriors outside the Owsla.

Ayanna was not convinced—the coincidence was too great—but there was nothing she could do.

She called for Chippaminka. The girl—a joyful, fresh, clever companion—had not been far from the empress's side since the day that Chamberlain Hatho had been killed.

She skipped into the private court a few moments later.

"Yes, Swan Empress?"

"In your travels with Yoki Choppa, did you come across any towns or cities with a surfeit of good warlocks?"

"You seek to replace Vong Wapun and Kawunger."

"I do."

"I saw nobody suitable within a thousand miles, but I could be your warlock until Yoki Choppa returns. I have talent and I'm trained in alchemy."

"I thought you were brought up by traders on the Water Mother?"

"I was. But my father had the talent and he'd been taught divination and other skills, but after a few years serving as a warlock he'd decided to become a trader."

"Why?"

"I don't know, he didn't talk about it. I got the impression he'd fled from a difficult situation. I don't know where he trained and practised, or who trained him, but he discovered that I had the talent, too, much more than he did, and he trained me."

"Why did you not mention this before?"

"You didn't ask."

"I see. Can you use hair to see a person's location?" This was a difficult procedure, one that had been beyond both Vong Wapun and Kawunger.

"With ease, but I'll need herbs and other equipment."

"Will Vong Wapun's alchemy bag and bowl do?"

"May I have Kawunger's, too? If I combine them I might find what I need."

A short while later, following a brief burning of herbs and hair in an alchemical bowl and consultation with a geographer, Chippaminka declared that the Owsla were in Goachica territory, twenty miles west of the main Goachica settlement, and travelling west at great speed. Ayanna guessed that they were chasing down survivors, which shouldn't take them too long.

"You may all go," she said. Her stomach was painful and she wanted to lie down.

"Would you like me to soothe you, Swan Empress?" asked Chippaminka. "With Innowak's blessing, I can make a salve that will ease the pains?"

The empress looked at the cheerful girl. She wanted to be alone, but the idea of having her pains eased...

"Stay, make your salve."

The empress manoeuvred herself into as comfortable a position as she could on the cushions and watched as Chippaminka pounded and mixed ingredients in an alchemical bowl and heated it with the rays from the sun crystal.

"Lift your dress so your stomach is exposed," the girl ordered.

Ayanna found herself doing as she was told. Chippaminka sat astride the reclining empress's legs and first stroked, then massaged the gel into her enormous stomach, using her hands at first, then her forearms, then all of her arms in wide sweeping circles.

Ayanna closed her eyes, feeling more comfortable and at peace than she had for months, while the girl caressed the stress from her stomach and her mind.

Chapter 18

Bad Musicians

"So can we go home and let the animals finish our mission?" asked Paloma Pronghorn.

Sofi Tornado smiled.

"But really, a little black bear? One adult getting killed by a black bear might be put down to bad luck, if you're being generous, but *two*? We don't need to chase these people. They'll all be squeaked apart by chipmunks or wafted over cliffs by butterflies before we catch them."

Sofi looked at the bones on the smouldering pyre. It might seem like everything was a joke to Paloma Pronghorn, but she took the business of tracking very seriously. By the time the rest of the Owsla had caught up with her, she'd analysed the surroundings and deduced how the two Mushroom Men had been killed. She'd also found when and how the fat woman who'd called herself Frossanka had left the group, where she'd jumped into the lake and where she'd crawled out.

Frossanka's aquatic exit posed more questions than it answered, but Sofi Tornado didn't need to answer them. She needed to eradicate the Mushroom Men, not study their oddness. Three down, fourteen to go.

"Don't worry, Pronghorn. If they carry on at this pace, we'll catch them tomorrow or the next day at the latest."

"If they haven't already been tickled to death by caterpillars or pecked to bits by hummingbirds."

"Indeed."

* * *

That evening, the Calnian Owsla and Yoki Choppa walked along a broad central road through the Lakchan town. Their immediate surroundings were deserted, but, judging from the cacophony of reed trumpets, pipe flutes, rattles, whistles and drums, all the people in the world who'd ever wanted to try a musical instrument but had been deemed too talentless to be allowed to thus far were gathered just out of sight up ahead, all having a go at the same time.

Morningstar resisted the urge to put her fingers in her ears. The noise was simply *awful*. It was difficult to produce good music, and they were a long way into the provinces so one couldn't expect instrumentalists to be as tight as Calnia's finest ensembles, but, really, there were *limits*.

The Lakchan artwork was as bad as their music. Dotted between the shabby huts and tents of the town were large representations of Rabbit Girl and Spider Mother, made of corn, buffalo skin, branches and various other materials. They looked like they'd been knocked together in an afternoon by apathetic children. The most inept apprentice artisan in Calnia would have been embarrassed by the best artwork here, and advised to find another calling.

Morningstar's father, the Emperor Zaltan, had once sent her and an entourage of guards to a village near Calnia to prove to her that her city was much better than everywhere else and that she was blessed to be Calnian. The Lakchan town reminded her of that village.

It was shit.

She knew that people couldn't change where they were born, and she guessed that people could call a place like this home and be content with it, but she couldn't help curling a lip. Why couldn't these people build themselves a *proper* town with pyramids and a plaza? Surely it wasn't that hard?

The road turned a corner and the "musicians" came into sight, still scraping, banging and farting out their dreadful din. There were maybe fifty of them, all dressed in rabbit ears and strips of leather which Morningstar took to be an attempt at spider's legs.

In the centre of the group, an elderly man with the craggy face and turkey neck of someone who preferred tobacco to food was leaping from foot to foot, tooting on a reed trumpet. With larger rabbit ears than the rest and more competently tailored spider legs, Morningstar took him to be the leader. There were a couple of warrior types next to him, but other than that all the people were either old or young. Had there been a war with another tribe that she hadn't heard about that had killed all the warrior-age adults? Was that why the town was so shit?

The Lakchans carried on playing their cacophonous non-song. The Owsla marched towards them.

They knew, through Paloma Pronghorn's tracking, that one of the Lakchans and her child had met the Mushroom Men, and that the Mushroom Men, thirteen of them anyway, had continued. They'd found yet another Mushroom Man killed by a gigantic bear—those people really were idiots with animals—and, even though none of the Mushroom Men had come to the Lakchan town, the Owsla had followed the tracks of the woman and the child who'd met them right to it.

So, it was clear that the Lakchans knew that the Mushroom Men had walked across Lakchan lands, and it looked like they hadn't tried to stop them, in direct contravention of Calnia's orders. That meant that they needed to be punished. Morningstar shivered in anticipation. She hadn't killed anyone for nearly a week. And, after a day's running, she was hungry.

Sofi Tornado signalled for her women to stop and took a few paces towards the waiting Lakchans.

The man with the largest reed trumpet stepped to meet her. "Good evening," he shouted over the racket. His voice was a wet, raspy rattle which complemented his pallid, going-to-die-soon skin. "I'm Kobosh, chief of the Lakchans.

Who the fuck are you and what the fuck can I do for you?"

Sofi nodded. Sitsi Kestrel, had warned her that the Lakchans liked to fit a vulgarity or two into every utterance. "There is a Mushroom Man living here. Where is he?"

"Sorry?"

"Can you quieten your musicians?" she yelled. "I asked where your Mushroom Man is?"

"Can't stop the musicians, we always play for fucking visitors. Answer my fucking question first. Who the fuck are you?"

Sofi Tornado's hand twitched on her hand axe, but she suppressed the urge to leap forward and smash the teeth out of the man's foul mouth. There'd be plenty of time for that.

"I'm Sofi Tornado, captain of the Calnian Owsla," she shouted. "I am under orders from the Swan Empress Ayanna, my ruler and yours, to find and kill any Mushroom Men, and to kill and eat anyone who has aided their escape."

"All right, no need for threats. We used to have one of the cunts, living near here. But we got the message to kill him, so we did. I fucking killed him myself, didn't I?"

"Unfortunately, it seems there is a need for threats. You may have killed your Mushroom Man, maybe not, we'll find out. What I do know is that fourteen Mushroom Men crossed your land three days ago. One was killed by a bear, thirteen walked on unharmed. You had been ordered by Calnia to kill any Mushroom Men you saw. The penalty of failure is death and consumption after death, which you knew. Your actions, or more accurately your inactions, have brought death to your tribe. We will kill you all now. Do you have any final words?"

"I do. Coooooo——EEEE!"

The musicians stopped. Immediately Sofi Tornado heard the heartbeats and breathing that had been masked by the music. She resisted the urge to slap her own forehead as she realised the trap.

All around them the crappy Rabbit Girl and Spider Mother models fell forward. Each revealed two or more archers, arrows strung and pointed at the Calnians.

Without the music, she'd have heard the waiting ambushers as they walked into the village. But surely Kobosh couldn't know her skill?

There were at least a hundred of them. If she dived for Kobosh her women would follow and get among the musicians, making it almost impossible for the archers...

"Forty of my archers," said Kobosh, "are aiming at you, Sofi Tornado, or near you. Some I've told to aim high, some low, some left, some right. You jump at me, or look like you're going to jump at me, they shoot. No matter which way you dodge, you will be hit. Ten archers are aiming at each of the rest of your women. You are, my dear, fucked."

"You are more than meets the eye, Kobosh," she said.

"Always try to be."

"But you do know that if you kill us, Ayanna will send an army to destroy you?"

"That's why I'm not going to kill you."

Surely he wasn't going to let them go? The idiot. They'd simply return that night and slaughter the lot of them.

"And you won't just come back and fucking kill us tonight," continued Kobosh. "You see, I've got this." He reached into a pouch, produced a large sun crystal and tossed it to her. She caught it.

"You're going to burn your hand with Innowak's power and swear that you and your women will never harm a Lakchan."

Any other god, she'd make the vow and break it. But Innowak was Calnia's chief god almost to the point of monotheism. She'd never break an oath to him. It wasn't a massive surprise that Kobosh knew this, the Calnians made no secret of their religion.

What was a surprise, and a serious worry, was that the

nature of the trap meant that he must know about her hearing. She couldn't think of another explanation. Three people knew about her super-hearing—herself, Yoki Choppa and the exiled warlock Pakanda. Could Pakanda have passed through here and shared her secrets? Maybe he was still here? It was possible. Either that, or Kobosh had watched her fighting in the Plaza of Innowak and worked it out himself. She did sometimes wonder why everyone just accepted that she could see into the future without seeking a more likely explanation.

"And if I don't make the vow?" she asked.

"My warriors will shoot you where you stand."

Sofi shrugged. Leaving the Lakchans alive was annoying, but it wasn't actually that massive a deal, especially if it saved their lives, because their mission was to kill the Mushroom Men.

She angled the stone to focus the sun's rays and burn the skin on the back of her hand, while vowing that the Calnian Owsla would not harm a single Lakchan.

Shortly after they'd left the Lakchan village, Paloma Pronghorn ran back from her scout ahead and cheerfully reported that the Lakchans had been lying more than they knew about their encounters with the Mushroom Men. A large number of Lakchans had ambushed their quarry and let them go. Just to make things more confusing, the big man and the colossal bear whose tracks she'd found earlier had put in an appearance, then left with the Mushroom Men.

"He's the same size as the biggest Mushroom Man from Goachica lands. Got to be the exile who lived with the Lakchans," smiled Paloma Pronghorn. "On the bright side, they're all together so we should be able to kill 'em in one go!"

"Thanks, Pronghorn."

Chapter 19
Ak Oo

The world was sodden.

Water dripped from everything that water could drip from and the very air was so wet that the Hardworkers knew what it was to be crayfish walking across a lakebed.

At least the rain had stopped, but Finnbogi the Boggy's skin was still puffed and white with dampness, his leather battle trousers had chafed his inner thighs raw and caked mud had bulked up his light leather shoes into weighty clogs. The wet straps of Foe Slicer's thick leather baldric were digging into one shoulder and his backpack, water-logged and three times as heavy, was digging into the other.

Up ahead, Sassa Lipchewer didn't seem to be affected by the same dank encumbrance. She seemed affected by something else. In Hardwork she'd always been verbally feisty but deported herself with a languid grace that Finnbogi had intermittently found hot as Hel. Now she was prowling along silently, bow in one hand, arrow in the other, head flicking from side to side to scrutinise every rustle and squeak. When she spotted a squirrel or some other unfortunate beast, she strung, drew and let an arrow fly. Nine out of ten times she missed, but she had three squirrels hanging from her belt and two of them had been skewered by her last two shots.

Finnbogi didn't know where she got the energy. They'd built another shelter the previous night, but Wulf had woken them what seemed like a few minutes after they'd gone to sleep. They'd breakfasted and left before the sun had even thought about beginning to lighten the eastern sky.

Finnbogi had never known hardship like it.

Ottar and Freydis were traipsing along behind him. Ottar was gabbling away, even whinier than usual.

"Just put them down, they'll be fine!" squeaked Freydis.

Ottar wailed.

"What's up with him?" Finnbogi asked.

"He's too tired to carry Hugin and Munin any further, but he won't put them down because he thinks they'll drown in the mud."

"Here, Ottar, I'll take them." Finnbogi held out his hands.

The boy looked from Finnbogi to Freydis and back, mouth open. He tilted his head back and moaned.

"What?"

"He thinks you'll hurt them."

"I won't, Ottar. I really won't."

Ottar peered at him suspiciously and Finnbogi nodded and smiled. The boy held his gaze, then shrugged and handed over the cubs. Finnbogi clasped them to his chest. They poked their noses up at him with expressions of offended enquiry, seemed to deem him an acceptable method of carriage and settled into his grasp.

An hour later they came to a river lined with tall, whispery-leaved trees. Two deer drinking at the crossing point ran off along the bank, embellishing their flight with high back leg-kicking leaps for no reason that Finnbogi could see, other than to show how good they were at leaping. An otter with a fish in its mouth watched them from the opposite bank, a couple of orange-eyed, yellow striped turtles stared at them from a log, and a thrillingly green frog sat on a submerged stone smiling at the sky and croaking his incongruously deep and loud croak, apparently oblivious to the arrival of fourteen humans and two racoon cubs.

The river was only ten paces across, but it was treacherous after the recent rain.

"Chnob, boat!" hollered Keef.

"We've got this larger boat," said Erik, pointing at a buffalo-skin boat resting high on the bank, "and there's one on the other side, too, thanks to some excellent man who's left them like this."

"Mine is better! And quicker!"

"By all means use it, but the other two are bigger, and—"

"Come on, Chnob!" Keef pulled his boat from Chnob's back, pushed Chnob into it, jumped aboard and ferried the bearded man across the river, paddling like a frenzied elf. By the time Garth, Sassa and Erik had squeezed into the larger buffalo-skin boat, Keef was on his way back, shouting: "Who's next? Come on!"

While Finnbogi crossed—in the larger boat, since Keef was taking only the lighter people, he saw Erik's bear lumber into the river a hundred paces downstream. It went up on two legs and waded across, forelegs in the air like a bather walking into Olaf's Fresh Sea in winter. The water, at least as deep as Finnbogi was tall, reached the animal's midriff. It really was a very large bear.

In the end, half of them crossed one at a time in Keef's boat, and half crossed in the larger boat. Keef's little boat had indeed proved to be a lot faster, but it wasn't clear how much of that was down to the boat's construction and how much was a result of Keef paddling like Fenrir the Wolf was after him.

"Wait, wait," said Erik when they'd crossed. "Who'll help me take this boat back across? We've got to leave it so there's a boat on either side."

"No we don't," said Garth.

Erik shook his head. "It's attitudes like that, young man,

that lead to tribes being massacred. The boat was here for us because some supremely decent fellow went to the bother of assuring it would be. We have a duty to make sure there's a boat on both sides for the next traveller. It's the code of the wild, something you need to learn now you've left Hardwork's cosy little walls."

"I totally understand you, Erik," said Wulf, "and I'd help you back with the boat—"

"Grand, let's—"

"If it weren't for the goddess warriors on our tail. Perhaps we could make an exception this once, and all promise to stick to the 'boat on either side' rule when we're not running for our lives?"

Erik sighed. "Fine, as long as Garth stays here manning the boats in case anybody who's not trying to kill us wants to cross the river."

"What?" said Garth.

On the other side of the river it was soggy as a fish's arse for a quarter of a mile, then they headed up a gentle hill and the path, which had a secondary role as a stream during the heaviest downpours, became stony rather than muddy. Finnbogi turned to Ottar, who'd been at his heels ever since he'd started carrying the racoons.

"I think they'll be fine to walk now."

Ottar looked at the ground, back up at Finnbogi and nodded. Finnbogi crouched and detached the animals from his chest. They were confused for a moment—both had been asleep—then they ran to Ottar, yickering.

The boy bent to stroke them, then looked up to Finnbogi. His eyes were a little askew, his cheeks ruddy. "Ak oo," he said.

"You're welcome. Let me know if you want me to carry them again."

Ottar nodded.

268   *Angus Watson*

Finnbogi smiled, and suddenly felt that it was time to talk to Erik the Angry. Or "dad," as he couldn't imagine ever calling him. It was the joke Erik had made about Garth staying behind to wait for any river crossers that had swung it—the joke that Finnbogi wished he had made himself and that Garth hadn't got.

He caught up with Erik, who was leading with Wulf.

"Hi," he said.

"Hello there," said Erik, his eyes flaring like a startled deer's then narrowing again.

"Hello, Finnbogi," said Wulf. "Would you mind taking the lead with Erik for a while? I'd like to go back and check on everyone."

"Sure."

They walked in silence. The sun dissolved the cloud and lanced down in beams that dazzled silver from leaves and boiled tendrils of mist from the wet ground.

"What kind of bear is your bear?" asked Finnbogi after a while.

"Astrid? She's not my bear."

"Astrid? You named her after . . ."

"Your mother."

"So you know it all?"

"I found out yesterday. If I'd known, I would have come back, but—"

"They would have killed you."

"There was that."

"Gurd Girlchaser still wants to kill you."

"Yeah? Hardwork law says he should and some people prefer rules to sense."

"How would you know about people after twenty years alone?"

"I've been with Scraylings. They're people, too."

"They're different."

"Nope. People are pretty much the same as far as I've seen."

"What do you remember about my mother?"

"Well, she was hot, but, by Spider Mother's eight-legged trousers, was she a bitch."

Finnbogi giggled.

Erik laughed. "You know, she probably wasn't a bitch, she was just young and young people are idiots."

"Great. I'm young. I've been talking to my newly discovered dad for one minute, and he's told me that I'm an idiot and my mother was a bitch."

"We're all idiots. Show me the man who doesn't know that and I'll show you the biggest idiot."

"I guess...What do you know about The Meadows?"

"Nothing. It's more of a sense that we should head west and a little voice saying 'The Meadows,' a bit like how I know to go to the larder when the little voice in my head says 'honey cake.'"

"Whose voice is it?"

"Not a clue. Could be luring me to my death for all I know."

"What's the voice like?"

"Feminine, possibly. Maybe an effeminate guy or a boy. But it's different from the voice I heard calling me back to help you lot."

"Ottar's."

"So I've gathered. He's a funny one."

"He's a nice little guy. Do you know his story?"

"I do not."

Finnbogi told him. Erik made suitably amazed and disgusted noises. At the end he said, "And I thought I was a bad dad."

"At least Ottar's dad showed him some attention."

"You know, don't you, Finnbogi, that I never knew about you?"

"Can you call me Finn?"

"All right, Finn. It never crossed my mind that you existed. I know theoretically it takes only one...um...shag to make a kid, but...if I'd even half guessed I had a son I really would have come back and at the very least spied on you."

"You could have watched me from the bushes, maybe freaked me out by throwing stones at me every now and then or something."

"It would have been the least I could have done as a father."

"Look over there," said Erik a while later.

There was a family of buffalo lying among the trees next to the path—what Finnbogi took to be a large bull, a cow and two calves. It was the closest Finnbogi had been to the creatures. He'd thought that they were furry all over, and the paler calves were, but the male and the female had bald back ends. The adults were different from each other, too, the male wasn't just larger, his head was proportionally much bigger, almost ridiculously huge.

The bull was staring straight ahead. He could doubtless see Finnbogi and Erik in his peripheral vision, but in so little regard did he hold them that he didn't even turn his head. The mother and calves also seemed indifferent to the passing humans.

"Aren't they scared of us?" Finnbogi asked.

"Should they be?"

"No, but they don't know that."

"Are you scared of them?"

"No."

"Why not? They're huge."

"I don't know. I just feel that they're not going to trouble us."

"And they probably feel the same about us. The Lakchans

reckon all animals are just as intelligent as humans, they just don't bother with all the running around, talking crap and agonising over pointless bollocks that we do. I think they're probably right."

Finnbogi nodded and they walked on, Finnbogi trying to work out if animals could be as intelligent as humans, and whether his father really believed that or not.

"In all seriousness, Finnbogi, I am sorry," said Erik a short while later.

"In all seriousness, it's fine. I've quite liked being the hero orphan."

"Yeah, I get that."

Finnbogi smiled. He couldn't think of any of the Hardwork survivors who would have got that, with the possible exception of Sassa Lipchewer.

"So," said Erik, "are any of the chicks with you single?"

"Erik!" Finnbogi could *not* bring himself to call him Dad.

"I'm joking. It looks like we've got enough woman trouble on our tail without me creating my own."

"What do you know about the Calnian Owsla?"

"If they catch us, we won't stand a chance."

"But we've got Wulf, Garth, you...and they're... women?"

"So is Thyri and she's one of your best warriors, apparently."

"Fisk beat her and I didn't rate him at all."

"I saw that. She was the better fighter. He was lucky."

"So it was you who saved her?"

"It was Astrid."

"And we might be lucky against the Owsla, even if they're better?"

"No. What they've got, and we haven't, is magic."

"You believe that?"

"The Lakchans believed it. Their chief, Kobosh, believed it, and he's a great deal cannier and wiser than any

Hardworker I ever met. He was fascinated by the Calnian Owsla and used to drag me over to hear travellers' tales about them. He was full of theories about how they got their powers, and what those powers really were."

"So what are the Owsla?"

"You Hardworkers did not take much interest in the world around you, did you?"

Erik told him about the creation of the Owsla, about its members and how they got their names—the super-fast Paloma Pronghorn, the giant Chogolisa Earthquake—and more tales he'd heard about the Owsla killing entire tribes and beating impossible odds. Finnbogi didn't know whether to be terrified that such creatures were after them, or thrilled to know that these goddesses existed.

"Can't we reason with them?" he said when Erik had finished. "Surely they won't kill the children?"

"That's the thing. At the same time as they were developed physically, they had all human compassion removed. You might as well hurl a rock at a wasp's nest then ask them not to sting you. The Owsla are bred to kill everyone the empress asks them to, without question. That's why we have to escape."

"But how?"

"We should be safe once we cross the Water Mother."

"Why?"

"The Calnians don't cross the Water Mother."

"Why not?"

"Because what's on the other side of the Water Mother is apparently a whole lot worse than the Owsla."

"So why are we going there?"

"The Meadows are there, and we don't have anywhere else to go."

Chapter 20
The Hair Trick

On the bright side, they'd avoided the worst of the rain. On the dark side, it had rained so hard on the Mushroom Men that even Paloma Pronghorn couldn't track them. One interesting thing, though: the Mushroom Men had walked along a stream, which meant that they knew they were being followed. That posed some questions.

"I can tell you exactly where they went into the stream, and that they headed north, upstream," said Pronghorn.

"But not where they left it?" asked Sofi.

"Not a clue, or even the beginnings of one. They've been relatively clever covering their tracks. Relative to people who let two of their number get killed by a black bear, that is. With so much rain it would have actually been quite hard to leave tracks if they'd been trying to. Chances are, they turned west again."

"Unless they knew they were being followed, in which case they might have headed north, or south or east."

"That is true," smiled Paloma.

Sofi looked around. Magnificent storm clouds hung heavy in the north-west but the local weather was a uniform drab. They were on a plain of grassland fringed by trees. Buffalo grazed to the south, white-tail deer and elk to the north. Her Owsla stood about her. Usually they'd be sitting to rest, but the ground was soaking. Somehow Yoki Choppa had lit a fire and was preparing their morning sustenance.

Although she could see for miles, this was only one infin-itesimal part of the vast land, and even though it looked flat she knew it would be riven with gullies that could have hidden entire tribes for years. She could either assume that the Hardworkers were carrying on west and head that way, too, or she could use a spiral search pattern from their last known location, hunting for traces and interrogating any people they met.

"Yoki Choppa, where do you think they've gone?"

The warlock looked up from his smoking alchemical bowl, bone in hand. "West," he said.

"Why?"

"One of them has been leaving deposits of hair."

"They have?"

"I've found hair several times in the low branches of a tree on their route."

Sofi nodded. "It's definitely Hardworker hair?"

"Yup."

"How do you know?"

"It's light but not albino, and it's been left recently by the same person, in a trail from Hardwork."

"He couldn't have snagged his hair repeatedly by mistake?"

"No."

"So they have a traitor?"

"Yes."

"Can't be. Why would anyone betray themselves? It must be a ritual."

Yoki Choppa shrugged.

"Why didn't you tell me about it before?"

"Pronghorn's tracking is quicker and more accurate that the hair trick."

"When she can track them."

"Yes."

"So where are they now?"

Yoki Choppa pointed west. "That way. Could be twenty miles, could be forty. Not more than fifty."

"So we should catch up with them tomorrow, or the next day at the latest. Pronghorn, run west and come back when you've found the trail."

"Will do!"

A short time later they caught up with Paloma Pronghorn. She was standing at the edge of a swollen river, hands on hips. There were two buffalo-skin canoes hauled up the bank on the other side.

"They crossed here and left both boats on the far bank!" She shook her head. "No manners. I'm glad we're going to kill them."

"Maybe they didn't want us using the boats?" suggested Talisa White-tail.

"You know, you may be on to something there," said Paloma.

"Can you swim it, Sadzi?" asked Sofi Tornado. Sadzi Wolf was from a tribe that lived off the Water Mother and spent most of their waking hours swimming in it, so could move through the water like an otter. The rest of them were more like cats than otters in the water. Swimming. That was something else to look at when they got back to Calnia. Swimming and teamwork.

"Of course I can swim it," said Sadzi Wolf, already stripping.

Chapter 21

Rock River

The Hardworkers set off in the dark again, after almost no sleep. Finnbogi's mind was strangely zippy and clear. Screw the pursuing Calnian Owsla and screw Garth Anviltwat. He'd woken to a revelation that changed everything. He tripped along the starlit path with a new nimbleness, inhaling the sweet and woody odours of the night.

He'd realised that it was by no means over between him and Thyri, in fact it hadn't even begun. He was certain that she'd liked him, and any objective observer would surely have agreed. If a girl didn't like a bloke, did she place his hand onto her naked breast and leave it there all night? She did not. His mistake was not making a move.

He should have been brave.

Then it had been just Tor-awful double shitty luck when the Lakchans had attacked that Bodil had come onto him so weirdly and so publicly, and that Garth had been next to Thyri.

So, Finnbogi reasoned, as an owl hooted nearby and a wolf howled in the distance, clearly Thyri fancied Garth a little, or else she wouldn't have reacted to his advances, but not as much as she fancied the nearer-her-age-but-wise-beyond-his-years Finnbogi. It was as if Sassa had come onto him when they were certain to die. Sorry, Wulf and Thyri, but he'd have gone for it, even if he much preferred Thyri.

So it was the same deal with Thyri and Garth. She'd kissed

him, then started this relationship with him only because her true love Finn the Hero looked like he was taken by Bodil and because Garth Anvilcock, curse him to Niflheim and beyond, had had the balls to go for it.

So, there was an obvious answer to all his problems. He'd sleep with Bodil Gooseface.

He'd enjoy it. Bodil might be dumber than a bucket of wet fish, but she was pretty and she had a good figure. Then Thyri would get jealous. She'd see the smile on Bodil's face, know what she was missing and come running to Finnbogi's arms.

The plan was foolproof.

Hang on, said a voice from somewhere low down in his mind, are you sure you're not sleep-deprived and a bit crazy and perhaps this is the most stupid idea you've ever had, which is going some for the man who once tried to pop a spot by banging his head against a tree?

No, said Finnbogi to himself, that's the point. The chance is still there.

Or could it really be the worst idea ever...He resolved to discuss it with Erik—surely this was what fathers were for—but Erik was way ahead with Wulf. Gunnhild was much closer. She'd have to do.

Gunnhild Kristlover replied so cursorily to his attempts at starting a conversation that he gave up trying and walked along next to her, planning his conquest of Bodil and thinking about what it would be like to sleep with her.

As the sky lightened, he saw why Gunnhild had been such a useless conversationalist. Her eyes were narrow, her skin flushed a blotchy red and her mouth drawn in a humourless skull's grin. She was exhausted.

"Can I carry your clothes beater for you?" he asked.

"It's called Scrayling Beater, and no thanks. *Always keep your arms at hand; it is hard to know when you will need a weapon.*"

She was too tired to discuss the most important thing in Finnbogi's life, but not too tired to dredge up a dreary old world saying.

"Do you think you'll need it today?"

"'Need' is probably the wrong word. The Calnian Owsla will catch up with us today and I'll want to have Scrayling Beater with me, but it won't be much use."

"It worked well against the last lot of Calnians."

"They were human. The Owsla are devils."

They walked on, Finnbogi looking over his shoulder repeatedly, expecting to see the gang of Calnian women charging at them like a pack of lions. But he saw only Keef and Bjarni bringing up the rear, plus the odd deer and other furry beasts stepping onto the path to watch and wonder after the Hardworker exodus.

He felt like a deer himself, fleeing predators. It wasn't an entirely unpleasant sensation. After Erik's descriptions of them, Finnbogi had built pictures of the Calnian Owsla in his mind. They were savage and powerful but beautiful— basically ten versions of Thyri mixed with bits of Sassa plus a hefty dose of lascivious imagination.

"What could you have possibly found to smile about?" asked Gunnhild.

"I'm looking forward to seeing the Calnian Owsla."

Gunnhild shook her head. "Stupid boy," she said.

Paloma Pronghorn ran faster than her namesake, skimming over the dawn-lit land, singing a song her mother had sung to her. She could feel the glow of strength in her feet, calves, thighs, buttocks and swinging arms as they powered her on, faster and faster. She was quicker than any living thing, with the possible exception of some of the faster birds when they tucked their wings and dived, but that was actually falling and didn't count. Nobody, nothing, could run as fast as her. She leapt, held her arms by her side and twisted in the air, to feel what it must be like to be a bird. Not bad, she thought as she landed lightly. But not as good as running.

She sprinted on.

Racoons, squirrels, deer, chipmunks, snakes and all the other animals looked up startled but didn't have time to flee before she'd zoomed past. She ran up to a recently woken humped bear, ruffled the hair between its ears, dodged a paw swipe and was gone as it roared after her.

She spotted a footprint on the path, swung her arms and dug in her heels to stop. She jogged back to it.

She was coming to know the Mushroom Men by their tracks. This was one of the younger men who was usually found towards the back of the group, carrying more supplies than most of the others. She'd thought he was heavier at first, but his tracks around their camps showed that he put down his burden in the evening and spent his time exercising, at first with a woman and latterly on his own. This man interested Paloma most of all the Mushroom Men. She felt a connection with him. Perhaps they shared a spirit animal? It was interesting, but it didn't matter. He'd be relieved of his current burdensome existence and be on to the next life by the end of the day, the lucky fellow.

The other Owsla women enjoyed killing. Paloma Pronghorn didn't so much, but she did love helping people on to a new life. Her original tribe believed the dead were instantly reincarnated into a better life, or at least into an animal or person with a chance at a better life. When her older sister had been killed out hunting, her mother had told her again and again that it was a good thing, her sister was in a better place, and this notion became Paloma's central philosophy. She was like a fat person, she told herself, who didn't like cooking but loved food. She didn't like killing much, but she loved making people dead.

The footprint was fresh, so she'd be on them in moments, and shortly afterwards the rest of the Owsla would catch them and that would be that. They were making good speed now, the Mushroom Men, for a group of refugees with two children and at least one older person. They hadn't slept long the previous night, poor things, but soon they'd all be dead and a great deal happier.

Even though Keef and Bjarni were meant to be rearguard, it was Finnbogi who spotted the Calnian Owsla first—one of them, at least.

"Look!" he shouted.

They turned. Standing on the brow of a hill three hundred paces back was a solitary woman clad in leather leggings, breechcloth and short jerkin. She was too far for him to see her features, but by her shape, stance and outfit this had to be one of the Owsla.

The Hardworkers held their breath. Finnbogi expected a gang of similar warriors to crest the rise and surround the lone figure at any moment, but instead the woman waved cheerily, then turned and ran back the way she'd come.

"She must be the forward scout. I'm going to catch her." And Keef was gone, sprinting back along the path.

"Come back, you idiot!" shouted Gunnhild, but Keef ignored her. She shook her head. "Finn, run ahead and tell Wulf what we saw. Everyone else, let's speed up and see if we can get somewhere defendable before the rest of them catch up."

"What about Keef?"

"He's an idiot."

Keef ran back a while later and said, "She's gone. Vaporised into nowhere. I could see miles down the track and she wasn't anywhere. Are we sure we saw her?"

Paloma Pronghorn skidded to a halt.

"They're five miles ahead."

Good, thought Sofi Tornado. The sooner the Hardworkers were wiped out and this mission was over, the better. She was looking forward to Calnia and a few weeks of normality executing people in the Plaza of Innowak.

She thought of speeding everyone up, but, no, she wanted to begin the return journey as soon as the Mushroom Men were dead, so there was no need to exhaust them with a sprint.

"Pronghorn, run ahead and keep an eye on them, but keep back and don't kill any until the rest of us get there, understood?"

"Understood!"

Finnbogi jogged along, sweating like Frossa the Deep Minded at the top of a hill. Wulf had told him to toss his pack and he'd done so with glee, but then Freydis had been falling behind, so he'd picked her up, copying Erik who had Ottar on his shoulders.

Judging by the song she was making up as they ran, Freydis wasn't aware that they were running for their lives.

> Oh a robin a robin is lovely too,
> With an orange chest and speckly poo
> He'll sing a song to make you smile
> Even if you're Finnbogi and you've run a mile
> With a girl on your shoulders who's hard to bear
> Cos she's got heavy knees and heavier hair—

"Here, I'll carry her for a while," said Wulf, catching up to him.

No, no, it's no effort, I can take her for miles more, Finnbogi wanted to say. Instead, he stopped, panting and unable to speak.

Wulf plucked her off his shoulders, and Finnbogi staggered.

"Come on, Finn, we're nearly there!" said Erik, leaping round and running backwards. Hugin and Munin, who hadn't left his heels since he'd picked up Ottar, jinked about to keep clear of his huge feet.

He was hardly underweight, Finn's dad, and he was over forty years old, and he had Ottar on his shoulders, but he had a spring in his step and not so much as a bead of sweat on his tanned brow.

Ottar bounced happily.

The "there" that Erik was referring to was a wide river, which, according to him, was just ahead.

They ran on. White cloud rolled in. The sky stayed bright as the land became darker and darker, which was odd. Finnbogi hoped it wasn't going to rain again. He didn't want to die on a rainy day.

He saw Bodil ahead and ran to catch up with her.

The path ended in a wooden jetty protruding into the widest river that Sassa Lipchewer had ever seen. It must have been a hundred and fifty paces across.

"This is Rock River," announced Erik the Angry, swinging Ottar the Moaner onto the ground. Ottar's racoons trilled admonishment at him for being out of reach for so long. "There was a village last time I was here. I thought they'd have boats."

Mature trees with small, whispery, yellow-green leaves leant over both banks up and down the river. The new growth in the Hardworkers' immediate vicinity, the jetty and a gap in the trees on the far side of the river were the only traces that there'd been a settlement here. As well as the lack of village remains, there was also a glaring absence of boats.

"So we swim?" asked Wulf.

The idea did not thrill Sassa. The river was silty brown and swift after the recent rains and, perhaps most ominously of all, slicing through the surface towards the centre of the river were the fins of three large fish.

"We don't swim," said Erik, "because of them." He pointed at the fins.

"What are they?"

"Sharks."

"Sharks?" said Wulf. "Sharks are monsters that live in the salt sea."

"And big rivers. This village used to worship them, so they'd feed them. That's why there were always so many here, and by the looks of it they didn't leave when the people did."

"Only three of them."

"That we can see. They spend most of their time underwater."

"Ah. And they attack people?"

"The Rock River tribe fed them live sacrifices, so they learnt that humans are food."

"I see. How big are they?"

"The big ones are double the length of a tall man. The smaller ones aren't much bigger than a big dog, but still big enough to kill you."

"Spunk on a skunk," said Sassa. "Will they attack a boat?"

"I'm pretty sure they won't."

"So we'd better get going with Keef's," said Wulf.

"But that'll only fit two." Sassa shook her head.

"So we get started. Chnob! Chnob! Where's Chnob?"

The bearded man came puffing along the track, ahead of the rearguard Bjarni and Keef. Sassa expected the Calnian Owsla to be at their heels, but she could see two hundred paces up the path and all was clear. For now.

"Keef, can you fit Ottar and Freydis in your boat at the same time?"

"With me as well?"

"Yes."

"Across this river?" Keef was prolonging the moment of his boat being elevated from quite useful to vital.

"We're in something of a hurry, Keef. We need to shuttle us all before—"

"Why didn't you say! Come on, let's go!"

Keef wrenched the boat from Chnob's back, dropped it off the jetty and set off with Ottar and Freydis in the bow, paddling like a fury. Two more fins appeared next to the three holding place in the middle of the current. Other than that, the sharks didn't seem to pay them any mind.

"Treelegs, you're next in the boat," said Wulf. "You paddle across carrying Keef and let Keef paddle back. That'll be the form from now."

"No," said Thyri.

"There's no time to argue. We're going in age order, apart from me."

"And you?" asked Sassa.

"I'm going last."

Sassa's signed. There'd be no arguing with him and, besides, annoyingly, it was the right thing for the leader to do.

"We should send Hird across first," said Gurd Girlchaser.

"Who's older out of you and Gunnhild, Gurd?" asked Sassa.

"Gurd is forty. Both Erik and I are a good bit older than him," said Gunnhild. "I don't mind waiting."

Wow, thought Sassa. She would have put Gurd at the same age at least as Gunnhild and Erik as ten years younger. The years had not been kind to the sour-faced Hardworker Gurd but, then again, as her mother had always told her, ugly thoughts make you ugly.

"Gurd, we've had this chat a couple of times now," said Wulf, sounding a lot more grown up at twenty-five years old than Gurd ever would. "There is no Hird."

"But the Hird will paddle faster, we'll get more across. And the Owsla will be here any minute. Better if more useful people survive."

"Well, it's all moot now," Wulf sighed, looking over Gurd's shoulder "Because here they come."

Gurd leapt around, terror on his face. "Where? I can't—"

"I'm joking," said Wulf. "And much as we'll need heroes like you on the other side, we will be going in age order."

"What do you think, Garth?" Gurd snarled.

"I agree with Wulf," said Garth Anvilchin, who was younger than Bjarni Chickenhead, Keef the Berserker, Gurd Girlchaser, Erik the Angry and Gunnhild Kristlover.

"Who's next?" hollered Keef, paddling back across the river with exaggerated, mighty strokes.

Wulf nodded at Thyri Treelegs. She jogged to the jetty.

Sassa waited her turn, watching the path to the east. After Thyri it was Finnbogi. Sassa would have enjoyed his false protests about wanting to wait until last if it had not delayed them vital seconds. In the end it had been her who'd shouted: "Just get in the fucking boat, Finnbogi!"

He had, ashen-faced, and she'd felt guilty.

"What about Astrid?" she asked Erik as they watched Finnbogi paddle across while Keef yelled technique-improving commands at him.

Erik pointed to the north, where the giant bear was clambering out of the river, pulling a thrashing shark almost as long as herself by its tail. The bear swung the shark around her head a couple of times, whacked it against a tree, then set about eating it.

"She looks after herself," said Erik.

Bodil was next, then it was Sassa. Several of the sleek, grey fish passed under the canoe, twisting as if to get a better look and show her their horrible mouths. She'd never seen such evil-looking creatures, with their repulsively strong-looking, bendy bodies, ridiculous amounts of teeth and eyes that looked right into your soul and said: "I don't care about your soul, I want to bite you in half and eat your guts."

Twice her paddle struck a yucksomely springy but solid shark's back, but the terrifying creatures allowed them to glide above unmolested, and soon she was standing with

Finnbogi, Bodil and the children on the other bank as Keef zoomed back across.

"Where's Thyri?" she asked.

"Scouting ahead," said Finnbogi.

"And you didn't go with her?"

"No. I'm looking after Bodil and the children here."

Erik had one nervous eye on the Hardworkers ferrying each other across the Rock River, and the other on the track they'd come along. He guessed that the forward scout must have been Paloma Pronghorn, the fastest person in the world. But just how far ahead of the others had she been?

He closed his eyes and tried communicating with the sharks again, in case the Owsla came and he needed to swim the river. Again he succeeded, but the answer was the same—a primitive, fishy invitation to jump in and be eaten.

Still the Owsla didn't come and finally only he, Gunnhild and Wulf were left and it was his turn to cross.

He turned to Gunnhild, knowing she'd expect him to insist that she took his place. He almost did, but then decided it would be more fun to see the look on her face when he said "see ya!" and jumped into the boat. So he did that.

As Sassa watched Keef power back across the Rock River to pick up Gunnhild, Ottar groaned loudly.

"What's he saying, Freydis?" asked Sassa.

"One of the Calnian Owsla is over there, hiding in a tree."

"Over where?"

"Up the road on the other side. Can you see that taller tree where the track goes out of sight over the hill?"

"Yes."

"She's in that."

"He's sure?"

Freydis gave her a "when is he not sure?" look.

"Root a coot," said Sassa, scanning the trees. She couldn't

see anybody, but the thickly leaved tree could have hidden twenty Owsla.

When Keef and Gunnhild pushed off and Wulf was left on his own, she saw a figure drop lithely from the tree and saunter towards the jetty. One part of Sassa was terrified for her husband, another miffed that a lissom lady was sashaying so sexily towards him.

Paloma Pronghorn watched from the branches of a leafy tree as the Mushroom Men shuttled across in their canoe. It was a speedy little vessel, for one not powered by a magically strengthened Calnian Owsla.

She'd been told not to kill any of them until the others got there, and she didn't fancy it anyway. Odd. She wasn't mad about killing at the best of times, but today the idea of slaughtering those funny looking people repulsed her, even if Sofi Tornado was going to be pissed off that she'd let them cross the river.

But what was she going to do, ask them to wait? No, Sofi had told her to keep back and not to kill them, and that's what she'd do.

Having thought that, she was intrigued by these weird looking people that they'd followed for so long. She wanted to speak to at least one of them, to hear what he sounded like as much as anything. So she waited until the second to last one had disembarked in the tiny canoe, then leapt down and walked along the track.

The Mushroom Man smiled at her; an easy, genuine smile. He was tall, one of the tallest men she'd seen, even though he hadn't looked the tallest when the others were standing next to him. His hair was the colour of corn, golden even in the drab day and curled in a way that had been in fashion when she'd first arrived in Calnia but was now seen in only the most backward provinces and on Calnian youngsters who were trying to be ironic.

His skin was pale but he didn't look ill. He looked supremely healthy in fact, with big white teeth not unlike a buffalo's. He was well muscled, more so than any of the women of the Owsla apart from Chogolisa Earthquake. He had shaggy boots and the leather trousers that a male Calnian warrior might wear, but his jacket was strangely padded and his weapon looked like an enlarged smith's hammer with a head of iron—but that was impossible; nodules of iron were never as large as that weighty looking lump.

His eyes were maybe the oddest part. They were blue, strikingly so, like lake ice in the sun. He held her gaze as she approached, not even glancing at her figure. So he was obviously homosexual, which was a shame, as despite his startling appearance he was an attractive man. Not as perfect as Kimaman, who'd been Calnia's finest, but not a long way off.

"Hello," she said, "I'm—"

"Paloma Pronghorn. The fast one."

"Well deduced."

"Nice to meet you. I'm Wulf the Fat."

"The Fat?" She looked down to his midriff and back to those blue eyes.

"It's because I have a fat cock."

She shook her head and blinked at him."...Do you?" she stammered.

He grinned. "Not really. It's because I was a fat kid. Got the name then."

"Oh!" A joke! She laughed. "Sorry, I didn't expect you Mushroom Men to be funny."

"Some of us aren't."

"In fact I expected you to be *really* stupid."

"We're not exactly geniuses, but why did you think we'd be stupid?"

"Because the Goachica had to feed you and clothe you for a hundred years."

"They didn't have to."

"So you let them even though they didn't need to? I can't decide if that makes you more or less stupid."

"I've often wondered that myself. So...are you going to kill me now?"

"No. I'm waiting for the others."

"And they'll kill us?"

"They will. They enjoy it more than me."

"I see."

"But you shouldn't worry about death. You'll be reincarnated before you know it. You might come back as something great, maybe even Calnian Owsla."

"Lucky me."

"You mock, but you'd love it. We're the most powerful people in the world."

"Just how fast can you run? Are you really as fast as a pronghorn?"

"Quite a lot faster."

"How?"

"I put one leg in front of the other, then repeat."

"No, how did you get your...talents?"

"Magic."

"That's not an explanation."

"I guess not. I don't know how we got our powers. They made us eat things and smoke some odd things when we were young, so I've always assumed that was the alchemy that gave us our magic. I've asked a couple of times but the warlocks are secretive."

"I see. And why are you so keen to kill us?"

"A prophecy from the empress. Pale-skinned people are going to destroy the world. That's you."

"You think? The fourteen of us?"

"It's not my prophecy. But you're the only pale-skinned people. Plus I've seen the wasteful way you build, and you must have hunted far too much because there are hardly any animals in the woods around your town. Maybe it's your descendants who are going to destroy the world, but you've made a good start."

"Do you know where we come from?"

"Yes. I just said. I've been there." Paloma glanced over Wulf the Fat's shoulder. The older woman had disembarked and the man was paddling back. Another of the Hardworkers, also pale-haired, was pacing the bank and watching them, raising and lowering her bow. Paloma Pronghorn made sure that Wulf was between herself and the archer. She'd be able to dodge an arrow if she saw it coming, but it was best to be safe.

"A hundred years ago our ancestors travelled from thousands of miles away," said the Mushroom Man, "across what you call the Wild Salt Sea. There are thousands more like us where we came from. Hundreds of thousands. Millions even. All with pale skin."

The canoe bumped alongside the jetty at the same moment as Wulf's eyes widened at the sight of something behind her. She turned and saw Sofi Tornado leading the Owsla over the rise, with Talisa White-tail on one shoulder and the huge shape of Chogolisa Earthquake looming behind.

She realised immediately that she'd have to kill Wulf the Fat and the man in the boat, or at least hurt them enough to hold them. There'd be no excuse if they all saw her letting two of their quarry and their easiest way across the river paddle away.

She jumped high and flicked her killing stick at Wulf's head.

Amazingly, he'd read her move. He ducked and batted her legs out from under her. She fell and rolled away from his likely follow-up blow, but that blow never came because he'd fled for the jetty. No matter, she'd catch him. She sprang to her feet but then felt as much as heard the arrow. She threw herself to one side. She rolled and was back on her feet, but there was another arrow flying, not at her, but at where she needed to be on the jetty in order to catch Wulf the Fat.

She looked across the river at the blonde woman. There was already one more arrow on the way and she was drawing to shoot yet another. She was no Sitsi Kestrel—the Owsla's archer would have had six or seven arrows zipping across the river—but she was far from useless.

The big man jumped into the canoe, managing to not quite sink it and to push it out of her reach in one move. The Mushroom Man already in the boat, a funny looking fellow with a long blond beard, small head and straight, corn-coloured hair all the way down his back, began to paddle furiously.

"Goodbye," called Wulf the Fat. "I enjoyed meeting you, but I hope we don't meet again."

"We'll swim across. I'll be seeing you again in a couple of minutes."

"Don't swim across, there are—"

"Swim across!" interrupted the other Mushroom Man. "And take your time. It's lovely once you're in!"

"You watched them cross," sighed Sofi Tornado.

"One by one in that little boat. You said not to kill them."

"And you didn't think to run in and hole the boat?"

"No. There would have been a fight and I'd have had to kill one of them at least. So I'd have been disobeying orders. What's the problem? This river's not nearly so fast as that last one. We can swim across."

"Oh, Pronghorn," Sofi sighed. She liked being in charge because she couldn't stand being ordered about by anyone, but sometimes she wished she was the lowliest warrior, standing around waiting to be told what to do.

"What?" said the speedy woman.

"Can you see the creatures in the river?"

"Big fish. So what?"

"They're sharks!" piped up Sitsi Kestrel. "Man-eaters. The Shark Clan used to have a village here but they moved south last year to the mouth of the Water Mother, in search of bigger sharks. They fed live human sacrifices to the sharks, so those fish think people are food. Get in the water and they'll attack."

"Ah. Sorry," said Paloma, her face flushing.

"I know how to deal with sharks," said Sadzi Wolf. "I fought off my first shark when I was five years old. It's all about punching them in the face."

On the far side of the river, the last Hardworker was climbing out of the canoe. The rest of them were gathered on the bank, goggling at their pursuers.

"These sharks are different from Water Mother Sharks," said Sitsi.

Sadzi put her hands on her hips. "I grew up on the Water Mother. I can tell by the fins. These are exactly the same animals."

"Same type maybe, different attitude."

"They are fish. I am Owsla." Sadzi unbuckled her jerkin.

Sofi was torn. If Sadzi came back with the Mushroom Men's boat, they'd finish their mission within the hour. If she didn't let her swim, they'd have to build a boat, which would put them a day behind their quarry again. However, if she let her swim and she was killed, nothing would be gained and she'd be down yet another Owsla. And, although she was keen to get back to Calnia, they weren't actually in a hurry. They could spend three days making a boat and they'd still catch the Mushroom Men before they reached the Water Mother.

"No, Sadzi, don't risk it. We'll—"

But Sadzi, already naked, jammed her stubby flint knife between her teeth, sprinted to the end of the jetty and dived in.

Well, that wasn't what I was going to suggest, but let's see how it pans out, thought Sofi Tornado.

Finnbogi the Boggy, standing in the gap between the trees with the others, was gaping at the huge Owsla woman, towering above all the others and wide as the church's door, when he noticed that another was stripping.

"One of them's coming!" he shouted as she dived in.

There was a long silence after the splash and he thought a shark had got her already, but she surfaced and cut across the river towards them with a scything overarm stroke, powerful kicks churning the water white. She didn't seem affected by the current. But the current wasn't her problem. Her problem was the five shark fins headed straight for her.

The smallest of the Owsla produced a bow and shot at the sharks. Two fins disappeared after arrows struck home, but the other three reached their target. Woman and sharks disappeared. Hardworkers held their breaths on one bank; no doubt the Calnians did the same on the other.

There was an explosion of water and blood.

All went quiet.

The swimmer surfaced with a gasp and charged on, now more than halfway across.

"Shoot her, Sassa."

A week before, thought Finnbogi, even a few days before, Sassa would have questioned the command. Now, grim-faced, she raised her bow, drew the string back further than Finnbogi would ever be able to, and shot the swimmer. The swimmer went down. She didn't come back up.

"Not a bad shot, for a woman!" said Gurd Girlchaser.

"I think she'd still coming, underwater." Wulf turned to Finnbogi. "Take the children west along the track. Chnob, she'll be after the boat, get it away from here. Bodil, Gunnhild, get clear. Sassa, get back but cover us with your bow. Hird, back from the bank, mad-lion formation. Erik, join the Hird. Remember mad lion?"

"Yes."

"And can you get your bear here?"

"It'll be hard to pull her away from the shark she's eating, but I'll try." Rather than hollering as Finnbogi had expected, Erik closed his eyes and lowered his head. Could he talk to the animal with his *mind*? And if so, were skills like that inherited from father to son?

Finnbogi began to bundle the children away, but he heard a whoosh of water, forgot about Freydis and Ottar and turned to watch.

The Owsla woman burst out of the river and landed, feet apart, hands splayed, breathing hard. Blood pulsed from several ragged wounds and there was an arrow sticking out of her shoulder, but she stood strong and ready. And naked. Finnbogi's jaw fell open.

She looked, he guessed, like Thyri would look if she hadn't eaten so much maple sugar and had trained hard every day for a few more years. She was lean but far from thin, her dark skin taut against muscles that slid around each other like fish and eels sewn tightly into the finest leather. Her features were regular and her lips full. Her narrow black eyes, shining with what looked like cruelty mixed with lust, stopped her from being beautiful, but, added to the whole, made her more physically attractive than Finnbogi had thought it possible for a human being or indeed any creature to be. He gulped.

Wulf charged in, hammer aloft. The Owsla woman slapped the hammer aside, grabbed Wulf two-handed by his jerkin, heaved him over her head and hurled him into the river.

Keef and, to Finnbogi's surprise, Gurd, went in next, Keef with his long-handled axe Arse Splitter and Gurd with hand axe and shield. Gurd charged first, turning the woman so that Keef could stab with his weapon's spear-like end. At the same moment Sassa shot an arrow.

Somehow the Calnian twisted to avoid Keef's thrust and Sassa's arrow, grabbed Gurd's wrist and snapped it. Gurd yelped and the hand axe fell. Catching the axe, she drove a foot into Gurd's groin. He folded forwards and she brought the axe upwards in a blur. Gurd fell back, his face cleaved from jaw to forehead.

Behind them in the river, Wulf surfaced.

Garth charged, brandishing the Biter Twins, while Keef swung Arse Splitter from behind at knee height. The Calnian leapt, knocked Garth's axe attack away with one foot and kicked him in the temple with the other. He went down.

Landing, the Owsla woman immediately jumped again, jinked around Arse Splitter and slammed the side of her foot into Keef's head. He pirouetted away and collapsed.

Erik put out a hand to hold Thyri back, but she slipped under it and ran in. Bjarni Chickenhead advanced, too, his beautiful sword Lion Slayer held aloft.

Wulf, already taken ten paces downriver by the current, struck for shore.

"Stay back, Bjarni!" said Thyri. "No point rushing in with this one." She was tossing her slim-bladed sax from hand to hand, her shield on her back.

Sassa shot another arrow. The Calnian dodged it. She spun Gurd's axe around on one palm. "You'll find I'm just as tricky if you take me slow," she said, "but I will be happy to show you, girl. So know the name of your killer, I am Sadzi Wolf."

"I am Thyri Treelegs."

Sadzi Wolf's eyes flicked down and settled on the Hardworker's bare thighs for a moment. "So you are. Well, you mustn't let it worry you. You'd probably have lost that puppy fat if you'd lived beyond today. I like your weapons by the way. They'll be a useful addition to our Owsla."

The Calnian strode forward, swinging Gurd's axe with impossible speed. Its head was visible only as a flashing glint in the dull sun. Thyri stepped to meet her, swinging her own blade. Sadzi Wolf, laughing, caught her wrist, turning as she did so to avoid another arrow from Sassa. While she forced Thyri to her knees with her iron grip, she looked up at Sassa. "Keep firing, beauty, because when I'm done here, I'm going to come over there and ram any arrows you've got left up your arse." She smiled. "You might enjoy it."

Bjarni charged, but, without turning and still holding Thyri by the wrist, Sadzi Wolf swung her axe backhanded and caught him in the temple. He fell on top of the prone Garth.

Finnbogi pulled his sword from its scabbard and looked at it. It felt like it was very much the wrong tool for the job, like trying to kill a bear with a feather.

Sadzi Wolf forced Thyri further towards the ground. Treelegs slammed a hard punch into the Calnian's kidneys with her free hand, which made the Owsla woman wince. It was the first blow that any of them had landed, but she responded strongly. She switched her grip to the back of Thyri's head, kneed the girl with a stunning blow to the face, then raised her axe for the kill.

"That's enough now," said Erik, hefting his club. "You kill that one, and I'll eat your flesh when I've killed you. Let her live, and I'll just kill you."

"What are you, her daddy?" Sadzi Wolf held Erik's eye, tilted Thyri's head back, pursed her lips and dribbled saliva into the unconscious girl's open mouth. "Do you like it when I do that, Daddy?"

Finnbogi crept forward, still wondering what he was going to do. There was a roar and someone thundered past. It was

Chnob the White! Sadzi Wolf turned to meet him and slashed her axe across his neck. Somehow Chnob ignored the wound and clasped his arms around her. Blood gushed from his gaping neck up into her face. Erik bounced forward and swung his club into the side of the Calnian's head. It connected with a noise like a log dropped onto rock from a height.

She collapsed, Chnob fell away. Erik swung his club twice around his head, up and down and CRUNCH onto Sadzi Wolf's skull.

He wiped his weapon clean on the grass.

"Arrggghh," Astrid the bear moaned, arriving on the scene in time to be no help whatsoever at all.

"Do you want me to go across?" asked Chogolisa Earthquake. On the far side of the river a Mushroom Man prodded a prone Sadzi with his toe.

"No, stay here," said Sofi Tornado.

"Shall I shoot them?" Sitsi Kestrel had her bow ready.

"No."

"We're not letting them go?"

"For now." Sofi was suffering from the strangest emotion. She felt *sad*. She hadn't felt this emotion before, at least since she'd been a child. She wasn't sad for Sadzi Wolf. She'd never liked the woman, and she'd told Sadzi not to swim the river. No, it was the Mushroom Men who were getting to her. Last of their tribe, a mixed bunch of men, women and children, and still they fought as if their lives were important. They shouldn't have beaten Sadzi Wolf, but, instead of fleeing like they should have done as she'd crossed the river, or at least after the first couple had been felled, they'd refused to give up against impossible odds, and somehow triumphed.

How *had* they beaten Sadzi? She shook her head.

"Are you all right?" asked Sitsi Kestrel.

"Of course I am."

"You said we were letting them go for now?"

"Talisa, go north. Paloma, head south. Look for boats. Come back if you find one, return before dark if you don't. They rest of us will start building one."

Part Three

To the Water Mother

Chapter 1

Romance in the Mud

"I didn't think. I acted. For a moment I wasn't Chnob the White, philosopher and lover, I was Tor himself, driven by instinct and, although this word is used too easily these days, I think you'll all agree it applies here—heroism." Chnob spoke quietly, one hand on his bandaged throat, drawing attention to the wound he'd sustained saving them all. "Did I consider my safety for a moment? I did not. Did I have a lifetime of battle training like all the Hird who'd attacked Sadzi Wolf and fallen before me? I did not. Did I know that my action might save the day and save us all? I did not. Did I dare suspect that I, Chnob the Thinker, would slay one of the famed Owsla? I did not."

Bjarni listened to Chnob, his eyes closed because the light from the campfire was a bit much. His head felt like it had been whacked by Tor's hammer. Gunnhild had given him a herby drink which might have helped a little, it was hard to tell. What he needed was a bucketful of mushrooms to take him to another world. Fat chance of that round here, miles from home and stuck on the banks of a river across from a gang of murderous superwomen who wanted to kill them all.

There was a funny mood in the camp, now that they knew they were certain to die soon. The Owsla had come all the way from Calnia and found them in a matter of days. It wouldn't be long before they crossed the river and caught up with them again. Once they did, given how one of them, naked and unarmed, had taken them apart, they didn't stand a straw man's chance in a tornado against the remaining six. It was a miracle that Sadzi Wolf had killed only Gurd Girlchaser.

With nothing else to do, since so many of them were injured and needed rest, Chnob had suggested that they try out the custom from the old world sagas of each describing their roles in the day's battle. Wulf had thought it was a great idea and gone first. He'd told and shown them how he'd been bested in a trice and thrown into the river, where he'd been terrified of the sharks. His description and antics were so funny that despite their predicament they'd all laughed, which had made Bjarni's head hurt all the more.

Now it was Chnob sounding off, ignoring the old world custom that you never exaggerated your role in a battle. There was another custom from the sagas that if anyone did exaggerate then everyone else was supposed to take the piss mercilessly, but nobody was bothering with that. Had it been anyone else but Chnob, they would have done. But you only take the piss out of people you like.

Bjarni closed his eyes, stopped listening to Chnob and thought about Wulf the Fat. That was the best pain reliever he knew.

"I saw the foe and knew what I had to do," Chnob continued. "I pushed past Finnbogi the Boggy, who was dithering on the periphery like an ugly girl at a Thing dance, and I charged."

An ugly girl. You'd think that someone with no mates in the world would try and befriend someone who was also on the social periphery, but no. One of the many reasons why Finnbogi hated Chnob was that he tried to curry favour with the inner clique that he'd never be in by attacking others who weren't in that clique. It was a wanker tactic, alienating the people most likely to be your friends, but Chnob was king of the wankers.

Annoyingly, because there was no fairness in the world and the gods hated Finnbogi, Chnob *had* won the fight against Sadzi Wolf. He'd done it by blinding her with his own blood so that another could deliver the death blow, which wasn't exactly a classic. How many heroes in the sagas used that manoeuvre? However, they all knew the victory was his and he had made it all the more noble by almost dying in the process. If Erik—helped by Finnbogi—hadn't treated his horrible gash immediately, then they would have built a funeral pyre for Chnob alongside the two for Gurd Girlchaser and Sadzi Wolf that were burning away merrily down by the river. Finnbogi hadn't been a fan of Gurd, but he would have swapped him for Chnob in a trice. He would have swapped Sadzi Wolf for Chnob. She'd certainly looked about forty thousand times better.

"Who knows why some men act and others don't?" Chnob droned on. "Perhaps Boggy was gawping and gulping like a fish and waiting for an invitation to attack Sadzi Wolf, when I simply saw a job to be done and got on with it?"

Oh the cock. That was enough. Finnbogi stood up.

"Chickening out of the tale of the fight like you chickened out of the fight, are you, Boggy?" crowed Chnob.

Finnbogi patted the sword at his hip. "I was about to take her down with Foe Slicer here when a silly little traitor skipped past, got whipped but was lucky enough to spurt blood in the right direction. It was my father who stepped in to do the hero's job of attacking her with a weapon rather than his own bodily fluids. That's my tale of the fight."

Several people laughed. Wulf even rocked forward and slapped his thighs with mirth.

Finnbogi turned to go, thrilled at his successful verbal spar and keen to be away before Chnob could think of a clever reply. He was a fool, Chnob, but he wasn't stupid.

As he turned, he caught Bodil's eye, and, without thinking, gestured with his head for her to follow.

She smiled prettily but uncomprehendingly, which was how she always smiled, and looked back to Chnob.

Finnbogi walked into the darkness alone.

He stood for a moment while his eyes adjusted, then followed the path which ran parallel to the river, sometimes alongside it, sometimes through the trees. After a while he stopped where the bank had collapsed and packed earth sloped directly into the water. There were animal tracks everywhere which meant, he guessed, that a bear or a lion might happen along for a drink at any moment. Before all this had begun, that thought would have scared the crap out of him and sent him scuttling back to the others. Now? He didn't feel brave, but he wasn't scared. The hoots and whistles of nocturnal animals sounded all around and any number of them might have been on its way to attack him. But he didn't mind.

He sat on a log. Light from the Calnian campfire flickered on the leaves across the river. The women were going to catch them soon and there'd be no escape. That was the consensus, even if nobody was saying it.

A snapped twig made him jump. There was something large coming along the path towards him. His heart raced. So much for his newfound bravery. A shape appeared at the edge of his little clearing. A woman. Bodil Gooseface.

"Bodil," said Finnbogi, standing. "What are—?"

She put a finger on his lips and a hand on the small of his back, pulled him gently and pressed her groin into his. Her brown eyes were huge in the moonlight, blinking up at him. He kissed her finger. She pulled it away, closed her eyes, opened her mouth and lifted her face.

On their way back to camp, maybe an hour later, maybe twenty hours later, they met Wulf and Sassa, walking hand in hand along the path towards them.

"There's a good spot for it about two minutes' walk that way," said Finnbogi, hoicking a finger over his shoulder, winking, then immediately wishing he was dead. What did he say such dumb things?

Bodil wanted to share a sleeping sack, but Finnbogi mumbled something about that being impossible without disturbing everybody else and climbed in next to the irregularly snoring Bjarni.

So, he thought, no longer a virgin. He'd pulled Bodil, two years older than him, and gone all the way with her. He grinned himself to sleep.

Chapter 2

A Tool

The next day was hard. Wulf the Fat woke them before dawn. With most of the Hird injured he took the forward scout role with Erik the Angry and sent Finnbogi the Boggy, Sassa Lipchewer and Chnob the White to be rearguard.

"He's pretty desperate if he's got untrained women guarding the rear," said Chnob to Sassa as the others headed off and the three of them waited to follow at a rearguard distance. "Still, I'd guard your rear any day."

"You're right, Chnob, you're so much better suited to this than I am," said Sassa. "How about you hang a hundred paces behind Finnbogi and me and be the real rearguard? You can call if you need us."

"I won't need you."

"I'm sure you won't. We'll call on you if we need you, though. So, you wait here for a bit, we'll head off now."

"Right."

"It's a mountain!" said Finnbogi, a short while later.

"I think mountains are quite a lot bigger than this," said Sassa, but it was the steepest and highest slope that she'd ever had the misfortune to walk up.

"So..." she said as the slope evened out. "Bodil?"

"What about Bodil?"

"I didn't know you liked her."

"Who says I like her?"

"Funny that you should switch your affections from Thyri so quickly."

"Is it?"

"Be careful, Finnbogi. You can't mess with people's hearts."

"It wasn't her heart I was messing with." He chuckled, a bit disgustingly.

"Finnbogi, don't be a dick about this. Bodil likes you."

"I noticed."

"If you don't like her in the same way, it's wrong to encourage her."

"But she doesn't really like me? I mean she might fancy me a bit, but surely that's it?"

"That's not how Bodil works. It was her first time, too."

"What makes you think it was my first time?"

She looked at him and he had the good grace to go red. "It was her first time and it was important to her. Was it important to you?"

"I...It was really good."

"So you'll be doing it again tonight? You didn't in any way use Bodil to get at Thyri?"

Finnbogi opened his mouth to say something and closed it again. They walked along in silence for a while. She could almost hear him thinking.

"I've fucked up," he said, a good few minutes later, "haven't I?"

She liked Finnbogi. He was insecure, maybe because he'd grown up without proper parents. That insecurity could come across as arrogance, even nastiness, but, pick the twatty crust off his character and you found a decent, sensitive young man underneath.

"Sounds like you have fucked up," she said.

"What should I do? I'm a tool."

"You've been a tool, but at least you can see your mistake. What do you think you should do?"

"Be cruel to Bodil so she goes off me."

She looked at him. He didn't seem to be joking. The twatty crust was quite thick in places.

"Wrong, you dong. You have to explain to her."

"Tell her the truth?"

"No, don't be stupid. Tell her a good lie."

"Like what?"

"Like you were terrified by the situation we're in and were looking for comfort. You like her a great deal, but you've always seen her as a friend, even a sister, and, although it was the best thirty seconds of your life—"

"It was more than thirty seconds."

"So although it was the best thirty-five seconds of your life, it was a mistake to take the friendship further and you won't be doing it again."

"I've got to say that to her?"

"Yup, unless you can come up with anything—"

"They're coming!" shouted Chnob from behind. "The Owsla are coming!"

They spun round.

"Got you!" Chnob laughed.

"That guy is the biggest dickhead," Finnbogi muttered as they walked on.

"Not today. Today he's the second biggest dickhead." She raised an eyebrow at Finnbogi and he looked at his feet.

The other problem with Finnbogi shagging Bodil, of course, was that Keef was in love with Bodil. Maybe Bodil would have reciprocated if she hadn't been holding a flame for Finnbogi, a flame that Finnbogi had probably just fanned into an inferno. There was no point telling Finnbogi about Keef's affections, though. That would be a disservice to Keef.

She really was lucky with Wulf the Fat. When they'd made love by the river the night before—further upstream from where Finnbogi and Bodil had rutted and beyond the scavenger-busy remains of the shark that Erik's bear had eviscerated—she'd been more certain than ever that they'd created a new life.

Did that make up for taking a life? She thought about Hrolf the Painter often; his ruined, leering face before she'd pushed the knife into his neck, the gush of warm blood over her hand, his eyes showing surprise, then terror, then nothing.

She thought of him often but she could not, no matter how hard she tried, feel guilty about killing him.

Finnbogi resolved to speak to Bodil, but he'd have to wait until a good time, which wasn't while he was rearguard.

It was a joy to walk next to beautiful Sassa Lipchewer. Wulf was a very lucky man to have such a problem-free love life with such a wonderful girl. She'd been right about Bodil. He'd been thoughtless, but he would make amends by talking to Gooseface as soon as the right moment presented itself.

He and Sassa chatted about other things as they walked— about their childhoods, about people in the group, about others who'd died at Hardwork—and it was more like they were best of friends out for a summer stroll than two people facing certain, imminent and violent death.

He asked her how he should win Thyri, and she said he should be himself. He said he'd been trying that for years and it hadn't got him anywhere and she laughed. He told her how much he regretted saying "There's a good spot about two minutes' walk that way" to her and Wulf the night before. She said, yes that had been a dickish thing to say, but that's what happened when, like him, you tried to be funny the whole time. Either he could be more careful about what he said and be less funny, or he could accept that every now and then he was going to upset people and embarrass himself. She said that she preferred the latter Finnbogi, and when he did say stupid things he could look at her and know that she'd be on his side.

It was at that moment that he decided he might love Thyri Treelegs sexually, but his deep fraternal love for Sassa Lipchewer was almost as strong.

The hill that he'd called a mountain proved to be the first in a set of ridges, so Wulf pushing them to keep up a strong pace and take no breaks was made even worse by the fact that they were going uphill most of the time, with wet feet from the streams they had to cross at the lowest point between every ridge.

They walked on and on. They passed a stark stand of dead trees at the top of one of the rises, their branches heavy with hundreds and hundreds of red-faced vultures watching them pass. Minutes later, as if to counteract any bad omen from the vultures, a thousand-strong flock of gigantic white pelicans flew overhead.

At the lunchtime break when they sat down together, Wulf congratulated them and said they'd covered about twenty-five miles, their best morning so far. Finnbogi's feet certainly felt like they'd gone further than ever before, and it looked like everyone else was feeling it, apart from Ottar and Freydis who were running around full of the joys of life, having been carried most of the morning by Erik and Wulf.

Thyri sat silently throughout the lunch stop. She was leaning on Garth's arm, one hand on his wrist, which tore at Finnbogi a little. However, on the bright side, her nose was a swollen and angry purple from Sadzi Wolf's knee the day before, and she looked sour as a cat with a pine cone recently inserted up its arse. Garth, who had a big bruise on the side from Wonderful Wulf's kick, didn't look any happier. Neither of them spoke.

For the afternoon, to Finnbogi's joy, he was put back on rearguard with Sassa and Chnob, and again Sassa persuaded Chnob to hang behind.

They talked about The Meadows, and what they hoped

to find there. Sassa said there'd be streams, beautiful hills they didn't have to walk up unless they wanted to, and they'd all have lots of children to entertain them and look after them when they were older. Finnbogi wondered briefly why she and Wulf didn't have any children and almost asked, but then they were talking about something else.

Finally the series of rises ended and they could see for miles and miles, across prairie dotted with stands of trees on hilltops and divided by lines of trees marking out watercourses. Far, far to the south they could see the smoke.

Bodil fell back to join them, "Look at the view! That smoke...Is it Muspelheim, the land of fire where the giants live?"

"Yes, Bodil, I'm sure it is." He gave Sassa an "isn't Bodil stupid?" look.

The look she gave him in reply made him shiver. "It's a prairie fire, Bodil," she said, "they happen every now and then, otherwise this would all be trees and not grassland."

"What, really?" asked Finnbogi. "How do you know?"

"I grew up on a farm. Now look, I'm going to join Chnob for a while, so you can say anything you need to say." She stopped to wait for the bearded backmarker.

Finnbogi walked on with Bodil, waiting for a pause in her chatter. But in the very few pauses it seemed ridiculous to suddenly announce that he loved her like a sister and not a lover, so the words went unsaid.

That night when they'd finally made camp and eaten, Finnbogi saw Bodil trying to catch his eye, but he headed off to his training. He could feel Sassa glaring at him, but what was her problem? It was important for everybody in the group that he trained. Maybe just this little bit would make the difference in the coming battle against the Owsla.

By the time he finished, he was far too tired to be talking to Bodil about serious things, so he slid into the sack next to Bjarni and fantasised about living in The Meadows in a house with Thyri Treelegs. Wulf and Sassa lived across the shallow, flower-filled valley and the two couples' children played in the middle.

It took all day to build the boat. They didn't have the tools, and Sofi Tornado wanted it done properly. Sadzi Wolf may have survived the sharks, but she didn't expect that the rest of them would, and there were many more fins in the river now. Perhaps news of the few chunks they'd taken out of Sadzi Wolf had spread and all the sharks had returned, thinking the human sacrifices had resumed.

The craft was ready as the sun was setting. Sofi decreed that they'd camp in the same spot that night and head across the river first thing in the morning.

At a good pace, they'd catch up with the Hardworkers by the early afternoon.

Chapter 3

Heartberry Canyon

"Wowsa in *wootah*!" Ottar the Moaner leapt about, pointed at the ground, flicked his fingers towards everyone as if he was trying to spatter them with invisible mud, then pointed back at the ground and nodded vigorously. "In wootah. Wootah!" he insisted. "Woooo-tah!"

"The Calnian Owsla are crossing the river," explained Freydis the Annoying.

Everyone looked at everyone else with varying degrees of determination and fear, apart from Erik the Angry who sighed and Wulf the Fat who grinned and said: "Did he say 'wootah'?"

"He did," said Freydis.

"I like it. *Woo*tah. Woo*tah*. Woo...tah! I'm going to use it. Do you mind, Ottar?" But the boy was already bouncing away, following a grasshopper. "Can you ask Ottar if he minds, please, Freydis?"

"He won't mind."

"Good. Wootah. Woooo—TAH!"

Sassa poked his chest. "What do you mean you're going to use 'Wootah'? What are you going to use it for?"

"I dunno. I just like it. Battle cry? Expletive? Perhaps I'll shout it as I ejaculate. *Woooooo—taaah*!"

"Well, whoopee for me, that'll enhance orgasm. Come on, though, those women move a lot faster than us. Let's get the wootah out of here."

*   *   *

"How far to the Water Mother?" Garth asked Erik as they trudged up the first rise of the day.

Erik didn't know. He'd been lost in thought when he'd made the journey before and hadn't noticed the days passing. But he knew they weren't nearly close enough.

"A day and a bit's walk," he said, thinking it was probably more.

"We shouldn't have stopped for the night," said Garth.

"We had to stop."

"Not all of us."

He was right. They'd gone maybe forty miles the day before, which was far too far for anyone to walk in a day, but Erik himself could have kept going. In fact he could have sped up, even run, if his life had counted on it, which of course it did. All of them could have run all the way to the Water Mother if they really had to, with the exception of Gunnhild and the children. So Garth had a point. But it was a wanker's point and Erik didn't bother answering.

"Wulf, I've got an idea!" shouted Garth, jogging off to catch up to the leader.

Erik walked on. At their current pace, the Owsla were going to catch up and chances were the Hardworkers weren't going to be so lucky this time. If they ditched Gunnhild and the children, and anyone else who couldn't trot along at jogging pace all day, they really might get across the Water Mother before they were caught. If they split up, there'd be an even greater chance that some of them would make it.

Funny, though, those ideas didn't interest him. He'd been with this lot for a couple of days, but already he was certain that they had to live together or die together.

Up ahead, Garth clearly didn't get the reply he wanted from Wulf. "We're all fucked then!" he raged, and stormed off ahead.

*   *   *

Around lunchtime, Erik reckoned the Calnians would be on them any moment. Keef and Bjarni, who were rearguard that day, said they'd seen something that could have been Paloma Pronghorn darting around behind them.

Erik jogged to catch up to Wulf. "How about I call in Astrid and we take the rearguard? I don't know if I'll be much use against the Owsla, but the bear should slow them up for a bit."

"I can't ask you to do that." Wulf scratched his chin.

"You won't stop me, though?"

"No."

"See you then."

Erik fell back, told Keef and Bjarni that he was replacing them as backmarker, and called for Astrid.

"We'll be on them in an hour," said Paloma Pronghorn.

"They're heading into the Big Bone tribe's territory," said Sitsi Kestrel.

Sofi Tornado looked at Yoki Choppa, who shrugged.

She agreed with the warlock. The Big Bone tribe would probably kill the Mushroom Men. If they didn't, the Owsla would. It made no difference; by sunset the Mushroom Men would be nothing more than an odd little story which might be told for a generation or two.

Finnbogi had been watching the sky to the south become steadily darker. Now, although it was a sunny day where they were, to the south was ridge after ridge of cloud, darker and darker until it was the same wounded purple-black as Thyri's nose.

"Should we be looking for shelter?" he asked nobody in particular.

"Why?" It was Bodil. She'd been walking behind him and he hadn't noticed.

He nodded at the sky.

"Looks like we're in for a bit more rain," she said.

"It looks like the end of the world to me." Could she not see the awesome weight of those clouds? Could she not feel the suffocating danger pressing down like an uncaring, unseeing foot driving down on a team of ants?

"It'll be good for the flowers," she assured him.

Sassa Lipchewer and Thyri Treelegs crouched between two trees, at the top of a wall of rock overlooking the village. The woods around them sang with the cheeps and chirrs of myriad tubby woodland birds, all unafraid or unaware of the hawks gliding above. Bright, tiny frogs hopped about on leaves.

The village was maybe fifty conical hide huts spread sparsely along a flat clearing at the confluence of two shallow rivers. Both sides of the valley were steep, wooded in places and vertical, bare rock in others. Dotted about the huts were large animal sculptures made of struts that looked like bones but were too large to be the bones of any animal Sassa knew. All was lit by a bright sun, despite the ominously dark clouds to the south.

The people were dressed in the usual Scrayling kit—men in breechcloths and shirts, women in bead- and quill-embroidered dresses, children varying degrees of naked. Several of the adults carried the sticks that looked like giant bones, and many of the men, women and children had bones in their hair. Off to the right, next to a slab-sided outcrop of rock in the middle of the valley, a group of older children were rolling a wooden hoop and trying to spear it with a hurled pole.

Nearer, a proud-chested man strutted along wafting a martial air, one of the great bone-like things over his shoulder. He stopped and looked up, directly at their hiding place. Both women held their breath. The man was maybe Erik's age, with small eyes and fat lips the same colour as his face.

His hair was shoulder-length at the back, but was shaped on top into a towering, centre-parted bouffant. He smiled—directly at them, it seemed to Sassa—then he walked away.

"Those kids are crap at hoop and pole," said Thyri when the man had gone. Not one of them had managed to spear the hoop while they'd been watching.

"Yes," Sassa agreed.

"And how did they build those walls of rock?" She pointed to a grey rock face on the other side of the valley. It was comprised of horizontal slabs, as if it had been laid down by giants.

"They're called cliffs. They're natural, not built." Sassa had heard about cliffs in the stories from the old world and was surprised Thyri hadn't, but then again Thyri had spent a great deal more time learning to fight than she had listening to the elders. And who was Sassa to blame her? Excellent fighting skills were more useful to the group right then than an ability to put a name to topography.

"I'd like to climb it," Thyri grinned.

Sassa couldn't think of anything worse. "Maybe you'll get a chance."

"What do we do?"

The track that they'd been following led into the village, bridged the river then disappeared into the trees on the southern side of the valley.

"Come on, let's head back and tell Wulf."

Sassa and Thyri found the rest of them walking along, marvelling at how weird the sky to the south was becoming. They told them about the village.

"Do they look friendly?"

Sassa looked at Thyri. "I suppose."

Thyri nodded. "They don't look unfriendly."

"We should skirt around," announced Garth. "They'll

Angus Watson

have the same instructions as the Lakchans and we won't
be so lucky a second time."

Ottar yelped and pulled at Wulf's hand.

"Ottar says we should go through the village," said Freydis.

Wulf ruffled her hair. "Let's go then."

"For the love of Tor!" said Garth, throwing his arms in
the air and storming off.

If they'd wanted to pass by unnoticed, they were in trouble.
What looked like an entire tribe had gathered to block the
path through the village. Foremost of the Scrayling welcoming
party were three people, standing in a row.

Leftmost was the high-haired man who'd looked at Sassa
and Thyri. He nodded and smiled at Sassa as if to say, "yes,
I did spot you hiding in the trees." Close up, his long club
looked even more like a bone.

On the right was a tall, overweight, convivial looking
fellow with a shining mane of hair who managed to be both
handsome and toad-like. Between them was an elderly lady—
she might have been sixty years old. She looked from
Hardworker to Hardworker, blinking nervously. In contrast
to the brightly dressed women behind her, she was all in
black, apart from a colourful and heavy-looking loop of what
looked like painted back bones draped over her shoulders.

"Hi there," said Wulf.

"Oh, hello, hello," said the woman, blinking as if she was
in a competition to see how many times she could blink in
an allotted timespan. "Sorry."

"What for?"

"Oh, you know. Just sorry!" She waggled her hands and
looked up at the sky as if the answer lay there.

"We are the Big Bone tribe and this is Heartberry
Canyon," said the portly man. "I'm Big Hinto, the Food
Chief, this is Balinda, the Home Chief, and the serious
looking fellow with the hair is Chucknor, the War Chief.

Who are you, please, where have you come from and where are you going?"

"We are the remainder of the Wootah tribe," said Wulf. Sassa gave him a look but he carried right on. "We come from the banks of the Lake of the Retrieving Sturgeon, where most of our tribe were recently massacred by the Calnians. We are currently fleeing the Calnian Owsla, who should catch up with us any moment."

At the mention of the Calnian Owsla the three chiefs looked at each other, and there was murmuring from the gathered villagers.

"We are headed," Wulf continued, "across the Water Mother and beyond, where we will found a new homeland in a place called The Meadows."

"How do you know of this homeland?" asked Chucknor.

"This boy told us about it." Wulf indicated Ottar, who was off to the side with a pensive look on his face, touching his chin repeatedly with alternate thumbs as if to find which he preferred. "He is a great seer. He warned our tribe that the Calnians were coming to kill us but no heed was taken. His guidance has saved us a few times since."

"Did he say we'd give you safe passage?"

"Pretty much, yes."

"I see. Would you mind waiting while we discuss whether he was right?"

"Sure."

"Do sit," said Big Hinto, indicating a swathe of grass. "There's some weather on the way but right now it's nicer to be out in the open. And you can tell your friend and his big bear to come out from under the trees. We don't fear that type of bear here." He turned to his own villagers: "You, you and you, fetch heartberry drinks and...let me see...some of my smoked rabbit, wild rice and berries that we had last night."

"Shall I heat the rabbit?" one of them asked.

"No, for the love of the Great Fox, no! Have you learnt nothing? *Never* reheat my rabbit and berry dish, and, besides, cold food is more palatable on a hot day."

The Hardworkers sat and waited, while the three chiefs stood at a distance, conversing and looking over at them every now and then.

"So," asked Garth, "Wootah tribe?"

"I think it's time we left the past," said Wulf, "and I reckon Wootah is as good a name as any."

"Have you no respect for the ancestors?"

"Recent ancestors? Not much. Olaf the Worldfinder and his cronies were the last lot who did anything worth respecting."

"Olaf named Hardwork. You're disrespecting him."

"I think the Worldfinder would appreciate the need for a break from the immediate past. But listen, I'm not set on it. We'll discuss it later. Maybe even take a vote."

"If we have a later. This lot might kill us. This food," he pointed to the three Big Bone tribeswomen who were returning with laden trays, "is probably poisoned. I can't believe we followed idiot boy again."

"He's a long way from being an idiot, Garth," said Sassa.

"He can't speak."

"And yet he warned us all about the Calnians. You can speak and you didn't. Who's the idiot?"

"Woooo-tah!" said Wulf.

The heartberry drinks and the cold stew were the most delicious thing that Finnbogi had ever eaten, even if he had one eye out for the Owsla bursting into the valley behind them, one eye on Garth and Thyri, another eye on the dark clouds to the south, and yet another eye on the Big Bone tribe's chiefs, wondering what they'd decide.

After what seemed like an age, they finished their deliberations and moseyed over. The Hardworkers—or the Wootah tribe, Finnbogi quite liked the new name—stood.

"I'm really sorry," said Balinda, "but we do know all about you. We know that you are the Mushroom Men and why the Calnians want you dead. We also know what they've promised to do to tribes that don't kill you. Sorry." She shifted from foot to foot and wrung her hands like a good girl reporting a breakage to her parents.

"I see," said Wulf.

"Yes, I am sorry, but a Calnian runner came here."

"Right."

"Right. But the thing is we don't *like* being ordered about, and we're not part of the Calnian empire. And we never eat *anybody*. Or at least I don't think we do... Big Hinto?"

"We don't."

"Oh good. So, the Calnians have no right to tell us what to do, even though they try to sometimes. You could say we have a duty *not* to do what they tell us."

"That sounds like a great thing to say."

"On the other hand, we also know about their Owsla. We would have to be crazy as toad bugs to take them on. Do you know how far they are behind you?"

Wulf looked at Erik. He looked up at the sun. "I thought they'd be here already."

"I see."

"You could let us pass through, then hide in the woods?" suggested Erik. "You shouldn't take them on and they'll be too busy following us to go out of their way to trouble you," suggested Erik.

"Nice idea, nice idea, but do remember we don't like being told want to do." Balinda suddenly looked a lot less nervy. She even looked a little threatening. "We are not without resources ourselves, and it wouldn't be the first time that we'd been as crazy as toad bugs."

"What did she say?" Bodil Gooseface whispered to Finnbogi the Boggy.

"They have resources and they've been crazy as toad bugs in the past."

"Oh. What does that mean?"

"I don't know yet. I have no idea how crazy toad bugs are."

"I see," said Bodil, nodding wisely.

The Wootahs (Bjarni Chickenhead loved the name, Woooooootah!) passed through the ranks of the Big Bone tribe.

Keef the Berserker, Erik the Angry and his bear Astrid were staying behind, standing shoulder to shoulder with the Big Boners (tee hee, thought Bjarni). He wasn't sure why they felt they should but both had been adamant. Bjarni considered standing with them for a moment, but he had something else on his mind.

He'd spotted the guy straight away. For Bjarni he stood out like a buffalo painted orange standing on its hind legs and blowing a trumpet. While most of the Big Boners (tee hee) had clean, intricately managed coiffures, scraped into place and set with wax, this man had unruly long hair and a centre parting that had just happened without the agency of a comb. That wasn't what gave him away, though. It was his contrary eyes, weary but wary, and his paradoxical body language, relaxed but furtive.

Bjarni slipped away from his tribe and approached him.

"Hi, I'm Bjarni Chickenhead."

"Hello there, friend," the man said, his voice a little slurred, "I'm Libbacap but everyone calls me Pipes Libbacap, on account of the large variety of smoking pipes which I own, most of which I made myself."

Bjarni smiled. "I'd like very much to see your pipe collection."

"That, my large woolly headed friend, is very easily arranged."

Finnbogi felt a bit shitty that Keef the Berserker had stayed with the Big Bone tribe and even more shitty for leaving his dad behind, but Erik had insisted. This tribe were risking their lives so that they might escape, so it was only right that one of them should stay to help. Since he'd already lived many fine years, and because he had a giant bear watching his back, Erik had said it might as well be him.

Wulf had tried to change Keef's mind, but the Berserker hadn't wavered. Finnbogi knew he was desperate to make up for being felled by Sadzi Wolf. Had Finnbogi been in Keef's boots, he'd have seen his failure against Sadzi Wolf as a reason for buggering off sharpish—there were at least six more Owsla coming at them, and these were dressed, armed and hadn't been savaged by sharks moments before like Sadzi Wolf had. But Finnbogi was not Keef.

He turned to look back at the waiting warriors, but the towering rock of the valley sides already blocked his view. He'd never seen anything like these rock walls, bright white in the sun. He wondered if the scenery might get even more impressive as they travelled west. Surely not? The cliff on the edge of the Big Bone village must have been ten times the height of a man.

Something weighty struck his cheek and he thought one of the hawks circling high above had shat on him, but he touched his face and discovered it was the first fat raindrop of the coming storm. Another struck him on the forehead. It was more like being hit with a rotten grape than a normal raindrop.

Erik, Astrid and Keef stood next to the three chiefs of the Big Bone tribe. Astrid was sniffing the air and moaning.

She'd been behaving very oddly since they'd come into the valley. Erik guessed there were other bears nearby. That's what freaked her out the most, although she'd never been quite this weird before. He hoped she wasn't going to bugger off before the Calnians got there. He tried to ask her about it but she was being obtuse.

Behind them were about twenty warriors, all armed with clubs that looked like bones but were too long and heavy to be bones. The rest of the tribe had retreated to caves in the cliff on the south side of the Heartberry River. He was grateful for their help but, scanning the warriors and the three chiefs, he didn't see how they were going to have a hope against the Calnian Owsla. It was possible though—likely?—that they wouldn't need to fight. The Calnians were few and far from home. Their leader would be reluctant to lose another Owsla member, so surely they'd retreat rather than take on this number of people? That's what he told himself, anyway, but he was far from convinced. The Calnian Owsla lived to fight. The idea that they'd back down from this because one of them might get hurt was like thinking a glutton would pooh-pooh a feast because it might give him indigestion.

"What wood is your club made of?" Erik asked Chucknor.

"It's bone."

"It's a very big bone."

"Twenty thousand years ago on this very ground, a tribe of monsters called kraklaws came from the endless forests to the north and enslaved our ancestors. For twenty generations our people toiled under the monsters' yoke, until a young man named Stonefinger came along and turned the beast to stone, freeing our tribe. This is one of those beasts' bones."

"The thigh bone?"

"No, one of the wrist bones. I can't lift the thigh bones."

"Must have been huge, these monsters?"

"They are. They're maybe three times your height on their hind legs. They make your short-faced bear look small."

"Short-faced?" asked Erik, noting that either Chucknor didn't speak the universal Scrayling language very well, or he wasn't good at differentiating past from present.

"That's what we call that type of bear."

"You've seen more?"

"Oh yes. They're not common, but I've seen a few."

"I thought Astrid was the only one."

"There's always more than one of every animal. That's how it has to be."

A huge raindrop splashed off Erik's own war club. Oh great, he thought. They were probably about to be torn apart by unstoppable Valkyrie warriors *and* he was going to get wet again.

Chapter 4

Weather

Sofi Tornado strode in front and Yoki Choppa jogged along at the rear, poking about in his smoking alchemical bowl with his bone. Sitsi Kestrel thought the warlock looked even more furrow-brow and pouty-lip worried than usual, but she wasn't sure. He never looked exactly carefree, that one.

Sofi Tornado wasn't worried. You could see her excitement with every prancing step and each flick of her hair. Sitsi had noticed that the promise of killing always made the captain more girlish. She was spinning her hand axe around on one palm and her knives were bouncing off her thighs; her obsidian dagger on one side, and her newly carved dagger-tooth cat tusk on the other.

They were finally going to catch up with these slippery Mushroom Men, finish them off and head home—hopefully. Usually Sitsi would be be as excited as Sofi to be heading into battle, but she had a gnawing nervousness in the pit of her stomach about this one.

The Big Bone tribe was not part of the Calnian empire. The official line was that they had nothing Calnia wanted, so Calnia hadn't bothered to conquer them. Time was, she believed everything she'd learned, but she'd seen enough to know that sometimes political expedience had more influence than truth on history and even the reporting of current events. Calnia had conquered plenty of tribes who were further away than the Big Bone tribe and had no obvious benefit to the empire, so there had to be another reason why this lot hadn't been conquered. She had a horrible feeling that they were about to find out what it was.

She closed her eyes and asked Innowak to watch over them. They'd lost two of their number on this mission already. That was two too many.

They reached the edge of the clearing as rain began to splat down in drops the size of bumble-bees. The base of the valley was broader and flatter than she'd thought it would be given the steepness of the approach, and held a sizeable village. Much of the valley side was made up of white cliffs and there was a weighty outcrop of rock in the centre of the valley floor. Overlooking all of this from the south was a towering black cloud.

Sitsi Kestrel did not like the look of that cloud. She'd learnt quite a bit about weather, and this sky looked an awful lot like the precursor to a tornado; yes, there we go, the cloud was beginning to spin.

Her uncle had been killed by a tornado. He'd been having a nap against a tree and by the time the roar of the twister had woken him it was too late. Her aunt, who'd been running to warn him, had seen him spiral up and up into the sky. They'd found his battered body three villages away.

Sitsi Kestrel didn't like weather that got you wet. She hated weather that lifted you high as the summer clouds and dashed you down three villages away. She was so busy gawping at the cloud that she didn't notice the Big Bone tribe welcoming committee until they were almost on it.

Spread in a line facing them, on the far side of the bridge across the Heartberry River, were four men, one woman and the gigantic bear that had travelled with the Mushroom Men since Lakchan territory. Two of the men were Mushroom Men, including the one who'd finished off Sadzi Wolf, which was good news. It would be satisfying to make him pay for that. Behind them were twenty club-armed warriors, holding big bone clubs, as one might expect from the Big Bone tribe. So far, not too scary.

Sitsi breathed a long sigh of relief and her stomach lightened. Thank Innowak, she thought. It was a lovely feeling when you dreaded something and it turned out to be nothing like as bad as you thought. Sofi Tornado or Chogolisa Earthquake could have dealt with this lot solo—any of the women probably could, including even herself.

She strung an arrow. She'd shoot one of the warriors first, she decided. Chogolisa would want to fight the bear, and Sofi would be keen to kill the leaders, or possibly take her time on the one who'd killed Sadzi.

She raised her bow. The elderly woman in the centre of the Big Bone tribe walked forwards. Did she want to talk? There was nothing to discuss. They were blocking the path of the Calnian Owsla. Even if they crawled away on their faces now in abject apology, the offence had been committed. They had to die.

She changed her aim and drew. None of the others would mind if she killed this crone, and an arrow to the face of the clearly favoured lady would be a pretty start to the battle.

"Here, have a go on that. Careful, though, it's delicate." Pipes Libbacap's voice was the squeak of a man holding his breath to keep that goodness in his lungs. He handed the pipe to Bjarni Chickenhead. Creamy smoke poured over the edge of the pipe's oversized bowl, too thick and mushroomy to billow up to the hut's smoke hole like everyday smoke. The rugs and furs that made the domed hut into a warm little nest were infused with years of excellent, pungent, mushroomy smoke.

Bjarni cupped the warm bowl in both hands, breathed out all his breath so that he might breathe in all the more, and placed the narrow pipe stem between his lips.

He inhaled, and inhaled. Lovely. More like drinking than smoking.

Pipes Libbacap grinned at him through the haze. "Mellow, isn't it? The smoke cools in the long stem. Trick is to make the clay thin as you can. It's not easy, but then nothing worthwhile ever is. It does warm up after a while but by then you don't care."

Bjarni nodded. This was the best smoke ever.

"Careful. It's stronger than it tastes, man. You may want just half a toke to start."

Bjarni was still nodding. He carried on inhaling.

"You've got lungs, man."

Bjarni filled himself to the soles of his feet with that lovely smoke. After what seemed like a few hours he reached his capacity and handed the pipe back. As Pipes Libbacap reached for it, his neck elongated and his warmly smiling face lifted towards the hut roof, then widened and loomed until his face *was* the roof.

Good, thought Bjarni. It had looked like rain outside, and skin was one of the most waterproof things around. Sitting under the happy Scrayling's face, he'd be kept dry and he'd be warmed by that cheery smile.

A banging crackle registered somewhere in his mind, followed by the roars of animals a short while later. It didn't seem to matter. He sank back on the cushion, looking up at his new friend who was also a roof.

"Did anybody see where Bjarni went?" yelled Wulf the Fat in a lull. Ottar, on his shoulders, poked out his lower lip and spread his arms with palms upwards in a "where's Bjarni?" gesture.

Freydis, who was holding Sassa's hand, said, "Ottar doesn't know."

The deluge that had looked imminent hadn't come. After the first few drops, the rain had been sucked back up into the black, black clouds. Sassa didn't like it at all.

They'd emerged from the gorge onto the scenery they'd become very used to—an undulating plain with the odd lone tree and a few spinneys. It had been blowing a gale and about to piss it down. Now it was a dead calm. All around them were the Big Bone tribe's maize fields. Patches of the plants were swishing and swirling like waves in an irregularly stormy sea while other patches were still.

Wulf sighed and looked at the sky, clearly wondering whether to head back for Bjarni.

"Either he decided to stay with Erik and Keef, or he found a Scrayling with mushrooms and joined him," said Sassa. The gale resumed, whipping her hair around her face and she had to shout: "Either way, he's a big man who made his own decision and can look after himself! Your responsibility lies with this lot! We've got to keep going! I do not like this storm!"

Wulf nodded. Sassa could see lighter sky to the south and she wanted to be under it. The gale calmed for a moment and she heard a deeper, thundering, terrifying roar.

She turned. A spinning column was stretching down from the cloud to the east like a probing grey pointy penis on the underside of a cloud beast. It thickened and darkened. Its tip stabbed the ground, immediately sucking up a skirt of dirt and—shag a stag—were those *trees* spinning up into the sky? They were full-grown trees! That meant the twister was further away than she'd thought, but it was bigger, too. A lot bigger. And it was growing. Was that a bull elk she could see, tumbling through the air, already as high as a hunting eagle and flying higher? That was something you didn't see every day.

The twister's tail whipped from side to side as if it was choosing which way to go. Then it decided. Of course, as she'd always known it was going to, it headed straight towards them, ripping the earth apart and swirling it upwards in a vortex of mulched debris, roaring like a billion berserk bears. Lightning flashed inside it and stabbed the ground around. Nature was coming for them, and nature was angry.

Freydis pulled her hand free of Sassa's and ran west. Chnob the White followed her, overtaking her in a moment.

"No, Chnob! No, Freydis! Not away from it, we've got to run clear of its path!"

Freydis changed direction to run southwards but Chnob was already too far away to hear her. He was sprinting west between two rows of maize, directly away from the twister, or, put another way, exactly in the twister's current path. He stopped for a moment, and Sassa thought he'd heard them or seen sense, but he wrestled Keef's boat from his shoulders, tossed it aside and ran on.

Everyone else but Sassa, Thyri and Wulf with Ottar on his shoulders was running south, at right angles to the monster's path, as fast as people could run when the alternative is being mashed to pieces in the maelstrom of a tornado. Gunnhild had shown an especially nifty turn of heel and was outpacing the lot of them, but then she yelped and went down, victim of an unseen hole. She stood, but immediately fell again. Bodil hauled her up, put an arm around her waist and both ran on. Finnbogi, who'd diverted to catch Freydis and lift her onto his shoulders, was bringing up the rear.

"I'll go after Chnob!" Wulf shouted.

"No, I'll do it," yelled Thyri.

Sassa shook her head.

"Wulf, you've got to get Ottar out of here. And I'm faster than you, Treelegs. Here, take this." Sassa glanced up at the approaching twister, handed her bow to her husband, turned and sprinted after Chnob.

She could *feel* the tornado bearing down on her. How long would it take to catch her? Minutes? Seconds? By the way the roaring was getting louder and louder, it was seconds.

She didn't dare turn. She was catching Chnob, but she was still a good thirty paces back.

"Chnob!" she shouted. "Chnob!" But the fool kept running.

Sofi Tornado held up a finger to stop Sitsi Kestrel from shooting. Sitsi lowered her bow.

The old woman blinked at them; possibly it was a tic, possibly terror. "Hi, um, hello Calnian Owsla," she said, her voice high and shaky. The valley was still in bright sunlight but a huge twister had formed under the black clouds in the distance. Sitsi had thought it was tornado weather! By the way it was heading, it wasn't going to trouble them, but she would keep an eye on it.

"Good afternoon," said Sofi.

"You must be, er, Sofi Tornado."

"I am."

"I'm sorry, I don't mean to be, um, personal, but you are *very* beautiful. I'd heard you were striking, but I hadn't expected you to be this, ah, lovely."

"Don't apologise, I'm used to it."

"And your figure...amazing. So strong. I think you are probably definitely the most attractive woman I've ever, um, seen."

"I daresay. We're here for the Mushroom Men."

"The who?"

"I can see two of them."

The woman looked round at the two Mushroom Men and started as if seeing them for the first time. "Ah! I see, yes. Yes, you're right. I am sorry. If you could bear with me just a moment. Bear with me! There's a bear with him. Ha ha! There we go, nearly got it, just—" she spread her arms.

"Sitsi, shoot her now!" shouted Yoki Choppa. It was so urgent, so out of character, for Yoki Choppa to yell like that that Sitsi Kestrel hesitated. It was a bad moment to hesitate.

*   *   *

What had Finnbogi ever done to Tor to deserve this? Weighed down by Freydis on his shoulders, he was the slowest of the lot.

"The thing about tornados," his Uncle Poppo Whitetooth had said back in Hardwork on the day they'd watched a waterspout out on the lake, "is that they're full of rocks, branches, squirrels, bears and whatever else the bugger's picked up, all whipping around faster than a stone in a sling. Get caught in a tornado and you'll be killed by a branch through the gut or a squirrel to the face before you can say 'By Oaden's great big salty balls, I'm flying.'"

"Surely you'd be going at the same speed and direction as all the debris around you in a twister, so it wouldn't hit you at all?" Finnbogi had reasoned.

"Good point," Uncle Poppo had replied, "maybe you'd just fly as high as the moon, then drop and splat onto the ground like a rotten squash hurled at a rock. Either way, you're dead."

Finnbogi turned to look at the twister, no easy job while running with a small but increasingly heavy girl on his shoulders. Loakie's bellend, the tornado was something! A sky-high screaming beast, lightning cracking across its black, swirling body, larger than any monster he'd ever imagined. It was like the whole world had reared up to roar and chase him.

It was going to be close . . . wasn't it? Who was he kidding, no it wasn't, the tornado was going to get him. On the bright side, he was going to find out how they kill you and in next to no time he might well be telling Uncle Poppo about it in a god's hall. Was that how it worked, he wondered? One moment on the earth about to die, the next chatting to an ancestor with a big horn of wine in your hand? Or was there some kind of orientation period, when you were shown around your afterlife by a goddess or a dead relative?

He felt bad that he'd be dragging little Freydis down with him, or, more accurately, up. He tried to run faster but he simply couldn't. The wind was stronger every second. A head of maize spun by like a tumbling, barrel-bodied, wing-less bird, followed by another and another.

"Ow!" shouted Freydis. "Ow! Stop that!" as maize whacked into her. One advantage of carrying a little girl on one's shoulders, thought Finnbogi, is that she acts like a sort of helmet, protecting one's head from the—

"Fuck!" he shouted as a maize head flicked up by a counter-eddy punched into his bollocks.

"Language, Finnbogi the Boggy!" shouted Freydis.

Only for the briefest of moments did he consider throwing the girl to the ground. He might have made it without the burden. But he ran on, Freydis bouncing on his shoulders and shouting encouragement.

"Sitsi, shoot her now!" Sofi Tornado heard Yoki Choppa shout. She had never heard him shout before. Something was seriously amiss.

Sitsi Kestrel raised her bow to take the old woman down. Paloma Pronghorn was running, already halfway to her.

Before arrow or speedy Owsla struck, a huge, cracking bolt of lightning lanced from the sky and struck the old woman square in the back.

She wasn't knocked down. She stood, lit up as if her insides were ablaze, shaking like a child's toy between taut strings. She lifted her head and spread her hands. Sofi saw what was going to happen and leapt for cover, but there was no cover. As she dived, lightning struck her midriff like a giant hammer and sent her flying.

Finnbogi the Boggy's foot jarred into a hole. He stumbled. He managed to keep running, but he was getting farther and farther behind the other fleeing Hardworkers.

"Come on, Finnbogi the Boggy!" shouted Freydis the Annoying, squeezing his head with her legs.

"Squashing my head does not help!"

"Sorry. Is this better?" She yanked his hair.

"No! Stop it! How are we doing?" he shouted. Turning round the last time had slowed them down momentarily. Now every moment counted.

"It's closer. It will be on us pretty soon if you can't go any faster." The strange little girl did not sound overly concerned.

Up ahead, Garth Anvilchin and Wulf the Fat—who was carrying Ottar the Moaner—stopped. After a moment Wulf and Ottar carried on, but Garth came running back.

Wulf had sent him to help with Freydis! That would save them both! Finnbogi found a secret reserve of energy and sped up. He'd rather it wasn't Garth, of course, but he could deal with being indebted to that arse later. Right now, he just had to reach him . . .

"Give me the girl, Boggy!" commanded Anvilchin, reaching out for her. The wind whipped his hair about his big, helmeted face and Finnbogi could not help but marvel just a little at how heroic he looked.

The larger man clasped the girl to his mail-clad chest with one hand, looked around as if to see if anyone was watching, then swung back and punched Finnbogi in the side of the head.

"What the . . . ?" thought Finnbogi as he fell.

Erik the Angry wondered why Big Hinto and Chucknor had sent Balinda out to meet the Calnian Owsla. The nervy woman did not seem the ideal choice for facing down a murderous band of magic-charged killers.

He jumped when she was struck by lightning, although not as much as she did. Then he stared agog as, instead of falling to the ground a smoking husk as any normal person would have done, Balinda absorbed the lightning into her slender frame and glowed and grew.

One of the Owsla shot an arrow at her, but her coat of

lightning deflected the arrow into the sky. When it seemed Balinda must explode, seven strands of lightning, one for each Owsla and one for their strange little warlock, blasted out of her hands and into each of them.

All of them were knocked flying, apart from the big one, Chogolisa Earthquake. She took two steps back, then strode forward, coming at them. Balinda, still out in front, swayed on her feet as if dazed. Erik had heard plenty about Chogolisa Earthquake and her tricks—like pulling spines out of backs or squashing heads with one hand—but he'd always assumed that tales and the reports of her size had been exaggerated. Now he saw that she was a real giant, at least a head taller than he was himself, and he was the tallest person he'd ever met. She must have been twice his weight, too, and she was not fat. Despite her size, she was fine-featured—pretty even. Erik had expected a girl that large to have a face like a half-melted snowman. He wasn't sure why.

She was unarmed. He guessed she didn't need a weapon.

The rest of the Owsla were climbing to their feet. Only their warlock stayed down. The lightning attack had not been a battle ender.

Chucknor ran in to defend Balinda from Chogolisa Earthquake, followed by a yelling, axe-aloft Keef the Berserker and the twenty Big Bone warriors. Big Hinto stayed back, lifted a bone whistle to his lips and blew.

Erik also held his ground. He was no coward, there was simply no point crowding the centre of a battlefield, especially when all your own side apart from you had trained together, so knew how each other was going to fight and what was expected in terms of support and so on. So Keef, although displaying admirable enthusiasm, was probably going to get in the way. Judging by his battle yell, there was no point explaining that to him.

Chogolisa Earthquake reached Balinda and grabbed the

old woman by the head. There was a bang and a white light
flash and Chogolisa was blown back again. Chucknor leapt
like an acrobat, swinging that great bone club into the Calnian
giant's head. The club exploded against her skull as if it
was made from dried earth. Chogolisa didn't seem to notice
the blow. She caught Chucknor by the foot in one hand,
flipped him upside down, grabbed his other foot and lifted
him as if he was a doll.

Smiling, sweet-faced as a happy baby, she pulled his legs
apart and kept pulling, ripping him apart from arse to neck.
A wash of blood and guts splashed onto the packed earth.

Then brave Keef was in there, prodding at the giant with
Arse Splitter. Chogolisa swung the half of Chucknor with
the head on like a club, but Keef ducked and stabbed. It
looked like he would surely strike a death blow, but the
woman was as quick as she was large. She jinked clear and
batted him away backhanded. Keef tottered and fell. He
jumped back up again, but Big Hinto grabbed his shoulder
and shook his head for him to hold. Keef, to Erik's surprise,
nodded and held back.

Instead of piling into the rest of the warriors and finishing
them in a moment, as she surely could have done, Chogolisa
Earthquake herself retreated to where the other Owsla stood
in a battle line. The women seemed to have recovered from
their lightning blasts. Their warlock didn't look quite so
well. He pushed himself onto all fours, scrabbled around as
if looking for something, then howled like a bereaved mother.

Order had been restored. Out-and-out battles did happen,
but most Scrayling tribes favoured a more orderly form of
one-on-one combat, and it looked like the Owsla and Big
Bone tribe were no different.

Sofi Tornado said something that Erik didn't hear and
nodded to the woman on her left—a tall, strapping lass—
and she jogged forward. Like the others she was dressed in
a short jerkin, breechcloth and leggings tied above the knee.

Like the others, she had her own weaponry, in her case a short, double-ended club.

"I am Morningstar!" she cried. "Who will fight me?"

Big Hinto held Keef back as a Big Bone warrior walked out to meet her. The Big Bone man's heavily styled and waxed hair looked like a couple of ravens towards the end of a well-matched fight to the death. By Rabbit Girl's sweet innocence, thought Erik, the Scraylings had some horrible hairstyles. The warrior was young and fit, though, just a little shorter than Morningstar, armed with two bone clubs, one with a hooked, sharpened end, the other coated with resin and sharp little white spikes that could have been chipmunk's teeth or, indeed, the teeth of any small, sharp-toothed animal.

The Big Bone warrior flung his clubs about like a performer might swing burning torches at a tribal gathering, swishing them around his waist and over his head.

Morningstar watched him come, then, picking her moment, hurled her own club at him underarm. It flew hard and true into his midriff. He doubled over, winded and perhaps worse. The Owsla woman nipped in while he was occupied trying to breathe, grabbed him by his horrible hair and punched him.

Erik had seen a punch break a nose. This punch broke the man's face. It pulverised nose, cheeks, eyes sockets and more. He would surely have fallen, but the Owsla woman held him up by the hair to examine her damage and nodded, smiling. She dropped him, raised her leg and stamped, obliterating his already crushed skull.

The Big Bone tribe looked on, slack-jaw stunned, but Keef the Berserker roared and sprinted forward, swinging his broad axe Arse Splitter two-handed around his head, as berserk as his name implied he should be.

Morningstar picked up her double-headed club and waited

YOU DIE WHEN YOU DIE

for the charging man. Keef lunged with the sharp prow of
his axe blade, but the woman knocked it aside with one
hand and darted in at him.

Erik sighed. Hadn't Keef had Hird training? One of the
first things Erik had learnt about fighting, long before he'd
even been old enough to join the Hird, was how to use a
short weapon against a weapon with a longer reach, and
vice versa. A long weapon has a danger zone, located around
its pointy end. Your goal with a short weapon is to get inside
that zone. The easiest way to do that is to knock the long
weapon aside and step in—exactly as Morningstar had just
done. Exactly as Keef had just let her do! Once you're between
the long weapon's effective zone and your opponent, their
long weapon is useless and you can chop or whack away
with your short one until they're dead.

The way to counter this if you're the long weapon warrior
was to make sure that the short weapon holder never got
past your danger zone. So Keef, in his Berserk excitement,
had done exactly the wrong thing by rushing in like that,
and Morningstar had capitalised like a trainer showing the
basics to trainees on their first day.

She swung her club for the death blow and Erik clenched
everything in anticipation. But Keef dropped to a crouch,
swung his axe, hooked her foot and pulled. Her feet flew
up and she was down, onto her arse.

Erik and the Big Bone tribe cheered. Keef, the genius,
had not been nearly as Berserk as he'd fooled Morningstar
and everyone else into thinking he was. With one clever
moved he'd proved that the Calnian Owsla were not as invincible as everyone said they were.

Keef swung Arse Splitter for a death strike to her chest,
but Morningstar kicked the shaft away and Keef's blade
struck dirt. Morningstar might be down but she was far
from out. She convulsed her body like a muscular worm

and sprung to her feet. Erik had never seen anything like it. She smiled at Keef and beckoned him to run in again. He circled, wary.

At that moment something caught Erik's eye and suddenly he realised he had his own problems. Sofi Tornado had ordered another warrior forward. This time he was the target. He couldn't really complain. The Owsla were here to kill the Hardworkers, after all.

A girl—a young woman—was coming at him. Her weapon set was two flattened iron knives, one in each hand. They were short, no longer than daggers, more like tiny canoe paddles than weapons, and did not look as if they could be particularly effective. Erik guessed she'd learnt how to use them pretty effectively, though.

More striking than her weapons, however, were her looks. Erik had always thought that he'd never again meet anyone as beautiful as Astrid (his former lover, not the bear). But this warrior was breathtaking. Her hair was shoulder-length and parted. Her lips were slightly open, revealing white teeth. She had sparkling eyes which seemed to say: "If I weren't about to butcher you like a deer for a feast, then you would have had a good chance with me, you really would have done."

"Stay back," he said to Astrid, and walked to meet his challenger. He hoped he looked brave, because he wasn't feeling it. He'd learnt many things from animals, but how to fight was not one of them, because animals are crap at fighting. The most inept human is a better fighter than an animal because a human puts thought into it. A bear will lunge with its claws and hope to hit. It beats a human only because its claws and teeth make it better armed and it's about a thousand times as strong. If Erik tried those tactics against this Owsla woman (who was so attractive it made him want to sing) he'd be dead before he knew it.

He swung his club, intending it as a feint to force her to duck before reversing its direction and driving an arm-disabling blow into her shoulder. But she slipped to one side, then the other, fast as a wasp in a whirlwind, punched him in the stomach and swung a fist into his jaw an instant later. He was winded and pain burst in his mouth as the punch made him bite his tongue.

His vision was blurred to buggery. He shook his head. They never covered this in Hird training, the way pain could totally disable you for a moment, even ignoble pain like biting your own tongue. Sight returned. She was standing five paces away, hand on hip, regarding him coolly. She could have finished him off while he was dazed. She could have used her blades instead of her fists for either of the two blows she had landed and made them killing strikes. She was toying with him. He was in trouble.

"My name is Talisa White-tail," she said, smiling at him like a mischievous girl who's recently discovered the effect of a saucy smile on older men. "I am about to kill you."

"My name—"

"—is unimportant to me." The smile didn't falter. "Soon you will be dead, and even more of a lump of useless flesh than you are now."

Well, that wasn't very nice, and Astrid felt Erik's indignation. The bear roared and reared, towering to twice the Calnian's height.

Talisa dived between Astrid's legs, her paddle knives flashing. Astrid roared in pain. Red blood shone in brown stomach fur. She fell back into a sitting position, moaning and holding her wounds.

"No!" shouted Erik. The Calnian danced into sight from behind the bear. He hefted his club.

There was a terrible bellowing. Both he and Talisa turned. Both their jaws dropped, and by mutual unspoken consent they paused the fight to stare at the animals wading across the Heartberry River. Astrid took a break from her pained moaning to turn and look, her little bear eyes widening.

There were two types of beast coming towards them. The first were half a dozen very large, short-faced bears, the same kind as Astrid. Three of them were quite a bit larger than her, with darker fur. Erik guessed these were males.

The other animals were the cause of their wonder. There were four of them, hairy like the bears, and with faces like the longer-muzzled humped bears, but they were stupidly big, much much larger than even the largest bear. They towered on hind legs to maybe three times Erik's height. He couldn't see fangs, but their great, brawny arms were tipped with three curved claws, each as long as a man's arm.

He realised in a moment what they must be—kraklaws, the monsters that Chucknor had said once enslaved their tribe.

He reached out to them with his mind, but all he could feel was a vast, overwhelming sorrow; not for themselves, but for the brevity of man's time of earth.

He shook his head. Wow. That had been very depressing. He would not try to communicate with them again.

"Reform!" the captain of the Owsla shouted.

Talisa White-tail smiled at him and bowed. "Another time."

"My name is Erik the Angry!" he shouted after her as she ran. Then he turned to Astrid.

The bear had her paws clasped across her wounded stomach. She moaned, streaming eyes staring at him accusingly.

Finnbogi the Boggy rolled over then over again. He pushed himself onto his knees and elbows. The wind was so strong he didn't dare rise higher. He tried to look around but the tempest was as much soil and stones as air, and it felt like the skin was being flayed from his face. He buried his face between his shoulders. The roar was agony in his ears. He managed to angle his head away from the onslaught and open his eyes. All was dark, all was rushing away, as if he were looking down a well shaft at night as a mountain of soil was poured over his head.

He staggered to his feet and was immediately shunted along by the incredible gale. He had to run to stop himself from falling. He tried to angle his flight away from where he guessed the twister's core must be, trying and failing to find purchase on the shifting ground. He lurched on, falling and pushing himself back up, willing his feet to stay earthbound but knowing that his crazy sideways stampede was only the beginning. Soon he'd be off his feet and up, up, up.

A clod of earth whacked into his head.

The wind toppled him, rolled him and he was back on his feet. He felt a new force in the wind monster, hoicking at his legs, trying to pull him upwards, away from the ground. He threw himself down, clawing at the soil, desperate to stay in touch with the ground that had been such an underappreciated but steadfast friend for his nineteen years alive.

His legs lifted. He was cartwheeling along, still in contact with the ground but no longer attached to it. Something, a rock probably, thumped into his head. Well, there's that question answered, he thought as consciousness slipped away.

Chnob the White, the idiot, was not going to turn. Sassa Lipchewer shouted, but he was drawing away and she could hardly hear herself. She tried to speed up, but the crosswind was so strong that she was running sideways as much as forwards. The twister must be almost on her. Pole a mole, if she'd had to choose a way to die it wouldn't have been death by tornado while trying and failing to rescue Chnob the White from his own stupidity.

She might as well see the thing that killed her, she thought. She stopped and turned.

"I knew I was faster than you!" shouted a grinning Thyri, holding Keef's boat. Behind Treelegs all was a mad whirl of earth, rock and maize. Why by Fraya's tits did she have Keef's canoe?

Thyri stooped and pressed the boat onto the ground. "Here! Wrap one arm around me and one arm around the boat bench and hold tighter than you've ever held anything!"

Sassa did as she was told. She didn't see why, but she wasn't blessed with time to argue.

"Okay!" shouted Thyri in her ear, "we're going to lift the boat and run north! The boat will act like a kite, lifting us off our feet! Hold on for your life! When I shout 'now,' let go and roll into a ball! If I get it right, we'll be flung clear!"

Sassa nodded. It made some sense in theory. In practice? When they were both children, Wulf had broken his leg jumping from Olaf's Tree holding his mother's cape, having convinced himself that the cape would act like birds' wings and that he'd surely fly at least as far as Olaf's Fresh Sea. In a ranking of dumbest ideas ever, Thyri's boat idea was probably just a little ahead of that me.

Bjarni Chickenhead wobbled out of Pipes Libbacap's hut, crouching under the low door. He stayed bent over for a good few extra strides to be sure he didn't hit his head. That was the thing about getting messed up on mushrooms. The world was more dangerous than usual and you had to be careful. Very careful. When he was one hundred per cent, totally confident that he wasn't going to whack his head on the doorframe, he straightened.

He looked around.

There were a few unusual things going on, none of which surprised him. That was the other thing about getting messed up on mushrooms. You saw some strange things. There was no point being surprised.

Least strange of the strange things, he was a good twenty

paces from Eats Too Many Mushroom's hut, or so he reckoned—all these huts looked the same. How had he got so far? He'd only just walked out of it. Maybe he'd kept his head down for longer than he'd thought? That was a good thing, better than hitting his head. You had to be careful when you were on mushrooms. Very careful.

Next on his agenda of unusual things to deal with was an enormous tornado, sucking the land up into the sky to the south of the white cliff. Wow, he thought, staring at its swirling majesty. Then he remembered that there'd been a third even more unusual thing going on that he really ought to check out. How could there be anything stranger than a giant twister?

Oh yes, there you go. Weirdest of the lot were the giant animals clambering out of the river, great sheets of water sloughing off enough fur to keep everyone in Hardwork warm for a millennium. Six of the beasts were Erik's big bear. He couldn't remember there being six of her, so that was confusing. Did animals multiply like that? Maybe. One had to keep an open mind—that was probably rule two when on mushrooms, after being careful. Perhaps that trickster god Loakie had been involved. Grrrrr, that Loakie. Still, no point worrying about the multiplying bears right now, because the other four animals were more amazing. They were giant, upright bears with claws like swords.

Bjarni felt a surge of warm love for the super-bears. They'd make good friends. He walked towards them.

"Hold up! Hold up!" he said out loud. *What* was rule one about being as messed up as he was? To be careful. Very careful. Would it be very careful to try and befriend monsters three times his height with claws like swords? It would not. He would *not* try to make friends with them. Nope. He giggled. "Well done me," he said, and giggled some more.

The safest thing to do, given all the weird stuff out here, would be to go back to Pipes Libbacap's hut and smoke more of his mushroom mix. Now, which one was it? No idea. They were all the bloody same, as if Loakie had built the whole village purely to flummox him. That Loakie!

A solution. He'd look in all of the huts until he found the right one. The simple ideas were the best ones. That should be rule three. Rule three of what? He couldn't remember, but it was something important. He put on his serious face, blurted a giggled, then forced his features back into a sensible expression.

He crouched—you had to be careful of those doorframes, very careful—and he hopped like a rabbit towards the nearest dwelling. The skin that served as a door lifted before he got there. A small girl who wasn't Pipes Libbacap looked at him as if *he* was the oddest thing around. The girl needed to get some perspective.

"Run!" shouted Thyri.

Sassa Lipchewer and Thyri Treelegs sprinted, holding each other and Keef's boat. Flying maize stalks whipped into them and Sassa's hair thrashed around her face as if it was trying to beat her to death. The extraordinary gale so nearly wrenched the boat from their grip but they held on. It was a good thing the canoe was so well constructed, thought Sassa. Keef's lecture on exactly how he'd made the boat began pouring from her memory. She beat it back, trying to cram the dreary splurge of information into the recesses of her mind and close a door on it. She did not want her final thoughts on this world to be Keef's detailed description of the superiority of birch bark over all other forms of bark and the necessity of making the paddles out of—

"Jump!" shouted Thyri.

They jumped, flew a good ten paces with their feet skimming the wildly whirling maize stalks, then landed running.

"Again, on three!" Treelegs yelled. "One. Two. THREE!"

They leapt. This time Sassa's legs kicked in space. Her stomach, she was fairly sure, stayed on the ground. Her arms screamed with the effort of holding onto Keef's stupid little boat.

"Now!" shouted Thyri. They let go. She was falling, the ground rushing to meet her. Time slowed. How should she land, she wondered? Arms out to break her fall and she'd surely break her arms? But she hardly wanted to cushion her fall with her head. She spread her arms out in front of her. The ground came, faster and faster. What was it Thyri had said? Oh yes, roll into a ball. She wrapped her arms over her head and tucked her knees up to her chest.

WHUMP! The air whacked out of her and she was rolling in a mess of earth. Finally she crumpled to a stop, then flopped out so she was lying on her back, earth in her ears and mouth, something pulling at her arm.

The something was Thyri Treelegs. "Come on!" she shouted.

Crouching, holding each other up, the two women stumbled through the maize, clear of the twister.

"Did you see what happened to Chnob?" shouted Sassa above the roar once they were safe.

Thyri pointed back at the twister. High, high above the ground a tiny spread-limbed figure was whooshing upwards. He was visible for a good few seconds before he disappeared in the maelstrom.

"Jab it in a rabbit," said Sassa. "I'm sorry."

"Don't be. I'm more upset about Keef's boat."

Sassa followed her gaze, and they watched the little boat that had saved them follow Chnob's trajectory, up into the unknown.

Her Owsla reformed around her and Sofi Tornado bounced on her toes as the six bears and four giant creatures advanced.

Here was an exciting battle for once. There were too many

of the creatures for any strategy that wouldn't go to shit in a moment, and no obvious way either to counter their claws or to bring them down. Their weapons and their training were based on fighting humans, not monsters.

They'd simply have to go at them and see what happened, and they really might not prevail. Every other fight she'd been in she'd known she was going to win. A new feeling grew in her stomach, a thrilling, rushing feeling. Was this fear? If it was, she liked it.

"Sitsi, fall behind, focus on the large creatures. Take their eyes. Chogolisa to me, I'm going on your shoulders. Talisa and Morningstar, you—"

"Stop," said Yoki Choppa.

"What?" Her axe twitched in her hand. She'd brained people for less than interrupting her.

"We have to retreat."

"Oh no we don't."

"You cannot risk losing more women. There is nothing to be gained from fighting these monsters."

She looked at the warlock's sensible face, then back to the most exciting adversaries the Owsla had ever faced.

Chapter 5

Powerless

Finnbogi the Boggy blinked. Ahhhh! Big buffalo buggered by a bigger buffalo, his head hurt. His everything hurt. He was face down, his mouth full of soil. He lay still. Why move? He had no reason to move.

After ten seconds or ten days, something crawled into his ear. He squashed its crunchy and gooey body with a finger, dug it out, then rolled onto his back. It was easier than he'd thought it would be. So many parts of him zinged with pain that it would have been quicker to list the parts that didn't hurt, but nothing seemed to be badly damaged.

He was in a trench maybe ten feet deep, looking up between earth walls at a dark sky full of blowing debris. Mostly it was leaves, maize and earth, but a couple of bright red finches somersaulted by, in some trouble by the look of things. He thought that animals were meant to know when things like tornados were coming and get clear? Maybe most animals did. Maybe these two birds had been betrayed by some bastard animal like Garth.

Garth Anvilchin had tried to murder him! He'd known the guy was a shit, but murder? What a bastard!

He tried to sit up but that made his head spin. He lay back down, felt consciousness slipping away and let it go.

"Finnbogi the Boggy!" someone hissed. "Finnbogi the Boggy!"

He opened his eyes.

Freydis the Annoying was looking down at him over the edge of his trench, blonde hair shining around her worried little face. Two young racoons' sniffing noses appeared next to her.

"Hello," he said.

"Why are you lying down there? We all came back to look for you. Well, some of us did. Bodil Gooseface is too tired after the run and Aunt Gunnhild Kristlover has hurt her leg and Garth Anvilchin said we'd leave tracks for the Calnians to follow and you were dead anyway."

"So Garth made it?"

"Made what?"

"He escaped the tornado."

"Everyone escaped apart from Chnob the White and you."

"Chnob's dead?"

"I don't know. The tornado caught him and took him to the top of the sky. Garth said he was dead. He said you were dead, too, and he said it proved that tornados only caught crunts—I think that's what he said. But Ottar knew you weren't dead so we came back to look for you. But come on now, you've got to get up and we've got to go."

Louder, she shouted: "Wulf the Fat! Sassa Lipchewer! Thyri Treelegs! Ottar's found Finnbogi the Boggy! He's over here! He's been sleeping in this ditch the whole time!"

Finnbogi rubbed his sore chin, dug his sore hands into the earth walls of the trench and pulled himself to his sore feet. Wulf appeared, grabbed his wrists (sore), hauled him from the trench and bear-hugged him, laughing with manful joy. Behind him, Sassa and Thyri were beaming.

"Well done, Finn," said Wulf, releasing his grip and clapping him on both arms. "What a great hole you found! And good on you, Ottar," he ruffled the boy's hair. "If you hadn't insisted he was alive we'd be long gone."

"Garth punched me," blurted Finnbogi before he realised he was saying anything. His rescuers' smiles morphed into brow-knitted concern.

"He did what?" said Wulf.

"When he came back to take Freydis off me, he..." He stopped. They were all staring at him—the children, Sassa, Wulf and Thyri. Perhaps he was imagining it, but in the eyes of the women at least, he thought he could see disapproval. Hardworkers did not tell tales.

"He...he didn't do anything now I think about it. Sorry, something hit my head and knocked me out and it must have been a dream. He didn't hit me. Sorry."

Wulf's eyes bored into his. "Tell me what happened, Finn."

"Nothing. Really."

"You said Garth punched you."

"He didn't. It's...things have happened and I don't like Garth at the moment, and it was a dream, a vision. He didn't hit me."

"All right." By the expression on his face Wulf thought it was far from all right. Sassa, too, was looking concerned, and Thyri suspicious.

They headed south. All around, the ground was churned rock and earth. The few trees were jagged ruins of splintered wood, as if a giant hungry goat had stripped the trunks with a toothy, sucking bite.

There was a wide band of flattened maize, then all was completely normal, maize shifting in the wind, even a bird singing in a leafy tree, entirely as if a devastating weather ogre hadn't passed by just minutes before.

"Hang on," said Finnbogi after a while, "what about Erik and Keef? And where's Bjarni?"

"Bjarni, we hope, is with Erik and Keef," said Sassa.

"What, why?"

"Don't worry," said Wulf, "Erik knows where we're headed. They'll catch up."

"Unless they were killed by the Owsla."

"I'm sure they weren't, but, either way, they move faster than us so it would be crazy to wait."

Sofi Tornado strode along, woodland to the south of her, prairie busy with deer and buffalo to the north, but she noticed neither. It had been the right thing to do, of course it had, but thinking about the retreat from the Big Bone tribe made her shudder with rage and shame.

Their mission was to kill the Mushroom Men, she told herself, and they were still on course to do that. They just needed to skirt the Big Bone tribe's territory, cross the Heartberry and pick up the trail again. And there had been one gain from their ignominious flight.

Now they had a hostage.

Trussed in a couple of woollen ponchos and slung over Chogolisa Earthquake's shoulder was the long-haired Mushroom Man who'd attacked her with the axe. When they stopped for the evening, the Mushroom Man would tell them his group's plans.

This was a positive, she told herself. Great generals know when to retreat. Even quite good ones do, she added. But all she could hear were the jeers of the Big Bone tribe as her women had fled. She had to put it from her mind; to forget old problems and deal with new ones. There was one thing, though, that still troubled her from the events at Heartberry Canyon.

"Yoki Choppa," she called.

"Yup?" said the warlock, jogging up.

"Shortly after the lightning woman knocked us down, why did you wail like an injured calf?"

The warlock looked at her levelly, then jinked his head, indicating that they should fall back, out of the other women's earshot.

"The lightning thrower destroyed my alchemy bag and its contents," he said once they were clear.

"So you won't be able to track the Mushroom Men?"

"That I can still do; the hair wasn't in the bag and the ingredients I need for the procedure are common."

"So what's the problem?"

"I can no longer sustain your powers."

Sofi stopped and turned to the warlock. Three nearby deer that had been watching them bolted.

"My powers or the whole Owsla's?"

"The whole Owsla's."

"But our powers were beaten, trained and poisoned into us when we were children."

"They were. However, they need to be sustained. You weren't told—"

"In case we left, or rebelled."

"Yes."

"And our powers are sustained by something we eat. That's why you always cook."

The warlock nodded. "Power animals. You share three base animals, then each of you has your own animal to give you a specific power. You need to ingest only a tiny amount of desiccated matter from each. I could hold enough for all of you for a month in one palm."

"What happens if we stop eating them?"

"You'll notice a difference in two or three days. Within a week your powers will be greatly decreased."

"These animals cannot be found locally, I take it?"

The warlock shook his head. "The three base animals, which you all eat, are caribou from the frozen north, diamondback rattlesnake from the mouth of the Water Mother and tarantula hawk wasp from a few hundred miles to the west. The caribou gives you stamina. I'm also conditioned to caribou power, which is how I run all day to keep up with you. The snake and the wasp give you strength and speed."

"And cruelty. Heartlessness."

The warlock nodded. So did Sofi. She knew this. Not the details, but she'd always known that the lust for killing and causing pain was not in her nature. She just hadn't ever admitted it to herself. Or cared much.

"What's my personal animal?"

"Burrowing owl. You have its hearing."

Burrowing owl? She thought. *Bit shit.* "Where do we find a burrowing owl?"

"Similar territory to the tarantula hawk wasp, a few hundred miles to the west."

"Are anyone's power animals local?"

"Chogolisa Earthquake's strength comes from dung beetles and I've already found one." Burrowing owl suddenly didn't seem like such a bad power animal. "She'll be weaker without the snake and wasp, but she'll still be the strongest human we're likely to meet. Paloma Pronghorn's comes from pronghorns, which live around here, of course, but are not so common, nor so easy to catch."

"Her nickname...?"

"Made sense because she's fast. It's a coincidence that it's also her power animal."

"And the others' animals?"

"We tried to use geographically disparate animals to make it harder for you to find them yourselves if you ever discovered your powers' source. Sitsi Kestrel gets her sight from a lizard called a chuckwalla and Talisa White-tail's reaction speed comes from a certain type of hummingbird. Both those animals are found on the far side of the Shining Mountains. Morningstar's punch comes from an oceanic shrimp."

"Can we all eat dung beetle and pronghorn?"

"You can, but it won't have any effect unless you've been conditioned to it, and you haven't."

"Can any of the power animals be substituted?"

"No. You have to eat the specific animal you've been conditioned to. Yours has to be a burrowing owl. Even another type of owl won't do."

"Why are you telling me this now?"

The warlock shrugged.

"And your entire stash of these animals is gone?"

"Yes."

"No backup?"

"In Calnia."

"That was an oversight."

"It was."

"So we have two days to catch these Mushroom Men, then we need to go back to Calnia."

"There are no warriors better trained than the Calnian Owsla, and you will keep a measure of your powers. If we didn't catch them for a month, you would still beat them with ease."

"In theory."

"Theory is all that can ever be applied to the future."

Garth Anvilchin, Gunnhild Kristlover and Bodil Gooseface were waiting on the path for Finnbogi the Boggy and his rescuers. Bodil and Gunnhild hugged him. Garth watched.

"How did you survive?" gasped Bodil.

Finnbogi smiled. "Let's just say that when you mix strength, perseverance and a refusal to die with a little magic, you can—"

"He fell into a hole," interrupted Thyri Treelegs.

"How fortunate," said Garth, flinty eyes narrow. Finnbogi held those eyes. Before, he'd disliked Garth and been a little afraid of him. Now he despised him. The man had tried to kill him for, as far as Finnbogi could see, no reason other than he didn't like him much and the opportunity had arisen. How dare he treat his life so cheaply!

Finnbogi would have his revenge.

They set off. Bodil fell in next to him, all wide-eyed and full of screamingly obvious observations about the tornado and questions that a four-year-old would know the answers to. He told her that his head hurt, so would she mind awfully if he walked on his own?

They continued south for an hour, then turned southwest and, to Finnbogi's annoyance, uphill onto a rolling upland. Prairie stretched as far as they could see on both sides, pocked by copses of young trees. Several times hawks passed overhead, each one mobbed by a pair of tiny birds. The smaller bundles of feather were flitting above the hawks, diving down at them, flying off upwards, then diving again.

"The big birds are quicker, but they can't fly up," said Freydis, taking Finnbogi's hand and emphasising her point by thrusting a finger skyward. "The little birds are slower, but they're *good* at going up. So the little birds can drive the bigger ones away and stop them finding and eating their babies, so long as they stay above them."

"I see. Thanks," said Finnbogi.

"This is a very old track," said Gunnhild in a voice meant to be heard by all, "trodden by the Scraylings for thousands of years."

"How do you know?" asked Garth.

"I can feel it," said Gunnhild. "*The young disparage, then follow the footsteps of the ancients.*"

None of them bothered to challenge her. They walked on in weary silence, Garth leading the way, Thyri next to him.

Finnbogi looked over his shoulder. No sign of Keef, Bjarni or Erik.

There were nine of them now, and two baby racoons.

Chapter 6
Vulpine Appropriation

"Okay, okay, I'm fine now! That's enough! I'm fine! Man!" Erik the Angry helped Bjarni Chickenhead up from the washing spot where he'd been dunking him and led him to a riverside bench.

After the ravages of the day the evening sky was almost too calm a transition of blues, powdery oranges and pinks, as if an ashamed weather god was overcompensating for its unforgivable earlier behaviour. Eagles soared high, geese bobbed on the river and a family of racoons were splay-legged on the opposite bank, muzzles poked into the water for their evening drinks. Erik could feel that the racoons weren't threatened by him and Bjarni. The Big Bone tribe did not interfere with their lives, so humans were about as dangerous as trees for them.

"What did I miss?" asked Chickenhead.

"Where did you get to?"

"You and Keef were staying behind, the rest were going."

"And you?"

"I met a guy with some mushrooms. Thought I'd pop into his hut for a minute. That was what, fifteen minutes ago?"

"Eight hours."

"Ah."

"Yes."

"Sorry."

"Nothing to be sorry for. I'm glad you're here. You can help me rescue Keef."

"What?"

"The rest of our lot buggered off up the cliff. Hopefully they got clear of the tornado that started up shortly afterwards."

"I remember a tornado, and...monsters?"

"I'll get to them. So, the Calnian Owsla arrived, six of them plus a warlock. Before they did anything, Balinda blasted them all with lightning."

"What?"

"This is the sort of thing you miss when you're indoors taking mushrooms."

"You sound like my dad."

"Your dad sounds like a sensible...hang on, your dad was Brodir."

"We didn't get on."

"Fair enough. Anyway, the lightning only delayed the Owsla. Their big one killed Chucknor, then another killed a Big Bone warrior."

"Oh dear."

"Could have been worse. Would have been worse, but then the Big Bone lot revealed their secret."

"The monsters."

"Just animals, apparently. Six big bears like Astrid—"

"Ah!"

"And four kraklaws."

"I saw them. Terrifying, man. What were they?"

"They're big animals, apparently. They used to be as clever as humans—not that that's any great achievement—and they conquered this tribe a few thousand years ago. A guy called Fingers of Stone turned half of the kraklaws to stone, so the story goes, and he took the human wickedness away from the rest of them, leaving them no smarter than your average bear. He banished them to the endless forests way to the north of here, apart from a few which the Big Bone tribe kept and trained as guards."

"Wow, they live a long time."

"The four that helped out today are descendants of the originals."

"Makes sense. How did they do against the Owsla?"

"The Owsla took one look at them and buggered off."

"Sensible."

"But they took Keef. The big one grabbed him and slung him over her shoulder."

"Shitbags."

"So we're going to go and get him."

"Double shitbags. Are we going to follow them?"

"No need. Balinda has a seeing eye duck."

"A what?"

"A duck whose eyes she can see through. The Calnian Owsla stopped for the night a while back. They're next to this." He pointed at the Heartberry River. "We're going to borrow a boat, wait until they're asleep and rescue Keef."

"Okay...but..."

"You'll wait in the boat while I get Keef."

"That is a sensible division of labour. But what about Astrid? How will your bear follow us?"

Erik felt tears prick his eyes. He shook his head. "She was hurt in the fighting; not too badly, thank Rabbit Girl, but she can't travel."

"So she'll catch us up?"

"She won't. There are six other bears like her here. She's been looking for her own kind all her life. She'll be happier and safer in Heartberry Canyon. She'd going to stay. It's for the best."

"Shit, man, I'm sorry. Do you want a hug?"

"I do not."

Erik told himself he wasn't going to cry, not in front of Bjarni and the Big Bone tribe, but as he hugged Astrid the bear and she moaned and rocked, tears gushed, flooded down his face and he sobbed like a toddler denied a promised treat. He told Astrid to recover quickly and swore to return even though he knew he never would. The bear looked at him and told him that he mustn't go, he must stay here with her, which made him cry all the more.

He was still sobbing while he made his goodbyes to the Big Bone tribe, apologising through the tears and snot. He was still weeping gently with the odd snort when they climbed into the canoe and paddled away. Through his grief he wondered whether it was just the bear, or whether he was weeping for the other Astrid, for the missed years with Finnbogi, for the life he might have had if he hadn't tried to march off from Hardwork like a damn fool...

He was almost glad when they found the corpse and he could finally get on with something that stopped him crying. The body was marooned face down on an islet, along with a mass of tree debris, twin globes of its arse glowing in the moonlight.

Erik swivelled his paddle, the canoe nudged ashore and he climbed out. There was rarely much dignity in death, but face-planted in the mud with one's bright white arse thrusting skyward was a particularly inelegant pose. Erik heaved the naked body over. His head was staved in at one temple, wrist snapped at right angles, stomach and thigh gashed open, beard tangled with sticks and silt.

"It's Chnob the White," he whispered.

"Oaden's chopper," said Bjarni. "He must have..."

Both men looked up into the night sky, then back down at each other, eyes wide.

"We should burn him," said Bjarni.

"No time. We have to rescue Keef before they kill him. The river will bury Chnob."

They left dead Chnob the White on his island perch and paddled on.

A while later they came to a beaver's dam blocking the way. Erik steered for the bank.

"Hold up," said Bjarni. "What's that?"

Bobbing against the twigs and mud of the dam was a small boat. They steered for it. It was Keef's canoe.

It was beaten about but intact. They took it, walked around the dam and continued, Erik paddling the larger boat and Bjarni in Keef's. There was no need to say what Erik guessed they were both thinking. If they'd found Keef's boat and Chnob, had the tornado picked up the rest of their party, dashed them to death and strewn them across the land?

They paddled on under the full moon, through a night almost as bright as day. To Erik, every stump and eddy looked like the body of his son, but they found no more Hardworker corpses nor equipment. Finally they came to the place Balinda had described. They could see the Calnian camp's fire through the trees.

Bjarni stayed with the boats and Erik crept towards the flames.

The Calnian Owsla ate a hearty but power animal-free supper. Sofi Tornado hadn't told the women about their imminent decline of abilities. She had told Sitsi Kestrel to shoot a pronghorn if she saw one. Hopefully they'd be on their way home before any of them realised that they were weaker than usual.

They were camped in a clearing used by previous travellers. The only sizeable creature that Sofi had heard in the vicinity was a fox that had gone to ground nearby. Good luck to him, she thought.

"Chogolisa," said Sofi when the eating was done and they settled to rest, "please can you fetch our captive?"

The big woman plonked the relatively little man next to the fire.

"Stand him up, please."

She did. He stood straight, arms and legs trussed in two woollen ponchos and tied tight with leather thongs.

"Remove his gag."

"Hello!" said the Mushroom Man. He jumped round so he was facing Chogolisa. "Thanks for carrying me, it made a fine change from walking. You have a very comfortable shoulder, madam." He bowed.

His long blond hair and beard was like a wig intended to entertain or perhaps terrify children, and his facial features were small, even in the context of his small head. He was not a pretty man. But he was brave. For now. Soon they'd see how brave he really was.

"What's your name?"

"Oh, I'm so sorry, where are my manners? I'm Keef the Berserker. And you are?"

"I'm Sofi Tornado, captain of the Owsla. This is Talisa White-tail. She's going to make you tell us where the rest of the Mushroom Men are going."

Talisa stood, grinning, holding one of her short iron paddle knives.

"Mushroom Men?" said the captive.

"That's you and your kind."

"Oh. Weird."

"It's because you're the colour of mushrooms. Apparently you smell like them, too, but I don't get that. You don't smell as bad as you look."

"Thanks. And you're going to torture me?" asked Keef.

"Yes."

"I'm just a guest, so not for me to say, but you needn't bother. I hate pain. I'll tell you whatever you need to know before you even begin to torture me. I'll tell you things you don't need to know. Anything! Ask away."

"You'll betray your tribe?"

"I'll betray whatever you want me to. And they won't mind. There's not much to tell."

"Don't you want to try at least a pretence at honour?"

"Nope. Just the other day I stubbed my toe and it hurt like a bastard and I thought 'I could not withstand torture.' So, there you go, I could stand here and refuse to tell you anything, and Tease a Shite-snail could tickle me or whatever it is she has—"

"*Talisa White-tail.* And I won't be tickling you."

"I'd guessed that, but I didn't want to give you any ideas. Anyway, point is that I'd tell you everything you want to know pretty much immediately. So let's skip the middle man and get straight to it. What do you want to know?"

"You're pathetic." Talisa White-tail shook her head.

"Sorry to disappoint you, and maybe I'd give your torture a go if I could tell you anything that might benefit your search, but, given that at least one of you is bound to be an excellent tracker who can follow my group without any help from me, I can't. So, let's save your effort and my pain. What do you want to know?"

Sofi Tornado quite liked this bizarre alien and his logic. It wasn't going to stop her torturing him, but it did make it less appealing, which was annoying. "Tell us where your people are now and where they are going."

"They went south from the Big Bone tribe's village. That's the last I saw of them and I don't know their route. Erik and I were going to help see you off, then we were going to head south and pick up their trail."

"And where are they headed in the longer term?"

"North-east. We've been heading west so far to throw you off track. But our final destination is a couple of hundred miles north-east of here. Place called The Meadows."

She heard Yoki Choppa lift his head. The fat woman back in Hardwork territory had told them that the Mushroom Men were headed for The Meadows. He'd tried to mask his interest then.

"Why are you going there?" asked the warlock. He was

trying to sound blasé, but that was the problem, thought Sofi, of hardly ever speaking. When you did, people knew you had a reason.

"We've got this guy called Garth Anvilchin with us. He's a soothsayer. He predicted that you lot were going to attack, so we trust what he says. He reckons there's a place called The Meadows where we'll find peace."

"What else do you know about The Meadows?"

"That's it. If Garth knows anything more himself, he hasn't told me."

"Really."

"Really really. He'd have told me. We're tight, me and Garth. The other day when I'd made a hole in my—"

"It's time you told me more about this Meadows place, Yoki Choppa," interrupted Sofi.

Yoki Choppa stood and walked away. Sofi followed. The warlock stopped in the trees.

"Well?" she asked.

"For more than a year I've been having dreams about The Meadows."

The warlock was positively haemorrhaging secrets today.

"Is it a place?" she asked.

"Possibly."

"Come on, Yoki Choppa, out with it."

"It's more than a place. It's a destructive force and a serious danger. I think it's linked to the recent extreme weather—today's tornado, for example."

"So..." The reason that Ayanna had sent her best troops on this mission was a little clearer. "These Mushroom Men plan to reach The Meadows and use it to destroy the world."

"Maybe."

"Ayanna saw Mushroom Men destroying the world. And now we hear they're heading right for this destructive something? It's pretty clear, isn't it?"

"Maybe."

She stared into his black eyes. He was hiding something.
"I'm going to find out what these people want with The Meadows." She turned to go.

"Sofi."

"Yes?"

"Don't kill him. Don't disable him."

"Why ever not?"

"We can use him to lure the others, and it will be helpful if he can walk."

"Thanks, Yoki Choppa, I'll bear that in mind." She wouldn't bear it in mind. He was her prisoner. She would do what she liked with him. Besides, she didn't need him walking. If Talisa severed every sinew in his body, Chogolisa could carry him.

Sassa Lipchewer and the Hardworkers who'd escaped the tornado sat silent for once, so filthy and weary after their flight that it looked like the twister had in fact whisked them up, whirled them around in a maelstrom of muck and splatted them down around their meagre fire.

Although they'd only just finished eating and wouldn't usually sleep for a few hours, Sassa Lipchewer had the strange sensation that her body was already asleep. Annoyingly, her mind was defiantly and resolutely awake, like a fire raging on top of a sodden haystack.

Why had Finnbogi claimed that Garth had punched him? He'd said he'd dreamt it and was confused, but Sassa was far from convinced that there wasn't more to it. And how had Ottar known Finnbogi had survived? How did Ottar know all these things?

But neither Finnbogi's feud with Garth nor Ottar's oddness was the source of her troubled mind. There was a deep, dark melancholy lurking beneath all her thoughts like sharks circling under a canoe. She tried to tell herself that its roots were her failure to rescue Chnob the White, but that wasn't it. His death had been his own fault and she'd tried her best. For a while she convinced herself that it was guilt at killing—murdering—Hrolf the Painter, but that wasn't it either. He'd been on the brink of death. If she hadn't finished him off then the Owsla would have caught them before they'd reached the Rock River. And it wasn't her annoyance that Thyri Treelegs had caught up with her and proved to be the faster runner—the big-bummed girl had a lower centre of gravity and was better at running in high winds, that was all.

No, the real sadness, the deep, never-to-fade, desperate sadness was the conviction that she'd killed her baby. She had been certain that she was pregnant. Now she was just as certain that she wasn't. Falling so far—she had no idea how high Thyri and she had flown—had killed the tiny person that had begun to grow in her. It proved she could get pregnant and she'd be able to do it again, she told herself. But the idea of that tiny life, the minuscule child deep in her womb, growing and struggling to survive until birth, that spark of life being snuffed out all because she'd tried to rescue the idiot Chnob when she'd never had a chance of doing so and hadn't even wanted to? She pictured her dead baby's miniature face, its tiny hand—

"So, shall we change our name to the Wootah tribe?" Wulf boomed cheerily. She glared at him for disrupting her important thoughts with his inane frivolity and he winked at her.

"No, never," grunted Garth.

"I agree," said Gunnhild. "We are Hardworkers."

"Wootah!!" said Ottar.

"I agree with Ottar," said Finnbogi.

"I agree with Finnbogi," said Bodil.

"The idiots don't have a say," Garth snarled.

"So that rules you out," Finnbogi snapped.

"Easy, easy," Wulf stood, spreading his hands for calm.

"This is a big waste of anger. It's just something to discuss, not to attack each other over. Now, does anybody apart from Garth and Gunnhild think we should keep the name Hardwork?"

"What do you mean?" said Bodil.

"Loakie's tits," muttered Finnbogi and Sassa felt a flash of anger. Since he'd slept with Bodil—or shagged her in the mud to describe it with all the romance it deserved—he'd behaved badly. He'd told Sassa that he'd talk to her and let her down kindly. He hadn't and she was pretty sure he wasn't going to.

"Do you think we should change our tribe name from Hardwork to Wootah?" Wulf explained to Bodil.

"I don't mind. It's just a word. I don't think it's important."

Bodil, thought Sassa, had made the most intelligent point yet about the matter. Sassa would always support Wulf, but they could call themselves the Squirrel Fuckers for all she cared. There were more important things and she was tired.

"I think we should change our name," said Thyri. "I think Olaf Worldfinder was proud of the ancestors' journey and the town they founded, but I don't think he would have found many—any—of those qualities that made him proud in the Hardwork we left behind. Hardwork was decaying— dead even. We should start afresh. So a new name is a good idea, I think. Wootah is as good a name as any. Wooooooo—tah! It works."

Finnbogi smirked at Garth, who ignored him.

"Nicely put, Treelegs. Has that changed anyone's mind?" Wulf looked at Garth.

"Not mine," said the big-chinned man.

He turned to Gunnhild. She sighed. "Can we really leave a hundred years of history behind?"

"Olaf shook off several thousand years of history when he left the old world, and he changed the name of the tribe.

I don't even know the name of the tribe that sailed from the old world."

"I don't either," admitted Gunnhild. "You make a good point."

"What would Uncle Poppo have thought?" asked Finnbogi.

"Oh, he wouldn't have taken it seriously. He didn't take anything seriously."

"I think he would have liked it. Wootah is certainly a less serious name than Hardwork."

"Perhaps...but *man cannot change the name of dung and make it meat.*"

"Let's leave it for a while," said Wulf, "until we meet the others. I'd prefer the decision to be unanimous, so everyone have a good think about it."

"I'm not changing my mind," growled Garth. "Wootah? Fray's cock. You are a bunch of children."

Erik squatted behind a bush and watched the Calnian warlock cook as the women sharpened their weapons and tended to their kit. Keef was trussed and propped against a tree in the middle of it all, so Erik's desired course of action—immediate rescue and successful flight before there was time to get nervous—wasn't an option. Oh well, he thought, it had been an unlikely hope. Perhaps, he mused, if he walked through them all saying "evening," "wonderful day for it" and so on, picked Keef up and walked out, they'd be too surprised to do anything. So far, that was his only plan. He was not proud of it.

The women ate and the warlock poked about in his smoking alchemical bowl. They didn't talk as they dined. In fact they'd hardly said a word to each other since he'd crept up to their camp. Erik approved of that. His gang of Hardworkers—Bodil Gooseface in particular—were always chatting away about nothing as if they felt that silence was a hole in a hut wall that needed to be filled. This lot filled the silence, quite adequately as far as Erik was concerned, with their looks. Talisa White-tail, the one who'd attacked him, was the most jaw-droppingly desirable of the Owsla, although perhaps Paloma Pronghorn was more beautiful, and actually Sofi Tornado was a fine looking woman, perhaps the finest of them. Sitsi Kestrel's huge eyes, although definitely odd, were also enchanting. Point was, they were all lovely, even the oversize Chogolisa Earthquake.

When Erik had lived with the Lakchans and people had talked about Emperor Zaltan's magic-powered fighting squad, it had been with half a curled lip of disgust that the elderly pervert had chosen only attractive women. However, Erik thought if he'd been emperor of the Calnians creating an elite bodyguard, and the choice had been between the most eye-poppingly gorgeous girls in the empire or a bunch of burly blokes... well, he could see where Zaltan had been coming from.

Yet, for all their magic, Erik thought to himself, he'd been able to use his fox-learnt stealth to creep up and hide just a few paces from their camp.

Just as he was congratulating himself, the warlock started, as if he'd seen something surprising in his bowl, and looked up. His keen eyes seemed to pierce through Erik's hiding bush.

Erik held his breath and willed himself invisible, but the magic man clambered to his feet and walked towards him.

"Anything amiss, Yoki Choppa?" said Sofi Tornado.

"Nope." Yoki Choppa stooped, plucked a twig off the ground, returned to his seat and didn't look in Erik's direction again. Thank Rabbit Girl, thought Erik as, very cautiously, he began breathing again. He'd been certain that the little man had rumbled him.

He had been cocky and lucky to get away with it. He'd approached like a fox well enough and remembered to breathe like a fox, but he was squatting like a man. Slowly, thinking foxily, he folded his limbs and collapsed himself until he was curled on his side in a foxy nose to arse circle, halfway under the bush. Now nobody looking at the bush would see him. They could have stepped on him without realising he was there.

He nearly fell asleep waiting for the women to finish eating, and then enjoyed listening to Keef's valiant attempt to feed misinformation and avoid torture.

Then there were more important things to worry about, as the warlock and Sofi Tornado came to stand a pace away on the other side of his bush and discuss The Meadows in whispers that he could hear perfectly clearly.

Erik thought fox, fox, fox. He pulled his lips back over his teeth, became one with the leaves and the loam and fantasised briefly about stalking a giant turkey. Then he listened.

So Yoki Choppa knew about The Meadows, too. What, by Loakie's beard, he wondered, *were* The Meadows, and why did the voice in his dreams want him to go there? Finally, after Erik learnt that Yoki Choppa had a very different take on The Meadows from the Hardworkers' ideas of a milk and honey-soaked sanctuary, the two Calnians headed back to the fire.

"Now, Keef the Berserker, please will you tell me why you've been lying to me?" said Sofi Tornado.

Erik shuddered (like a fox).

"What? Lying? Me? I never lie. My mother taught me—"

"Now you're lying about lying. Try again." She sounded very certain, the Owsla captain.

Keef retold his story. It was true, apart from he said that they were going north-east instead of west, and he claimed that Garth was the soothsayer. Presumably that latter lie was to divert attention from Ottar if the Owsla caught the Hardworkers. If? Let's face it, thought Erik, they'd been very lucky so far. It's a when.

"Talisa, cut his ear off, please," Sofi commanded.

"Which ear?"

"Surprise me."

With his face pressed into the earth, Erik couldn't see what happened next, but he heard it.

Talisa kicked the legs out from under the captive, gripped his hair and held the knife to his ear.

Sitsi Kestrel stood.

"Where are you off to?" asked Morningstar. "You'll miss it all."

"Pee."

"That's bad timing."

"I've seen torture before and it'll probably last a while."

Sitsi followed the track down to the river. She didn't need to pee. She hadn't wanted to watch the amusing, cheerful Mushroom Man being tortured. She wondered why. She'd never minded torture before.

Bjarni Chickenhead heard a yell that sounded a lot like Keef, then he heard someone coming through the woods towards him.

Please be Erik and Keef, please be Erik and Keef, he said to himself, lying back into the soggy bottom of the canoe. He was in the larger craft, holding onto Keef's smaller boat with one hand and the branch of a bankside tree with the other. The boats were in between two half-fallen trees which jutted halfway across the seven-pace-wide river, perhaps twenty paces downstream from an old wooden bridge. The water was silver in the moonlight, and the moon itself was like a perfect circular mirror gathering all the light in the world and beaming it onto Bjarni's hiding spot.

The steps came closer, then he heard someone walk onto the bridge. He lifted his head, slowly, slowly. It was one of the Owsla! She was pacing back and forth on the bridge, looking down as if lost in thought.

From Sadzi Wolf and the women he'd seen across the river, he'd thought they were all tall and stocky. This one didn't look too massive. She was petite even. But she did have a bow in one hand, and he had no doubt that she could use it.

She stopped in the middle of the bridge and turned her delicate face towards him. All she had to do was look in the right direction and she'd see him lying there in the boat like a crippled deer in a ditch. There was no way he'd be able to scramble clear before she plugged him with an arrow.

The Owsla girl looked up at the sky and stared like a love-sick teen at the moon with bright, preternaturally large eyes.

Bjarni's nose twitched. He was going to sneeze.

"I am telling the truth," said Keef. "I meant what I said. I'm a complete pussy. Please don't hurt me any more. There's no point, I've already told you everything! If you have any other questions, any, I will answer them. I will tell you things that I have never told anyone! I once stole a precious stone from an aunt I didn't like and threw it into Olaf's Fresh Sea. When I was young I found some of the other boys sexually attractive. I have masturbated halfway up a tree. One time I ate—"

"Quiet!" Sofi Tornado smiled. She couldn't help but like this one. But she could tell by the way he shifted his feet, by the way he clasped and unclasped his hands and by a dozen other signs that he was lying about the direction the others were headed, and about their soothsayer. And about the aunt's precious stone. The rest was true.

"You lied about the direction that your group is headed in. I know they're going west."

"But they're not! The direction so far was all a ruse to throw you off. They've turned north-east now, I promise on all the gods and their relatives, and their friends and their relatives' friends. Please don't hurt me again."

"Talisa, eye, please."

"My eye? No, that's too much." Keef shook his head. "You're just doing this because it's expected of you as captain of the Owsla. I don't think you want to. Come on, break the mould, be your own person."

Talisa gripped him by the hair, pulled his head back and pushed the tip of her finger into the corner of his eye.

"Ow! Stop that! It really hurts! They're going north-east, they really are. They still will be after you take my eye out. Think about it! Do you really want a captive with no depth perception? I'll be a burden!"

Talisa looked at Sofi. She nodded. The Calnian shoved her finger deep into the Hardworker's face, twisted and scooped. Keef screamed.

Usually Sofi got a thrill watching one of her women inflict pain on an inferior being. Was she missing the diamondback rattlesnake in her diet already or was it psychosomatic?

Or...she'd definitely been feeling less ruthless of late. She'd let the Goachica survivors live. Sure, she'd made a vow not to kill the Lakchans and told herself that it was binding, but would a vow usually have stopped her murdering someone? Surely not.

Had Yoki Choppa cut the rattlesnake from their diet before the Big Bone tribe had disintegrated his supplies? Did he want them less vicious for his own reasons?

If he had a scheme, she'd get to the bottom of it. If he'd been messing them about for his own purposes, he was dead.

Keef's scream echoed through the trees. Bjarni shuddered. He considered running to help, but the woman on the bridge would put an arrow in him the moment he moved, then he'd be dead and Keef would be in the same predicament. He was stuck, one hand holding a branch, one hand holding a boat, blinking and wrinkling his nose and trying not to sneeze.

The little Owsla woman with the big eyes drew in a long breath. For a second he thought she going to cry, but she began to sing in a high, sweet and tuneful voice.

The tune crescendoed towards a long note and Bjarni sneezed.

The lonely moon shone. An owl hooted. It was all rather magical. Sitsi Kestrel wasn't an invader in this strange land of monsters and tornados any more, she was part of nature's cycle, at one with the ebb and flow of the earth.

She lifted her head and sang a song about lost love. The wavelets on the river twinkled in rhythm with her words, the soft wind shivering through the trees' broad leaves accompanied her song.

Just before she reached the chorus she heard a racoon or possibly a squirrel sneeze, which bolstered her idea of being one with nature.

Her song sung, she felt a great deal more cheerful and headed back to camp.

They were done with the torture. The man was trussed again and Yoki Choppa was dressing his wounds. Sitsi sat down next to Paloma Pronghorn.

"What did I miss?"

"Talisa cut off the Mushroom Man's ear and scooped his eye out."

"Did he tell us anything useful?"

"Nothing that he hadn't said before we started torturing him."

"Oh. Why did we stop?"

"Maybe Sofi decided he was telling the truth after all. Maybe we'll try again tomorrow. I don't know."

In all the tales of the Hardworkers and the Lakchans, Erik had never heard of a more heroic display. Keef had shouted a little and screamed once but mostly remained calm and stuck to his story as Talisa White-tail had cut off his ear and gouged out his eye.

It seemed that he'd finally satisfied the Owsla captain, because she'd stopped the torture. Talisa had been disappointed, which, thought Erik, made her a little less attractive. Or maybe a little more...?

The women of the Owsla went about their evening business, Yoki Choppa was put on watch and, as far as Erik could tell, all the women went to sleep. Soon the only sounds were the whistles, snorts and rustles of the animals of the night, the soft snores of most of the women and the loud snuffling grunts of one of them. Erik guessed the latter noises came from Chogolisa Earthquake, even though in his experience there was no positive correlation between size of woman and loudness of snore.

A new sound arose, a soft sucking. The smell of burning tobacco tickled his nose.

He uncurled from his fox ball and lifted his head, fox-style. Yoki Choppa was sitting on a stump at the edge of the camp, facing away from him, puffing out clouds of smoke into the moon-bright sky. Slowly, foxily, Erik rose into a crouch.

The women of the Owsla that he could see were asleep, as was Keef, trussed and propped against the same tree as before. Sofi Tornado was on one side of him, Chogolisa Earthquake on the other. The loud snores weren't coming from the large woman, they were Keef's. Erik guessed that Yoki Choppa must have given him something powerful for the pain.

There was a tapping sound as the warlock knocked out the burnt tobacco from his pipe. He stood, stretched, and walked away into the trees on the far side of the camp.

Erik stood too. Now or never. He fox-crept around the bush, into the camp and over to Keef. A real fox screamed nearby, as if protesting the human's appropriation of vulpine ways. The big man froze. None of the women woke.

Keef was breathing raspingly with intermittent snorts. Half his head was bandaged. His spear, Arse Splitter, lay next to him.

Erik leant forward and gripped the man by the leather thongs that bound him.

Six feet away, the Owsla captain stirred. Her eyelids flickered.

Finnbogi had heard the phrase "so tired I couldn't sleep" and consigned it to that group of sayings that adults spouted because their lives were so boring that they had to make up crap to talk about, and they were so dumb and unimaginative that they couldn't make up their own phrases. It came from the same dull bucket as choice lines like "too cold to snow" and "you can have too much of a good thing."

But now, knackered beyond knackeredness, he *was* too tired to sleep. Or, possibly, he was too nearly-murdered-by-a-twat to sleep.

He knew that he should have been worrying about his father, Keef and Bjarni, but he couldn't drag his thoughts away from Thyri Treelegs.

The thing was, he could see Thyri didn't actually like Garth. She always disagreed with him, like she had tonight about the Wootah renaming. When they were together they didn't just not talk to each other, they actually looked unhappy. They'd kissed when the Lakchans had been about to kill them, sure, but it was only because they'd been about to die and Garth had lunged. Thyri, because she was so stubborn, had carried on the relationship. She simply couldn't admit to anyone, least of all herself, that she'd made a mistake.

He wanted to talk to her, to explain how wrong she was, to tell her she had an alternative and that nobody would think any the worse of her for taking it (apart from Garth, of course, but screw him). Finnbogi was sure that she'd rather be with him if only she knew it was a possibility, and she was capable of admitting to herself that she'd been wrong to go with Garth. But he couldn't think of any way of telling her which wouldn't make her react like an armadillo poked with a stick. He knew what was best for her— he knew *he* was best for her—but she was so wilful that if he told her he was the one it would make her all the more determined that he wouldn't be.

There had to be something he could do or say that would make her go off that lunk Anvilchin.

Or, better, he could remove Anvilchin.

It was straightforward revenge. Loakie and all the gods would approve, and, even if they did meet in Valhalla, Garth wouldn't have a leg to stand on. He'd tried to kill Finnbogi, so Finnbogi was allowed to kill him. Any god would agree.

But how to do it? He could engineer a situation when they were apart from the others but, having tried to kill him once, presumably Garth would be on the lookout for an opportunity to do so again. And Garth, let's face it, would beat Finnbogi in a fair fight ninety-nine times in a hundred. Or even a hundred. So he'd have to make sure it wasn't a fair fight...

And now he was losing sleep so he'd be even less able to deal with the problem in the morning. It was impossible. Why did bad things always happen to him?

Sofi Tornado settled. Erik the Angry tightened his grip on Keef the Berserker's straps. There was no avoiding it, this next bit was going to make some noise. He prayed to Spider Mother and Tor that Sofi Tornado and the rest of them were heavy sleepers and heaved the Hardworker up and onto his shoulder. Keef wasn't as big as Erik, but he was heavy enough.

Keef oofed quietly but stayed asleep. Erik stood and

listened, expecting the camp to wake and kill him any moment. Nothing happened. He squatted and picked up Arse Splitter. Keef would be upset if he didn't rescue the axe as well.

He turned and almost shouted with surprise. Yoki Choppa was back, sitting on his tree stump. His alchemical bowl was smoking in his hands, but he was looking, with a mildly bored expression, directly at Erik.

He stared back. The warlock jinked his head almost imperceptibly towards the river.

The exiled Hardworker did not need to be asked twice. He crept out of the camp, fox-style, speeding up as he neared the river.

"Nice one," said Bjarni Chickenhead, sitting up in the canoe.

"Shhhh," said Erik. They weren't clear yet.

He lowered Keef, still sleeping, into Bjarni's boat— Chickenhead could paddle with the extra load since he'd been lying about all evening—and climbed into Keef's little canoe.

They set off. Erik expected an axe to the side of the head at any moment. Why had the warlock let them go, if not for the fun of chasing and killing then? But no axe came. When they'd rounded three bends in the river, Erik the Angry let himself believe that the rescue had succeeded.

He felt every muscle relax as he paddled on through the moonlit night, south-west along the Heartberry River towards the Water Mother.

Chapter 7

No Excuses

"It is very odd that I didn't wake up, wouldn't you say, Yoki Choppa?" Sofi Tornado sounded calm, but Paloma Pronghorn recognised the tone. It was the same one she'd used ordering Chogolisa Earthquake to tear off Malilla Leaper's arms.

The warlock shrugged.

Paloma looked from one to the other. She did not like this. It was like her parents fighting.

"And when you returned from checking the periphery it's strange that you didn't notice the prisoner was gone, wouldn't you say?"

"Yup."

If Paloma had been in his position, she would have said that it had been dark, that she had nothing to gain from freeing the prisoner, that the person who'd taken him must have been another warlock using magic, and any number of other excuses. But Yoki Choppa wasn't saying anything.

The whole thing *was* a bit odd.

When the warlock had woken Paloma to take her turn on watch, it had taken her about a quarter of a heartbeat to notice that Keef the Berserker was gone. Why hadn't Yoki Choppa spotted it?

By the tracks, the largest of the Mushroom Men had crept up and lain behind a bush, waited until Yoki Choppa went off into the woods, walked into the camp, picked up Keef and walked out again, down to the river and a waiting boat.

Then Yoki Choppa had sat for two hours before waking Paloma. It was all *very* strange, but the idea that the warlock had somehow colluded in the escape was even stranger.

Sofi seemed to reach the same conclusion and the menace evaporated from her voice. "All right, I suppose it's possible I might have missed the intruder. I don't suppose we have any of his hair to trace his whereabouts?"

"Did you clean your knife after cutting his ear off, Talisa?" asked Yoki Choppa.

"I did, in the river. I tossed the eye and ear in, too."

"Then we can't trace him."

"We have his blood on the ground."

"No good."

"Okay, please use the hair we do have to find the other Mushroom Men."

The warlock nodded, mixed his ingredients, set fire to them, poked about a bit then said: "The Mushroom Man who owned this hair is two miles upriver."

"What is he doing there?"

"He's dead."

Sofi shook her head. "Paloma, see if you can find him. Oh, and if you see any pronghorns, bring one back."

"Dead or alive?"

"Dead."

Paloma ran, glad to be away from the camp, glad to be running, and glad to be looking out for pronghorns. She wondered why Sofi wanted one.

Early morning was her favourite time to run, so it was a disappointment when she found the corpse not long after leaving. He was on an island in the middle of the shallow river, naked and torn open by scavenging animals.

For a moment she thought he was alive because his stomach was moving, but it was an otter with her head buried in his side and chomping away.

"Yuk!" she said out loud, then waded across, hissing and waving her arms to shoo the munching mustelid.

"Do you remember the one who launched that novel attack on Sadzi—getting his throat slit on purpose then blinding her with the blood?" said Paloma Pronghorn, reporting back.

Sofi Tornado nodded.

"That's the chap who's dead in the river. As well as the cut to his neck, his head was staved in, one thigh and his stomach ripped open, a wrist, both legs and his nose were broken, and he was bruised all over."

"Twister," said Yoki Choppa.

"Yup," said Paloma. "Twisted to death."

Sofi nodded. "Let's hope he was the only one it got."

"Don't we want them dead?" asked Morningstar.

"We have to know they're dead. If the twister has thrown them all over the woods, lakes and prairies, we'll have a job finding the bodies."

"So what do we do?"

"Our escapee and his rescuer will have rendezvous plans with the rest of them. So we find them and follow them. Paloma?"

"Consider them found!" She sprinted away again.

"And catch any pronghorns that you see!"

"Sure thing!" she yelled. What was Sofi's sudden obsession with pronghorns?

"I never knew the world was so *big*!" cried Bodil Gooseface. "*Is* it the whole world, do you think? Where are The Meadows? Is that them over there?" She pointed to a shining stretch of prairie.

"Yes," said Finnbogi the Boggy. "We can see the whole world and that bit is The Meadows."

"It is? So we'll be there today?"

"Yes."

"Shush, Finnbogi." Sassa Lipchewer shook her head. "It's not really the whole world, Bodil, nothing like it, and I don't think that's The Meadows. But it is a big view."

It was certainly the widest view Sassa had ever seen. They'd been walking steadily uphill since they'd left the Big Bone tribe the day before, and now arrived on a ridge where it seemed the land lost all the height it had gained in one go and they could see woods, lakes and prairie stretching southwards as far as the horizon.

The pace was good, the mood not so much. Chnob the White had been the opposite of popular, but it was still a shock to lose one of the group. The bigger worry was whether they'd lost three more. If they'd simply seen off the Owsla, then Keef and Erik would have caught up. However, if the Owsla had defeated the Big Bone tribe, surely they'd have been on them by now? So what had happened? Had Keef and Erik succeeded in stopping the Owsla but died in the process? Bjarni was even more of a worry, since he'd simply disappeared.

Whatever had happened to them, Sassa wasn't going to worry about it and let it put her into a sulk, as had happened to everyone else. You die when you die. She was going to focus on living and keeping the people around her alive. She looked over her shoulder. No sign of pursuit, just Thyri and Garth, today's rearguard. She gripped her bow. She'd shaken off her lethargy and bad mood and practised again the night before, as she had every night since leaving Hardwork. She was pleased with her progress.

Paloma Pronghorn might have been the fastest runner in the world, but following the canoes wasn't as simple as it might have been, because there was no track running along the river. Why would there be? If you wanted to go where the river went, you went along the river. But you needed a boat for that. Quick as she was, Paloma could not run on water, nor through the overgrown tangle of woods that lined so much of the watercourse.

The other problem was that Keef and his rescuer could have left the river, so she had to go slowly enough that she wouldn't miss their tracks if they had. She was assuming that if they'd left the river they would have headed south to join the rest of their group, so she kept to the river's left bank as much as possible, leaping downed tree trunks and whacking her way through choking vegetation with her killing stick. It was painfully slow going.

If they'd gone north, which they might have done if they were being clever, or if they'd walked carefully up one of the many little streams that fed into the Heartberry River, which they'd have done if they had any sense at all, she'd miss their tracks. Her only real hope was that they'd been stupid enough to stay in the canoes.

It was well past noon when she spotted the boats. The river was wider here and the canoes were on the far side but there was no mistaking them—Keef the Berserker in his head bandage and the big one with the light brown, shaggy hair. There was another one with them, the one with the ball of curly black hair.

She pirouetted around and sped back to report.

Chapter 8

Old Man Water Mother

Massbak and Galenar, two young men of the Water Divided tribe, were out hunting. As usual, animal quarry was a secondary pursuit to discussing their tribe mates.

"I don't understand," said Massbak. "Cavanar asked me—practically begged me—to come to his new Shark Clan gathering yesterday evening. When I got there, he looked at me like I'd crapped in his alchemical bowl, then blanked me."

"And he's usually all right?" asked Galenar.

"We're friends, far as I'm concerned, good friends. Have been ever since we did our vision quests together."

"I bet—"

"Hold on." Massbak lifted his bow, peered into the trees, then lowered it. "Thought I saw a deer."

"I bet I know what it was. Was Sabula Derinda at this Shark Clan thing?"

"She was."

"And were you talking to her?"

"Of course I was."

"There you go."

"What?"

"That's Cavanar for you. Sabula Derinda was the hottest girl there, right?"

"Sabula Derinda is the hottest girl anywhere."

"She certainly is. And you were cock blocking Cavanar."

"But there were loads of other people, and I didn't talk to her all evening by any means."

"He would have organised the whole thing just to show off to Sabula Derinda and you got in his way."

"Surely not. She's practically married to Big Keller."

"Was Big Keller asked?"

"Not his sort of thing. He's much more Buffalo Clan."

Galenar chuckled. "He certainly is. And Cavanar knows that. His sole intention in creating the Shark Clan was to prise Sabula Derinda away from Big Keller and you pissed him off by speaking to her when he could have been speaking to her."

"But he's an idiot. He doesn't have a hope."

"I agree with you on both counts. He's the worst kind of idiot, one who's quite clever but thinks he's a genius. He's clever enough to know, deep down, that he's not really a genius, so, as well as being conceited, he's sickened by self-loathing. He's arrogant and insecure—a double twat."

"You've put some thought into it."

"Some people are twats, but nobody needs to be. So why be a twat? That's why people like Cavanar fascinate me and why, yes, I have put quite a lot of thought into it."

"Are you studying me?"

"You're not a twat because you have a degree of humility and self-awareness and that governs your actions. The conclusion of my twat studies so far—and this may change, I've got a long way to go—is that all people are fools. None of us, even the cleverest, is actually clever. The greatest warrior chief or infallible warlock can trip over a tent rope and land face first in buffalo dung. It's when we can't accept our ineptitude and try to cover it up with bluster and posturing that we become conceited and paranoid: twats, in other words."

"Good theory."

"I'm not convinced yet, I need to study more examples, but it certainly fits for Cavanar and—"

"Shush. Hide."

The young men melted off the path, nipped between trees and lay down. Massbak was glad he was with Galenar. Other people might have stood in the road asking what he'd seen and why he wanted them to hide. But the fact that Massbak had told him to hide was enough for Galenar, and now he lay silently, waiting either for the all clear or for the danger to make itself apparent.

They didn't wait long. A man and woman came along the path. The man was a little older than them—in his twenties—tall, muscled and carrying a club with an impossibly large iron head. The woman was elderly, carrying a wooden club set with colourful gems. Their strange weapons, however, were not the thing that made Massbak almost gasp with wonder. He'd never seen such odd-looking humans. Their skin was a weird hue, shiny and light. The man's hair was curled and the colour of yellow petals.

There were seven more, each odder than the next. There was an even larger man in a hat that looked a lot like iron, a young girl with hair that shone like gold and another woman with yellow hair. This latter woman, despite her freakish locks and skewed lips, was perhaps even more lovely than Sabula Derinda.

Massbak knew immediately who they must be. He waited until they were well out of earshot before turning to Galenar and whispering, "Mushroom Men."

Galenar nodded. "We'd better get ahead of them, warn the tribe."

"Do you think we'll kill them?"

"Of course we'll kill them. Calnia wants us to kill them and we do what Calnia tells us."

After several hours' slow progress along the path-free banks of the Heartberry River, Sofi Tornado, Paloma Pronghorn, Yoki Choppa and the four other remaining Owsla women ran from the trees onto buffalo-grazed prairie. The land sloped down to the winding, sun-sparkling Heartberry River. Silhouetted neatly on the near point of a broad meander were three large Mushroom Men in two canoes.

Sofi sped up. The river was narrow. There was no way they could escape.

"That's not a river, it's a long sea!" said Finnbogi.

"Is it?" asked Bodil. "What do you mean?"

He didn't bother answering. He looked at the view. For a moment he forgot that his true love was sleeping with his arch enemy, forgot that his arch enemy had tried to kill him and was bound to try again, forgot that his father and two friends were missing, and forgot that any moment now the world's finest killing squad was going to catch up and slaughter them all. He forgot it all and looked at the river.

Could there be anything more magnificent?

This was the reason he'd wanted to leave Hardwork. He wanted to see amazing things. Here, surely, was the most amazing sight in the world.

From his cliff-top standpoint he could see miles across the insanely wide valley. Flowing along that valley was a body of water too huge, too majestic, to share the word "river" with all the piddling streams that Finnbogi had considered to be rivers thus far. He'd thought the Rock River had been wide. The Water Mother made it look like a ditch in a dry spell.

There'd been a small island in the Rock River, but the islands in this river could have held entire towns. Indeed, by the trails of smoke rising peacefully into the still evening light, it looked like there were settlements on some of them. A river wide enough for islands that you could live on... It was like something from the sagas.

There were a handful of canoes near the banks. In the river proper, a couple of larger boats glided downstream at a lick that made Keef's canoe seem pedestrian. Finnbogi guessed that it must be the current swishing them along so quickly, even though the great body of water looked like it wasn't moving at all.

While the Hardworkers' gods inhabited a far-off world that few saw before they died, the Scraylings' gods were often visible: a particularly large tree, a white buffalo, a bird—that sort of thing. If the Water Mother was not a Scrayling god, Finnbogi would eat his dad's breechcloth. He'd always thought that their religion was a little silly before. Now he absolutely saw the sense of it.

"Wootah!" cried Wulf the Fat behind him, playing with the children and the racoons. They'd made camp next to the rocky promontory overlooking the Water Mother. There wasn't much daylight left, and Wulf wanted to wait until the following morning to approach the riverside town that they could see from the cliff and ask to borrow boats. People were more helpful in the morning, he'd said. That had seemed like a really dumb reason to Finnbogi when they had killers on their tails who they could escape by crossing the Water Mother. He'd been about to say something when he realised that Wulf wanted to wait for Keef, Erik and Bjarni, but he didn't want those three to take the blame if the Owsla did catch up ... Once again Finnbogi thanked Loakie that he wasn't in charge.

"Wootah! Wootah!" yelled Ottar and Freydis.

Wootah indeed, thought Finnbogi, looking back across the river. No other Hardworkers had seen a sight like this for at least five generations. The enormity of what they'd done, and what they were going to do, made Finnbogi giddy. Already they were very different people from the ones who, just a few days before, had been happy to stagnate next to a lake for the rest of their lives. No longer were they Hardworkers. They were heroes and adventurers. They were the Wootah tribe.

"Two canoes tied together," said Gunnhild, walking up to join him and Bodil on the overlook.

"Tied together?" he asked.

"Those larger boats, heading downstream, they must be two canoes fixed together. I imagine they separate them to paddle back upstream. Our ancestors were great boat people, don't you know?"

Finnbogi did know. It was pretty obvious. You couldn't cross thousands of miles of salt sea without knowing one end of a boat from the other.

"Oh yes, they had great boats, with the heads of dragons—"

"Oi, Boggy!" came a welcome call. It was Thyri.

He leapt round like a ravenous dog called for dinner.

"What's happening, Treelegs?" he asked, scrabbling to regain nonchalance.

"Fighting practice, you and me, now."

"Sure. If you want." This was the first time she'd asked him since she'd got together with Garth, five days and a million years before.

Don't ask her about Garth, don't ask her about Garth, he told himself as they walked along a path busy with butter-flies, the warm woodland air almost overbearingly heavy with the scent of flowers. He fantasised that they were out for an evening stroll from their home at The Meadows. They were having a break from the kids, enjoying the evening air and heading for their secret moss-lined shagging glade.

Back in the real world, they found a suitable training area in a clearing near the edge of the cliff, and Thyri cut two slender but sturdy branches with her sax.

She handed him one of them as if everything was normal and there hadn't been a great gap in their training and she hadn't made love to a monster even though Finnbogi had to be her true love.

"What's going on with Garth?" he asked.

"Can you block this?"

"Ow!" Before he'd realised she was moving, she'd whacked him on the thigh.

"How about this?" She hit his other leg.

"Ow!"

"And this?"

"OW!" That was his arm.

"And this?"

"OW!"

"And this?"

"Ahhh! Stop!"

"And this?"

"OWWW!" That was his ear!

He fled. She chased him. He ran in circles with his hands over his ears. She was laughing, flicking him on the arse with her wooden cane.

"Stop, stop, stop!" he cried, laughing despite the pain.

"You don't want me to!"

Whack, whack.

"Ow! Ow! I do! I really, really do."

She stopped and he stood panting and laughing, bent double with his hands on his knees.

"Now," she said, "stop pissing about. As I have demonstrated, you need to learn some blocks."

"Racoon's cocks!" cried Paloma Pronghorn, "I'm really, really sorry."

"What, why?" Sofi Tornado looked at the Mushroom Men's canoes, then hung her head. She'd spotted what was wrong.

"Those boats haven't moved since I found them a couple of hours ago," gushed Paloma. "I was so keen to get back to you that I turned as soon as I spotted them and didn't check and—"

Sofi held up her hand to halt the group. The boats were shifting in the current but making no progress. The three Mushroom Men were motionless.

She walked down to the river to investigate. She was too disappointed to run.

They'd tethered the canoes' sterns to rocks on the riverbed, so that they swung with the flow. To make the three figures, they'd stuffed clothes with vegetation, made balls out of twigs for the heads and, by the looks of it, cut off all Keef's and the curly black-haired one's hair to decorate the fake skulls.

There were no tracks on either bank, so they'd swum away downstream.

"Get some of that hair," Sofi ordered Paloma Pronghorn. "Yoki Choppa, prepare to analyse it."

"They've headed south-west," said the warlock a short while later.

"But Keef said they were going north-east!" said Talisa White-tail.

"Yes," sighed Sofi. She looked up and saw the sun touching the horizon in the west. "Make camp here. We'll catch up with them tomorrow."

Sassa Lipchewer had heard Garth Anvilchin arguing with Thyri Treelegs on the march earlier in the day and sped up to hear the details. If they didn't want people eavesdropping, she'd reasoned, they should argue in private. She hadn't caught every word, but the gist seemed to be that Garth wanted to leave the group and wanted Thyri to go with him.

So it wasn't a huge surprise when Garth waited until Sassa and Wulf were sitting on their own by the fire, walked up and said: "I think we should leave now. Us three and Thyri, none of the others."

"That's an interesting idea," said Wulf.

"It's our best chance. Without the old woman and the children we could go at three times the pace."

"Has Thyri agreed to it?" asked Sassa.

Garth glowered. "She'll change her mind if you two come."

"And Finnbogi and Bodil?"

"She's an idiot and he's a weak idiot. They're both dead weight. We stay with them, we die. On our own, we've got a chance."

"Do you remember," said Wulf, "that game we used to play in Olaf's Fresh Sea, when we'd throw a stone to each other, getting further and further apart?"

"I do..."

"We could have made that a lot easier by sitting on a log and handing the stone to each other. But then we wouldn't have been playing the game. It's the same deal here, Garth. We're getting everyone to The Meadows, that's the game. Take the 'everyone' away from that and the game's ruined."

"We've lost that game. If we'd made it Hird only, and you, Sassa, from the start, then Ogmund would be alive, Gurd would be alive—Hrolf would probably be alive—and we'd be well clear of the Owsla by now."

Sassa felt a twinge of guilt that she didn't feel guilty about killing Hrolf the Painter.

"We wouldn't know where to go without Ottar," said Wulf.

"We don't know where we're going with him, apart from west, which we could have done on our own. We may have evaded the Owsla for now, but they'll catch up tomorrow or the next day and we don't need to be around when that happens."

"We'll be across the Water Mother tomorrow," said Wulf, "they won't follow us."

"Won't they? Why not? And have you thought about how we're going to cross? The river and both banks are teeming with Scraylings."

"They won't follow us because Calnians don't cross the Water Mother."

"Who told you that?"

"Everyone knows Calnians don't cross the Water Mother."

"Hmmm."

"And we're going to cross in the boat that the Scraylings who live in the town to the north of here are going to lend us."

"*That's* your plan?"

"Yup."

"That's shit. We know the Calnians sent runners telling all the Scraylings to kill us. Our only hope is to sneak down tonight and steal a boat."

"We need rest and Ottar says the Owsla are nowhere near."

"Gunnhild and the children need rest, we don't. And I know the boy's been right a couple of times, but can we really risk our lives so completely on his word? He didn't know the tornado was coming. And why do you think the Scraylings by the river will help us? The Lakchans wanted to kill us. The Big Bone tribe were an exception. The chances of another tribe defying Calnia are zero. You cannot save all these people, Wulf. Our only chance of preserving anything of Hardwork— to continue our line—is to leave now, the four of us."

"Maybe I can't save all this lot, but I think *we* can. I need you, Garth. You're a good fighter and a better man. Sleep on it. Tomorrow we'll be across the Water Mother and safe from the Owsla."

"We will attack the Mushroom Men's camp the moment the sun rises tomorrow and kill them all," said Dyas Bellvoo, chief of the Water Divided tribe.

The tribe's territory was the shifting islands of the Water Mother and its eastern and western banks—if it could be called their territory. They paid tribute to Calnia and did what Calnia told them, so really the land was Calnia's and they were not much more than slaves, or, as Galenar would have put it, they *were* slaves.

"Why not in the night?" asked Sinsinawa, head warlock.

Massbak was amazed that anyone would question Chief Dyas Bellvoo. It would certainly never happen in public, but it seemed that everyone had their say in these leadership moots; everyone apart from him and Galenar, of course. They'd been asked along as a reward for spotting the Mushroom Men and tracking them to their camp, but they weren't meant to speak, as had been made emphatically clear when Galenar had tried to make the case for letting the Mushroom Men live and Sinsinawa had invited him to shut up if he valued his life.

Initially Chief Dyas Bellvoo had wanted to help the Mushroom Men, too, but the warlock Sinsinawa and the others had been against it. Their point was that the Calnians would exterminate them all and damn their souls to oblivion if they didn't kill a small group of strangers. It wasn't a bad point, Massbak had to admit.

"I don't like this at all, killing travellers. And killing children! Two children, was it, Massenar?" said Chief Dyas Bellvoo.

"Yes, two," said Massbak, chuffed that the chief knew half his name.

"Yes, a shame. Reluctantly, I do see the sense in it. But it is a bad business and we will not slay them in the night like murderers. We will kill them in the day, and give them the chance to die like warriors with the sun on their skins." Dyas Bellvoo blinked his piercing eyes and looked at them all over his heron-bill nose.

"But some of us might be killed," said Sinsinawa.

"By people called Mushroom Men? I hardly think so. If some of us are unfortunate enough to fall, it is the price we will pay to maintain our pride. Anything less, I could not live with."

Sinsinawa had raised his eyebrows but said nothing. Massbak wondered if he was thinking what he himself was thinking. Dyas Bellvoo wouldn't be one of the attackers, so was being free with others' lives to satisfy his own principles. He looked forward to Galenar's opinion of Dyas Bellvoo's vicarious sacrifice.

"You said they were seven adults as well as the two children?" Chief Dyas Bellvoo asked Massbak.

"Yes. An older woman and six of fighting age. Two of the men and two of the women looked like warriors. The others did not," Massbak answered, trying to sound tough and wise and a good candidate for becoming a permanent member of the leadership circle. That would impress Sabula Derinda. He hadn't told even Galenar, but he was very much in love with Sabula Derinda, even if she was with Big Keller.

"To ensure none of ours are killed, we will send twenty-one warriors. Massenar, you will tell the warriors where to find their camp."

"I could lead them?"

"No. You'll only get in the way and get yourself, or, worse, someone else, killed."

Massbak looked at Galenar, who nodded and pressed his fingers to his pursed lips as if he made plans with the chief every day.

"And will we give these Mushroom Men to the Water Mother?" asked Sinsinawa.

Good question, thought Massbak. All the Water Divided tribe's dead were tied to posts and lowered into the river so that fish might eat them and return their spirits to the Water Mother. Enemies of the Water Divided tribe—plus rapists, murderers, child molesters and people who took offence on behalf of others—were burnt, so that their souls wouldn't sully the sacred waters. By Sinsinawa's tone, he did not think the Mushroom Men deserved the watery option.

"We will give them to the Water Mother and I will mourn them as if they were my own second cousins," declared the chief. "We do not know these people. We are killing them to save our children. I only hope the Water Mother will forgive us."

"They have the skin and hair of demons. Should they really go to the Water Mother?" Sinsinawa snapped.

Dyas Bellvoo looked down his long nose. "It is natural and enjoyable to demonise those who look and act differently from us, Sinsinawa, but also ignorant and juvenile. I am surprised that you haven't grown out of it."

Chapter Nine
Cliff

"Where's Garth?" asked Wulf.

"He left in the night," Thyri replied.

Wulf nodded as if he'd been expecting it.

"What do you mean, left?" asked Finnbogi.

"Get yourself ready to go, Finnbogi," said Wulf, "and help Freydis and Ottar once you're sorted."

Finnbogi nodded and went back to his kit, wide-eyed with happy wondering. Had Garth *gone* gone? He hardly dared to even begin to believe it. Could Garth have buggered off for ever? Could this be the best day of his life?

"Ottar says twenty-one people are coming to kill us," announced Freydis. "They'll be here very soon."

Perhaps not the *best* day.

"Any idea which direction they're coming from, Ottar?" asked Wulf.

Freydis looked at her brother, then pointed to the north along the cliff line. "From that way." Then she pointed south. "And that way."

"Knob in a robin," said Sassa.

"They're very nearly here," added Freydis.

Wulf looked about. Their campsite was next to a cliff-top path that ran south to north, or north to south depending on your perspective. To the west was a promontory and a rocky certain-death drop down to the Water Mother's flood plain, to the east was scrub-choked woodland.

"Can you ask Ottar for an earlier warning next time?" asked Wulf.

"He's only just woken up."

"Fair enough."

"So we go down the cliff," said Thyri.

"Not an option."

"Into the woods?" asked Sassa.

"That will split us up, slow us down and they'll be able to hunt us one by one. Nope, this one's a fighter. Thyri and Finn, cover the south path. I'll take the north, Sassa, back there, cover both entrances to the clearing with your bow. Gunnhild, over there with Sassa. Brain anyone that comes for her. Bodil, you're with Freydis and Ottar, behind Sassa and Gunnhild."

Ottar was leaping about and pointing.

"Ottar wants to know where Hugin and Munin should go?" said Freydis.

"Good question," said Wulf, scratching his chin. "Ottar, send your racoons into the forest. They're in charge of biting any Scraylings that try to escape."

The boy shooed his racoons away. The animals fled with unseemly haste, making no attempt to hide their relief at being excused from the fight.

Finnbogi stood by Thyri at the edge of the clearing, where the path emerged from the woodland. It's funny how things can change so quickly, he thought. A minute ago he'd been the happiest man in the world because Garth had gone. Now he wished that Garth was still with them. His dad, Bjarni, Keef and his dad's bear would be pretty handy, too.

"We stay two paces away from each other at all times," Thyri Treelegs told him out of the corner of her mouth, sax drawn, shield in the other hand, eyes fixed on the path, "so we don't hamper or hit each other. Try not to move from your spot too much; we can't let any through. If you have to move to avoid dying, do. Hopefully Lipchewer will plug any that get past us."

"Okay." Finnbogi was breathing hard. His sword Foe Slicer was heavy. It wasn't his sword, of course. It was Jarl Brodir's and it wasn't really his either, it was Olaf the Worldfinder's. Point was, he didn't know how to use it. He shouldn't have a sword. Fighting wasn't his thing and he was going to die.

"You'll be fine, Finn," said Thyri. "Remember the blocks I taught you last night. If you get a very clear opening, go for it, but other than that don't worry too much about killing them, I can do that. Block and stay alive."

"Shame we didn't get to the hitting lesson."

"We'll do that next time."

"If there's a next time."

"There will be. Relax. Tor is with us. You'll be fine. Don't get yourself too wound up before they get here. Try to think about something else."

There was only one other thing he could think about. "What's going on with you and Garth?" he asked.

She gave him a look that would have made Tor himself flee the field, and did, happily, make him forget the approaching enemy for a moment.

"Here, take this." Sassa Lipchewer handed Bodil her iron knife. Bodil looked at it as if it were a week-dead fish. "If the Scraylings get past all of us, you have to protect the children."

"Right-o," said Bodil.

Sassa wasn't sure that she'd understood, but surely she'd work it out once they were under attack.

It was strangely quiet at the top of the cliff. Njord the Wind God was still asleep. Sassa looked down and across the vast valley. Tendrils of smoke rose straight up from cook fires on islands, and on both sides of the river. Funny to think, she thought, that while she'd been waking and break-fasting and living her life in Hardwork, these people had been doing the same, without knowing or caring about her. After she was gone they'd carry on, as if she didn't matter at all...

She tried to focus on the coming fight. Wulf stood ready on one side, Thyri and Finnbogi on the other. Assuming the attacking force was evenly split, they'd have to face ten warriors on each side. Oh well, she thought, no point getting worked up about it. You die when you die.

The first two Scraylings appeared silently at Wulf's entrance to the clearing. One moment it was leaves and twigs, the next there were two Scraylings in warrior garb, brandishing stone hand axes. They stood clear of her husband's hammer's reach, hopping warily from foot to foot. They'd probably never seen such a large man, let alone one armed with a great lump of metal on a stick. Sassa took aim.

"What do you fellows want?" asked Wulf.

They didn't say anything.

"Only I don't want to kill you if you're here to welcome us to the area with a basket of cakes."

"Sorry, mate," said the nearer one, a small man with a squashed, pointy, narrow-eyed face. "It's not cakes." He whipped his axe into a swift strike. Wulf parried. The Scrayling weapon's stone head shattered on Hardworker iron. Wulf swept his hammer up and into the face of the second man, who fell.

The first Scrayling leapt back, scrabbling for his belt knife. Wulf glanced back to Sassa and nodded, then stood out of the way. She loosed an arrow at his chest. It hit. The man looked down at the arrow, then up at Sassa. His horrified eyes reminded her of Hrolf's, when she'd killed him. For a second she thought she might be sick, then she recovered.

Then the rest of the twenty rushed in, on both sides.

Finnbogi went down almost immediately, his legs swept away by clever club work. Thyri slashed and sliced with her sax and blocked and whacked with her shield, keeping them at bay and sending a couple staggering back, bloodied. Finnbogi scrabbled to his feet. He swung his sword at a Scrayling—a woman who looked about Gunnhild's age—but she sidestepped the blow and jabbed Finnbogi in the chin with a bony little fist. He staggered. She raised her axe for the death blow.

Wulf had told Sassa not to shoot into groups of fighters, but a woman shouldn't do everything her husband tells her. Her arrow took the Scrayling in the throat.

"Block, Finnbogi, block!" shouted Treelegs, whacking her shield into another attacker.

On the other side of the clearing, Wulf the Fat fought like Tor himself, leaping and swinging his hammer and roaring.

But there were too many.

Wulf was pressed back and back by three capable warriors, all of whom were careful to keep him between themselves and Sassa's bow.

Finnbogi was on the ground again and now Thyri too was forced back. Soon she was next to Wulf, just a few paces from Sassa, both defending more than attacking.

Sassa sought a target, but it was so frantic and they were so close now that she didn't dare shoot for fear of hitting Wulf or Treelegs.

More Scraylings poured into the clearing.

Gunnhild ran forward with a yell, swung her club and felled one, two, three attackers before a stone axe whacked into her temple with a crunch and she went down. Finnbogi was back on his feet but dazed and nobody was paying him much attention.

An axe sliced into Wulf's shoulder. Blood sprayed and he staggered, harried by two Scraylings. Thyri's legs were taken from under her and she went over. She lay on her back, lashing out with shield and sax and kicking like an upended beetle.

They'd done well. They'd killed or disabled half of the attackers, but now half a dozen stood facing Sassa, breathing hard. She was all that stood between the Scraylings and the children and Bodil. She knew they'd charge the moment she raised her bow.

To her left, Wulf finally fell. Thyri was still on her back kicking and slashing, but there were five of them circling her now.

Sassa Lipchewer raised her bow.

A Scrayling charged and she loosed an arrow at no range into his chest but there were already two more coming at her.

Behind her, Bodil screamed so loudly that it hurt Sassa's ears. Thanks, she had time to think, that's really helpful.

Erik the Angry, Keef the Berserker and Bjarni Chickenhead strode north before it was light, partly because they were keen to catch up with the others, but also because they were cold. They'd left their shirts behind on the decoys then waded a good way along the Heartberry River to put off their pursuers and never quite warmed up.

Since they'd carried on well after dark the night before, it was only now as the sun rose that they saw the vast view over the Water Mother valley.

Bjarni voiced his amazement.

Erik, keen that the other two should remember that he'd been there before, said: "The river's fuller than it was last time I was here."

"We'd be across it in no time if we'd kept my canoe," Keef muttered.

With the growing light, Erik was amazed all over again at how different the other two looked without their hair. It has taken a while to persuade them that they needed to be shorn, and even longer to persuade Keef that they had to leave his boat behind. However, going by the fact that they were alive, it seemed that his plan to fool the Owsla's forward scout with decoys had worked, so they hadn't lost their coifs or Keef's craft in vain.

But they did look very different.

Bjarni Chickenhead, shorn of his cloud of curls, had become a good-looking man, clear-eyed and strong-jawed, but he looked a lot less interesting. With his big ball of curly hair, he'd looked appealingly approachable. Now he looked like just another guy.

The effect on Keef the Berserker was less positive. The bandage over one eye and ear didn't help, but, before, when Erik had looked at Keef, he'd thought, "there's a man with long blond hair and a long blond beard." Now, he thought, "there's a man with a head that's *way* too small for his body." Blue eyes made most of the Hardworkers look more striking to Erik, especially after twenty years spent with the dark-eyed Scraylings. However, Keef's little blue eyes—well, little blue *eye* now—deep-socketed and staring out of his little round head, simply made him look all the more like a nocturnal animal forced from its den at noon.

"Bjarni, you should have kept your hair," said Keef as the track swung uphill. "You look like Baldur the brave and boring."

"And you look great," said Bjarni.

A short while later, the path forked and they had to choose between staying up on the ridge or heading down to the valley floor.

"We might find some people who've seen our friends in the valley," said Erik. "We might even meet them by the river and cross together."

"Or we might meet some people who've killed our friends

404 Angus Watson

who'll kill us, too, so we can all walk into Valhalla together,"
said Keef.

"That's also a possibility, but I think we should head
downhill."

"Yeah, you're probably right."

"I honestly don't mind," said Bjarni.

"Downhill it is."

Shortly after they'd finished their descent and were
walking through a younger, brighter, animal-noisier woodland than the one that had fringed the ridge, they heard
the scream.

They all looked at each other.

"That came—" said Bjarni.

"From up the hill. I reckon it was—" said Keef.

"Bodil."

"Yup."

"Cunt fucking cuntfuckers," said Erik. The other two
gave him strange looks and he realised that he'd reverted
to his adopted Lakchan in his frustration.

"Sorry, I mean oh no, what a blow, that came from up
the hill and we decided to take the low road. But it also
came from ahead of us, right?"

The other two nodded.

"It'll take us ages to backtrack. There must be another
way up. Come on!"

Erik ripped his club from its belt loop, not because he'd
need it immediately but to stop it banging against his leg
as he ran, and sprinted down the woodland path. The other
two thundered behind him.

They were going at such a pace that they didn't see the
Scraylings until they rounded a corner and ran right into
them.

The Calnian Owsla set off at dawn. Paloma Pronghorn zoomed
ahead as usual with the now normal request to catch and

kill a pronghorn ringing in her ears. The others followed at a fast jog. Sofi Tornado led, followed by Sitsi Kestrel, Talisa White-tail, Morningstar and Chogolisa Earthquake. Yoki Choppa trotted along at the rear.

Following Yoki Choppa's divinations, it wasn't long before Paloma skipped back with news that she'd found their trail but no pronghorns.

"All things being equal," she said, "we'll be on them in about two hours."

But all things were not equal. Yoki Choppa had said it would take between two and three days not eating their power animals for them to notice a waning in their powers.

It was day three.

Bodil Gooseface screamed with rage, jumped past Sassa Lipchewer and sank her knife into the attacker's neck. Woman and stabbed Scrayling went down in a mass of limbs and Sassa had a moment to blink in surprise that Bodil had saved her.

But things were still far from whuppity-doo.

Four more Scraylings advanced on Sassa. Wulf was sitting to one side, one arm useless, the other using his hammer to deflect the relentless blows of two Scraylings. Thyri was still on her back. One of the attackers had got hold of her foot and was battling to bring her thrashing leg under control while she kicked him with the other one. Two more were whacking away at her splintering shield with axes.

Finnbogi seemed to gather his wits. He raised his sword and charged. Sassa felt a rush of hope. He swung at a Scrayling, the Scrayling ducked, punched Finnbogi in the stomach and grabbed his sword hand. The two men wrestled.

Sassa swung her bow at the three men and one woman moving in on her. They were taking their time because they had time, but here they came, it was the end and—

"WOOOOOO-TAH!"

Garth Anvilchin charged into the clearing like an armoured buffalo, battle axe in each hand. He sliced one Biter Twin through the neck of the man struggling with Finnbogi, felled two of the Scraylings who had Thyri pinned down with a double undercut, sliced the throat out of the other, then set upon Sassa's attackers.

"Wootah!" shouted Wulf, launching himself back into the fight like a toy wooden warrior shot from a sling. He thumped his hammer into the head of one of his attackers. "Wootah!" he roared at the other, who backed away.

"Wootah!" yelled Thyri, kicking the man who held her leg in the face with her free foot. She flipped herself onto her feet, punched the Scrayling with the boss of her ruined shield then sliced her sax sideways in an almighty blow that chopped through ribs and lungs.

"Wootah!" yelled Bodil, but stayed standing next to Sassa.

The Scraylings were routed. The four who were still on their feet looked at the blood-covered, advancing Hardworkers, then at each other, then fled away up the northward path.

The Hardworkers stood, panting.

"I think maybe Wootah does work," said Garth, grinning.

Finnbogi the Boggy blinked and walked over to Gunnhild. She had a gash on her forehead from the axe blow but it had not bled overly much and she was breathing. Wulf's cut to his shoulder was nasty and deep, but not overly serious. Thyri was limping but insisting she was okay.

Nobody had been killed or badly injured, which was astonishing and showed that the silly Hird training Finnbogi had always mocked was maybe not so silly. In fact he felt pretty silly now. He'd contributed nothing. If anything, he'd got in the way. Sweat was running down his back, not from exertion but from embarrassment at how useless he'd been. Everyone else had contributed more, including Gunnhild—and Bodil!

"We have to chase those Scraylings down and stop them

bringing others," said Garth. "Finnbogi, you're fast, come with me!"

"I'll come, too," said Sassa.

"No, stay here and tend to the wounded. We'll be back soon. Come on, Finnbogi!"

You tried to kill me. I'm not coming with you. I may just have been completely useless in a fight, and you might think that I'd want to make amends, but I don't care how I look in front of Wulf, Sassa and Thyri. I am not coming—was what Finnbogi wished he had the courage to say. Instead, he said, "Let's go! Wootah!" and ran up the path. He heard Garth follow behind him.

Sofi Tornado hoped it was her imagination, but soon she knew it wasn't. She was tiring. Caribou for stamina, tarantula hawk wasp for strength. Both of those were needed for them to run all day and they'd had neither for three days. After an hour, she was slowing. She even had a twinge of pain in her hip. The hope that all the others were doing better than her was dashed when they found Paloma Pronghorn sitting on a tree trunk in a clearing, elbows on knees.

She looked up, wide-eyed and red-cheeked. "I'm sorry, I think I must be ill. I had to rest."

"I'm feeling tired, too," said Morningstar.

"Me, too," said Sitsi Kestrel, "and I think Chogolisa and Yoki Choppa have fallen behind. We all must have eaten something. I bet it was that fawn last night. I thought it looked unwell."

"Actually," sighed Sofi, "it was something we didn't eat."

"What?"

"Have a rest and wait for the other two to catch up. I'll explain when they get here."

"Oooof!" said Erik, bouncing back half a yard. The Scrayling was knocked off his feet. He lay, looking up at Erik, brown eyes enormous. Behind him another Scrayling was tiptoeing backwards, as if he hoped they hadn't seen him yet and he might sneak off. Both of them looked to be in their late teens. Neither looked like a warrior, nor a warlock. They were just everyday Scraylings.

"Sorry about that," said Erik, reaching down a hand to the felled one. "I'm in a hurry." He hauled the young man to his feet. "Have you seen a bunch of people who look like us—paler skin and lighter coloured hair than your average person? There are, what, nine of them? Couple of women, two children..."

"I'm Galenar," said the righted Scrayling. "This is Massbak. We have seen them and they're in danger."

"I'm Erik the Angry, these are Keef the Berserker and Bjarni Chickenhead. How come they're in danger?"

Galenar sighed. "Look, we're not bad people, but our tribe is going to kill them because Calnia wants them dead and we're scared of Calnia. I guess they'll want you dead, too. It was us who saw the other lot coming. We told the chief and he didn't want to kill you, but under pressure from the ruling council—which we were on—"

"We're not usually on the ruling council," interrupted Massbak.

"Shush, Massbak, that doesn't matter."

"Let's torture them, Erik, might speed things up," said Keef.

"No!" said Galenar. "We're on your side! A squad was send to kill them at sunrise. Massbak and I decided it was wrong to slaughter children and such a, well, hot woman, so we decided to warn them."

"But it's well after sunrise now," said Bjarni.

"I *know*." Galenar's head fell. "It's my fault. We tried the drink-loads-of-water-the-night-before waking method and it didn't work. It's always worked before."

"We've never tried it before."

"*Shut up*, Massbak."

"Can you give us a bit more detail?" asked Erik.

"Sure. It's based around the idea that needing to piss will wake you up. The night before—"

"Not about that. Where are our friends?"

"Oh sorry, they're on the cliff top, but it's probably too late. There's a secret path to the top. We were going to take it and see if we could save any of them. It starts about fifty paces back the way you came. It's easily missed and—"

"And you're showing us where it is, now. Come on!"

"Hang on," said Bjarni, "I know this neat trick to fool anyone tracking us. You walk backwards in your own footprints like this." He headed off backwards, gingerly stepping in his own tracks.

Not a bad idea, thought Erik, and did the same.

Garth and Finnbogi ran along the same broad path that Finnbogi had walked along the night before with Thyri. If anything, there were even more butterflies and the stink of flowers was even stronger. It wasn't nearly so lovely, though.

They passed the place where Thyri and Finnbogi had trained and ran on to another, wider clearing which was clearly some sort of shrine, with a couple of really very good giant fish woven from reeds, both looking through a gap in the trees, across a craggy cliff top and over the vast Water Mother valley.

Standing between the two fish were the four Scraylings. They looked a lot more capable than they had when they'd fled. Two had hand axes, two had stone-headed spears. Finnbogi hauled his heavy sword free of its scabbard and tried to look menacing.

"Out of the way, Boggy." Garth shouldered past and ran at the Scraylings. All hope that the big man might have genuinely wanted Finnbogi's help evaporated. The huge, armoured warrior intended to kill the Scraylings, then, surely, he'd turn on him. What could he do?

Garth whacked a spearhead away with one axe and chopped into its holder's head with the other. The other spear glanced off Garth's mail shirt. The Hardworker swung round and opened the spearman's stomach. The Scrayling fell hard onto his arse, looked down at shiny guts unravelling sloppily from a torso-wide wound, then tried to stuff them back in with both hands.

Finnbogi gagged, then coughed. He really was not much use in a battle, he thought, blinking away tears brought on by his coughing.

"Wootah," snarled Garth, heading for the other two Scraylings who cowered at the edge of the cliff.

Not a great place to cower, thought Finnbogi.

The first Scrayling yelled and ran at his armoured attacker. Garth whooshed his axes upwards in a double undercut and sliced both arms clean from the man's body. Letting his axes swing by their lanyards, Garth caught the armless man by neck and waistband as he fell, heaved him above his head, marched to the edge of the cliff, showered by his victim's blood, and hurled him off.

Wow, thought Finnbogi, despite himself.

Enjoying his own warrior magnificence a little too much, Garth had perhaps assumed that the other Scrayling would wait for death at his god-like hands. The Scrayling had his own plans. He charged. He dived and flung his arms around Garth's waist just as the Hardworker was turning to look for him. Both men went over the edge of the cliff.

Brilliant, thought Finnbogi. Not exactly how I would have done it, but well done that Scrayling. He crept to the edge of the cliff.

There was a gap in the trees and Erik saw that the path was heading straight for a cliff. He could see no obvious way up. Were they going to climb?

He gulped. The great thing about Lakchan territory, and

Hardwork, too, was that there was pretty much no way one could fall to one's death, so long as one avoided climbing trees. There were no secret paths that climbed up cliffs, for example, which, given their secret nature, were bound to be rarely trodden and badly maintained.

Something caught his eye over to the south. There was a person flying from the top of a rocky promontory, spraying dark liquid as he tumbled. The figure's arms seemed to be trussed. Or was he missing his arms? That would explain the spray. Whatever it was, it was an untimely reminder of the hideous power of gravity.

"Tor's tits," said Bjarni. "You seeing this?"

"I am."

"Good, just checking."

"I guess the fight's started."

"We'd better hurry."

"I guess we'd better," said Erik, looking up the cliff and gulping again.

Finnbogi the Boggy edged as near as he dared to the top of the cliff. He craned his neck to peer over. The Scrayling was nowhere to be seen but Garth Anvilchin, Loakie curse him, was clinging to a resilient shrub a few feet down and scrabbling his feet against loose rock.

Garth heaved like a birthing buffalo, but to no avail. He could not pull himself up. The rock was too loose and while the shrub seemed to be aggravatingly unbreakable, it was also slippery. Garth lifted his eyes to meet Finnbogi's. His meaty face was twisted with exertion, but his eyes shone with unflappable, handsome confidence. No beseeching, no pleading, only the certainty that the cowardly, does-what-he's-told loser Finnbogi the Boggy was going to help him up, even though Garth had tried to kill him two days before.

Behind Garth, and a long way down, the Water Mother flowed muddily by, the early morning light orange-brown on the mighty river's waters and golden green on its islands. Already there were several boats out. A large craft was floating downstream at a good clip and half a dozen or so smaller ones were crossing. The smaller craft seemed unaffected by the current and Finnbogi guessed that there must be a rope running right across the river. The rope must be freakishly long, light and strong, he thought, better than any rope the Hardworkers could have made.

He stood.

"What are you doing?" demanded Garth. "Where are you going? Come here now!"

"I'm fetching something to help you up." Finnbogi was shaking with hatred and excitement. This man had tried to kill him. This man had slept with Thyri.

For once, Finnbogi was going to do something brave. Although not necessarily noble.

"You can reach me with your hand, you idiot. Or use your sword, it's not like you'll ever use it for anything else. Come back here, Boggy. Now."

A spasm shook Finnbogi. By Loakie's little dick, he hated that nickname.

The Scrayling that Garth had eviscerated was whimpering and fighting a losing battle to stuff his entrails back where the Scrayling gods had put them. He saw Finnbogi coming and scrabbled for his axe. Finnbogi circled him and found the arms that Garth had chopped off his unfortunate friend.

He picked up an arm. It was surprisingly heavy. He circled the dying Scrayling again and returned to Garth.

"Here, I'll give you a hand," said Finnbogi. He jabbed the arm at his enemy's face.

Garth jinked his head to one side and grabbed the dead Scrayling's wrist. Before Finnbogi had the wherewithal to let go, Garth hauled himself up. He stood, smiling.

Finnbogi still held the other end of the arm. Skunks' tits, how ridiculous, he thought. With a jerking pull, Garth ripped the arm from his grasp and tossed it behind him, off the cliff.

Finnbogi reached for Foe Slicer's hilt.

"Go on," said Garth. "Draw."

"I've only learnt blocks so far." Finnbogi heard himself stammer. Heroic lines in difficult situations was not a strong point.

"Draw, or die unarmed."

Strike first, strike hard, that's what Thyri Treelegs had told him in his first lesson, a few days and a million years before.

Finnbogi heaved the heavy sword free of its scabbard and swung it at Garth.

Before the weapon even reached the top of its arc, Garth stepped in, grabbed Finnbogi's wrists and twisted. The sword clattered onto rock. The much taller and heavier man pushed him back, away from the cliff edge, still twisting his wrists. He felt bones grind.

"Hilarious, Boggy. You are hilariously shit."

He looked up at Garth's smiling face. He felt both enraged and weakened with hatred. "I..." he attempted.

"Don't worry," said Garth, releasing his grip and pushing him away. "I get it. I don't even blame you for trying to kill me."

"You tried to kill me first, you dick!"

"You wanted to kill me before that. You know it. I know it. You love Thyri. But she loves shagging me. She's great, by the way. The things she does, the things she begs me to do to her... some of them are disgusting, frankly, but I do it because you would not *believe* what she does in return." Garth smiled and shook his head.

Finnbogi was so angry it was an effort to stop himself bursting into tears. That would not look good. "She doesn't love you," he shouted.

"She does, Boggy, in so many ways."

Finnbogi roared and ran at Garth. A fist came from nowhere and he was reeling back, head swinging around like a toy bird on a string. He spat blood.

Garth stood, hands on hips, mail-clad chest proud and broad, early morning light glinting from his helm. He looked, as he so often had, like a hero from a saga. "You know what I really hate about you, Boggy?" he said.

"That I'm cleverer than you?"

"No! By Tor's hammer, no. It's because you think you are. You think you're cleverer than everybody. You strut around looking superior, but you have nothing to be superior about. You can't do anything. You can't fight, you can't make clothes, you can't cook, you can't even carry food without losing it. And you're not clever. What fresh or witty insights have you made to delight and amuse the rest of us? None. How many gags have you cracked recently that have left the whole group helpless with mirth? Not one. How many ideas have you contributed to accelerating our flight, avoiding the Owsla or constructing better camps? None, none and none.

"But *still* you think you're better than everyone else. You're not. You're dead weight. You're hampering our escape and, for the sake of the others, I'm going to end that now."

Garth raised his hands, big as bears' paws.

Finnbogi tried to slap his attack away, but he might as well have been trying to fight off a dagger-tooth cat. Garth grabbed the shoulder of his jerkin in one hand, the waistband of his leather trousers in the other, and swung him up, above his head, exactly as he'd done to the armless Scrayling. Finnbogi bucked and kicked and beat at irritatingly well-muscled arms, but Garth held him high.

Finnbogi couldn't do anything. He considered pissing. It was the only defence he had left. He squeezed. Nope, nothing. He couldn't even piss. Garth was right. He was useless.

Garth turned, the world spun, and Finnbogi was looking

out over the vast Water Mother valley. Yes, he found himself thinking, those boaters crossing the river are definitely pulling themselves along on ropes.

Garth took one step towards the top of the cliff, then another.

Sitsi Kestrel listened as Sofi Tornado explained where her powers came from. Sitsi had always thought that their powers were due to the years of punishing exercises, beatings and poisonings that had been their long and unpleasant Calnian Owsla induction. She'd been right about that, but she'd never guessed that they also had power animals that they had to eat every day. So this was the secret Morningstar hadn't told her.

She heard that her eyesight and resulting ability with the bow came from a western lizard called a chuckwalla. She'd been hoping for something less fat and slithery. A kestrel would have been good.

Her extensive education had taught her all the world's known animals and she'd seen many of them in Calnia's menageries, so she knew all about her chuckwalla and the other power animals. The only one that could be found in the wild anywhere near their current location—and the only power animal that was less glamorous than her own— was Chogolisa's dung beetle. Yoki Choppa had a stock of all the other animals back in Calnia. But they were a long way from Calnia.

"We should go back now," said Morningstar. "We can run to the Water Mother, take a boat and supplies. We'll be safe on the river and back in days."

"No," said Sofi. "We are still the best trained warriors in the world without the power animals, and our powers will persist—in a lesser form, but they will still give us an edge; much more than an edge. We're only a couple of miles behind Keef and the other two men, and we can be almost certain that they have arranged to meet the others to cross the Water Mother. We will carry on, we will catch them and we will kill them. We will travel at a fast walk instead of a run, we will fight as a team rather than solo exhibitionists, and we will complete our mission with ease."

"I'm not disagreeing with your rule, Sofi, and I will do what you order," complained Morningstar, "but surely our value is such to the empress and the empire that we should protect ourselves? We should go back and get the power animal flesh and this time split it into two or even three bundles like any sensible person would do with something so vital," she shot a look at Yoki Choppa that might have drilled a hole in a tree, "then come back."

"I have considered that," said Sofi, "but Ayanna thinks the Mushroom Men are going to destroy the world. Going to Calnia and back will take at least ten days. By then the Mushroom Men will have disappeared into Badlander territory and we will have lost them. If Ayanna is right, that will mean the end of the world."

"But the prophecy is a nonsense," said Paloma.

Sitsi gasped. The others all turned to stare at her. Even Yoki Choppa looked up from his alchemical bowl.

"Well, it is. Do you really think half a dozen people and a couple of children are going to destroy the world? They'd need the most amazing magic and if they had that they'd have used it against us, or at least to escape. Maybe the prophecy isn't total nonsense, maybe Mushroom Men are going to destroy the world, but do you know where this lot came from? They came across the Great Salt Sea from a land that's *teeming* with Mushroom Men. If any Mushroom Men are going to destroy the world it's the millions they left behind, not the gaggle of losers that we're pointlessly chasing."

Sitsi expected Sofi to fly at Paloma, or at least upbraid her severely, but instead the Owsla captain said: "The accu-

racy of the prophecy is irrelevant. Our orders are to kill
them. If there was a serious risk I might consider breaking
those orders, but there's hardly any more risk than there
was before. You may feel weakened, but you are all still far
more powerful than anyone else. You are also better trained,
and more then equipped to deal with a tiny group of people
famed for their laziness. Innowak willing, we will catch up
with the Mushroom Men before they cross the Water Mother.
We will kill them swiftly and mercilessly. Then we'll return
to Calnia and put this whole crappy business behind us."

Gunnhild had come to and was bandaging a poultice on
Wulf's cut shoulder. Sassa squatted to help her.

"Hugin, Munin!" came Freydis's high voice from the woods
as she and Ottar searched for the racoons.

"Where's Finnbogi?" asked Wulf.

"He's gone to chase down the surviving Scraylings with
Garth, said Sassa."

He nodded. "Go after them, will you?"

"But I'm needed here and they'll be fine, Garth is more
than capable of—"

She was stopped by Wulf's level gaze. "I'll go," she
said.

The path was worse than Erik the Angry had imagined it
could be. If you could call a vertical climb a path. It started
innocuously enough—a foot-wide track cut into the rock
face—but then that path had ended and Galenar said: "You
see the handholds here?"

"Do you mean those finger divots?"

"Yes. They're not made for giants, sorry. They're also
footholds." The young Scrayling looked at Erik's feet. "Or
at least they're meant to be. I'd take those shoes off if I were
you, then follow me."

Galenar scurried up the rock wall like a squirrel. He

reached a ledge some thirty feet above, looked down and said, "Come on!"

Erik removed his shoes, slung Turkey Friend over his shoulder, jammed three fingers into the first hold and heaved.

It wasn't too difficult to begin with, even though he could get only three fingers and two toes in most of the holds. However, by halfway up his arms felt as if they were made of soggy reeds. He pulled his face into the rock and breathed heavily. He was high enough up now that a fall would be life-ending, or at least life-altering.

"Arms tired?" shouted Massbak from a mile—or ten paces—below.

"They seem to have turned to fat."

"Happens to everyone, first few times. Rest for a minute, you'll be fine."

Erik wasn't sure they had a minute. It had been a good while now since they'd seen the Scrayling fly from the cliff, and he wasn't sure his useless arms could hold on that long. But finally some strength flowed back and he climbed to the top.

It wasn't the top, of course, that would have been too easy. It was barely a third of the way up. At least the next section was path again; not really path so much as a ledge about as wide as his hand span, but still preferable to climbing.

"Is it like this to the top?" he asked.

"No," said Galenar, pulling a plant-fibre rope away from the rock wall and shaking it. Erik looked up. The thing snaked and jiggled all the way to a point maybe thirty paces above them. "How are you climbing a rope?"

Sassa ran through the butterfly-busy, flower-scented woods, skimming over the leaf-strewn path, bow in one hand.

She stopped, heard voices ahead, and ran on.

There were three dead Scraylings in the clearing, two

large fish woven skilfully from reeds, and Garth, holding
Finnbogi above his head and striding towards the cliff edge.

"Stop!" she shouted.

Garth ignored her, walked on and stood at the top of the
drop. It gave her a sharp feeling in her groin just to see
them so near the edge. She did not like heights.

"Garth Anvilchin!"

He turned. "Hello, Sassa."

"Will you tell him to put me down?" Finnbogi asked.

"Take a few steps this way, Garth, and put him down."

"I will not."

"Please?"

"No."

"Why not?"

"Because I'm going to throw him over the edge." He bent
his arms.

Sassa pulled an arrow from her hip quiver, strung it,
drew and aimed at Garth.

"Why?"

"He's useless and he's annoying. We're better off without
him. The world's better off without him."

"He's different, Garth, not useless. He may not have found
his role in life yet, but he will. He's a good guy, let's keep
him."

"I know what his role in life is. It's to be thrown off the
cliff by me."

"I don't want to shoot you, Garth."

"Don't then. If you do, we'll both go over. It doesn't
matter about Boggy, but you don't want to lose me. All of
you would be dead if I hadn't rescued you just now. I
stopped that Scrayling from killing you back in Hardwork,
too. I've saved your life twice, Sassa Lipchewer. Don't you
dare fucking shoot me."

It was true. She would be dead twice over if it wasn't for
Garth Anvilchin. Finnbogi's greatest achievement in relation

to Sassa was shagging and upsetting her friend. She lowered her bow.

Objectively, there was nothing in it. The sole design of her life was for her and Wulf to live and have children. It had to be. Who was going to be more help to that end? Who was going to be more useful on the long trek through dangerous territory? Was it the trained-for-a-lifetime, iron-clad warrior who could dispatch two enemy warriors with one double-axe move, who'd already saved them all, or the introverted teen who'd upset her friend and been beaten by every Scrayling he'd ever fought, including an elderly woman?

Garth turned, squatted and bent his arms. He wasn't just going to drop Finnbogi off the cliff, he was going to hurl him.

"Shoot him, Sassa! Shoot him now!" shrieked Finnbogi.

Garth straightened. Finnbogi screamed.

Erik watched Galenar hold the rope, place the flats of his feet against the cliff and pretty much run up.

He copied the Scrayling, albeit more slowly. His hand-over-hand work was confident and he placed his feet firmly. It wasn't too bad to begin with.

It was like walking, only all his weight was held by the rope. The rope...

One day the rope will snap. That's a certainty, not just because everything decays but because ropes are chewed by chipmunks and other gnawing creatures. Now this particular rope, being on a secret route, is probably neglected, almost certainly never checked for signs of animal nibbling. And the rope would have been selected to bear the weight of the heaviest Scrayling. In other words someone about half his weight. If it ever does break, and it is going to, it will be when someone particularly heavy is climbing it. Someone like him. And if it breaks, when it breaks, that person will fall backwards for an age, past the pissy little path and on, to thump to the ground at the very bottom, where his back will snap and he'll lie in agony, unable to move, waiting to die.

Erik pulled himself into the cliff face and gripped onto it as tightly as if a giant eagle had squawked its intention to swoop in, rip him off, carry him up to the clouds and drop him on a rock.

"Get on with it!" yelled Keef from below.

Erik gripped his handholds all the harder. He wasn't going to get on with anything.

"Move your fat arse!" encouraged Keef.

Erik could feel snot running over his lip, but to wipe it he'd have to move.

So you're going to stay here for ever? asked an internal voice, this one sounding like Astrid, not the bear but the human who'd betrayed him then died giving birth to Finnbogi.

Piss off, he told it.

A girlish shriek cut through his musing, this one real, not in his head, coming from the top of the cliff.

It was Finnbogi! His son! In trouble! He thrust himself away from the cliff and shinnied up the rope spider-style. At the top he bounced onto his feet, pushed past Galenar and sprinted southwards.

"Wait for the others!" called Galenar.

Finnbogi's fall was interrupted by the ground sooner and less life-endingly that he'd expected. He opened his eyes.

He'd fallen away from the edge, and thumped down onto the body of a Scrayling. He sat up. Garth was at his feet, eyes crossed, looking downwards at the dully glinting, bloodied iron tip of the arrow that protruded from his mouth like a metal-tipped, fly-catching frog's tongue.

"Lucky he fell this way." Sassa was walking towards him, bow in hand.

"It was," he said.

"You're welcome," she said.

"I can't believe you did it."

"He's not the first cunt I've killed."

What!? Finnbogi's mind screamed. For a hot and confusing flash he fancied Sassa Lipchewer about a thousand times more than he'd ever fancied Thyri Treelegs. Who else had she killed? And she'd said cunt!

"Are you all right?" said Erik, running into the clearing.

"Just in time, Dad," said Finnbogi.

"Looks like you dealt with the Scraylings."

"Yup."

"Shame they killed Garth."

"He fought well."

His father walked over to the big corpse and poked him with a toe. "That Hardwork arrow through the back of his head must have hampered him a bit, though." He looked at Sassa.

"He was about to throw me off the cliff," Finnbogi blustered. "Sassa saved me."

"I don't believe you."

"It's the truth, I swear."

"I'll never believe you. I believe he fell off the cliff saving you from Scraylings."

"I got here just in time to see it happen, but too late to help," said Sassa.

Finnbogi held Garth's head while Erik wiggled and wrenched the arrow out of his skull, then the two of them rolled the corpse of the man that a gorgeous woman had killed to save his life off the cliff. It was bonding activities like this, he thought, that he'd missed, growing up without a dad.

When she arrived with Finnbogi, Erik, Bjarni, Keef and the two Scraylings, Wulf the Fat's face cracked into the first genuine Wulf smile that Sassa had seen for a good few days. The giant smile gave way to concern when he saw Keef's bandages.

"A scratch," said Keef. "Just a flesh wound."

"A flesh removal more like," said Bjarni. "The Owsla took an ear and an eye."

"*The lame can ride a horse, the one-handed can drive cattle; tis better to be blinded than be a corpse,*" said Gunnhild.

"Did they take your hair, too?" Wulf asked.

"No, that's a different story."

"I look forward to it," said Wulf, then: "Where's Garth?"

Sassa went to busy herself with the children and their racoons, so Wulf couldn't look her in the eye while Erik lied to him.

She wasn't sure that she'd done the right thing. She'd shot Garth and saved Finnbogi out of instinct. Would she have made the same decision if she'd had more time...? Probably. Letting Garth live and letting him kill Finnbogi would have made more practical sense, and maybe she'd regret her decision when all that stood between her and a dozen murderous Scraylings was a trembling Finnbogi the Boggy, but saving him had seemed the right thing to do. Despite it all, she liked Finnbogi.

"I see," said Wulf at the end of Erik's explanation, sounding grim. He knew. She'd tell him what had happened one day, and he'd understand. After all, he'd pretty much sent her off to do it.

"And who are these two?" He gestured at Galenar and Massbak, who were staring with horror at their dead tribe mates.

"They're from the Water Divided tribe. They're going to help us cross the Water Mother. Unless this has changed your minds?" Erik nodded at the corpses.

"Well, it's not great," admitted Galenar, "but they shouldn't have attacked you. We'll still help, won't we, Massbak?"

"Sure, providing we don't run the slightest risk of getting caught."

"Why do you want to help us?" said Wulf. He didn't sound combative, only interested.

Sassa tensed, expecting someone to rush forward, call Galenar and Massbak Scrayling scum, put a knife to their throats and demand a motive, but Thyri, Keef, Bjarni and the rest of them all waited with open expressions, ready to listen and to consider their answers.

Gunnhild said: "*I was journeying and I lost my way, then I met another; Man is the joy of man.*"

Sassa realised with a sense of surprise and guilty relief that all the narrow-minded, aggressive men who'd turn a meeting like this into a confrontation—Garth Anvilchin, Gurd Girlchaser, Fisk the Fish and Hrolf the Painter—were dead. She felt bad about it even as she admitted it to herself, particularly as she'd killed two of them, but the idea that she'd never have to deal with those argumentative, mean pricks again made her feel a lot lighter. Chnob the White and Frossa the Deep Minded were gone, too...

It was almost like someone, Finnbogi, for example, was killing all the people he didn't like. Ridiculous theory, of course, when he'd had nothing to do with any of their deaths and she'd topped two of them herself, but still, he'd been nearby every time...

"We're part of the Calnian empire," said Galenar. "We're meant to be a semi-independent tribe that pays tribute to Calnia, but really we are very much what one might call their bitches. Calnia has ordered us to kill you, so we do, with no respect to your spirits, your spirit animals or your gods. We don't know who or what you are, so we really should not kill you as if we were gods ourselves, dropping wanton death from a great height. That would be evil. So, I am sorry that one of yours has died, and, honestly, I'm

more sorry that so many of ours have, too. However, we see
it as our duty to help you to escape the Calnians."

"Provided we can get away with it," added Massbak.

"That is a secondary consideration, but, yes, our tribe
must not find out."

Wulf gripped the young Scrayling's shoulder. "Good news
and we're grateful."

The friendly Water Divided tribesmen pointed out the
two lines of boats crossing the Water Mother and explained
that there were two ropes across the river, strung between
islands, for people to pull boats across.

"I knew it! But why two ropes?" asked Finnbogi.

"Because you can cross the river in two directions," said
Galenar.

Finnbogi coloured a little.

"How come they don't break?" asked Keef.

"We make good ropes."

"How?"

"Not now, Keef," said Wulf.

The eastern ends of both ropes were in the main Water
Divided settlement, so they couldn't start there. However,
said Galenar, they could find boats further south, paddle
these across the narrow channel to the first island, then
carry their canoes along the island to the rope, wait for a
gap, and go. Once on the rope, provided they didn't arse
about, they should look like any other boat. On the far bank
they'd find a small settlement.

"The Other-Siders won't be a problem. Anyone bright or
capable moves to this side of the river. The Other-Siders
won't do anything except gawp at you."

"What's the best way down the cliff?" asked Wulf.

"The best way is to the north. There's a good path there.
However, unfortunately for you, it runs down to the main
village and is visible for most of the way to people who'll

be working in the fields or out performing their morning rituals. You'll have to go back the way we came, down the secret path."

"Great," said Erik the Angry.

Chapter Ten

She Just Keeps Rolling Along

"Big cat's pissflaps!" said Paloma Pronghorn. "I thought their prints were odd. They've done the walking back in their own footsteps thing. Why didn't I pick that up?" She shook her head. "Outfoxed by Mushroom Men. Whatever power animal made us clever, we need to find it again, now."

"We're near the Water Divided tribe's chief settlement," said Sofi Tornado. "We'll press on and see what they know."

"Have you seen the Mushroom Men?" demanded Sofi when they arrived in the centre of the village shortly afterwards. A group of Water Divided seniors had assembled hastily to meet them.

"You hold on right there!" A small, purple-faced warlock with about six hairs of beard broke from the group and bustled up to the Calnian captain. "There are protocols. You may be the Owsla but you cannot march into *our* territory and—"

Sofi Tornado swung her axe backhanded into his jaw. He flew for a couple of paces, crashed down onto packed earth and lay still.

Yup, thought the captain, I am definitely weaker. She'd had to put strength into the blow. A few days before it would have needed only a flick. The lack of tarantula hawk wasp was telling.

Another idiot charged, a woman red-faced with rage, presumably the little man's wife or daughter. The Owsla captain stepped aside, tripped and pushed her towards Chogolisa Earthquake. The giant Calnian encircled the Water Divided woman's head with the long, strong fingers of one hand, and looked at Sofi.

Having her head crushed like a robin's egg would have been a fitting punishment for attacking the Owsla. However, Sofi shook her head. Chogolisa shrugged and let the woman go.

"Everybody calm down!" cried a wise-looking older fellow. "I am Chief Dyas Bellvoo. Calnian Owsla, please don't harm any more of my people. And my people, stay back and stay quiet. The Mushroom Men are camped on yonder bluff." He pointed at the cliff to the east. "Following the request of a Calnian runner, I have sent a squad to kill them. They should have returned by now. I was about to send scouts to find out what has happened. Perhaps you would like to go instead?"

Canny, thought Sofi. She'd bumped off one of his tribe in front of him, and instead of panicking he was not only controlling his own tribe, but ordering her about, too. They didn't make any old idiot their leader, these little northern tribes.

"One of your warriors will show us the way."

"All the available warriors are already up there."

"Then you will show us the way." She may have been lacking some of her normal aggression, but there was only so much that Sofi Tornado was prepared to put up with. "And while we are gone, you," she pointed at the most capable looking member of their greeting gang, "will find me any parts of the following animals: caribou, diamondback rattlesnake, tarantula hawk wasp, burrowing owl, pronghorn, broad-tailed hummingbird, mantis shrimp and chuckwalla."

"Uh, what?" said the slack-jawed provincial, "what do you...? Caribou? Uh?"

"Never mind," she sighed, "Yoki Choppa, stay here and see what you can find in their stores, from the river merchants, whatever. Talisa, stay with him. And find the biggest canoe you can. If Innowak is with us for once our mission will be complete and we'll be heading down the Water Mother to Calnia before noon."

Bjarni enjoyed the climb down the cliff even less than he'd enjoyed the climb up it, but watching Freydis and Ottar descend like happy chipmunks helped. If two children weren't scared, then neither was he. At one point he missed a handhold, almost fell and had to swallow hard to prevent himself from vomiting in terror, but apart from that it wasn't too bad.

Erik the Angry came down last, white as a winter hare in a blizzard, insisting he'd enjoyed the descent.

Galenar and Massbak led them through the woods. They ducked under branches and held back bushes for each other, following the stony course of a dry stream. The woods either side were busy with turkeys which freaked Bjarni out with their sudden fluttering and gobblings. The females skedaddled but the fat males stood their ground and fanned their tails pompously.

At the edge of the woods they waited while the two Scraylings checked that there was nobody about, then headed out, blinking in the morning light, onto a wooden pontoon which was chock-a-block with neatly arranged, upside-down canoes. Below the pontoon the muddy river churned.

Wulf insisted on hugging Galenar and Massbak, which Bjarni thought was appropriate, but which the two young Water Divided tribesmen did not seem to enjoy at all, and then the Wootah tribe were off, in two boats.

The current was stronger than it looked, but it was only twenty paces to the first island and they powered across easily enough.

Safely ashore, they waved a final goodbye to their two Scrayling helpers and carried their boats up the island to join the rope.

Bjarni crouched in the bushes next to Wulf while they waited for a gap, watching the technique of the people pulling themselves across.

The east to west rope ran through a hoop on a post at the end of their island, twenty paces from their hiding place. The west to east rope was a couple of hundred of paces to the north, running between a different set of islands.

"They'll be able to see us from the other rope," said Bjarni.

"Yes," said Wulf, "but to check us out they'll have to let go, come down on the current, catch our rope, catch us up, then go all the way back across on our rope, then back across on theirs. That's too much of a shag; we're not that interesting. Here, we've got a gap. Let's go."

Finnbogi waited while Wulf, Sassa, Erik, Bjarni and Freydis launched in one boat, then carried the second forward with Keef, Bodil, Gunnhild, Thyri and Ottar.

"I'll go at the back," he announced.

Keef shook his head. "Ah-ah. Strongest at the front, that's me. Second strongest goes at the back."

"Which is me," said Thyri.

"Are you sure? I listened to the tips you gave me when we crossed the Rock River and I—"

"Quiet, Finnbogi," said Gunnhild. *"The man who is never silent utters many futile words; if not checked, he will often sing himself to harm."*

*   *   *

The Calnian Owsla reached the top of the cliff path. Morningstar was distraught. She wasn't exhausted by any means, or even tired after the climb, but her legs felt like they'd done *some* work. Usually she'd have to run a hundred miles to feel like this. Normal people must feel *even worse* than this after a bit of exercise, she thought. How *awful* to be them. She could not wait to be back in Calnia with their power animals.

"Where are you, Mushroom Men?" she called. "Come out, come out to play!"

"Nearly there!" called Chief Dyas Bellvoo. "But it's something of a worry that we haven't passed my own people coming back."

Sofi Tornado nodded, grim-faced. *She* didn't look at all tired, Morningstar noticed. She looked mean as a bobcat whose tail has been in a snare for a day and a night. There'd be no mucking about this time. The Mushroom Men would all be dead moments after they caught up with them.

They jogged along the cliff-top path until they came to a clearing full of dead people in warrior garb. None of them were Mushroom Men.

"Who are these demons?" said Chief Dyas Bellvoo, staring at his attack squad, voice catching in his throat.

"*Where* are these demons?" snarled Sofi.

"There they are," piped up Sitsi Kestrel, standing on a rocky promontory. A pair of young whitecap eagles was gliding lazily above her. Beyond were the brown river, green trees and blue sky of the Water Mother's immense valley. She was pointing at the two canoes near the beginning of the rope-pull across the Water Mother.

"You're sure?" asked Sofi.

"It's so strange," the little woman blinked her big eyes, "I can't see clearly, but I am very nearly certain it's them."

"Good. Let's go."

"But if they get to the other side of the Water Mother...?" asked Talisa White-tail.

"They won't get far."

"But Calnians don't cross..."

"We're the Owsla. We go where we want."

They ran, leaving Chief Dyas Bellvoo standing among his dead.

Pulling the boat across was trickier than it looked. The vast body of brown water was more like moving land than a river, determined to carry the tiny canoes downstream on its eternal flow. It did not make for easy boat handling, and by the time Finnbogi and the others in the second boat worked out that pulling against the current was as important as pulling across it, the first boat was a hundred paces ahead.

"This will not do!" declared Keef. "Come on everybody. Heave! Heave!"

Finnbogi pulled until his arms hurt. He wanted to slow the pace, but Bodil, in front of him in the boat, was pulling on the rope with lean, tanned arms, as if she'd been born on the river.

He still hadn't had the talk with her that Sassa had insisted that he must, but Bodil had stopped pestering him, so he reckoned that ignoring her must have done the trick just as effectively as telling her he didn't like her, with a lot less meanness to her and a lot less effort on his part. So everybody was happy.

By the time they'd reached the second island, perhaps halfway across the river, they'd narrowed the gap with the forward Wootah boat to fifty paces.

"Perhaps we should reduce the pull rate a little for the next section?" said Finnbogi as they manoeuvred around the rope's holding post. "We'll have a long way to walk on the other side and—"

"Look behind you, Boggy," said Keef.

He turned. "Loakie's cock..." he said.

*　　*　　*

The first Owsla canoe was gaining on the Mushroom Men like a pack of wolves running down a broken-legged buffalo calf. Chogolisa Earthquake and Talisa White-tail in the second canoe were falling behind, but that wasn't a worry. Sofi Tornado, Morningstar, Paloma Pronghorn and Sitsi Kestrel would slaughter the Mushroom Men quite happily on their own.

Yoki Choppa had found two power animals in the Water Divided tribe's market—caribou and mantis shrimp—so their stamina would be boosted back to normal levels, and Morningstar's ability to punch people into a bloody pulp would be restored. It was more than Sofi had expected but not as much as she'd hoped.

On the bright side, they were catching the Mushroom Men. They'd be on the back boat easily before it had crossed the river and the others would not get far.

She heaved and heaved on the rope. Was her stamina returning already after the tiny morsel of caribou that Yoki Choppa had fed them all? She thought so. Her muscles were certainly singing with the joy of the work.

Heave, heave, they gained with every heave. So much water was coming over the prow that she had Yoki Choppa on permanent bailing duty, using the scooped paddle that served both as a bailer and emergency propulsion if they should lose the rope.

The nearest Mushroom Man boat reached the second island and she saw them turn to look at her. That's right, she grinned, we're coming.

Heave, heave, heave! Finnbogi's arms were burning hideously, striving to match the relentless rhythm set by Keef and Bodil in front of him. His back was screaming in protest with the twist and strain. His hands were stinging; blistered and bleeding from pulling on the wet rope.

They'd sped up a lot. Because the rope bowed with the

current, the Owsla had been obscured by the island last time he looked back, and now he didn't want to look because all he could do was heave, heave, heave! What they'd do the other side, he had no idea, but they *had* to get there.

Gunnhild was panting like a dying buffalo behind him. Behind her, Ottar was bailing water from the canoe and singing a high-pitched, strange but surprisingly tuneful song. Gunnhild and Ottar! Why for the love of Loakie was he in a canoe with those two dead weights? Although, to give them their due, they were both working hard, and they were catching up to Wulf, Sassa, Bjarni, Erik and Freydis in the forward canoe.

"Owsla coming in canoes!" shouted Keef when they were within earshot of the others.

The forward boat put on a sprint, and soon Finnbogi's canoe wasn't catching up any more.

"Innowak's burning beak!" Sofi Tornado cursed as they rounded the second island. The Mushroom Men had piled on the pace and were only a little closer than the last time she'd seen them. It was less certain that they'd catch up before they'd crossed the river. Still, the Owsla would land moments afterwards and have them.

Unless...

If the Mushroom Men did reach the other side first, there was something screamingly obvious that they could do to once again delay their inevitable capture.

But there was also something she could do to prevent that from happening.

"Sitsi, stop pulling and be ready with your bow!" she yelled over her shoulder.

"I am always ready with my bow," Sitsi replied, letting go of the rope and preparing her bow in direct contravention of her claim.

*   *   *

Sassa bent over, hand on her knees and sucked in heaving, panting breaths. The world span around her and she was certain she was going to die right there on the river bank. Finally her breathing calmed enough and she was able to stand straight and take in her surroundings. Foul an owl, the pulling had been an absolute duck fucker.

The boat containing Keef, Bodil, Finnbogi, Gunnhild, Ottar and Thyri was fifty paces from shore. The first Owsla boat was maybe a hundred paces behind that, and gaining.

"We are not going to cut the rope," Erik was saying to Wulf, fists on hips.

"Of course we're going to cut the rope, the moment the others reach the bank," Wulf replied. "They'll restring it easily enough."

"That will take an age, and bugger everyone about. No, we must respect the ways of the river crossing. Besides, you die when you die. It will make no difference to our fate whether we cut the rope or not."

Sassa thought this was pushing the "you die when you die" thing a bit. Sure, the Norns set the day of your death, but it didn't mean you could run off a cliff or drive a spike into your eye and expect to not die because it wasn't your day. Except, if you did, surely the Norns had known that you were going to be such a tit so in fact that *was* the day of your death...

"What do you think, Sassa?" asked Wulf. "Should we cut the rope?"

The river crossing rope sprang taut from the stump around which it was wound, in the middle of a mess of boat equipment. The chaos of kit was a stark contrast to the orderly pontoon that they'd set off from.

Several local Scraylings—"Other-Siders" Galenar had called them—were standing at a safe distance and staring at the newcomers as if they were sharks that had walked out of the river shaking tortoise-shell rattles and singing a song about ocelots.

She picked up the end of a coil of rope that was part of the riverside detritus. It was light and strong.

"Well?" asked Wulf.

"I'm sure Sassa agrees with me. We must not cut the rope," said Erik. "We've already killed a large number of the Water Divided tribe. If we ruin their means of getting across the river as well... What kind of people does that make us?"

Sofi Tornado was beginning to feel it in her arms and her back, so perhaps the gap in regular caribou consumption was taking its toll, but they were still gaining on their prey.

The woman, girl and three men from the first boat clambered out on the far bank. They could cut the rope now, but it would mean abandoning over half their group. They wouldn't do that...

"Sitsi, anyone on the shore looks like they're going to cut the rope, put an arrow in them."

Sassa Lipchewer saw the Owsla archer kneel up in the canoe and bring her bow to bear. The second Wootah boat was thirty paces from shore, the first Owsla boat not far behind. The second Owsla boat, containing the giant and one other, was a long way behind.

"Give me your hammer, now!" she yelled. Wulf proffered it to her questioningly and she snatched it. Pulling her obsidian knife from its sheath, she dived and sliced at the crossing rope. As the twine sprang apart, something hit her.

Sofi Tornado saw the woman dive. Sitsi Kestrel loosed an arrow. The rope, which had been so firm and vital in her hands, went limp. Everything was still for an instant, then the current had them and they were propelled sideways at a shocking speed.

"Give the paddle to Morningstar, Yoki Choppa!" she

ordered. "Morningstar, paddle as if your life depended on it."

All was far from lost. The second Mushroom Man boat was caught in the current, too. Keef the Berserker at the prow *was* paddling as if his life depended on it, which in his case it did, but it didn't matter. The mantis shrimp-powered Morningstar had more strength in her arms than twenty Keefs. They would catch up and put arrows in all of them. Then it wasn't far to shore and the others.

Sassa touched her head and found blood, but it was only a shallow cut. The Owsla arrow had nicked her and lodged in the stump. A tuft of her hair sprouted from its entry point like a decoration.

She looked up to call to Wulf, but he was already kneeling next to her, doing what she had been planning to do. While all the rest of them were still gawping at the second boat which she'd seemingly abandoned, Wulf had grabbed a spare rope and was tying one end to the shaft of his hammer. He winked at her, then whirled his hammer around his head.

Morningstar paddled like a god. The canoe sliced a white tear through the brown water towards the western bank of the Water Mother.

Paloma Pronghorn, freed from the irksome business of pulling on the rope, sat back and watched the Mushroom Men on the shore. Wulf the Fat—her friend from the Rock River, as she thought of him—was whirling his hammer on a rope above his head. Not a bad idea, she thought, but even if it worked perfectly and they towed their friends ashore, Morningstar would have the Owsla on the bank not long afterwards. The current was seriously powerful so they'd be a fair way downriver, but this time the Mushroom Men would not escape.

She turned to check on the other Owsla crew, just in time to see Chogolisa Earthquake reach for something outside the canoe, overbalance and plunge into the water with a great splash, taking Talisa White-tail and the boat over with her. The canoe's prow thrust above the surface then sank. Chogolisa's head and flailing arms emerged from the swift, silt-heavy water. Talisa's did not.

"Tornado!"

"Not now, Pronghorn." The leader's eyes were fixed on her quarry.

"We have to turn back."

"What?"

"The other boat is over. Chogolisa is afloat but I can't see Talisa."

The hammer flew over their heads, Finnbogi half leapt and grabbed the rope. Keef got a hand to it—which he was able to do only because Finnbogi had caught it—and cleated it to the front of the boat.

Wulf, Erik and Bjarni pulled like heroes and the craft bounced across the water. But the Owsla couldn't be that far behind. Finnbogi turned.

The Owsla *were* that far behind. They were heading back east, already taken a hundred paces south by the current.

"They've turned!" he shouted.

They all looked.

"But why?" Keef asked.

"Calnians don't cross the Water Mother," grinned Gunnhild. "They must have been hoping to catch us before we got to the far bank. When they saw they weren't going to, they turned."

By the time they'd reached the shore and clambered out, the Owsla boat was out of sight behind an island, far downstream.

"Erik was right!" shouted Bjarni. "Calnians do not cross the Water Mother!"

"I didn't know it was that hard a rule," said Erik, scratching his chin. "Maybe there was some other reason? We can't assume their pursuit is over." He looked warily at the Scraylings gathered around, but they were keeping a fearful distance.

"Don't worry, Erik, we'll still be careful," Wulf grinned. "Come on everyone, the chase is over! Let's go! Woooooo-tah!"

He then paused, not certain where they should go.

"You headed west?" asked the eldest of the Other-Siders, craning his neck at them. "Most strangers come out of the river are headed west." He spoke the universal tongue slowly, in an accent coated with river mud.

"We are," said Wulf. "Is there a path?"

"Walk a few hundred paces south of here, you'll find a little path off to the right, next to a dead tree with a big bees' nest in it."

"Right."

"You do not want to take that path, it's a nasty climb up the cliff and I doubt your little ones will enjoy it. Or the older lady."

"I see."

"You want to go north."

"Do I?"

"Yes. Nice road for three miles. Little bit after a walkway over some marsh, you'll find a lovely broad path turning back southwards and up the bluff. You won't miss it if you're looking for it. It's a longer way up the bluff, a good bit longer than the other path, but that way up the cliff, oh it's nasty. I haven't been up the cliff path myself for twenty years and I still remember the last time I did it."

"I see, thanks!" said Wulf.

"You're very welcome," replied the toothless man. "Did the Other-Siders send you?"

"They call you the Other-Siders."

"They do? Why's that?"

Sassa found herself walking next to Keef the Berserker on the path up out of the valley and away from their old lives. Walking? She was fairly bouncing.

They'd escaped the Owsla! She hadn't realised what a terrible weight the constant fear of death had been until it was removed. Now she felt like she could fly.

There was one niggle, or two to be precise. Two niggles called Hrolf the Painter and Garth Anvilchin. There was only one thing she could do about her two murders, she decided there and then, and that was to absolve herself wholeheartedly and unreservedly of any wrongdoing.

Several billion tons of sluggish brown, constantly renewing Water Mother separated her and the Wootah tribe from the old world of the Hardworkers. It was a fresh life on this side of the river, a new start, all their old problems left behind on the far bank. Goodbye, Hardwork—and anything she might have done as a Hardworker.

Goodbye Hardwork.

Hello, Wootah tribe.

Hello, dare she think it, babies.

Of course, some of them had left more than regrets and guilt east of the Water Mother.

"How are your missing ear and eye?" she asked Keef.

"I don't know. Haven't seen them for a while. Probably eaten by a badger or something by now."

"Bits of *you*? Surely not. They're going to be eaten by a lion at the least. Probably a dagger-tooth cat."

"You're right. Badgers don't eat hero."

"How are the holes where those bits used to be?"

"Healing nicely, thanks. I can see and hear just as well as before."

"Really? That's amazing."

"What? Who's there?"

Sassa laughed.

"Sight is odd, to be honest," said Keef, "kind of smaller. I've got to move my head around to see what's going on. And with my hearing, I have a bit of an echo and it's harder to work out where noise is coming from . . . but all in all it's not too bad. I reckon we should all chop off an eye and an ear. It would be a good tribal mark."

"I can think of better ones."

"Like both eyes and both ears?"

"I was thinking whole head. It would be an original look and we'd never have to worry about catching our hair on low branches again."

"Or poking ourselves in the eye when we're eating."

"Indeed."

"People would think twice about messing with people tough enough to cut their own heads off."

"And if they did attack we wouldn't have to duck any head shots."

They were quiet for a minute, then Keef said: "How do you think they'll string the rope back across the river?"

"I don't know."

"Here's how I'd do it. First I'd get a smaller rope. Made of what, you might ask? There are a few choices. First up—"

"Wootah!" said Sassa.

"What?"

"Nothing, just trying something."

"Right. Anyway, as I was saying, there are a few material options for your first, lighter rope, each of which has positives and negatives. The most obvious choice would be . . .'

Not everything, thought Sassa, was different west of the Water Mother.

* * *

They didn't find Talisa White-tail.

As Morningstar propelled them back across the Water Mother, they watched Chogolisa Earthquake dive down again and again, even though she was a terrible swimmer and had never dived under the water before. Eventually she'd had to give in and swim to an island, where Sofi and the others found her, sitting on the mud shore, exhausted and weeping into her hands.

"The rope slipped and I was trying to grab it and..." she stammered as they arrived. "I looked, but you can't see a thing under that water and—"

"It's not your fault, Chogolisa. The woman who cut the rope is to blame and she will pay. Come on."

Sitsi Kestrel watched her captain and saw what she expected—a darted, angry glare at Yoki Choppa. It wasn't just the Mushroom Man archer's fault. Talisa White-tail's blood was on four people's hands.

Chogolisa could be forgiven, because dropping the rope and reaching for it had to have been an accident.

The woman who'd cut the rope had done what anybody fleeing for their lives would have done, and the cutting of the rope hadn't directly killed Talisa White-tail. She could be forgiven, too. A moot point, perhaps, since they were going to kill her anyway, but a point all the same.

Sitsi had missed the shot that would have stopped the woman cutting the rope, but nobody could have made that shot. Nobody, apart from her perhaps, *if* she'd been eating her power animal every evening.

Yoki Choppa's negligence in keeping all their power animals in one place had slowed them down and prevented them catching the Mushroom Men on the Calnian side of the Water Mother. It had prevented them pulling fast enough to catch the Mushroom Men boats, and it had reduced her ability to put an arrow in a woman who was diving for a rope. He should have split his cache and given some to other people to carry.

The person who could be held accountable for Talisa's death was Yoki Choppa.

By the look in her eye, Sofi Tornado agreed. Once they'd caught up with the Mushroom Men yet again, and surely killed them this time, there was going to be a reckoning between Sofi Tornado and Yoki Choppa. Most likely, there was going to be a slaying.

Morningstar paddled to the west bank of the Water Mother with Chogolisa holding the back of the canoe and floating along behind. Nobody spoke. They ran north, to the west bank settlement of the Water Divided tribe.

"They went that away," said the eldest of the group of villagers who gathered to goggle at them. He pointed northwards out of the village.

"Thanks," said Sofi Tornado.

"You'll be hoping to catch them up?" The old man cocked his head and opened one eye wide, as if he'd asked an exceptionally incisive question.

"We will."

"Are they friends or do you mean them harm?"

"We mean them harm."

"Good. *Horrible* they were. Funny coloured skin. And that hair? It turned my stomach to look at them. Who knows what trouble those deviants will cause? Had two racoons following them. It was unnatural. They'll kill us all and defile our corpses, I wouldn't wonder. We won't sleep easy tonight knowing they're nearby. You going to kill 'em?"

"Yes."

"Good. Go back south a quarter of a mile and you'll find a path west next to a dead tree with a bees' nest in it. Fit young women like you will make it up that cliff without a bother. Three miles after the top of the cliff your path'll join a bigger one. That's the path they're on. Go now and go quickly and you'll get ahead of 'em."

"Thank you."

"I hope you do kill 'em all. When you're done, come back 'ere. I've fifteen grandsons, eight unmarried. Some of them might like you more muscly type women."

"How charming. We'll be certain to come back this way."

Chapter 11
Ambush

Usually Paloma Pronghorn would have been up the cliff and away before the others were pondering their second handhold, but she'd hung back to help Chogolisa Earthquake, who'd never been the best of climbers, and was rendered even more clumsy by her reduced power and by her distress at killing Talisa.

"It wasn't your fault," Paloma said when she saw a tear running down Chogolisa's smooth cheek. "I've explained why about nine times now, so I'm just going to repeat the words 'it wasn't your fault' until you've got it. Got it?"

The big woman nodded and sniffed.

"Good. It wasn't your fault."

They carried on up.

At the top they jogged along a vegetation-hemmed track.

"It wasn't your fault," said Paloma.

Paloma Pronghorn wasn't that fussed by Talisa White-tail's death. In all their years of training she'd never actually had a conversation with her and wasn't going to miss her too much. In fact, she felt positively cheerful. She was, despite it all, having a lovely day. She couldn't run as fast as before but it didn't matter. She was out in the beautiful world having an adventure with her friends. She was young, healthy and happy.

She had a bizarre urge to hug someone.

Her overhappiness was, of course, entirely a result of not eating power animals. If you ingest and assume the characteristics of a snake and a wasp, she reasoned, it's hardly going to make you more skippy. They hadn't made her exactly unhappy, but she did feel explosively joyful without them.

It did pose a problem, though.

They had to kill the Mushroom Men. She was fine with that, she wanted to get back to Calnia and the Mushroom Men had to die before she could do that. But the idea of actually physically whacking and slicing the Mushroom Men to death, especially the children and her friend from the Rock River, sickened her a little and was even in danger of souring her fine mood.

They arrived at the wider track that the old fellow had said the Mushroom Men would be taking. Nobody had walked on it for a couple of days, so they jogged west until they found a suitable ambush spot where the path followed a stream. The watercourse was bordered by hip-high grassland for about thirty paces, beyond which the valley sides were wooded.

Sofi sent Paloma and Morningstar into the trees on the north side of the valley and told them to wait for the signal, which would be Sitsi Kestrel shooting the leading Mushroom Man.

Sitsi was sent to the south side of the valley and Chogolisa further east along the path to block any retreat. Sofi headed to the west with Yoki Choppa.

"Will you kill the children if they're on our side of the valley, please?" Paloma whispered to Morningstar once they were hidden in the trees.

"How come you don't want to do it? You're usually overjoyed to send people into a better world."

"Not this time."

"I don't want to do it."

"You, too?"

Morningstar looked her in the eye and nodded. "I guess we're missing those power animals."

"I'm not sure I want the power to kill kids without caring."

"I don't know. The sooner we're back in Calnia and everything's back to normal, the better. It's a shame Talisa drowned. She would have killed the children. She didn't need to eat a snake to make her a bitch."

"But, ironically, she was too much of a bitch to eat snake. That's what one guy told me anyway. Talisa the Receiver he called her."

Morningstar snorted a laugh through her nose. "Seriously, though, let's leave the children to Sofi. If we kill an adult or two each, she won't notice."

"She notices everything."

"I suppose, but it's not our fault Yoki Choppa lost our power animals. So long as they all get killed she won't mind."

Sitsi Kestrel waited in the shade of the trees on the edge of the shallow valley, opposite Paloma and Morningstar. It was the perfect ambush spot and it was nice and cool.

After an age she heard the clang of metal on metal from somewhere down the valley. That surely meant they were almost there? By Innowak, the Mushroom Men moved slowly.

They appeared shortly afterwards. The tall man with golden hair led, alongside the woman with even shinier golden hair, the one who'd cut the rope. They were sauntering along, chatting away as if they were lovers out for a stroll. It seemed almost a shame to kill them. But Tornado had asked her to start the attack, and it meant that they could all go home.

She'd make it quick. She strung an arrow, drew, and aimed for the big man's heart.

West of the Water Mother, the grass was greener, the sky bluer, the air fresher and there were even more animals. A small mammal or bird perched on every rock and branch, staring at the passers-by. A black bear and her cub lolloped away into the trees. The big yellow and black bumble bees that had once terrified Finnbogi buzzed enchantingly between yellow, blue and pink flowers. A family of deer approached them with no apparent fear, but Hugin and Munin scared them off with sharp yickers.

This idyllic valley, thought Finnbogi the Boggy, was surely The Meadows. He could see himself being very happy here with the rest of them, especially with Thyri Treelegs...

"Tell me what happened to Garth," asked his true love to be, catching up.

"He was pushed over a cliff by a Scrayling."

"How did it happen?"

"There were four of them. He told me to stay out of the way while he took them on. He killed three of them, the third one by chopping his arms off and throwing him off the cliff. He was turning round after doing that when the fourth one hit him at a run. They both went flying over the edge."

"You're sure he died?"

"I looked over the edge. He was lying on bare rock at the base of the cliff, arms spread, puddle of blood around his head, dead as can be."

Thyri leapt in front of him. He stopped. She took both his hands and stared at him as if she was trying to see inside his skull.

Finnbogi congratulated himself. Everything that he'd told her was one hundred per cent true. She wasn't going to see any lying in his eyes.

"That's what happened," he said.

"All right, but Finnbogi—"

"Call me Finn."

"All right, Finn. If I find out that you killed Garth, Finn, or helped him to his death in any way, then I will kill you, Finn. Is that clear, Finn?"

"I'm sorry I couldn't do more to save him, but you've only taught me how to block so far. Can we start with some attacking moves when we train tonight?"

Thyri looked at him as if he was something large and shiny that someone seriously ill had sneezed into her breakfast bowl, then hurried ahead.

Finnbogi had just begun to contemplate the unfairness of it all when Thyri spun around and leapt, her sax flashing down towards him. He dodged the blow and drew his sword. She slashed. He blocked, their weapons met with a shocking clang and he took a step back, Foe Slicer high and ready for her next attack.

"Your blocking still needs work," she said, "but it has improved. We can look at some attacking moves at the end of tonight's lesson." She strode on ahead.

Finnbogi marvelled in her wake. Why was everyone else so much cooler than him?

He walked on to where Freydis had stopped.

"What's up?" he asked.

"Hello, Finnbogi the Boggy," said Freydis. "Have you see Hugin and Munin?"

He looked about. "Not for a while."

"They've disappeared. Ottar's not worried, but I don't like them going off on their own in a place they don't know."

"I'll keep an eye out."

"Thanks!"

He walked on, Freydis beside him. He ruffled her hair and she didn't seem to mind.

Was this life now, he wondered? Beautiful countryside, no Garth, great company like Freydis, Sassa, Bjarni, Keef, Wulf, and, let's face it, Erik, practice with Thyri, maybe a real romantic chance with her, and no Owsla pursuing them?

Surely it was too good to be true?

* * *

Sitsi Kestrel loosed the bowstring as something small and furry crashed down on her arm, knocking her aim awry. Her arrow soared harmlessly across the valley, high above the Mushroom Men's heads.

"What the..."

A small racoon scurried into the bushes.

That had been freaky. Were there any more animals waiting to drop on her? Sitsi looked up.

She didn't think so. And it looked like the Mushroom Men hadn't seen her shot fly over their heads. They were still walking along like a happy family on a feast day. She took another arrow from her quiver.

"I saw an arrow fly over our heads," said Bodil Gooseface.

"When?" asked Bjarni Chickenhead.

"Just now, just before I mentioned it."

"EVERYBODY DOWN! ARCHERS!" shouted Bjarni. He dropped onto the path, pulling Bodil with him.

"Are you sure it was an arrow?" he asked.

"Could have been a very skinny, very fast bird," she said.

Sitsi Kestrel missed by miles, which was about as unusual as a seven-legged bobcat, and a couple of heartbeats later the Mushroom Men went to ground, putting the long grass between them and Sitsi's arrows.

No matter, thought Sofi Tornado. They had them now. She strode down the path towards her cowering victims, stone axe in hand. Beyond the prone Mushroom Men, Chogolisa Earthquake appeared from the trees and jogged to meet her. Morningstar and Paloma Pronghorn emerged to the north and Sitsi came from the south.

Their prey was surrounded. It didn't stand a chance.

Finnbogi peered through the grass. He didn't dare get to his feet for fear of an arrow. One of the Owsla was striding down the path towards them, the warlock behind her. More women were coming from either side.

So, they'd finally been caught and here came death. It was strange to think that he'd be in another world within minutes. He hoped Garth wasn't there. He'd only just got free of the fucker.

Ottar and Freydis lay in front of him, brave little children.

He reached for the hilt of Foe Slicer and pulled the sword from its scabbard. He'd do what he could for the kids. He'd go down blocking.

Then silly, mad little Ottar stood up.

"Get down, Ottar!" Finnbogi squeaked.

"Wootah!" shouted the boy.

The boy stood. Sitsi Kestrel raised her bow. He looked at her. She drew. He had the pale skin and startling blue eyes of a Mushroom Man, but the dark, messy hair of a Calnian child. His cheeks were red and his chin was shining with saliva. By his overwide eyes and the spittle on his chin, she guessed that he had an underdeveloped mind like her brothers.

She lowered her bow. The boy smiled at her.

Sofi Tornado saw the boy stand and saw Sitsi Kestrel not shoot him. It wasn't a surprise; the little archer had always been the kindest of the Owsla, and, without diamondback rattlesnake and tarantula hawk wasp in her diet, the normal human reluctance to kill children had returned.

No matter. Sofi had a mission and no qualms. She walked to meet the boy, raising her axe.

The big blond man jumped up to stop the boy. Here we go, thought Sitsi Kestrel. I can make amends for letting the boy live. She whipped up her bow, aimed at his face and shot.

* * *

Before Sassa saw that Ottar was walking past, Wulf was standing. Sassa knew from grim experience the result of standing up when archers had their bows trained on you.

"No!" she kicked his foot, grabbed his padded leather jerkin and pulled him back down. The arrow that would have impaled his head zipped by.

Sofi Tornado quickened her pace.

The boy grinned at her.

I'll take that smile off your face, she thought, pulling her weapon back for the death blow.

Something took hold of her arm. And she hadn't heard it coming.

She turned.

Yoki Choppa was holding her wrist.

Gently but firmly, he pulled her arm back to her side, shaking his head. To her surprise, she let him.

He stepped around her. The boy raised his arms, Yoki Choppa bent down. The boy wrapped his arms around the warlock's shoulders. Yoki Choppa picked him up and hugged him tight, like a warrior returned from a long mission hugging his son.

"What," Sofi Tornado took a step back, "by Innowak's red-hot bollocks, is going on?"

Paloma Pronghorn looked to Morningstar, who looked as confused as she felt, then back to Yoki Choppa hugging the boy.

Wow, was all she could think.

Chogolisa Earthquake was staring like a woman who's come home to find her husband making love to a buffalo calf. Sitsi Kestrel dropped her bow. Even the Mushroom Men had lifted their heads and were looking on with mouths agape, no wiser than the Calnians.

The only person who reacted with any poise was the little

girl. She climbed to her feet and sauntered along to join the boy and the warlock.

Yoki Choppa jinked the boy round in his grasp so he was holding him on one arm, squatted, picked up the girl with his spare arm and stood. "There will be no killing here today," he said.

"Unless you tell me why in less than three heartbeats," said Sofi Tornado. "There will be killing, starting with one treacherous Calnian warlock."

"I'd be interested to know what's happening, too," said Wulf the Fat, looking up from the grass.

"I'll tell you all," said Yoki Choppa. "It's not complicated, but it will take longer than three heartbeats."

Chapter 12

There and Back Again

Yoki Choppa led Sofi Tornado and Wulf the Fat back towards the Water Mother. The Mushroom Man tried to make conversation but Sofi was a very long way from being in the mood for a chat. She was smouldering with a rage that she couldn't shift—that she didn't want to shift. The jovial, freakishly light-haired Mushroom Man was one joke away from being brained by an axe.

"Shut the fuck up," she advised.

He had the sense to do so.

Whatever Yoki Choppa was going to tell them, whatever the reason that the Mushroom Men weren't dead and they weren't on their way home to their power animals and normality, one thing was certain. The warlock had mucked her about and she did not like being mucked about.

She wasn't so psychotic that she wouldn't listen to what Yoki Choppa had to say, but it was very hard to imagine any other outcome than her smashing the warlock and Mushroom Man's skulls then killing the rest of the pale-skinned freaks and eating the lot of them.

Something that kindled her rage even more was that part of her *liked* these aliens. Look, said an annoying voice in her mind, the same one that had almost made her cry at the Rock River, these people are jolly and brave and kind, and surely the world is a better place with them in it.

But it was their *mission* to kill them. That was all that

mattered. They should be dead and Sofi should be glad of it. All this unwelcome "oh but they're *nice* people" stuff was because of the withdrawal of her power animals and it could fuck right off.

They reached the top of the bluff and the warlock found a rock that formed a natural bench overlooking the Water Mother valley. He asked the two leaders to sit.

"Right," he said, pacing. Behind him the Water Mother flowed sluggishly and the low sun lit the western boundary of Calnia's territory. The sooner Sofi and the Owsla were back over there, the better.

"Wulf the Fat, you are travelling west because Ottar the Moaner claimed that you will find a home in a place called The Meadows."

"That's right. You can call me Wulf."

"Sofi Tornado, you have been pursuing the Mushroom Men—that's your tribe, Wulf—because of a prophecy that the Mushroom Men will destroy the world."

"Do you want me to confirm that? You know I know this." This had already taken too long. She curled her fingers around her axe handle.

"You both need to know the full position."

"Get on with it."

"You can call us the Wootah tribe, not Mushroom Men, if you like," said the Mushroom Man.

"You shut up. Yoki Choppa, you have five heartbeats to convince me not to kill you both."

"You have both been misled. Ottar has misled you, Wulf, and I have misled you, Sofi."

The Owsla captain closed her eyes, opened them and breathed out heavily through her nose. "Four heartbeats."

"The Wootah tribe and the Calnian Owsla have been united by Ottar the Moaner to travel to The Meadows. The Meadows contains a force which has already begun to destroy the world. The recent freak weather—the huge tornado that killed one of the Wootah tribe, for example—are manifestations of it."

"So the boy will lead the Owsla to The Meadows and we'll defeat this force and save the world?"

"No. We're going to make sure Ottar gets there and *he's* going to save the world."

"You're certain of this?"

"No."

"But certain enough to betray Calnia."

"Yes."

"So we can kill the rest of the Mushroom Men?"

"No, we need them."

"Why?"

"I don't know."

"I see. So you expect me to betray Ayanna and follow a child who I have been ordered to kill, alongside the people I've been ordered to kill, away from Calnia?"

"Yes."

"For no reason other than your say-so?"

"Yes."

"And you've been planning this since we left Calnia." She'd suspected it. That slimy warlock. "You haven't fed us any rattlesnake since we left, have you?"

"Doesn't sound so bad," said Wulf the Fat.

"Quiet, you. Answer me, warlock."

"You have not eaten diamondback rattlesnake since two nights before we left Calnia."

"Without asking me, you have changed us. You have taken our ruthlessness—the very essence of what makes us Owsla. It's why we didn't kill the Goachica. It's why we let the Lakchans live. It's why we didn't battle the monsters at Heartberry Canyon, it's why I left Keef alive. The Mushroom Men—"

"Wootah tribe," said Wulf.

"Interrupt me again and I will kill you, got it?"

"Got it." He nodded solemnly but with a smile in his eyes. Did the fool take anything seriously?

She turned back to Yoki Choppa. "When we got closer you had to reduce our powers further to stop us catching the Mushroom Men. The lightning from the Big Bone warlock was no coincidence. You *colluded* with them to remove our powers."

"No. I saw the opportunity and I took it. I am not the shaper of events here. The Wootah boy is. I believe he persuaded the Big Bone tribe to hinder us. I believe he put the idea of destroying my alchemy bag into my mind and gave me the chance."

"And you couldn't just stop feeding us our power animals, because your predecessor Pakanda told Morningstar about them. If we'd weakened she'd have realised what was happening and confronted you or told me."

He nodded.

Sofi looked at her feet. Anyone else, anyone other than Yoki Choppa and she would have ripped his head off, beaten the Mushroom Man to death with it and thrown them both off the cliff. But the warlock was neither a liar nor a fantasist. He would not have done all this for the fun of it. And there was something else . . .

"So Empress Ayanna's prophecy is wrong?" she asked.

"It's not. Mushroom Men will destroy nature and kill us all, including themselves. But not, I believe, these Mushroom Men. As Paloma Pronghorn pointed out, there are millions more. There are eleven remaining of Wulf's Wootah tribe. Killing them to prevent Ayanna's prophecy from coming true would be like trying to stop a plague of ants by killing eleven ants."

Sofi nodded. She could accept that. But orders were orders and she was still far from convinced that she wouldn't carry them out, and kill Yoki Choppa for his treachery.

"Where are The Meadows?" she asked.

"Only Ottar knows. From what I've heard, they are on
the far side of the Shining Mountains."

"The Shining Mountains! They are, what, a thousand
miles from here?"

"A thousand miles?" asked Wulf.

"Shut up."

"It is about a thousand miles to the Shining Mountains,
mostly through Badlander territory. The Meadows are perhaps
another thousand miles beyond the Shining Mountains,
through the Desert That You Don't Walk Out Of."

Sofi Tornado was not easily gobsmacked, but now she
actually gasped. "It's an impossible journey. No—through
Badlander territory, over the mountains, across the desert—
it's three impossible journeys, each one worse than the one
before. Hang on, we've got to come back! It's six impossible
journeys. For the love of Innowak..."

"It will not be easy. Hence the boy needing the powers
of the Owsla."

"Powers which you've thrown away."

"Powers which will be regained."

"So, my women and I are to betray Ayanna and escort
the Mushroom Men on a journey that might take years and
is likely to kill us all?"

"Yes."

"All on your say-so?"

"On more than my say-so. Think about it. I know that
you know it's the right thing to do."

The tubby little bastard was right, of course. Not because
she could *feel* it or because the boy's magic was speaking to
her or any crap like that. It was simply because she trusted
Yoki Choppa more than she trusted anyone. If he said it was
the right course of action, then it was. Still, she was far from
happy about how he'd gone about it. His scheming had killed
Talisa, and she wasn't going to forgive him for that.

*   *   *

Wulf came walking back with Sofi Tornado and the warlock, through grassland lit golden by the setting sun. Sassa breathed a sigh of relief that her husband was alive, but, by the looks on their faces, all was far from settled.

Wulf bade farewell to the Calnians. The warlock reciprocated, but the captain of the Owsla strode on stony-faced, without acknowledging any of them.

"What happened?" she asked.

"Everybody sit down," said Wulf. "I have quite a lot to tell you."

They gathered around. Sassa watched Keef try to sit next to Bodil, who tried to sit next to Finnbogi, who tried to sit next to Thyri. It was reassuring to see that the Hardwork men's affections hadn't been too affected by the startling beauty of the Owsla women.

"First up, we are no longer the Hardworkers. We are now the Wootah tribe. I'm sorry, I know we were going to vote, but I told the Calnians that's what we're called and we're stuck with it now."

"Can you get to the part of why they didn't kill us, and why it should matter to us what the Calnians call us, please?" asked Sassa.

"Sure."

He told them everything.

"Deep-throat a goat," said Sassa when he'd finished.

Chapter 13

Persuasion

There was a flash from Chippaminka's alchemical bowl. The girl warlock fell back and cracked her head on the great gold statue of Innowak.

"See to her," Ayanna told her fan men. "No, just one of you. The rest of you keep fanning." The baby was due any moment and it was hot.

"What did you see?" she asked the girl when she was back on the cushioned seat.

"I saw bad news, Empress, but also an opportunity."

"I am far too pregnant for cryptic fooling. Out with it."

"The bad news is that Yoki Choppa has turned against you and tricked the Owsla into following him. He is taking them into Badlander territory. He intends to unite with the Badlanders to attack Calnia."

"Never!"

"That is what the bowl tells me."

"What is the opportunity?" Pain lanced through the empress's stomach. "Massage your salve into my stomach as you tell me."

Chippaminka picked up the bowl of the unguent that now sat permanently next to the empress's day and night beds. She warmed it in the rays from the great sun crystal, scooped out a handful, straddled Ayanna's legs and lifted her dress. The lithe, near-naked girl looked very slight next to the empress's preposterously massive belly.

"The opportunity is to bring a halt to the strange and worsening weather. It is being caused by the dark magic of the Badlanders," she said, her wonderfully cool hands gliding up the centre of the empress's stomach, outwards across her ribs and down her flanks. "The alchemy tells me that you should gather the army, cross the Water Mother, march to the Badlands themselves and destroy the Badlanders."

"Calnians do not cross the Water Mother."

"In that case you cannot do it. I am merely telling you what the alchemy tells me." The girl's hands circled her stomach again, then again, each time widening her reach.

The empress sighed and closed her eyes.

EPILOGUE

HERE COME THE BADLANDERS

The Badlander scout Nya Muka sat astride his moose and watched the strange procession. He was two miles away, in a copse of trees on a slight rise in the broad plain. His red-tailed hawk-powered vision allowed him to see the strange travellers as if they were twenty paces away.

"This is a new lot," he said to his companion an Empty Child sitting silently on his or her bighorn sheep.

The child's large, bald head tilted too far to the side then too far upwards. White iris- and pupil-free eyes looked up blindly. Nya Muka told the boy-girl creature about the pale-skinned people and the warrior women. The latter lot were Calnians and the first lot demons, by his reckoning.

The way the two groups were spaced reminded him of when he'd been perhaps eight years old, and his clan and another clan who disliked each other had travelled together. They'd walked across the Ocean of Grass close enough to benefit from each other's numbers if they were attacked, but not so close that anyone might be forced to have anything as unpleasant as a conversation with any of the other clan.

Twenty miles to the west, Tansy Burna watched as the Plains Strider prepared for the return to the Badlands. Riding her dagger-tooth cat across the Ocean of Grass was around a thousand times more exhilarating than travelling on the huge land craft alongside the Badlanders' captives, but the size of the Plains Strider and the staggering amount of magic needed to make it work were awesome.

The millions-strong flock of crowd pigeons took to the sky, each attached by a strand of spider's silk to the super-structure of the Plains Strider. With a dreadful creak, the nose of the vast vehicle lifted like an island leaving the land, shedding grass and earth like spring rain. The hundreds of buffalo tethered to its trailing edge strained and hefted the tail off the ground. At its prow were the six bald-headed Empty Children who commanded the animals and so controlled the Strider, all rigid with concentration. Aboard the land ship Badlanders milled about, checking bonds and cages. The captives roared and shrieked and shouted. As well they might. Tansy Burna did not envy the fate that awaited them back at the Badlands.

Flanking riders on dagger-tooth cats and moose took their positions alongside. Behind the Plains Strider, more Empty Children manoeuvred the herd of buffalo which carried fodder, catch nets, folded cages and all their other gear. There were too many folded, unused cages. It had not been an unsuccessful hunt—they had plenty of interesting takes, including their first ever Squatch—but it had not been one of the greats.

She looked across at Rappa Hoga. The expedition leader's strong face shone with its usual calm confidence, but could she see a hint of disappointment in his brown eyes and the slight downturn of his kissable lips?

She was startled by the drum of hooves. It was Chapa Wangwa, galloping up on his moose, his permanent, skull-like grin ablaze with cruel excitement. Tansy Burna shivered.

"Rappa Hoga!" he cried. "The Empty Children have found new quarry. Eleven pale-skinned and yellow-haired demons travelling with five female warriors and a man."

"Are the warriors Calnians?"

"The scout thinks so."

"Which scout?"

"Nya Muka."

Rappa Hoga nodded, his face giving nothing away. "There is more to the message." It was a statement, not a question.

"You are wise, O great leader." Was that sarcasm in Chapa Wangwa's voice? "The Child said that there is much magic in both the people and the demons, that they are more powerful than they look."

The leader's dagger-tooth cat roared. His eyes drilled into Chapa Wangwa's. The latter's cruel smile morphed into a grin of terror. There was a long and deliciously awkward silence, during which Tansy Burna fantasised about Rappa Hoga wrestling his horrible underling to the ground and pounding him into a dead mess.

"I shall lead the catch squad myself," said Rappa Hoga eventually. "Have all the dagger-tooth riders prepare, plus a hundred moose-mounted warriors with clubbed arrows, holding poles and catch nets."

Chapa Wangwa was surprised, and it looked for a moment as if he was going to protest that so many should be taken to catch so few, but instead he nodded.

"Tansy Burna, prepare your riders and tell the other cat captains," Rappa Hoga added.

Tansy nodded and squeezed her thighs on the great cat's flanks. She smiled as she bounded towards the squads of cat riders. Who were these people that Rappa Hoga was sending an army powerful enough to take a city?

She could not wait to capture them and find out.

The story continues in . . .

THE LAND YOU NEVER LEAVE

Book Two of the West of West series

Coming in FEBRUARY 2018

History

This book is a fantasy fiction novel, but it's inspired by Vikings in North America a thousand years ago.

Vikings

Vikings were in North America around a thousand years ago. Hard, provable history will tell you they got as far as Newfoundland. However, it's important to remember that history knows very little about the past. Whole empires have been and gone and done many things without leaving a trace of themselves. There's no physical evidence of Caesar's huge invasions of Britain in 55 and 54 B.C., for example (see *Age of Iron*). If a couple of people hadn't written about those invasions, we wouldn't know they'd happened (and, more importantly, there would have been no *Age of Iron*). Imagine what other huge things must have taken place about which we know absolutely nothing.

So, given that the Vikings were gung-ho adventurers with "you die when you die" at the forefront of their philosophy, I am certain that they didn't sit around in Newfoundland. They went further into America.

It is perfectly feasible that the great sailors and mad adventurers sailed and rowed up the St. Lawrence River, around the Great Lakes and down Lake Michigan to a spot about fifty miles north of modern-day Chicago (which they may or may not have named Hardwork). They would have had to portage around Niagara Falls on the way, but a little waterfall wouldn't have held back people like the Vikings for long. Once they'd established a base on the banks of Lake Michigan, it's possible that a group of them headed off, across the continent.

It's less likely perhaps that they met sabre-tooth tigers and were chased by magic-powered super-warriors, but, as I mentioned, this is fantasy fiction.

I've tried to be accurate with Viking technology and culture. Christian Vikings, for example, did bury their dead with a holy water tube poking down, Freydis's suggestion that Jarl Brodir tried and failed to encourage a bear to have anal sex with him would have been a normal Viking insult, and their tribal gatherings really were called Things.

Native Americans

For all their coverage, we actually know very little about the Vikings. We don't know how they worshipped the Norse gods, for example.

We know far less about pre-Columbian Americans.

The first important notion to grasp is that we're not talking about one group of people here, in exactly the same way that when we talk about Vikings we're not talking about ancient Egyptians. America, south and north, is a vast place, and it was populated by myriad diverse tribes.

(Similarly today, to think that two people are from the same culture because they're both Native American is like expecting someone from Glasgow to drink retsina, eat moussaka and play the bouzouki on the slopes of Mount Olympus.)

The second generally held misconception is that pre-Columbian Americans were stone-age savages. Technically, yes, their tools were predominately stone. But, for example, a thousand years ago the city of Cahokia, near modern-day St. Louis, was the same size as London (25,000 people). But, while London was a sprawling mess, Cahokia was a fully planned city, with broad boulevards, towering gold-topped pyramids and burial pits, some of which contained only the bodies of young women. Cahokia, of course, is Calnia in this book.

Over on the other side of the Rockies at Mesa Verde (we'll get there in book three), there are thousand-year-old stone towns built into the cliff sides (which you can visit today, and should if you're even slightly interested in that sort of thing).

Both Cahokia and Mesa Verde were abandoned about seven hundred years ago, well before the European invasion. Nobody knows why. People will generally suggest climate change, war or a combination of the two. But the Cahokians and Mesa Verdians might just as well have built a space rocket and headed off to populate another planet. We really don't know. It's mysteries like that one that make me write speculative fantasy historical fiction.

So, I've tried to be a realistic with the pre-Columbian structures and technology, but I've completely invented the tribes and their characteristics, based very loosely on the history books.

Flora, fauna and landscape

Bull sharks still swim up the Mississippi, at least as far as Illinois. The Rock River is a tributary of the Mississippi, so, believe it or not, it really is possible that a tribe fed people to sharks on the Rock River a thousand years ago.

I've tried to be accurate with the animals, landscapes and flora, with the exception of kraklaws, dagger-tooth cats and Erik the Angry's bear. These animals, more commonly known as giant sloths, sabre-tooth tigers and short-faced bears, officially died out about ten thousand years before the events in this book, but I've reincarnated them and enlarged the sabre-tooth tigers. The other two really were that big.

Acknowledgements

M assive and unrelenting thanks to my wife Nicola, without whom nothing would be possible.

Thanks to my sons Charlie and Ottar for the entertainment and the sleep deprivation which contributed so much to this book. (In case you're wondering, I named Ottar the Moaner in the book before our own Otty was born. I mentioned the name to my wife and she liked it (not the "the Moaner" bit)).

Thanks to Joyce Boxall and Danielle Evans for looking after Charlie and Ottar so that I could get some work done during the day.

Thanks to all at Orbit and Writers House for their ceaseless devotion and vehement striving, particularly my editor Jenni Hill and my agent Angharad Kowal.

Thanks to Dr. Mike Voorhies, University of Nebraska-Lincoln Emeritus Professor in Earth and Atmospheric Sciences and Robert E. Warren, PhD, Curator of Anthropology at Illinois State Museum for their help in working out what North America looked like a thousand years ago.

Thanks to beta readers Tim Watson and Amy Dean, both of whom have greatly improved this book.

Thanks to the states of Illinois, Iowa, Nebraska, South Dakota, Colorado, Utah and Nevada for your hospitality and jaw-droppingly beautiful landscapes. Particular thanks to the Nebraska state trooper who let me off with a warning for speeding, the doctor in Sioux Falls, SD, who pointed out that the tick I was worried about on what we'll call my lower back was in fact a mole that I'd scratched, and the farmers from California who rescued me when I got my car stuck on a rock.

Thanks to everyone who read *Age of Iron* and posted a favourable review. Thanks to everyone who emailed or Tweeted or Facebooked or whatevered me directly to say they liked it. Writing is a weird profession, in which you sit alone at home while everyone else in the world, it seems, goes out and has a jolly old time together. An email from someone saying that they liked a book I wrote is a massive boost at the beginning of the solitary writing day.

Please do write a review anywhere online if you enjoyed *You Die When You Die*. If you didn't like it, well done for reading this far, and please don't fuss too much about that review.

extras

meet the author

ANGUS WATSON is an author living in London. Before becoming a novelist, he was a freelance features writer, chiefly for British national newspapers. Features included looking for Bigfoot in the USA for the *Telegraph*, diving on the scuppered World War One German fleet at Scapa Flow for the *Financial Times* and swimming with sea lions in the Galapagos Islands for the *Times*.

Angus's first historical fantasy trilogy is *Age of Iron*, an epic romantic adventure set at the end of Briton's Iron Age. He came up with the idea for West of West while driving and hiking though North America's magnificent countryside and wondering what it was like before the Europeans got there.

Angus is married to Nicola. They have two young sons, Charlie and Otty, and two cats, Jasmine and Napa.

You can find him on Twitter at @GusWatson or find his website at: www.guswatson.com.

Find out more about Angus Watson and other Orbit authors by registering for the free monthly newsletter at www.orbitbooks.net.

if you enjoyed
YOU DIE WHEN YOU DIE

look out for

THE FIFTH WARD: FIRST WATCH

by

Dale Lucas

Humans, orcs, mages, elves, and dwarves all jostle for success and survival in the cramped quarters of Yenara, while understaffed watchwardens struggle to keep its citizens in line.

Enter Rem: new to Yenara and hungover in the city dungeons with no money for bail. When offered a position with the watch to compensate for his crimes, Rem jumps at the chance.

extras

His new partner is less eager. Torval, a dwarf who's handy with a maul and known for hitting first and asking questions later, is highly unimpressed with the untrained and weaponless Rem.

But when Torval's former partner goes missing, the two must consort with the usual suspects—drug-dealing orcs, mind-controlling elves, uncooperative mages, and humans being typical humans—to uncover the truth and catch a murderer loose in their fair city.

Rem awoke in a dungeon with a thunderous headache. He knew it was a dungeon because he lay on a thin bed of straw, and because there were iron bars between where he lay and a larger chamber outside. The light was spotty, some of it from torches in sconces outside his cell, some from a few tiny windows high on the stone walls admitting small streams of wan sunlight. Moving nearer the bars, he noted that his cell was one of several, each roomy enough to hold multiple prisoners.

A large pile of straw on the far side of his cell coughed, shifted, then started to snore. Clearly, Rem was not alone.

And just how did I end up here? he wondered. *I seem to recall a winning streak at Roll-the-Bones.*

He could not remember clearly. But if the lumpy soreness of his face and body were any indication, his dice game had gone awry. If only he could clear his pounding head, or slake his thirst. His tongue and throat felt like sharkskin.

Desperate for a drink, Rem crawled to a nearby bucket, hoping for a little brackish water. To his dismay, he found that it was the piss jar, not a water bucket, and not well rinsed at that. The sight and smell made Rem recoil with a gag. He went sprawling back onto the hay. A few feet away, his cellmate muttered something in the tongue of the Kosterfolk, then resumed snoring.

Somewhere across the chamber, a multitumbler lock clanked and clacked. Rusty hinges squealed as a great door lumbered open. From the other cells Rem heard prisoners roused from their sleep, shuffling forward hurriedly to thrust their arms out through the cage bars. If Rem didn't misjudge, there were only

479

about four or five other prisoners in all the dungeon cells. A select company, to be sure. Perhaps it was a slow day for the Yenaran city watch?

Four men marched into the dungeon. Well, three marched; the fourth seemed a little more reticent, being dragged by two others behind their leader, a thickset man with black hair, sullen eyes, and a drooping mustache.

"Prefect, sir," Rem heard from an adjacent cell, "there's been a terrible mistake..."

From across the chamber: "Prefect, sir, someone must have spiked my ale, because the last thing I remember, I was enjoying an evening out with some mates..."

From off to his left: "Prefect, sir, I've a chest of treasure waiting back at my rooms at the Sauntering Mink. A golden cup full of rubies and emeralds is yours, if you'll just let me out of here..."

Prefect, sir...Prefect, sir... over and over again.

Rem decided that thrusting his own arms out and begging for the prefect's attention was useless. What would he do? Claim his innocence? Promise riches if they'd let him out? That was quite a tall order when Rem himself couldn't remember what he'd done to get in here. If he could just clear his thunder-addled, achingly thirsty brain...

The sullen-eyed prefect led the two who dragged the prisoner down a short flight of steps into a shallow sort of operating theater in the center of the dungeon: the interrogation pit, like some shallow bath that someone had let all the water out of. On one side of the pit was a brick oven in which fire and coals glowed. Opposite the oven was a burbling fountain. Rem thought these additions rather ingenious. Whatever elemental need one had—fire to burn with, water to drown with— both were readily provided. The floor of the pit, Rem guessed, probably sported a couple of grates that led right down into the sewers, as well as the tools of the trade: a table full of torturer's implements, a couple of hot braziers, some chairs and manacles. Rem hadn't seen the inside of any city dungeons, but he'd seen their private equivalents. Had it been the dungeon of some march lord up north—from his own country—that's what would have been waiting in the little amphitheater.

"Come on, Ondego, you know me," the prisoner pleaded. "This isn't necessary."

"'Fraid so," sullen-eyed Ondego said, his low voice easy and without malice. "The chair, lads."

The two guardsmen flanking the prisoner were a study in contrasts—one a tall, rugged sort, face stony and flecked with stubble, shoulders broad, while the other was lithe and graceful, sporting braided black locks, skin the color of dark-stained wood, and a telltale pair of tapered, pointing ears. Staring, Rem realized that second guardsman was no man at all, but an elf, and female, at that. Here was a puzzle, indeed. Rem had seen elves at a distance before, usually in or around frontier settlements farther north, or simply haunting the bleak crossroads of a woodland highway like pikers who never demanded a toll. But he had never seen one of them up close like this— and certainly not in the middle of one of the largest cities in the Western world, deep underground, in a dingy, shit- and blood-stained dungeon. Nonetheless, the dark-skinned elfmaid seemed quite at home in her surroundings, and perfectly comfortable beside the bigger man on the other side of the prisoner.

Together, those two guards thrust the third man's squirming, wobbly body down into a chair. Heavy manacles were produced and the protester was chained to his seat. He struggled a little, to test his bonds, but seemed to know instinctively that it was no use. Ondego stood at a brazier nearby, stoking its coals, the pile of dark cinders glowing ominously in the oily darkness.

"Oi, that's right!" one of the other prisoners shouted. "Give that bastard what for, Prefect!"

"You shut your filthy mouth, Foss!" the chained man spat back.

"Eat me, Kevel!" the prisoner countered. "How do *you* like the chair, eh?"

Huh. Rem moved closer to his cell bars, trying to get a better look. So, this prisoner, Kevel, knew that fellow in the cell, Foss, and vice versa. Part of a conspiracy? Brother marauders, questioned one by one—and in sight of one another—for some vital information?

Then Rem saw it: Kevel, the prisoner in the hot seat, wore a signet pendant around his throat identical to those worn by the prefect and the two guards. It was unmistakable, even in the shoddy light.

"Well, I'll be," Rem muttered aloud.

The prisoner was one of the prefect's own watchmen.

Ex-watchman now, he supposed.

All of a sudden, Rem felt a little sorry for him...but not much. No doubt, Kevel himself had performed the prefect's present actions a number of times: chaining some poor sap into the hot seat, stoking the brazier, using fire and water and physical distress to intimidate the prisoner into revealing vital information.

The prefect, Ondego, stepped away from the brazier and moved to a table nearby. He studied a number of implements— it was too dark and the angle too awkward for Rem to tell what, exactly—then picked something up. He hefted the object in his hands, testing its weight.

It looked like a book—thick, with a hundred leaves or more bound between soft leather covers.

"Do you know what this is?" Ondego asked Kevel.

"Haven't the foggiest," Kevel said. Rem could tell that he was bracing himself, mentally and physically.

"It's a genealogy of Yenara's richest families. Out-of-date, though. At least a generation old."

"Do tell," Kevel said, his throat sounding like it had contracted to the size of a reed.

"Look at this," Ondego said, hefting the book in his hands, studying it. "That is one enormous pile of useless information. Thick as a bloody brick—"

And that's when Ondego drew back the book and brought it smashing into Kevel's face in a broad, flat arc. The sound of the strike—leather and parchment pages connecting at high speed with Kevel's jawbone—echoed in the dungeon like the crack of a calving iceberg. A few of the other prisoners even wailed as though they were the ones struck.

Rem's cellmate stirred beneath his pile of straw, but did not rise.

Kevel almost fell with the force of the blow. The big guard caught him and set him upright again. The lithe elf backed off, staring intently at the prisoner, as though searching his face and his manner for a sign of something. Without warning, Ondego hit Kevel again, this time on the other side of his face. Once more Kevel toppled. Once more the guard in his path caught him and set him upright.

Kevel spat out blood. Ondego tossed the book back onto the table behind him and went looking for another implement.

"That all you got, old man?" Kevel asked.

"Bravado doesn't suit you," Ondego said, still studying his options from the torture table. He threw a glance at the elf on the far side of the torture pit. Rem watched intently, realizing that some strange ritual was under way: Kevel, blinking sweat from his eyes, studied Ondego; the lady elf, silent and implacable, studied Kevel; and Ondego idly studied the elf, the prefect's thick, workman's hand hovering slowly over the gathered implements of torture on the table.

Then, Kevel blinked. That small, unconscious movement seemed to signal something to the elf, who then spoke to the prefect. Her voice was soft, deep, melodious.

"The amputation knife," she said, her large, unnerving, honey-colored eyes never leaving the prisoner.

Ondego took up the instrument that his hand hovered above—a long, curving blade like a field-hand's billhook, the honed edge being on the inside, rather than the outside, of the curve. Ondego brandished the knife and looked to Kevel. The prisoner's eyes were as wide as empty goblets.

Ingenious! The elf had apparently used her latent mind-reading abilities to determine which of the implements on the table Kevel most feared being used on him. Not precisely the paragon of sylvan harmony and ancient grace that Rem would have imagined such a creature to be, but impressive nonetheless.

As Ondego spoke, he continued to brandish the knife, casually, as if it were an extension of his own arm. "Honestly, Kev," he said, "haven't I seen you feign bravery a hundred times? I know you're shitting your kecks about now."

"So you'd like to think," Kevel answered, eyes still on the knife. "You're just bitter because you didn't do it. Rich men don't get rich keeping to a set percentage, Ondego. They get rich by redrawing the percentages."

Ondego shook his head. Rem could be mistaken, but he thought he saw real regret there.

"Rule number one," Ondego said, as though reciting holy writ. "Keep the peace."

"Suck it," Kevel said bitterly.

"Rule number two," Ondego said, slowly turning to face Kevel, "Keep your partner safe, and he'll do the same for you."

"He was going to squeal," Kevel said, now looking a little more repentant. "I couldn't have that. You said yourself, Ondego—he wasn't cut out for it. Never was. Never would be."

"So that bought him a midnight swim in the bay?" Ondego asked. "Rule number three: let the punishment fit the crime, Kevel. Throttling that poor lad and throwing him in the drink...that's what the judges call cruel and unusual. We don't do cruel and unusual in my ward."

"Go spit," Kevel said.

"Rule number four," Ondego quickly countered. "And this is important, Kevel, so listen good: never take more than your share. There's enough for everyone, so long as no one's greedy. So long as no one's hoarding or getting fat. I knew you were taking a bigger cut when your jerkin started straining. There's only one way a watchman that didn't start out fat gets that way, and that's by hoarding and taking more than his fair share."

"So what's it gonna be?" Kevel asked. "The knife? The razor? The book again? The hammer and the nail-tongs?"

"Nah," Ondego said, seemingly bored by their exchange, as though he were disciplining a child that he'd spanked a hundred times before. He tossed the amputation knife back on the table. "Bare fists."

And then, as Rem and the other prisoners watched, Ondego, prefect of the watch, proceeded to beat the living shit out of Kevel, a onetime member of his own watch company. Despite the fact that Ondego said not another word while the beating commenced, Rem thought he sensed some grim and unhappy purpose in Ondego's corporal punishment. He never once smiled, nor even gritted his teeth in anger. The intensity of the beating never flared nor ebbed. He simply kept his mouth set, his eyes open, and slowly, methodically, laid fists to flesh. He made Kevel whimper and bleed. From time to time he would stop and look to the elf. The elf would study Kevel, clearly not simply looking at him but *into* him, perhaps reading just how close he was to losing consciousness, or whether he was feigning senselessness to gain some brief reprieve. The elf would then offer a cursory, "More." Ondego, on the elfmaid's advice, would continue.

Rem admired that: Ondego's businesslike approach, the fact that he could mete out punishment without enjoying it. In some ways, Ondego reminded Rem of his own father.

Before Ondego was done, a few of the other prisoners were crying out. Some begged mercy on Kevel's behalf. Ondego wasn't having it. He didn't acknowledge them. His fists carried on their bloody work. To Kevel's credit he never begged mercy. Granted, that might have been hard after the first quarter hour or so, when most of his teeth were on the floor.

Ondego only relented when the elf finally offered a single word. "Out." At that, Ondego stepped back, like a pugilist retreating to his corner between melee rounds. He shook his hands, no doubt feeling a great deal of pain in them. Beating a man like that tested the limits of one's own pain threshold as well as the victim's.

"Still breathing?" Ondego asked, all business.

The human guard bent. Listened. Felt for a pulse. "Still with us. Out cold."

"Put him in the stocks," Ondego said. "If he survives five days on Zabayus's Square, he can walk out of the city so long as he never comes back. Post his crimes, so everyone sees."

The guards nodded and set to unchaining Kevel. Ondego swept past them and mounted the stairs up to the main cell level again, heading toward the door. That's when Rem suddenly noticed an enormous presence beside him. He had not heard the brute's approach, but he could only be the sleeping form beneath the hay. For one, he was covered in the stuff. For another, his long braided hair, thick beard, and rough-sewn, stinking leathers marked him as a Kosterman. And hadn't Rem heard Koster words muttered by the sleeper in the hay?

"Prefect!" the Kosterman called, his speech sharply accented.

Ondego turned, as if this was the first time he'd heard a single word spoken from the cells and the prisoners in them.

Rem's cellmate rattled the bars. "Let me out of here, little man," he said.

Kosterman all right. The long, yawning vowels and glass-sharp consonants were a dead giveaway. For emphasis, the Kosterman even snarled, as though the prefect were the lowest of house servants.

Ondego looked puzzled for a moment. Could it be that no one had ever spoken to him that way? Then the prefect stepped forward, snarling, looking like a maddened hound. His fist shot out in front of him and shook as he approached.

"Get back in your hay and keep your gods-damned head down, con! I'll have none of your nonsense after such a bevy of bitter business—"

Rem realized what was about to happen a moment before it did. He opened his mouth to warn the prefect off—surely the man wasn't so gullible? Maybe it was just his weariness in the wake of the beating he'd given Kevel? His regret at having to so savagely punish one of his own men?

if you enjoyed
YOU DIE WHEN YOU DIE

look out for

THE COURT OF BROKEN KNIVES

Empires of Dust: Book One

by

Anna Smith Spark

Merith is the newest recruit to the mercenary band hired by Orhan to assassinate the Emperor. Young, charming and impossibly handsome, he hides the worst secret of all. He is a direct descendant of the world conqueror—and half demon—King Amrath. Merith has made some powerful enemies in his short life, including his own father, and their reach is far longer than he imagined.

extras

Thalia had never wanted to be High Priestess, to appease the One God of Living and Dying by stabbing sacrificial victims to death in the great temple. Even those who volunteer to die falter at the end; so Thalia, who has to look into their terrified eyes, harbours growing doubts about the religion she serves. And as soon as her successor reaches adulthood, Thalia herself will be tied to the altar to await the knife.

Orhan Emereth wanted to avoid the lethal power politics of the capital; but risks everything—including his pregnant wife—by staging a coup d'état to save the Yellow Empire from itself.

Knives.

Knives everywhere. Coming down like rain.

Down to close work like that, men wrestling in the mud, jabbing at each other, too tired to care anymore. Just die and get it over with. Half of them fighting with their guts hanging out of their stomachs, stinking of shit, oozing pink and red and white. Half-dead men lying in the filth. Screaming. A whole lot of things screaming.

Impossible to tell who's who anymore. Mud and blood and shadows and that's it. Kill them! Kill them all! Keep killing until we're all dead. The knife jabs and twists and the man he's fighting falls sideways, all the breath going out of him with a sigh of relief. Another there behind. Gods, his arms ache. His head aches. Blood in his eyes. He twists the knife again and thrusts with a broken-off sword and that man too dies. Fire explodes somewhere over to the left. White as maggots. Silent as maggots. Then shrieks as men burn.

He swings the stub of the sword and catches a man on the leg, not hard but hard enough the man stumbles, and he's on him quick with the knife cutting. A good lot of blood and the man's down and dead, still flapping about like a fish, but you can see in his eyes that he's finished, his legs just haven't quite caught up yet.

The sun is setting, casting long shadows. Oh beautiful evening! Stars rising in a sky the colour of rotting wounds. The Dragon's Mouth. The White Lady. The Dog. A good star, the Dog. Brings plagues and fevers and inflames desire. Its rising marks the coming of summer. So maybe no more campaigning in the sodding rain. Wet leather stinks. Mud stinks. Shit stinks, when the latrine trench overflows.

Another burst of white fire. He hates the way it's silent. Unnatural. Unnerving. Screams again. Screams so bad your ears ring for days. The sky weeps and howls and it's difficult to know what's screaming. You or the enemy or the other things.

Men are fighting in great clotted knots like milk curds. He sprints a little to where two men are struggling together. Leaps at one from behind, pulls him down, skewers him. Hard crack of bone, soft lovely yield of fat and innards. Suety. The other yells hoarsely and swings a punch at him. Lost his knife, even. Bare knuckles. He ducks and kicks out hard, overbalances and almost falls. The man kicks back, tries to get him in a wrestling grip. Up close together, two pairs of teeth gritted at each other. A hand smashes his face, gets his nose, digs in. He bites at it. Dirty. Callused. Iron taste of blood bright in his mouth. But the hand won't let up, crushing his face into his skull. He swallows and almost chokes on the blood pouring from the wound he's made. Blood and snot and shreds of cracked, dry human skin. Manages to get his knife in and stabs hard into the back of the man's thigh. Not enough to kill, but the hand jerks out from his face. He lashes out and gets his opponent in the soft part of the throat, pulls his knife out and gazes around the battlefield at the figures hacking at each other while the earth rots beneath them. All eternity, they've been fighting. All the edges blunted. Sword edges and knife edges and the edges in the mind. Keep killing. Keep killing. Keep killing till you're all dead.

And then he's dead. A blade gets him in the side, in the weak point under the shoulder where his armour has to give to let the joint move. Far in, twisting. Aiming down. Killing wound. He hears his body rip. Oh gods. Oh gods and demons. Oh gods and demons and fuck. He swings round, strikes at the man who's stabbed him. The figure facing him is a wraith, scarlet with blood, head open oozing out brain stuff. You're dying, he thinks. You're dying and you've killed me. Not fair.

Shadows twist round them. We're all dying, he thinks, one way or another. Just some of us quicker than others. You fight and you die. And always another twenty men queuing up behind you.

Why we march and why we die,
And what life means... it's all a lie.
Death! Death! Death!

Understands that better than he's ever understood anything, even his own name.

But suddenly, for a moment, he's not sure he wants to die.

The battlefield falls silent. He blinks and sees light.

A figure in silver armour. White, shining, blazing with light like the sun. A red cloak blowing in the wind. Moves through the ranks of the dead and the dying and the light beats on to them, pure and clean.

"Amrath! Amrath!" Voices whispering like the wind blowing across salt marsh. Voices calling like birds. Here, walking among us, bright as summer dew.

"Amrath! Amrath!" The shadows fall away as the figure passes. Everything is light.

"Amrath! Amrath!" The men cheer with one voice. No longer one side or the other, just men gazing and cheering as the figure passes. He cheers until his throat aches. Feels restored, seeing it. No longer tired and wounded and dying. Healed. Strong.

"Amrath! Amrath!"

The figure halts. Gazes around. Searching. Finds. A dark-clad man leaps forward, swaying into the light. Poised across from the shining figure, yearning toward it. Draws a sword burning with blue flame.

"Amrath! Amrath!" Harsh voice like crows, challenging. "Amrath!"

He watches joyfully. So beautiful! Watches and nothing in the world matters, except to behold the radiance of his god.

The bright figure draws a sword that shines like all the stars and the moon and the sun. A single dark ruby in its hilt. The dark figure rushes onwards, screeching something. Meets the bright figure with a clash. White light and blue fire. Blue fire and white light. His eyes almost hurt as he watches. But he cannot bear to look away. The two struggle for a moment. Like a candle flame flickering. Like the dawn sun on the sea. The silver sword comes up, throws the dark figure back. Blue fire blazes, engulfing everything, the shining silver armour running with flame. Crash of metal, sparks like from blacksmith's anvil. The shining figure takes a step back defensively, parries, strikes out. The other blocks it. Roars. Howls. Laughs. The mage blade swings again, slicing, trailing blue fire. Blue arcs in the evening gloom. Shapes and words, written on the air. Death words. Pain words. Words of hope and fear and despair. The shining figure parries again, the silver sword rippling beneath the impact of the other's blade. So brilliant with light that rainbows dance on the ground around it. Like a woman tossing back her head in summer rain, hair throwing out drops of water. Like snow falling. Like coloured stars. The two fighters shifting, stepping in each other's footprints. Stepping in each other's shadows. Circling like birds.

The silver sword flashes out and up and downwards and the other falls back, bleeding from the throat. Great spreading gush of red. The blue flame dies.

He cheers and his heart is almost aching, it's so full of joy.

The shining figure turns. Looks at the men watching. Looks at him. Screams. Things shriek back that make the world tremble. The silver sword rises and falls. Five men. Ten. Twenty. A pile of corpses. He stares mesmerised at the dying. The beauty of it. The most beautiful thing in the world. Killing and killing and such perfect joy. His heart overflowing. His heart singing. This, oh, indeed, oh for this, all men are born. He screams in answer, dying, throws himself against his god's enemies with knife and sword and nails and teeth.

Why we march and why we die,
And what life means . . . it's all a lie.
Death! Death! Death!